A LITTLE BIT OBSESSED

CHRISSY HOPEWELL

Published by Fox Hollow Publishing LLC

Editing by Nicole Evans at Thoughts Stained Editorial thoughtsstainededitorial.com

Proofreading by Jenny Sliger at Owl Eyes Proofs and Edits owleyesproofsedits.com

Cover art by author

First US Edition: May 2026

ISBN: 978-1-968544-04-1 (paperback), 978-1-968544-03-4 (ebook)

CONTENT WARNINGS

While this dark romcom may be lighter than many of its dark romance cousins and Wes is a walking green flag (except for the murders and the stalking, of course), there are still dark topics, histories, and events in *A Little Bit Obsessed*. Please take care of your mental health and let me know if you have any questions!

- Poison pies / poisoning
- Restraint by zip ties
- Restraint by ropes
- Stalking
- Stabbing
- Outrageous male entitlement
- Explicit consensual sexual content
- On-page murder of bad guys
- Off-page murder of MMC's parents and teenage sister (off-page, in the past)
- Kidnapping
- On-page sexual assault (not by or between MCs, from a distance, and the guy dies right after)
- Off-page sexual assault of a minor (mentioned briefly, not by or between MCs, no details, and the guy dies shortly after)
- Spousal gaslighting, physical, and emotional abuse (not between or by the MCs)
- Divorce
- Swearing

ALSO BY CHRISSY HOPEWELL

Hart Sisters Trilogy:

If We Pretend

Unless It's You

Since We're Here

One Hundred Lights (novella)

Fort Collins Blizzard Hockey:

Just One Season

Any Second Now

Sign up to Chrissy's newsletter for extra content, including bonus scenes for each book and hockey romance novella *Zamboni Kiss*.

www.ChrissyHopewell.com

For those of us who love a golden retriever serial killer...
I'm as confused about it as you are.

CHAPTER 1

ALLIGATORS ARE
HELPFUL

WES

"This is messier than when we give them one of my pies." I'm in the doorway of a Fort Lauderdale apartment, staring at a very dead middle-aged white man on a beige area rug in the living room.

Fuck me. This isn't just messy. It's a disaster.

"Seriously? Death by your mince pie is disgusting." Noah casually lounges on the expensive gray leather couch, careful to avoid the red splatters that he put there during all the stabbing. Luckily, that should easily wipe off the leather. Noah pushes up his dark-rimmed glasses to rub his eyes. "They foam at the mouth."

"At least with pie, there's no blood," I grumble, adding a swear under my breath. This carpet is no longer beige. "And you're in no place to criticize my techniques right now." I wave my hand at the pile of predator on the ground.

This one was wealthy, and he'd lure young immigrant women to this shitty apartment where he'd beat and fuck them, and recently escalated to killing. He liked Venezuelan and Colombian women in particular.

1

"Did you fly down here to lecture? Or help?" Noah glares at me from across the room.

"Both. On the beige rug, Noah? Really?" I gesture at the large area rug that'll have to be disposed of.

"Well. It didn't go as smoothly as I had hoped."

"Oh really? You had an actual plan for where the blood would splatter?" I cross my arms and arch an eyebrow.

"A semblance of one."

"Be serious right now. What's the plan?"

This morning, my brother snuck out of our little Maine lake town, drove to the Boston airport, and got on a plane to Florida. He waited until I was elbow-deep in testing out a tweaked apple pie recipe for the Portland Springfest pie competition in March. I wasn't paying attention to my phone and must've missed the geo alert notifying me that Noah was out of the area. He'd counted on that. As soon as I realized it, I raced to follow him. He'd probably counted on that as well.

"I don't have a revised plan just yet. But I'd have figured it out without you, you know." He yawns to emphasize how unconcerned he is.

"You would have, huh." For fuck's sake.

"And anyway, I have a psycho younger brother who obsessively tracks me, so I knew he'd come eventually to help sort it out. That's you, by the way."

I close my eyes for a beat and pray for strength. Protecting my brother from himself is almost a full-time job.

"Are you sure there aren't cameras?" I say when I'm ready to face this.

He shrugs.

"Did you check the hallway?"

Noah blinks and pushes his glasses up the bridge of his

nose. One look at him and you'd think he has a boring desk job as an accountant or financial advisor, not a side hustle as a serial killer.

I swear to god.

"Not yet."

I just stare at him.

"It's an old-ass building. There's no way there are security cameras."

While Noah talks and justifies why he went off plan, I'm coming up with one that'll take care of this mess and get us back to Maine.

It takes three hours to thoroughly clean the apartment and drag the man's body and heavy rug out of the building and into the rental car for disposal. Noah was probably right —there was only one camera in the stairwell, and the lens was smashed to bits. I hacked into the city's closest street-view cameras, which are on a bigger road a few hundred feet from the apartment building's entrance. I don't think they would catch anything considering the distance and angle of the cameras, but just in case. By the time I've done the best I can to cover our tracks, it's the middle of the night. Dark is helpful cover when you're filling a trunk with a body and blood-splattered rug.

"You're getting sloppy." I let out a long breath and lower the window in the rental car as I pull away from the apartment building. This was a mess, but I'm enjoying the warm Florida air, even in the middle of the night. February is cold as fuck in Maine.

I hope we didn't miss anything and this little side quest of Noah's doesn't come back to bite us in the ass.

"Yeah. I know. Sorry." To his credit, Noah sounds genuinely remorseful.

"I need you to stop going rogue." I glance over at him in the passenger seat. "For your protection. And mine. You promised you'd be more careful, and we'd agree on targets and timing."

"I know. But this guy was scum, Wes."

I sigh. He's right.

Noah and I both spend too much time on the dark web. He canvases chat rooms and message boards for targets, and has an anonymous contact who feeds him information. I'm on there searching for information and clues so we can vet the targets and locate them. He's ideas, I'm execution.

The man Noah killed was named John Williams.

Williams fit all our criteria.

He targeted young women.

He was a rapist.

He'd already killed at least two of the women he assaulted.

Police don't often prioritize solving cases of assault or murder of immigrants, sex workers, or homeless women. Because the women Williams targeted were so far from home, they didn't have families here on the ground demanding attention to their missing person or homicide cases. Some of those families probably don't realize their daughters are even gone.

The cops are fucking it all up, as they often do in these kinds of situations.

We pick up what the police drop. Usually in a more organized fashion than this. I wanted to wait for more information on John Williams, but Noah never wants to wait once he has someone on his radar. He gets hyperfocused on eliminating them before *they* can eliminate anyone else.

Which, fair.

We've been doing this for a decade, but lately, Noah's gotten sloppier. He doesn't like that I try to slow him down.

My phone buzzes in the cup holder, and at the next red light, I click open a new notification on Gone, the highly encrypted app I use to communicate with clients.

CC95

Can you help me find someone?

The message fades and fades until it disappears completely within seconds. Screenshots are disabled within Gone, but obviously I've found a way around that when needed.

But I have no idea who this CC95 person is. Usually people find me through referrals. It's not like there's a directory of people who do my kind of people-finding work. I'll respond to CC95 later, after we finish cleaning up the mess in our trunk.

"I got directions to a spot," Noah says, staring at his phone.

"Yeah? Better be good."

"We're in Florida," Noah says. "Lots of creepy places to ditch bodies."

And he's right.

Two hours later, Noah takes over driving as we leave the Everglades and head to Orlando to catch a flight back home. You couldn't pay me to live in a state where you can toss a body into a swamp and reasonably assume that alligators will take care of the mess for you.

With Noah driving, I finally have a chance to open Gone again to respond to the message that popped up hours ago.

Noah and I both have multiple streams of income. I take cybersecurity project work for corporations via a freelance agency. It's boring as shit but I get paid well. On the side, I find people for significant sums of money. According to the IRS, Noah's main source of income is renovating cabins in the spring and summer.

And we're hobby serial killers, which I realize sounds a bit fucked up. No one pays us to kill people. We do it for the greater good.

Everyone's fucked up in their own way, I guess.

The sun is starting to rise as we approach Orlando, and I'm half tempted to suggest we keep driving west and get some beach time in before heading back to the freezing-ass Maine winter.

ME

Who are you looking for?

CC95

My husband

She responds instantly, and I'm not a huge fan of her answer. Domestic disputes aren't really my thing.

ME

Who is your husband, who referred you, and who are you?

CC95

His name is Shane Robertson, and I want to serve him divorce papers. My brother, Jake Callahan, referred me. My name is Callie Callahan

So much for keeping things cryptic via Gone. She's just throwing out full government names like she has no sense of self-preservation.

"Callahan," I say, turning to my brother. "I just got a job request from someone named Callie Callahan. Her brother is Jake Callahan, and he referred me."

"Callahan as in the crime family?" Noah glances over at me, eyebrows raised.

"I don't know. I guess." I usually don't do much work with crime families because of what happened a decade ago. And a crime family domestic dispute sounds extra dangerous. Still, my curiosity is piqued. Piqued enough to find out more information, not to necessarily agree to the job.

ME

Let's meet to discuss. I'm out of town right now. End of this week? You pick the place and time

CC95

Okay. Friday, Maine Coffee Co in Portland at 3pm?

I agree and put my phone down. I usually don't meet in person, but I want to be able to read body language while she explains what she needs. I can usually tell if someone is lying or being sketchy.

"While I have you as a captive audience, should we talk about the list?" Noah glances over at me.

"For fuck's sake, you just took a guy out. You want to plan the next one already?"

"Yes. Yes I do."

I can't imagine where Noah would be without me.

We weren't born like this. We were made into what we are today by shit that went down a long time ago.

I used to hate what we do way more than I do now. When I'm in doubt, I remind myself that without us, there'd be so many more women and girls hurt.

We couldn't save our sister, but we can save others like her.

"Alright. Let's talk about your list."

Noah nods to his backpack, and I pull out his notebook. As we talk, I make a mental list of things to work on later tonight.

Including researching Callie Callahan.

CHAPTER 2

HACKERS ARE ALSO HELPFUL

CALLIE

"Fuck you, Jake." I'm so angry at my brother that I'm seeing black spots at the edge of my vision.

"Callie. Please." Jake's standing in the kitchen of his apartment, elbows leaning on the bar-level countertop as I pace around the connected living room. "I don't know anything about Shane."

He's lying. Regardless of the fact that he threw some private detective's information at me last time we argued, I know he knows more than he's admitting. I growl at him and tug on my long, dark braid. Tears fill my eyes and I stop, turn to Jake, and cross my arms. His eyes shutter as he takes in my pathetic state.

This is not the first time Jake and I have had this fight. This isn't even the worst time. But I haven't gotten anywhere with the insults and the yelling and the guilt trips. Every time I've tried to ask people who should know where Shane is, I get stonewalled. No one will tell me anything. They say they don't know and give me a blank look. No one in the business is actively looking for Shane, so he must not actually be missing.

"You have no loyalty." My voice hitches, and I absolutely hate that about myself. I cry at the drop of a damn hat.

"First of all," Jake starts, then stops. He runs his hand through his short blond hair. He's so unlike me in appearance. Tall and slender and olive-skinned. Light hair and blue eyes. I'm all dark. Dark hair, dark eyes, but not a dark, criminal soul like the rest of my family.

"Jake." I plead with my voice and my eyes. "Shane is a terrible person. A bad husband. And he's got Mom's ring," I rasp, waiting for my brother to react. Shane knows how important that ring was to me. He took it to hurt me. To control me. Jake knows it too.

"Callie." Jake flinches, but doesn't break. "Don't you think he'll be back? Why would he take Mom's ring?" This last question feels like it's almost directed at himself.

Our father passed away three months ago, and it was a real wake-up call for me. I realized I wanted to live my life differently, not cringe in the shadow of my controlling, narcissistic husband. I don't think Shane wants to be married to me, but the fact that I was the one who asked for a divorce sent him over the edge.

That and the fact that he didn't get promoted within the family like he thought he would after my father died. Instead of having to continue to prove himself to my father—which drove him crazy—he now has to prove himself to Jones, my father's old colleague who was promoted into his place. That only fed into Shane's insecurity about his role. He loves the drugs and money laundering and fight clubs. At the same time, he's never felt deeply connected with the group. I get it. I feel bad for him. But I gotta get out.

We fought about getting divorced a month ago, and then Shane trashed our life and disappeared. He called me two weeks ago to ask about my father's inheritance money, and when I freaked out on him, he hung up on me. I haven't stood up for myself very much in our six-year marriage, but he stole the ring, everything in our joint bank account, and almost the entire contents of our apartment, so I can't just back down.

"You're covering for him." I poke at Jake's chest. "I'm your *family*."

"Which is why I gave you Hawk's contact information." Jake looks pained.

"Oh, the sketchy hacker who your criminal friend recommended? Thanks so much for that." I plant my fists on my hips and let the sarcasm drip from my words.

"Listen, I don't know exactly where Shane is." My brother sighs deeply and closes his eyes for a few seconds, probably realizing his mistake right away.

"Exactly? Where is he *approximately*?"

Jake groans and hangs his head.

Growing up, I didn't understand what my father did to earn a living. But when I was ten years old, my eighteen-year-old cousin went to jail for murdering a member of another crime family. He was killed in prison shortly after that. That's when I realized that this life was not it for me. Regardless of circumstances, I should've run instead of marrying Shane fourteen years later. I hate it all: drugs and money laundering and fight clubs.

My brother shuts his eyes and sighs. If it weren't for the fact that I've been staying with him since Shane disappeared, I'd leave and slam the door on the way out.

"Callie..." Jake has the nerve to look at me with tear-filled eyes. I hate how authentically upset he appears. I hate that he's got dark circles under his eyes and looks torn up about whatever is going on.

"Fuck!" I do the next best thing to leaving, which is stomp down the hall and into Jake's spare bedroom and slam *that* door. I freeze inside the room with my arms crossed tightly. Jake calls my name unconvincingly from outside the door, but I'm betting he really doesn't want me to open it. He gives up quickly, his footsteps echoing as he walks away.

Anyway, it's pointless to continue to have this conversation with him. I know that. I think providing me with Hawk's information was the most I'll get out of my chickenshit brother.

Now if only the sketchy hacker guy would respond to my messages.

I take the few steps to my bed and sink down onto the comforter, pink, soft, and with lacy hearts stitched all over. Shane didn't leave me much when he disappeared, and sometimes I wonder what he did with it all. Trash it? Donate it? Put it in a moving van and take it wherever? But I've created my very own space at Jake's. As soon as he offered me a room here, I took the meager funds in my secret bank account and bought a new comforter set, a used bookshelf for the books Shane left in the apartment, and new supplies for my folded art creations. Pink and black is my jam, so I basically have a bookshelf half filled with black-covered dark romance and the rest pink-covered fluffy romcoms. On top of the bookcase, I have a few of my book folding art pieces. A hedgehog, a rabbit, the word love... each page of an old book folded to create something new.

The divorce has been a long time coming. After love bombing the shit out of me at the beginning, years of controlling, neglect, emotional abuse, and abandonment followed. I had been stuck with a father who never protected me from the family lifestyle or his lowlife associates, but I realized I didn't have to be stuck with a husband like that.

Shane refused the divorce and then avoided me, spending more time than usual on out-of-town assignments before he disappeared. I just know it's because he was waiting for my dad's inheritance to clear. My father's estate was to be divided three ways between me, Jake, and our half-sister Meadow, who lives in New York City. Shane kept demanding half of the inheritance to even consider a divorce, and when I said no, he called me a *fucking boring-ass good girl.* And not good girl in a hot way.

A month ago, I took a weekend trip to get away from the drama with my best friend, Lola, who I met years ago back when we both worked at the library. I came home to an almost empty apartment. All that was left were my clothes and books.

My book folding art supplies and creations? Gone. Out of spite, because he always hated my hobby.

My mother's ring? Gone. To control me. I squeeze my eyes shut and think about the ring, willing it to reappear on my finger. It's a green emerald set in gold, with swirling vines of roses etched into the band. It was my grandmother's ring, and my mother wore it until she gifted it to me at the end of my senior year of high school, right before she died.

Honey Bunny was nowhere to be found. Shane fucked with my *rabbit.*

But as I cried to Lola on the phone with the door of the apartment wide open, the sweet old lady who lived next door popped out and told me she'd found my poor bunny hopping around the hallway unsupervised, so she took him in and gave him water and lettuce.

I probably could've convinced the landlord to let me stay

in our old apartment, but I didn't want to be alone there in case Shane decided to come back. And since Dad's fancy apartment in Portland sold right away, I ended up at Jake's.

A second later, I feel the comforter shift as my giant lop-eared rabbit jumps up from the floor and hops over to snuggle up next to my thigh.

"Hey Honey Bunny." I scratch the top of the rabbit's soft head and sigh. "I know you'll be happy never to see that asshole again, huh."

Finally, two weeks ago, the inheritance check arrived, and I deposited it to the account Shane doesn't know about.

Now all I want is to find that asshole and my ring, and get him to sign the divorce papers so I can be well and done before starting a new life far from here. Lola hates the idea of me leaving as she thinks I'm running away from my problems, but while Jake hasn't explicitly said how he feels about it, I bet he'll be happy to get rid of all my drama.

I'd picked a Master's in Library Science program across the country. With my share of Dad's estate, I can start over and get a degree to become an actual librarian, a big promotion from the library assistant job I do now. I'd wanted to do that for years, but Shane sneered at the idea.

It's time to move on.

I'm going to live a quiet, completely non-criminal life far from here.

My phone pings with a Gone message. I tap through to the message and breathe out in relief because Hawk agreed to talk. I send a day and time to meet at a coffee shop in Portland.

Lola thinks I'm nuts for reaching out to this guy. Of course, she's usually too busy making heart eyes at my brother to pay much attention. I did promise her I wouldn't do anything stupid, so I'm going to have to stretch the truth a little so she doesn't freak out.

Everyone ignores me anyway, so they'll probably not even notice.

And maybe starting Friday, when I meet up with Hawk, I can get some answers that lead me to Shane and my mother's ring.

CHAPTER 3

SINGLE FOR A REASON

WES

I'm not sure what she's trying to do here, but if it's watching me without me noticing, Callie Callahan is the worst fucking... stalker? I've ever encountered.

I spotted her the second I turned onto the Portland side street and ducked into Maine Coffee Co.

Thanks to her offering me her full government name, I know a lot about Callie. I don't blame her for thinking she's still mostly anonymous, as not everyone has my particular skill set, but lordy, she should be more careful. With my previous knowledge of the Callahan family and a little digging, I confirmed that her family is the organized crime group I thought it was, including her late father, her brother who she lives with, and the man she's looking for—her husband. The family is involved in fight clubs, smuggling, and drugs. Lovely people, I'm sure.

Callie's in a pink puffy coat leaning against the building across the street and blatantly staring at me. She's clearly freezing standing out there in the February bitter cold, and a few stray snowflakes drift down from the sky, a warning about the storm to come. She's wearing gloves and a black beanie hat and looks adorable, yet also like she might be on the verge of frostbite. For a second, I wish I were here to meet her on a date instead of as a client, but my line of work means I'm not able to have a normal dating life. So I basically just don't have one at all.

I order a second coffee at the counter from the barista, who has short blue hair and a nose ring. She scans my tattoo sleeves peeking out of my hoodie and the ink that snakes up the side of my neck. I nod politely but ignore her interested expression and return to the table. It's logical to assume most women don't want to date serial killers, so why bother? I prop my phone in front of me and open my baking-focused social media account.

Ruth Roy's latest Pinterest-worthy photo of pie distracts me. Fuuuuck me, that same perfect apple pie with rich streusel crumbles that has won her first place four years in a row.

That eighty-year-old menace hates me, but I like to think it's because she feels threatened as I beat her the first time I entered the pie competition five years ago. I make a mental note to swing by the winter farmer's market this weekend to grab some fresh fruit. I need to decide on what kind of top crust I'll go for this year.

Remembering my purpose today, I click off the screen so I don't lose track of Callie. The woman is still staring blatantly at the coffee shop, the least subtle person on the face of the planet. I know she's watching, so I make a show of tapping my phone again and opening Gone.

ME

You on your way? I'm here

Without turning my head, I watch Callie slip her phone

out of her pocket and make a distressed face. She glances my way, clearly indecisive.

I bite back a smirk and wait to see what she'll do.

CC95

So sorry, I need to reschedule. Something came up. Tomorrow?

The woman is standing me up? We're about a forty-five-minute drive from my isolated lakefront cabin in Lake Savage, so not exactly around the corner. Ballsy of her to stand up a hired people hunter.

She doesn't know about the serial killer part, of course.

Normally, I wouldn't mind making the drive again, but the forecast says we'll get hit with a pretty big snowstorm tonight.

What's her plan? Why not just talk to me?

ME

If the storm isn't too bad

I dramatically stand, shrug into my black jacket, and take a last swig of my coffee, giving her time to scatter, as I'm sure she'll do. When I get out of Maine Coffee Co and feel the icy cold on my face, I subtly observe her take two steps back. Trying to hide, maybe?

She can't actually be part of a crime family, because she isn't pulling this off very well.

My car's only a block away, and I slowly stroll to it and slide into the front seat, keeping an eye on her rushing to her own car across the street. Surely she's not going to follow me.

But when I pull my car out of the street parking spot, she makes a crazy U-turn, drawing all the attention to herself. I snort as I slow, stopping early at a yellow light so she doesn't miss it.

Her impulsiveness reminds me of Noah. I don't understand people who don't have a concrete plan in place before doing something potentially dangerous. But she seems harmless, and her nervousness intrigues me in a whimsical sort of way. So I guess we'll see what happens.

There's no way she'll trail me out of Portland once she realizes I don't live around here, right? I'm a stranger to her, communicate on an anonymous encrypted app, and might be willing to find someone who doesn't want to be found. Not the kind of person you casually follow out of the city.

But she does.

Callie keeps a bit of distance on the road out of Portland and toward the inner state lake areas, but subtlety is hopeless once' we get off the main road and snake along the small county routes to Lake Savage, a tiny town set on a large lake, very popular in the summer tourist season, but quiet in the off season. We're on a narrow two-lane road with houses set back from the street, a rough gravelly shoulder, and lots of trees.

So yeah, I can clearly see her following me. Eighty-year-old Ruth Roy would see her.

Then again, that old lady has the senses of a fucking hawk, and the murderous instinct as well. She's probably a fucking axe murderer.

Once I merge onto the even more sparsely populated lake road leading to my cabin, Callie drops farther back. I slow so she doesn't miss when I turn onto the long private driveway leading to my lakefront cabin.

I pull up to the cabin and into my garage and consider texting Noah, figuring my brother will be home at his own cabin just a mile down the road.

But I can handle this myself. Whatever this is.

And *this* isn't my fault. I didn't bring her here or try to get her to follow me. I might've made it easier, but the woman seems like she needs something but is too scared to talk to me, so really I'm helping her. Still, I probably should've tried to shake her on the drive home, or gone to Main Street in Lake Savage to get her to leave me alone.

Something about her intrigues me, and it only has a little to do with the fact that she's cute. I don't let myself talk to women very often because there's no point. I don't have many friends, and I definitely don't have girlfriends. Only some acquaintances in Lake Savage and my brother, plus the work we do.

The plan right now is to wait for Callie and then send her on her way after a quick chat.

I slowly get out of my car, forgoing the garage door entrance and instead whistling to myself as I stroll around the house and up the rocky path to my cabin's front door. I pause for a second to admire the view of the lake. I'm looking forward to the winter storm that's due to hit. There's a gorgeous silence and serenity that comes when the world— or at least my woodsy part of it—is covered in a thick fresh blanket of snow.

While I'm standing here, I click through to my extensive network of cameras around my property. It shows Callie's parked her car on the road and is slowly walking down the driveway. Like, just walking down the middle of it, crunching gravel, as if I'm not going to notice. Oh, look, she popped behind a tree.

I press my lips together to suppress a grin. I guess I'll go in and wait.

Once inside, I call out to Sir Fluffy. He comes ambling

over from the family room, where he was almost definitely napping in the crook of the old gray armchair.

Sir Fluffy showed up at my door a few winters ago half frozen and hasn't left. The elderly black cat limps over and meows, so I squat and pet his head. This sweet soul is a little mangy, with one ear looking like it was previously chewed on by something with big teeth. His fur isn't fluffy or particularly soft, but I didn't want him to get a complex, so I named him Sir Fluffy. For some dignity in old age.

"Come on, kitty." He follows me into the kitchen, and I pour a too-large portion of hard cat food into a bowl, then drop a treat on top. As he chomps away at his dinner, I admire the apple pie I baked this morning, under the glass and safe from the cat.

Then I throw a few fresh logs into the fireplace and poke at it until it's crackling with flame and warmth. All within sight of the large window in my family room.

It's a performance for the woman who has moved to another tree, closer to the house. At least she's not standing in the middle of my driveway. Sigh. Maybe I'll have to bring her inside to talk to her. I have a feeling she's not gonna knock on my front door.

I slip out of view of the window to grab the supplies I need from the closet by the back door, then pull on my jacket and balaclava. The last thing I do in the house is to click off the Wi-Fi and turn on the cell service blocker so it appears as if we're in a dead zone, except for my personal devices. Noah's got one too. We don't prefer to bring targets into our homes, but it definitely happens sometimes.

Then I slide out the back door, gently closing it behind me.

Snowflakes drift lazily down from a white sky. I guess I shouldn't worry about what the roads will look like tomorrow, when Callie wants to reschedule, because it turns out I probably won't have to go anywhere.

I trek down the wooded pathway to the shoreline, the frozen lake bright and still, then back up and around the house, approaching Callie from behind. She's still standing partway behind a tree in her pink puffy coat, staring at my cabin.

I take a second to consider what I'm about to do. Noah is the impulsive one, not me. He would just knock her over the head and tie her up without a second thought.

But Jesus Christ. Callie Callahan might as well have a neon blinking sign over her head. *Find me here! I'm watching you! I'm a terrible stalker!*

I shouldn't do this. I could just say, hey, what are you doing? And let her run away from me untouched.

But I don't want her to run away.

I want to know what she's thinking. What she's planning, if anything. I'm almost giddy with the thought of talking to her.

Callie's not even paying attention to her surroundings, so intent on staring at my cabin, where nothing at all is happening. So much so that I can walk up behind her, and she doesn't even notice me.

Not until I lift the syringe to her neck.

Fuck, this is why I'm single, isn't it?

CHAPTER 4

POOR DECISION MAKING

CALLIE

I am so not a stalker.

I'm also not a criminal, which is more than I can say for my late father, my brother, and my soon-to-be ex-husband.

What the fuck am I doing here? I'm fueled by anger and spite, which is what I'm mostly made up of these days. I'm like three rabid raccoons in a trench coat.

And I'm huddled behind a damn tree in the middle of the woods spying on this gorgeous but almost certainly fucked-up dude.

I shiver and rub my arms with gloved hands. I totally chickened out of meeting him back in Portland in public where I would have been safe. Safer. And then as he strode down the sidewalk toward his car—after I realized that yes, my first thought when watching him through the coffee shop window was correct, he's insanely hot—I panicked that he might not agree to meet me again. Maybe he'll think it's a trap or I'm the cops or something. Then Shane's words echoed in my head, calling me a boring-ass good girl. I might

23

be looking to get rid of all the criminal nonsense that surrounds me, but that doesn't mean what Shane said is true. I'm not boring.

And I can't let Hawk slip through my fingers.

I almost didn't even reach out to him. But what choice did I have? Just wait around for Shane to call me again or show up at Jake's apartment? Nightmare.

Hawk responded. And showed up. Tall and broad-shouldered and dark-haired with tattoos on his exposed forearms. He also smiled at the woman who walked by with her baby and said thank you to the barista who came to collect his empty coffee cup.

So I followed him. He might've been local, and I could learn something else about him. Maybe he'd go home, and his real name and social security number would be posted on his door for easy reference.

Instead, I'm in the middle of the woods, the sky heavy and the cold, wet smell of impending snow in the air.

Maybe if I'd been a part of the family business, I'd be good at this stuff. Finding people. Forcing people to do what I want. Sneaking around.

Maybe then my marriage wouldn't have crashed and burned.

Shane's father was part of a different crime family, and our fathers had been friendly. When his dad was killed in a job gone wrong and Shane ousted from the group, Dad offered him a place to stay, a low-level job with the family, and some mentorship. He even pushed Shane to change his name for safety. At that point, I was in the middle of getting my bachelor's degree at a community college and had already moved out into a tiny studio apartment.

Over the next year or two, I slowly got to know Shane. It had only been a few years since my mom had died, and I'd felt such empathy for his loss. We bonded. The summer we got together, I spent a lot of time at the house. At the time, Dad lived on a lake outside of Portland, and we'd sit on the dock side-by-side, letting our legs swing from the wooden platform and soaking in the summer. His sadness was deep and raw and drew me in.

That's when it got intense.

Shane wrote me love letters and called me five times a day and constantly texted. He brought me flowers and wanted every minute of my time. In hindsight, it was obvious he was love-bombing me, but I couldn't see it. He moved out of Dad's house and into my apartment, even though my father strongly disapproved.

Then I got pregnant, and Shane immediately proposed. My father was furious, but at that point, I loved pissing him off. It was the only time he actually paid attention to me. Ever since an awful incident when I was a freshman in high school, I knew that man didn't have my back. And clearly he didn't have Shane's, either.

Shane and I married quickly, and Dad reluctantly accepted him into our family.

I lost the baby.

Things turned fast. Shane became overly critical and withdrawn, claiming he was upset about the baby, pushing me to get pregnant again. He was emotionally abusive and manipulative. Shane was constantly chasing that feeling of belonging in our family. He wanted to *be* my father's son.

It took my father's death to shake me out of it.

It's fucking cold out here. I shudder and sigh loudly, then freeze. Shit. I should remember what I'm doing, standing in the middle of the woods behind a tree, spying on a man who is probably a criminal, just like my family. Someone I want absolutely no part of. How much noise have I been making?

What if he's looking out that window and sees me lurking in the woods?

I need to focus, both right now and overall. Find Shane. Finalize divorce. Get Mom's ring back. Move to Seattle. Get my master's degree.

Start my life over.

To get to that goal, I'm gonna have to wade through some nasty shit.

Like standing in the middle of the woods. Alone. With a snowstorm about to start, as illustrated by the large, lazy snowflakes drifting down through the trees.

This is exactly what Lola means when she talks about my poor decision-making. Which is why I didn't tell my best friend my new plan to find Shane. Her opinion was that he didn't want to be found, and I should just wait for him to reemerge.

Not go chasing after him by hiring another criminal to help.

I pull out my phone to text her, because maybe I *should've* told Lola about coming here, but naturally there is zero service. In the middle of the woods.

Which definitely means I need to get back to Portland before I get stuck out here. I shake my head and slip my phone back into my pocket. It's already dark, stupid February in stupid Maine. I want to go home and hang out with Honey Bunny.

The idea of snuggling on my bed with my rabbit and a book page art project spurs me to action. I adjust my beanie. I'll message Hawk when I get back to the apartment. I'll apologize profusely and ask to talk over the phone instead.

But as I start to turn, a branch cracks behind me.

Then I feel a prick in my neck, and everything goes dark.

CHAPTER 5

SINGLE FOR ANOTHER REASON

WES

Callie crumples, and I catch her, feeling instantly bad for sedating her. I might do some questionable shit, but I would never intentionally hurt a woman or a girl.

But my curiosity is too strong to just let her go without getting some answers. I want to have an innocent conversation with her.

And *she's* stalking *me*. It's not like I went out to kidnap her. I'm innocent here, for fuck's sake. This is not! A kidnapping!

I lift Callie into my arms, careful not to let her head loll back and hurt her neck. She's as light as a feather, although her coat is puffy enough that it feels like carrying a marshmallow.

The snow is falling heavier now, and the air is cold and crisp in the way that predicts a big storm, but my face is protected by my balaclava.

I only have a few minutes to get her situated inside before she comes to, so I half-jog to my back door. She's most likely going to freak out when she wakes up, and I want to be sufficiently prepared.

I push the unlocked door open and turn to sidestep into the cabin, careful of Callie's head and the doorframe. The heat feels good, and her cheeks pinken while I prop her on the wooden kitchen chair I have set in front of the fire. But fuck, she's going to be too hot if I zip-tie her while she's still in her winter gear, and then she'll want to take it off, and I'll have to cut the ties, and she might not be ready for that. *I might not be ready for that.*

Feeling kind of like a creep, I unzip her puffy jacket. The zipper gets stuck at the bottom, and I have to use two hands to hold the zipper together and tug it down. Finally it comes undone, and I shimmy her coat off one arm. Her head lolls to one side, and I shoot my hand up to catch her. Her cheeks are still so cold.

"Fuck me," I mutter.

Sir Fluffy, watching me from in front of the fire, meows with deep judgement.

I finally get her jacket off and toss it to the side. Underneath, she's wearing a tight long-sleeved shirt, and I'd be lying if I said I didn't take a second to admire the way her shirt is snug against her breasts. And when I pull her arms behind the chair and secure the zip ties, that does an even better job of showcasing her tits.

I'm not a pervert, so I don't let my gaze linger as I secure her legs. This situation has not arisen because I think she's hot—which she obviously is—it's arisen because she was on my property. But it has been a long time since I've even had a conversation with a woman I'm remotely attracted to. There aren't many eligible women under the age of sixty in Lake Savage, I don't go to Portland searching for hookups, and I'm not into online dating like Noah.

The last time I let myself get involved with a woman was several years ago, and she didn't appreciate the way I kept her safe.

By tracking her, obviously.

But that woman looked at it in all the wrong ways. Late one night when I was following her, I realized she was meeting up with another man for a drink. We weren't exclusive, but I was furious anyway. Furious and hurt. After their drink—during which I lurked in a dark corner of the bar, anger swirling inside me—they came out and walked down a quiet side street, then ducked into a dark alley. He pushed her against a building and began kissing her roughly. She was into it at first, and I probably should've walked away. I shouldn't have watched. But I stayed, hidden in a shadow. And she's lucky I did, because then she was pushing him away, and he wasn't stopping, and they were in a dark, isolated alley so what would've happened if I hadn't been there? My temper got the best of me, and I intervened. Everyone walked away from the incident, some in better shape than others.

She did not thank me for protecting her.

"There. Done." I stand, then kneel to acknowledge Sir Fluffy as he walks over and purrs against my leg. Then he meows.

"Yeah, I know, her head is totally tilting to one side." I tug Callie's black beanie off her head, setting free dark, wavy hair that hangs halfway down her back.

She's really beautiful. I have to clench my hand to stop myself from running my fingers through her locks, because that would be even creepier than this situation already is.

I'm not a creepy guy. Not really, anyway. But she'll definitely be concerned when she comes to.

I sigh and drop my head. *Focus.* I stand and watch her for

signs of waking up. Nothing yet, but her neck will not feel good if she stays in that position for much longer.

I don't normally worry about the people I zip-tie getting a neck ache, but she's different. Most aren't good people and don't have much of a future.

I shrug off my jacket, hang it on the hook by the front door, and pull my hoodie over my head before striding down the hall to my room. My airplane pillow—which I was in too much of a rush to remember to grab for the Florida trip earlier this week—is sitting right on top of the small suitcase in my closet.

Back by the fire, Sir Fluffy watches as I adjust the pillow around Callie's neck and fuck—I really am a psychopath, aren't I?

Then her eyes flutter open.

I'd seen pictures of Callie during my online stalking, but the depth of her dark brown eyes wasn't obvious in any of the images. Gorgeous.

"Hello." Best to start simple, right? Maybe if I act normal, she won't freak out.

Callie's eyes widen. Nope, definitely terrified.

Then she screams.

It's so loud and piercing that I wince and cover my ears. I guess I should've gagged her or duct-taped her mouth, but who knew she'd react like this?

Me. I did.

"Help. Help! Heeellllp!" Then she starts her piercing scream again, and I'm so fucking happy there's no one within screaming distance of my cabin. Sir Fluffy zooms out of the living room and disappears down the hall.

"Hey. Hey!" I wave my hands in the air.

But Callie doesn't stop. She shakes her body, moving the chair inch by inch.

What's she gonna do, fling her zip-tied self out the front door? She locks her eyes with mine and then I realize she's not just scared—although there's definitely a layer of fear there—she's also furious.

I stride into the kitchen, find a thin dishtowel, then dash back and attempt to wrap it around her head. She's whipping her head back and snapping at me like an agitated alligator. Even the airplane pillow falls to the carpet.

"What the fuck?" Now I'm sweating, but I finally get the dishtowel tied and the volume of the noise coming out of her decreases greatly.

I take a deep breath and walk back around to the front of her.

"You need to calm the fuck down."

She growls at me, and I take an involuntary step back, as if I'm not six foot three and two hundred pounds of muscle. Callie's gotta be a foot shorter than me and scrawny, except for those tits, the ones that keep bouncing as she shakes and squirms in the chair.

She's terrifying. And beautiful.

Embarrassingly, I feel my dick getting hard.

"Alright, listen. I don't want to have you zip-tied. I definitely don't want to have you gagged."

Callie growls at me again. I hold up a finger.

"But if you recall, I found *you* on *my* property." I point to her, then myself. I don't think she appreciates my charades. "You hired me to find someone, but you showed up here, which honestly wasn't at all what I expected."

She narrows her eyes at me.

"You were stalking me?" I nod, looking for her acknowledgment. "Well, I guess following me home once isn't really stalking, it's more like staking out. Like a complete amateur, I might add."

She has the audacity to roll her eyes. I sink down onto my couch and lean my elbows on my knees.

"And you followed me here from Portland. I don't know, you could be dangerous." I throw my hands in the air. "You could've had a gun. I hate guns."

It's true. As inconvenient as it can be for our line of work, both Noah and I avoid using guns as much as possible. They give us PTSD. The world would have far fewer problems if there weren't any guns.

She shakes her head, then shuts her eyes and takes a deep breath, her shoulders rising and falling.

"Mmmffffp." She opens and then narrows her eyes at me. "Rrrfff ifff offff."

"Sorry, I didn't understand that." I touch my ear and lean forward. "It's almost like you are asking me to take something off. What would you like me to take off?"

She just stares at me.

"My shirt? I get asked to do that sometimes. I don't go to the gym, but I do a lot of manual labor around the cabin." I flex my biceps for her. She sighs deeply instead of looking impressed, her eyes only fleetingly glancing at my bulging muscles. "Oh, *your* shirt?" I ask hopefully.

I wonder if I've gone too far in my attempt to make her smile. She said in her messages she's looking to serve her husband divorce papers, but who knows if they really are splitting up. Maybe she wants to find him and try to reconcile first. Maybe she's highly offended by me in general. I should back off.

"Fffff eww."

Or maybe she's just mad at her current situation.

"Fuck you? I think I'm starting to understand your language." I chuckle and stand, walking around to the back of her. "But if I take this off, no screaming. Just talking. Okay?"

She nods aggressively.

I untie the knot and tug the towel off her face, then step back around to the front of her. Not too close, though, because now her mouth—and teeth—are free.

"Are you fucking kidding me?" she shrieks and lets out a frustrated scream.

"Ahhh, you promised." I step away from her. Her screaming really hurts my damn ears.

She huffs and grinds her teeth, as if holding herself back from continuing to scream.

"But isn't this better now?" I ask, hope filling me. I pull a chair from my kitchen table and spin it around, sitting on it backwards a safe distance away from her. "Let's start over. I'm Wes."

Her eyes flit over my face, and I wish I knew what she was thinking. Now she looks anxious, like once I'm right here in front of her she loses her nerve.

"Wes? I thought it was Hawk?"

"That's my Gone name. You didn't use your real name on Gone, did you?"

Callie's cheeks flush even pinker, and not from the warm fire contrasting the cold outside.

"My name is Callie," she says through gritted teeth. "Which you know."

"Hm." I raise a single eyebrow at her.

"Hm what?" She puts extra emphasis on the *T* in *what*.

God, the attitude on this one? Amazing. And while I'm almost positive she's not flirting with me, maybe she is.

Nah. I need to get out more.

But while finding someone to flirt with is not super hard

—the barista from Maine Coffee Co comes to mind—dating someone is impossible.

I haven't been a normal human being since the murder of my family. Something broke in me that day, just like something broke in my brother.

Noah makes fun of me for never dating, but I'm not sure why he thinks his online-only dating is more respectable. The guy won't date a woman who lives within five hundred miles of us. That way, he can keep his dating life separate from his normal life, which is very much not normal. Five *hundred* miles.

"Hello? Where'd you just go? I need you to focus, Wes-Hawk, because I'm literally fucking zip-tied to your chair."

I blink out of my daydream and focus on the beautiful, angry woman in front of me.

"Just Wes. And we are—as you know because you followed me here—in my isolated cabin in the Maine woods."

"Oh fuck off, we're forty-five minutes from Portland."

I let out a chuckle, and she looks surprised for a split second, then one side of her mouth twitches, and I almost think she's going to smile. Then it's gone.

"I'm sorry. I didn't mean to say fuck off. I'm just a little unnerved by the situation. Can you pretty please un-zip-tie me?"

"No. You definitely did mean to say it, and I'm frankly pretty terrified as to what you'd do if I set you free." I tilt my head at her.

She sighs like I'm an infuriating child on the thousandth round of the why game.

I hang my arms over the chair back and don't miss how her eyes flit to my exposed forearms, tattoos partially visible due to my hoodie sleeves pushed up.

"Okay, so if you won't cut me loose, can you please let me know what you plan on doing to me?"

Her words sink in, and my stomach twists. I wouldn't do anything to her. To any woman. Men—bad men—sure. We fuck them all the way up. Noah and I might not like guns, but that's not the only way to take care of business.

But a woman? Our whole purpose is to eliminate bad men who target women and girls. Because what haunts both of us is the fact that the asshole who came for my father didn't blink an eye before he shot my defenseless mother and then turned on my innocent younger sister.

If only that man—the one who is already dead—had the same reservations we do about hurting women.

But he didn't.

CHAPTER 6

GORGEOUS MASKED KIDNAPPER

CALLIE

The briefest pain flickers over Wes's face, and then it's gone. But I don't have time to wonder about it because the plastic digging into my wrists is killing me. I won't be able to slip out of it, so I should just stay still and wait for this admittedly very attractive but dangerous man to reveal his plans.

This is all my fault. Shane doesn't want to be found. He'll reveal himself when he damn well pleases. Involving someone like Hawk in this was an obvious mistake. Thanks, Jake.

I can hear my best friend in my head. *But you actually followed him to his isolated Maine cabin, Callie.* Shut up, Lola! Also, I should've listened to her, my best friend who did not grow up in a crime family.

"Are you okay?" Wes asks, his voice dripping with what must be fake concern.

"What?" I snap out of my reverie and can't help but stare at his exposed arms, covered in bulging muscles and damn, those tattoos. Seeing them up close is intoxicating. His right forearm has ivy and roses covering all of the skin, snaking up into his sleeve and reappearing at the crook of his shoulder and neck. It's beautiful. His other forearm has a skull with a dagger through the eye and a thorny vine without flowers disappearing into his hoodie sleeve.

I got a tattoo after my father died. It was the start of my road to freedom from my family and Shane, and represents strength and transformation. It's a giant phoenix with its wings spread, ascending while facing upward, the image starting below my right breast and stretching out along my right side and onto my hip.

Shane disappeared before he even realized I had it.

That's two fucked-up men I'll be free of soon.

My brother, the third? I can't bring myself to cut him out of my life. Not yet, anyway. I don't think he's a bad person. He just needs to reassess his priorities.

"You just had about a million expressions cross your face," Wes says, again with the kind voice. He's examining my face as if he really wants to understand me.

"What, so you're an emotional mind reader?" I snap at him. Fuck him! He has me zip-tied. Zip-tied!

The asshole has the nerve to grin.

"I have been told I have a very high emotional IQ."

"Told by whom?" What on earth is he talking about? Emotional IQs? I almost forget to be mad and scared.

Wes shrugs, and we stare at each other for a full minute, him with an infuriatingly adorable little smirk on his full lips, and me giving my best scowl, but I'm sure it's coming off as confusion. He's got a sharp jawline and icy blue eyes that look almost clear. Broad shoulders, sinewy forearms hinting at muscles for days. He is truly a beautiful man.

"Alright, Callie Callahan," Wes says in a soft voice, licking his lips as he watches me examine his face. He sits up and crosses his arms, his shoulders pushing against his sleeves. "Why don't we talk about finding your husband?"

"Huh?" I twist my wrists, but the plastic bites into my flesh even more.

"You messaged me to meet up. Said you wanted me to find your husband—"

"Ex husband, as soon as I can make it happen." I interrupt him because I hate referring to Shane as my husband, even though it's technically true. And it feels important that Wes understands that.

"Right. Okay." Wes nods thoughtfully. "So let's talk about that."

"I don't want to work with you anymore." The nerve of this guy? I scoff. "Is this how you handle your business?"

But of course it is. Criminals and all.

Still, I kinda wish I hadn't just said those words. If Wes doesn't help me, then who will? I'll just head back to Jake's apartment, head hanging, and continue to wait for Shane to show up?

Wes raises an eyebrow, then glances at the fire, which is still glowing warm against my back.

"Why don't you think about it for a few more minutes before you make that decision? I need to grab more firewood." Wes nods outside. "We'll need it tonight."

"Tonight?" My voice is high-pitched, but when I glance out the large window, I have a sinking feeling, like an anchor slipping from my lungs to my gut.

It's dark, but an outside light illuminates the fact that there's a freaking blizzard outside.

Wes is already zipping up his jacket. He pulls on black

gloves and a full black balaclava. When his hand is on the front door to the cabin, he turns to me. Only his eyes are visible, and I can see the blue from across the room.

Oh my god. Why do I find him so hot right now?? Is it the freaking mask? I never knew I had a mask kink. I don't! No mask kink. No zip tie kink. No kink for bad-boy kidnappers. I'm not one of those girls.

But this makes me wonder if maybe I am? Because I like what's happening right now way more than a boring-ass good girl should.

"Don't go anywhere. I'll be right back." Then Wes fucking *winks*.

"Hey!" I shout, but then he's out the door.

At least his absence gives me a second to think, like he suggested.

I shouldn't have followed him home. I shouldn't have even contacted him. Of course he'd do something like kidnap me.

I get that I was on his property. Technically, I broke the law first. But he stabbed me in the neck with a needle, dragged me into his cabin, and—wait, where's my jacket? I spot it on the couch, my beanie neatly placed on top. He took my jacket off and then tied me up. In front of a nice, warm fire, which I have to admit feels wonderful. He even tucked an airplane pillow around my neck, which is now on the floor a few feet away. I mean, he didn't have to do that.

No! The kidnapper is not thoughtful. And I should not ask the kidnapper for help finding Shane.

But... what are my options? I have basically no survival skills thanks to my refusal to engage with my family's business.

I should've checked the weather.

I should've brought a friend.

I should've hired a normal private detective, not accepted a recommendation from my criminal brother. But I know I couldn't have done that, because it would expose myself and my family to extra scrutiny.

I'd happily throw my father to the authorities. I should've. But that would endanger Jake and most definitely myself. And I'm not like my father. I care if people I love are in danger.

When I was a freshman in high school, there was an incident at our house. Ever since my cousin had been murdered, I'd tried to steer clear of my father and his business. One night, Dad had a few associates over for some kind of meeting that involved a lot of alcohol and cursing and obnoxious laughing. As usual, I stayed away, quiet, and was getting ready to go to bed when one of the men cornered me in the upstairs bathroom, where he shouldn't have been. I smelled the liquor on his breath as he pressed me up against the wall—his disgusting erection pressed against my belly—and whispered vulgar things in my ear. I managed to kick him in the balls and slip out of his grasp as he doubled over in pain.

I didn't bother telling my father. Instead, I first told my brother, then sixteen, and he paled and said he'd install a deadbolt on the inside of my bedroom door and the bathroom. He did that, but was too chicken to confront my father. Aren't families supposed to stand up for you? My father and brother should be the ones protecting me. Maybe they weren't the ones that threw me under the bus, but they're definitely the ones that left me on the road.

I told my mother, and she at least tried to help. She picked a fight with my father about it and tried to leave him, but my father said I could go with her but not Jake. Mom relented, a sorrowful look on her face. She wouldn't leave her son. But I felt like I was being sacrificed.

That was an early lesson on how no one in this family would choose me first. Not even my mother.

So I have to choose myself.

Movement outside the cabin window catches my eye, and my jaw drops as I watch Wes stride over the snow-covered ground back toward the cabin with two arms full of firewood balanced on his shoulders. My mouth actually waters, and I try to swallow, but my throat is so dry I almost choke.

Fine. I might have a mask kink. And it would be even closer to my sort of new fantasy if he were shirtless. If Shane wore a mask and tied me up, I'd be terrified. I'd never have asked him to do that. I would want to experience it in a safe way, which sounds fucked up.

I can unpack that at a much later date. Or never.

There's a sound of firewood hitting the porch boards, then cold air and snowflakes rush in when the front door opens again.

Wes drops the remaining wood on his front mat as he strips out of his jacket, slips his boots off, and turns to me. Is he going to leave the mask on?

And maybe take off his shirt?

Shut up! Dammit.

I roll my eyes and look away from him, but out of the edge of my vision, I see him pull the mask off and run his hand through his longish dark hair.

Wes carries the logs over to the fireplace, and by the flare of fire and crackling sound behind me, I'm guessing he added one to the fire.

"My wrists hurt," I say. Not that my kidnapper will care.

"Hmm."

I feel his presence approach my back from the fireplace, and I turn my head to look over my shoulder.

"What are you doing?" He's close. So close. I can smell him, fresh air and smoke from the fireplace and some other woodsy scent. A shiver runs down my spine, and I feel his hands on my wrists, gently touching.

"That is red. I'm sorry." His voice is low and warm and close. And he sounds sincere.

I half expect him to cut the plastic strips off me, but he doesn't. A kind kidnapper is still a kidnapper. Instead, he heads to his kitchen, which is within my line of sight.

"Want coffee? Hot chocolate? Tea?"

"You're offering me a beverage?" I huff. "What the fuck kind of kidnapper are you?"

He freezes with his hand on the refrigerator, then turns around, hurt etched onto his handsome face.

"I didn't kidnap you."

"Um. I was walking through the woods minding my own business, but now I'm tied to a chair in your cabin. What would you call this?" I jiggle my arms a little to emphasize but regret it right away when the plastic digs into my wrists.

His brow furrows when I flinch. "Minding your own business?"

"Yes." How dare he? Fine. Maybe I wasn't quite minding my own business, but still. Zip ties.

"You were hiding behind a tree watching my cabin after following me home from Portland. What would you call that?"

I scoff.

"So you're afraid of me? Which is why I'm tied up?" I wiggle my body in frustration, moving the chair an inch forward.

His eyes flick down to the chair legs, then back up to my

face. Then Wes just… stares at me, clearly and shockingly concerned. Instead of answering my very logical question, he pulls out his phone, taps it a bunch of times, then slides it back in his pocket.

"What'd you just do? And where's my phone?"

Wes turns and takes two steps, then reaches for something on the kitchen counter and strides toward me.

It's a huge fucking knife.

"Wait!" Panic grips my body as he approaches me, his face blank.

I'm gonna die. Now's the moment. And it's my fault because I followed him home and then picked a fight with this psychopath while I'm tied up in his remote cabin. Shit! I squint my eyes shut just as the walls creak with whipping wind. Is he gonna cut my throat? Stab me in the belly? Cut off my fingers one by one?

Then I feel the smooth, cold metal on my hands.

Guess it's my fingers. I feel pinpricks of tears in my eyes.

"Please," I whisper, my voice pathetic.

But then I feel the pressure release on my wrists.

He cut the zip ties? I pull my wrists in front of my face. He cut the zip ties.

"Oh my god." I spring up, intending on, I don't know, running out of the cabin or attacking him or something, but then I immediately fall face first onto the thick rug, my cheek hitting the ground hard. The air's completely knocked out of my lungs, and I can't get a sound out or a breath in.

My ankles are still tied to the chair.

"Fuck!" Wes swears and falls to his knees next to me, the knife still in his hands. "Are you okay? I'm so sorry." He touches my back and peers down at me. "You're lucky you didn't hit the other chair with your face."

I struggle and finally manage to suck in a breath. Perhaps

I should just give up on life now. I can't get anything right. A single tear breaks free from my eye and drips down the bridge of my nose.

"Were you trying to run?" Wes wipes the tear off with a gentle touch. "It's a blizzard outside."

"Can you help me up and put down the knife?" I'm humiliated. Exhausted. Face-first in a surprisingly fluffy shag rug.

A second later, my ankles are cut free and the chair lifts off my back. Strong, knife-free hands wrap around my waist and lift me up, and for a second I'm in Wes's arms, like a bride on her wedding night.

Then he deposits me gently on the couch and sinks down next to me.

"Are you okay, Callie?"

My name on his lips is weird to hear, like we're friends, not the kidnapper and the kidnapped.

"I'm fine," I say, trying to sound tough, but when I lift my hand to my cheek, I wince.

"Your cheek might be sore. Let me get you ice so it doesn't bruise." He heads back into the kitchen and pulls a bag of frozen corn out of his freezer, walking it over. "Here, put this on your face."

Then he returns to the kitchen and pulls a half-gallon of milk from the fridge. I touch the corn to my cheek and watch him stick a pot on the stove, click it on, and pour milk in.

Now's my chance to run. Run from this... really not scary man? And run where? I'm not sure I could even make it to where I ditched my car. My car, which is shit in the snow, even though I live in Maine. At least I'm wearing sturdy boots.

Fuck, it's really snowing out now.

There's literally nowhere to go. I made a series of terrible decisions today, and now I have an aching cheek, sore wrists, and I'm sitting on the couch of this mystery dude, trapped here by snow. At least I'm no longer tied to a chair.

I consider my options.

I could leave anyway, fight my way to my car, and hope I can get off the side of the road. Maybe he'd let me, maybe he wouldn't. He's unhinged in a confusing way. Like he'll stab a woman with a needle and tie her to a chair, but then feel bad when said woman complains that her wrists hurt.

And why does he look so fucking good in the gray sweatpants and the snug hoodie that's hugging the hard lines of his body? He scoops hot chocolate mix into the pot where he poured the milk and pulls a whisk out of a drawer.

I shake my head. It doesn't matter how hot he is. Besides the fact that he's a kidnapper, I could never trust another man to keep me safe. I should never have depended on anyone to do so.

Shane kept me in my place, but not safe. He might not have hit me, but the gaslighting and the emotional abuse were intense. Over the years, he continued to try to convince me to have a baby, and when I resisted, called me selfish, a bad person, not a real woman, etc. Even right before my father died, Shane tricked me into meeting with my father's boss about working on the family's bookkeeping—as if that were something I'd ever want to do over my peaceful, safe library job. Luckily, the man let it go when I said no. But Shane flipped out and disappeared for a weekend. A few days later, someone slashed my tires, and Shane refused to give me a ride to work. I could walk or take the bus anyway.

That same week, I found a scrap of women's underwear shoved into the pocket of his jeans.

I contacted Hawk—Wes—so I could find Shane for the last time and be rid of him forever.

Maybe he'll still help me do that.

"I need to find the man I want to divorce," I say. "Can you help me?"

Wes freezes in the kitchen with his back to me, mid-whisk.

"Tell me more," he says, turning around to look at me.

CHAPTER 7

SERIOUSLY, SINGLE

WES

I'm not sure me helping her is a good idea. Domestic disputes like this can be so messy. And domestic disputes that involve the Callahan family? Extra messy. Also, I'm already not quite in control of how my body is reacting to her. It's just a physical attraction, obviously.

"How'd you lose track of him?" I sneak a look at her while I briskly whisk the hot chocolate, making sure all the cocoa mix dissolves as the milk heats.

Callie scoffs.

Sir Fluffy appears in the kitchen, stretching his legs, likely fresh from a power nap in his favorite spot in front of the heater in the guest bedroom. He meows and weaves himself in and out of my legs, begging for a treat or pets.

"You have a cat."

"I do." I glance over at her. "You're not allergic, are you?"

She narrows her eyes at me. "Why do you care?"

When I do interact with women, even pretty ones, I'm often met with flirting and interested, lingering gazes. This suspicion bordering on hostility is intriguing. Like she already doesn't like me, so I don't have to worry about impressing her. Maybe it was the zip ties.

"Noah is allergic, so he has to take daily allergy medicine and get shots so he can even walk in here."

"Noah?"

"My brother." I stop whisking and make sure the hot chocolate is lump-free. It smells delicious. "Do you have a cat?"

"No." She spits out her answer, then sighs.

I let the silence fall. What did I do to deserve her contempt?

"Sorry. I meant *no*." This time, she says the word with less force. I bite back a grin. "I have a rabbit."

"What's his name?" Given her feisty attitude, I'd have guessed she has something sharp like a hedgehog or a snake. I lay the whisk on a spoon tray shaped like a smiling moose head and pull out two mugs. The hot chocolate is the perfect temperature as I pour it—steaming, but not so much that it'll burn going down. I prepare a special serving for Callie. "Marshmallows?"

"Sure?" She half laughs, and I grin as I sprinkle in some small marshmallows. "My rabbit's name is Honey Bunny."

"That's cute." I walk over to the couch and hold out a mug. Shit. I didn't plan on a pet that might need to be fed. She's not going to like it when I insist she spend the night at the cabin for her own safety.

"You know what? You're really weird." Callie accepts the hot chocolate and wraps her hands around the ceramic, breathing in the sweet steam.

"That's not very nice." I settle on the couch an entire cushion away from her, prepared to fend her off if she attacks me. I probably shouldn't have handed her a mug of hot liquid.

"Sorry. I just—this has been a surprising evening." She glances outside, where it's already dark, but still bright because of the pure white snow blanketing the outside world. "Night?"

"What kind of rabbit is Honey Bunny?"

"A giant lop-eared." Sir Fluffy strolls over and sniffs at Callie's feet. She leans down and scratches his head. "And he would kick your cat's ass."

I chuckle. "Sir Fluffy's an old dude, so I don't doubt it."

"Sir Fluffy?" She shakes her head. "I feel like I'm in some alternate dimension right now."

"Because of the hot chocolate?" I furrow my brow. "Or because you have a rabbit named Honey Bunny, and I have a cat named Sir Fluffy?"

"Um, yes. Those things." Callie sips and moans. "This is so good."

I watch with fascination, trying to ignore my dick twitching at her moan. I'm not going to lie, I'm very much enjoying having a pretty woman curled up on my couch. It's nice to have company that isn't Noah. For a second, I picture her reaching over to rub her hand on my—

"Listen. Here's the deal. Like I said in my messages, I'm trying to divorce my husband, but I need to find him to sign the papers and return something very important to me. My mother's ring. He disappeared a month ago, then called me two weeks ago, but I have no idea where he is. And he doesn't want me to know for some reason."

Fuck. I clear my throat and adjust myself. I need to focus.

Her eyes dart down to my crotch, and she flushes. I guess I wasn't very subtle. She's definitely not thinking about touching my cock, but then I realize her nipples have hardened to little peaks beneath her tight shirt so maybe she is?

"What's the urgency?" I manage.

"I'm just… done." Callie clears her throat and smooths her hair. She pulls a thick chunk over her right shoulder. "My father died three months ago, and I realized that I want out of my marriage. I want to get away from my family and my old life. I want to start over and live a crime-free life, so I'm going to move to Seattle to get a master's in library science."

"Yeah?" I chuckle. "A librarian in Seattle sounds pretty wholesome." And the exact opposite of me. I'm the least wholesome person she could possibly connect herself to.

"I'm less going for a wholesome vibe, and more a safe one. Ethical. Legal."

"Hm. Got it." Also not words that describe me or my life.

"I already work at a library, but I'm a library assistant, not a full librarian."

"Which one do you work at?" I am very much enjoying the image of Callie Callahan in a long skirt and cute tight sweater carrying books pressed against her chest.

"The one on Congress." She shakes her head. "But that's not why we're here."

I nod, making a mental note of her workplace location, which she tossed out to me like it's nothing. I'd do just about anything to see her at work, but she should not have told me that. The woman has no sense of self-preservation.

I shouldn't agree to help Callie Callahan.

I'm too attracted to her. It's been a long time since the last weekend trip to Boston with Noah where I found a flirty woman at a bar and took her to my hotel room to fuck. She was more than happy to do whatever I wanted. She was pretty and sweet and made all the right sounds. But it was too easy. Boring. And I crave connection, not just fucking. Something tells me sleeping with Callie would be more complicated than that.

My motivation comes from protecting women and children in the way in which my mother and sister weren't. Ivy was only fourteen when she was killed. Fourteen years old. Some monster assaulted her and then looked her in her pretty blue eyes and shot her? And my mother, the kindest woman ever? My father shouldn't have done what he did to bring on the murders, but no one deserved what happened to my family.

After that first kill taking out our family's murderer, Noah and I hadn't planned to do it again. Or at least I hadn't. But my brother decided it was his life's mission, and I wasn't going to let him do it on his own. He's impulsive and gets distracted by shiny objects, so I need to protect him.

I've lost too many people. I can't lose him.

"Forget it though, I'm not sure we can recover from the way, uh, this started." She waves a hand between me and her.

"You mean you stalking me, me knocking you out, and the whole zip-tie situation? That's not the foundation for a beautiful relationship?" I sip from my mug and lick the extra chocolate from my lips. "I feel like we could move on."

She gawks at me, watching my tongue move across my upper lip.

Married to a criminal, the daughter of one, sister of one, yet she has no clue what she's doing. Callie Callahan is the world's most unlikely good girl.

She has no idea whose cabin she's in.

No idea what I'm capable of.

But... she needs my help. She needs someone's help, at least, and I think I need to be the one to provide it.

Callie needs someone to protect her.

And that's what I do best.

Callie's eyelids flutter.

Ah, good. The sedative I slipped into her hot chocolate is

taking effect. I'm feeling the slightest bit of remorse for drugging her. Again. But I'm not trying to do anything bad, I just don't want her to fight me so much on the next thing I'm going to suggest.

"So will you help?" she asks, her voice a whisper and her eyes fluttering.

"Let's talk about it tomorrow." She probably won't remember anything that happens in the next few minutes, so there's no point in agreeing. "But tonight? You're not going anywhere." I nod outside to the storm. White swirls tap on the window, the visibility to the woodpile I was at just a little while ago gone.

"I am not sleeping here." She shakes her head violently, even as she stares out at the storm, even as she fights to open her eyes.

"I have a guest room."

"No." Her eyes widen briefly and with great effort. "But I am *so* tired all of a sudden."

"You've been through a lot today. I promise I won't bother you."

She lifts her hot chocolate but doesn't quite get it to her mouth. I reach over and take the mug from her hands before she drops it, sliding it and mine onto the side table.

"I have a t-shirt you can sleep in. I'll even make you coffee in the morning."

"I don't need a t-shirt to sleep in," she yawns, leaning her head back on the couch and blinking her eyes at me charmingly. "And what about Honey Bunny?"

"Does he need to be fed tonight?" That'll complicate the situation, but I'll figure out how to get the rabbit some food.

"No he doesn't *need* food tonight, but he likes snacks and snuggles." Callie's eyes close. She's fucking adorable.

"So Honey Bunny will be okay without you for a night."

The very last thing I want to do is put her pet in danger, but at this point, I'm not sure if she's still capable of responding, or if she's already passed out.

"Yeah. He's okay for tonight." Callie lifts her head and opens her eyes one last time, smiling lazily at me. "Thanks, Wes."

Something shifts in my chest. Man, I'm so into that open smile. "For what?" I ask, but she's already passed out.

I scoot over and gently pull her in my direction so her head nods onto my shoulder instead of lolling uncomfortably on the other side. I let her press herself against me. Sir Fluffy stares at me judgmentally.

"What? I'm not going to do anything bad." I sigh and scoot out from beneath Callie and lay her body gently across the couch, then tuck a gray fuzzy fleece blanket on top of her.

Sir Fluffy meows as I deposit the mugs in my sink.

Callie should be out for the night, but I don't want to leave her alone for long. I quickly grab the supplies I need, fish her car keys out of her jacket pocket, and suit up in my boots, jacket, gloves, and balaclava.

It's bitterly cold and quiet outside, the snow carpeting the ground and covering the trees, making everything white and beautiful. I trudge through four inches of snow down my driveway and to the road to get to her car, clearing it off and driving it slowly to my cabin. I'm lucky I can even get it off the side of the road, and I'm lucky her shit car makes it down my snowy driveway.

Before heading back inside, I stick a tracker under the carriage of the vehicle, holding it in place for a few seconds to make sure it sticks.

I hurry back inside my cabin with her purse, which was on her passenger seat, and I'm satisfied to see she's still passed out on the couch. I unblock the cellular network, open the drawer next to my utensils, and pull out her phone. She uses face ID, so I wave it in front of her and get to work installing a stalkerware app—spyware but for stalkers—so I can keep track of her once she's gone. Then I stick a tiny tracker inside her phone case. It's not as powerful as the bigger ones but gets the job done.

I wish I could install cameras in her living space, but I can't get to Portland in this weather, and I don't want to run into her brother. I'll do that later. There's a text from someone named Lola cancelling drinks tonight because of the snow—that's damn convenient for me—so I respond to the text with a thumbs up.

I leave her phone on the counter and re-block her cellular network for another eight hours. In the morning, she'll find she can use her phone again.

My phone buzzes, and it's Noah.

NOAH

what did you do

I sigh. This whole situation is so not my fault, and of course I look like the bad guy. Yes, I'm intense with women, which is why I don't get involved. This one just showed up on my doorstep.

ME

I literally did nothing. She followed me home from Portland

and let's not pretend that I'm not the one usually cleaning up your messes

NOAH

yeah, sure, okay. Need my help?

nope. Just letting you know what's going on.
I'm sending her on her way tomorrow after
the storm clears

I gather Callie in my arms for the second time tonight and walk her to the guest room. She's in jeans and that long-sleeved shirt. I can't let her sleep in uncomfortable denim, and I have a fantasy image in my head of her in one of my t-shirts. I'm not gonna be satisfied until I see it in real life.

I lower her on the bed and stare at her, dark hair spread out around her head. Her shirt is tight around her ribs and has ridden up, exposing a soft, curvy section of skin. Ink peeks out, and I nudge up her shirt so I can see the whole thing. It's a beautiful tattoo of a phoenix, stretching from below her right breast down into her jeans. It's fierce and powerful and incredibly hot. And the underside of her breast peeking out from her bra? Fuuuuck me. I reach down and rub my cock, hardening in my joggers.

Nope. Don't be a freaking creep.

I let go of myself and focus on getting her changed. Am I still being creepy? Yes. But I won't touch her inappropriately, I swear.

It's been a while since I got obsessive over a woman. Guess I'm due.

I reach over and unbutton Callie's jeans, pulling the zipper down and groaning at the site of her low-rise white underwear. I tug the denim down her hips, swallowing hard at the sight of her underwear ridden up in the back, exposing the side of her ass cheek. I can't help but rub my cock once more after I pull the jeans off the rest of the way. Fuck me, the sight of her long, smooth legs and curvy thighs are too much for me.

I know I should stop, but I tug her shirt up her abdomen

and over her breasts, my breath catching when her thin, lacy bra is fully revealed, her nipples visible through the fabric. That's why it was so easy to see her arousal before. There's barely anything here. I rush to pull her shirt the rest of the way off, then tug on the oversized t-shirt I brought in. I reluctantly cover her breasts and pull the shirt down over her pussy. If I didn't have any integrity, I'd just swipe once between her legs to see if she's wet. Fuck, I'm tempted.

But I'm not like that.

I pull a blanket over Callie, turn off the light, and leave her to get some rest.

Now I'm left with a rock-hard cock and only my hand to take care of it.

CHAPTER 8

WARM APPLE PIE

CALLIE

I'm still half asleep when I reach down to scratch Honey Bunny's head, but when I go to stroke his long ears, I find them... short.

My eyes fly open, and I prop myself up on my elbows. Where the fuck am I? A black cat is lying along my side and while I'm watching, he stands, arching his back with a big stretch and yawning so wide I can see down his throat.

Oh my god.

I shoot to a full sitting position, and the cozy fleece blanket I'm under falls down. And what the flying fuck am I wearing? It's an old oversized concert t-shirt for—I pull out the front so I can examine it... Gin Blossoms?—and my underwear. That's it. Where are my clothes? Where the fuck are my pants?

I'm in a strange bed.

In a strange room.

In a strange cabin... oh.

I leap onto my feet, the blanket tangling in my legs and almost bringing me down onto the cool wooden floor. The cat hops down gracefully and casually strolls out the partially open door.

My heart's racing, and I take a second to get my bearings. The room is pretty stark, just a queen-sized bed, one tall dresser, and a desk that doesn't look like it gets used very much. On the wall there are paintings of... pies? The radiator along the wall turns on with a few loud ticks and I startle.

Then a man's voice sounds from the other side of the door.

"Would you like breakfast, Sir Fluffy?"

Sir Flu—again, what the fuck.

I place my hand on my thumping chest as everything comes back to me.

Standing outside Maine Coffee Co. Making the highly questionable decision to follow Wes to his cabin. Crouching behind a tree in the snow flurries and passing out. Warm fire. Zip ties. Capable hands helping me to the couch. Hot chocolate.

Oh. Hot chocolate? Is that why I don't remember the end of last night, or why I'm in a strange t-shirt and underwear? The drink tasted like heaven, and we were discussing finding Shane.

Then nothing.

I don't remember getting changed into this shirt or going to bed. I don't remember agreeing to sleep here. I dash to the window and push aside the curtains. I'm blinded by the bright sun. I'm looking out at the side of the cabin, with a partial view of the frozen lake. The sun is shining on a fresh layer of snow on the ice, and it glistens like a billion diamonds. If I had to guess, there's a foot of snow on the ground. I really didn't have a choice about staying here, unless I was going to snowshoe home or sleep in my car, both of which would've probably landed me in the morgue.

But he didn't have to fucking drug me.

"There you go, kitty. I'm going to go check on our guest."

Oh, fuck. My eyes dart around for pants. Nothing.

There's a light knock on the door.

"Callie?"

I dash over and reach for the fleece blanket, wrapping it around my waist like I'm a dude who just got out of the shower. Only a squeak escapes my throat. I stare at the door and watch in horror as it slowly swings open.

Wes sees me by the window and a wide smile crosses his face. He looks aggravatingly hot. Stupidly attractive in a fresh blue hoodie and the same gray sweatpants from last night. The hoodie hugs his broad shoulders just snug enough that I wonder if it's even comfortable. While I'm watching, he takes his hand, pushes up his sweatshirt, and scratches his abdomen.

My jaw drops at the brief sight of his chiseled muscles. I swallow the lump in my throat.

No. I am not hot for my kidnapper. Definitely not.

"Did you sleep okay?" he asks in a gravelly voice. "How do you take your coffee?"

I dart my eyes back up to his face, the one with a jawline that could cut glass and those crystal blue light eyes, and he's still smiling at me like this is a completely normal situation and I'm an invited guest in his house.

I want to strangle him. And fuck him? It's confusing.

And so I do what comes natural to me. I pick a fight. I stride over, attempting to look intimidating, even though I'm a foot shorter. The smile fades from Wes's face as I take one hand and push him as hard as I can. He doesn't move, obviously. My other hand is still holding up the fleece blanket.

"Did you drug me? Again?? And then did what? Got me naked? Played dress up? Did you..." The words get stuck in my throat as I picture myself naked on the bed behind me, Wes running his huge hands over my body, maybe using one of his thick fingers or his tongue—

Fuck!

"I didn't touch you in any inappropriate way. I promise. I would never." His holds his hands out, eyes wide and deeply concerned.

Annoyingly, I kind of believe him. And I'm the tiniest bit disappointed, which is interesting to me. It seems like my brain is wholly accepting a new side quest to break my good girl spell before I leave Portland. Anyway, touching me while I'm passed out would be a deal-breaker. When I'm awake? That's a different story.

"And I'm sorry about the sedative. I didn't mean to make you pass out completely. I just wanted you to relax." He twitches his face to one side. "No, that's not true. I did mean for you to pass out."

"What the fuck?" I push him again, and this time he steps back. But I'm ninety-eight percent sure it wasn't because of the strength of my one-handed push that he retreats to just outside the bedroom door.

"I'm sorry," he says. "It was poor decision making on my part. I have trust issues."

But when I step forward and go to push him again, he grabs my wrist and turns my body so my back is against the doorframe, and my wrist is secured above my head and against the doorframe in one of his hands. My other hand flies up to try to yank his hand off, but he just grabs that one as well.

And the blanket falls off my waist.

"Sorry? Fuck sorry." My last two words come out as a whisper. Heart racing, I stare up at him. I'm aware of the fact that with my hands above my head, the hem of the t-shirt is above my ass. My nipples harden and there's a tightening between my legs. I should not be getting turned on by this man roughhousing me. What the fuck is wrong with me?

He drops my wrists and steps back, hands out in front of him, palms up.

"I'm sorry about that." Wes's eyes flit down my body and land on my bare legs. "Last night, I thought you'd try to drive home, and there's no way I could allow you to leave my cabin in that kind of snowstorm. You wouldn't have gotten far."

"Because you were going to chase me?"

"No, I was thinking it would be because your car would've gotten stuck and what—" He swallows. "Would you want me to chase you?" The last words come out roughly.

I find myself leaning toward him, and for a second I really want him to chase me and kiss me and then hopefully fuck me until I die.

What? No. No!

"No, obviously not." Now *I'm* whispering again.

He shakes his head as if to get dirty thoughts out and steps backward toward the kitchen.

"So, coffee?" Wes clears his throat and I nod. "How do you take it?"

"Cream and one sugar." I bend down for the fleece blanket, re-securing it around my waist.

Wes raises his eyebrows before turning to the kitchen.

"What was that look for?" I touch the doorframe, sort of wishing he still had me trapped against it. "And where are my clothes?"

"What look?" Wes turns back to me, hand on the refrigerator door handle. "Your clothes are in the top drawer of the dresser."

I don't answer his question, instead shutting the guest

room door. I get dressed, then take my time straightening the bed, folding the fleece blanket and Gin Blossoms t-shirt, and giving myself a pep talk. Just act normal. He's kind of acting normal. Nothing bad happened, aside from him knocking me out twice. Undressing and dressing me. Looking sexy as hell.

It's the smell of coffee and something sweet that finally pulls me out of the bedroom.

Wes is sitting at his cozy table in a dining room area, which I hadn't noticed last night during all the chaos. He's got his fingers wrapped around a mug that says something about hackers. There's another steaming mug of coffee across from him, this one with Lake Savage written on it in script. Wes watches me approach the table. Not scrolling mindlessly or even looking at a phone. Just me.

"I should leave," I say.

"Have coffee first."

It's a suggestion, not an order, but I can't resist the hot drink, so I decide to stay. But first, I fold my arms and scowl at him.

"Am I allowed to leave? Have any plans to drug me or zip-tie me today?"

"No, Callie Callahan." He has the common courtesy of hanging his head and looking remorseful. "And I'm sorry about both of those things."

"Three of those things. You drugged me twice."

"Right. I'm sorry about all three of those things." He bites back what I'm guessing is an adorable smirk. "To make it up to you, I brought your car over last night and cleared the snow off it again this morning. Plus ran the snowblower so you can actually get out of my driveway. The roads have been plowed but are still shit, so you need to drive home carefully."

He did what now? I slide into the chair across from Wes

and blink at him as I take my first glorious sip of coffee. Amazing all around. Then another smell hits me. Something sweet and warm and sugary.

"What's that smell?" My stomach growls loudly to emphasize the question.

"Oh! Right." Wes heads back into the kitchen and pulls open his oven. "Perfect." He slides on an oven mitt and produces a gorgeous apple pie, the pastry top a perfect golden color crisscrossed on top of moist, sweet slices of apple pie covered in sugary goo.

"Holy shit. You made a pie?"

Wes nods. "I'm working through top crust options so I can beat Ruth Roy at the Portland Springfest apple pie competition in six weeks."

"There's a lot to unpack there, but let's start with who is Ruth Roy?" I hate myself for being interested in his life, but I can't help it. I tuck a leg underneath my butt and lean forward.

Also, this helps explain the pie artwork in the bedroom.

"She's a nasty eighty-year-old woman who has had it in for me ever since the first year I entered the pie competition and squeaked out a first-place win. She got second and has hated me ever since." His face darkens. "I also haven't beaten her since."

What the fuck is happening here? I'm not sure what to do. Commiserate? Encourage?

"Can we eat it?" I wave to the steaming apple pie on the stovetop and kind of hate myself for sounding so eager.

"Of course we can eat the pie." Wes grins and reaches up to pull out two plates. I can't help but watch how his shoulder muscles shift through his sweatshirt as he moves around the kitchen. He pushes up his sleeves, revealing sinewy forearms with those tattoo sleeves. "Whipped cream?"

"For the pie?"

"Yes, for the pie." I can see the asshole grin from the side of his face. "What else would it be for?"

"I don't know. And yes." I attempt to infuse absolute casualness into my tone, not let on that for some fucking reason my mind went sexual when he suggested whipped cream. Not that I've ever used food with sex.

By the time he turns to me with the slices of pie on plates, I'm still eye fucking him. Wes smirks and slides a plate in front of me.

This whole situation is so weird.

First of all, I'm married. To a scumbag asshole. But I'm not available for dating or fucking or whatever.

Second of all, this is the man who had me zip-tied to a kitchen chair yesterday.

Third of all, I have no interest at all in another man. In fact, I'll hopefully never date again.

Fucking Shane. Just thinking of him makes me mad. Actually, what would really make him mad is me having slept at this hot hacker dude's cabin and sitting down to have coffee and homemade pie with him.

Wes settles across from me, and I take another gulp of my delicious coffee. Oh. Oh no.

"Wait, you didn't drug the coffee, did you?" I've already chugged half the mug. Fuck!

"No, but wouldn't that have been a good question five minutes ago before you took your first sip?"

"I guess, but—" I narrow my eyes at him. "Is that what that look was for?"

"Yeah. I was wondering when you were going to make

sure the coffee was safe to drink. Not that last night's hot chocolate wasn't safe, but, well, you know what I mean."

"Stop drugging me, and I won't have to be so on guard."

"You should always be on guard," Wes says, a serious look on his face.

I'm an idiot. How many times will I let this man drug me? I should've questioned the coffee. And the hot chocolate last night.

"How about the apple pie?" I pull the plate closer, and my mouth waters at the smell of it.

"I would never drug one of my apple pies."

"Hmm." I scrunch my nose. "So you'd drug other pies?"

He shrugs but doesn't answer. Weird.

"Eat," he nods to the pie.

"Fine. Wait. Why is there a whipped cream heart?" It's actually pretty impressive, not some messy shape, but a very precise heart on top of a picture-perfect slice of apple pie.

"Because it's Valentine's Day."

"It is? Huh. Okay." I snort out a short chuckle, and he grins at me. I'm annoyed that my first thought was *that's sweet*. I'm starting Valentine's Day with apple pie that's homemade by a gorgeous masked kidnapper? Could be worse, I guess.

I scoop up a soft, warm spoonful of pie with some whipped cream and shove it in my mouth and oh. My god.

Wes crosses his arms and leans back, not biting into his pie, his eyes examining my face intensely. The thick sugary filling coats my tongue and explodes onto my taste buds. It's hot, but I don't even care. This man can sure as hell bake a pie.

"Do you like it?" Wes watches me eagerly.

"It's amazing." A sigh involuntarily escapes my throat, and he smiles broadly.

"Enough to beat Ruth?"

"Fuck that old lady. Of course."

"Exactly! Fuck Ruth." He grins even wider at me. Then Wes drops his spoon, leaning forward on the table onto his forearms, giving me a chance to really examine the ivy and rose tattoos I noticed yesterday. They disappear into his sweatshirt and reappear on his neck. The other side of his neck is bare. I wonder if he has anything on his chest?

Something is off about this guy. I have a good nose for sniffing out humans who are used to breaking the law or doing shady shit. Maybe it's the past decade of being in my family's criminal world without actually being a part of it. I witnessed a lot over the years, and Wes is definitely one of those guys. Therefore, I should be terrified of him. I should cut ties and run from this place, as associating myself with Wes goes against my entire plan to start a new, legal life somewhere far away.

But he doesn't scare me.

The Ruth-inspired scowl drops from his face, and he replaces it with a pleasant smile.

Something might be off about him, but he's probably the perfect person to help me find Shane. Normal people don't do the kind of work Wes does.

"So, Wesley, will you help me find Shane?"

"Wesley?"

"Isn't that your name?"

"Yeah, but it's been a long time since anyone called me that."

"Can I?"

Wes assesses me for a few seconds. He tilts his head and runs a hand along his jaw, the sound rough against the stubble, more pronounced than it was yesterday.

"Yeah."

"Yeah I can call you Wesley or yeah you'll help me find Shane?"

"Both."

I take a sharp breath. Thank god. What was I going to do if he said no?

"Thank you so much."

"No problem. I can't promise I'll find him, but I'm pretty good at this kind of thing."

I stare at Wes. It's on the tip of my tongue to ask him more about what he does. But maybe I don't really want to know. Maybe I should just work with this guy to find Shane, and then I'll be able to get that clean slate.

"So what happens next? Do I, like, Venmo you money?"

"Nah, you can pay me after. For now, I need a few days to do some research on your husb—I mean, your soon-to-be ex-husband. Then I'll get in touch about meeting up to discuss my findings."

"Are you sure?"

Wes nods. "More non-drugged coffee?" He reaches for my almost empty mug.

"No, I need to go." I shove half the slice of pie into my mouth and stand. I really don't want to walk away from what looks like a mouth-watering crust, but I've remembered—again—that I'm in the middle of the woods eating pie with a stranger. "Honey Bunny is probably freaking out."

"Right, of course. We don't want to freak out your bunny," he says with a completely serious look on his face. "Want a to-go cup?"

I blink at him. "You might be a psychopath."

"That's offensive." He furrows his brow and—god help me—actually looks hurt.

"I'm sorry? I didn't mean to offend you." I honestly just

apologized to this unhinged, beautiful man for calling him a psychopath. What is happening?

"Apology accepted." Wes winks at me and heads to the kitchen, opening a cabinet and pulling out an expensive, reusable coffee cup. Who gives one of those to someone they just met?

I need to finalize this divorce and get the hell out of here. Get away from my old life and start over. I want to be in a place where no one knows me. No more criminal husbands or brothers. No peeking into the underbelly of humanity.

No one like my father or Shane or even my brother.

Definitely no one like Wesley.

CHAPTER 9
YOU FED HER APPLE PIE

WES

allie carefully steers her car down my driveway, and I lift a hand as she navigates the curve that leads to the main road. I flip my sweatshirt hood up over my ears and watch the spot where she disappears.

Yesterday did not go as expected.

I didn't think she'd do something like follow me home from Portland and hide in the woods. I hadn't expected to say yes to helping her, especially after I found out the details of who and what.

But she surprised me. And I surprised myself with how much I enjoyed our time together. She might not say the same.

Not that I could ever be with someone like her. I'd always have to hide who I really am. But eventually it comes out. Not all of it, of course, but enough. Women realize I know their location at all times. Or they don't appreciate me following them.

And with Callie, I had the urge to help her. To protect her. And that's... not great.

Feeling protective of someone makes me too vulnerable. Too exposed. I couldn't protect my little sister or my mother. I couldn't keep my twin, Sia, in my life—not once she found out who I really am. Who I'd become.

I've lost too many people.

I walk down the path I cleared with my snowblower, then start it back up and clear a few more lines up and down the driveway and around my front steps, finishing just in time for Noah to pull up in his red truck, which he annoyingly calls Red Daisy.

My brother steps out of his vehicle, taller than I am but not nearly as muscular. It's just how we're built. He's big and strong but has nerd vibes, like he spends his days playing video games or studying history. Meanwhile, I look like a gym rat, but I don't go near one. Cutting firewood, shoveling snow, and helping Noah remodel cabins do the same thing.

"Howdy. Your new girlfriend gone?"

"Oh fuck off." I lean down and grab a handful of snow in my gloved hand, then toss it at Noah as he approaches.

"Dick." Noah pulls off his glasses and gives me a dirty look as he cleans the snow splatters off with the front of his hoodie. "I guess that means you scared her off already?"

"She's not my girlfriend. She's a client." But as I say it, I picture her on my guest bed, passed out with her underwear riding up her ass and her nipples pushing against her lace bra. I kept that image in my head last night as I violently jacked off in my bathroom, biting back the moans as I came harder than I had in months.

"Mmkay." Noah walks past me, bends to scoops up snow, then turns back and presses a handful on my cheek. I yelp. "Come on. We've got things to discuss."

～

I CAREFULLY LAY strips of raw dough over the top of the two mini mince pies I'm finishing up. The crust forms the word *no*. Once I get the design just right, I lay wax paper on top before wrapping them tightly with red plastic wrap. I slide the mince pies into the freezer.

"I find it funny you always have so many of them on hand." Noah chuckles and leans down to scoop a giant spoonful of apple pie into his mouth. "It's not like we use them that often."

"Gross. Don't talk with your mouth full." I scoff as I turn on scalding hot water to rinse the mixing bowl I used to make the poison pies. I use the same bowl every time, and only ever use it for my special mince pies, but I'm extra careful so Sir Fluffy doesn't get himself into trouble. "And you never know when we'll need more than one."

"Whatever, Wes. Come sit." Noah's impatient to discuss his top two targets. It's only been a few days since we talked about the list, but he's always super eager.

I settle down across from him and glance at the notebook. "You really want to do Chad Smith next?"

"Sure do." He taps the table in front of me, where his notebook is open to a page in the middle with a list of names, bits of information scribbled around each one. I made Noah promise to never put this on his phone or laptop or anything. No need to make a digital record of all the people we're planning to target. I'm not the only hacker out there.

Top of the list is Chad Smith, 26, Boston, Massachusetts. Hedge fund manager. Rapist. Likes his girls young. Targets sex workers. Smith graduated college after taking the six-year plan to get his undergraduate degree in Boston and has been working for a hedge fund for two years.

"Scorpion thinks this is the best next target." Noah taps his finger on the paper.

I grunt in response. I don't love that we learn about so many of our targets from a dude on the dark web who calls himself Scorpion. Sure, I vet all the tips, and we make sure we have a good case outside of what information Noah's anonymous source has given us, but still. For Chad Smith, we know a ton about him. His workplace address, his home address, his net worth, his friends and acquaintances, his social media presence—spoiler alert, he's an asshole online.

"This fuckwit's a rapist, and his girlfriend is sixteen years old." Noah adjusts his glasses.

I grind my teeth together. *Sixteen years old.* I found that out after I hacked into Smith's phone and found messages between him and a teenager, plus inappropriate images. Like fucked-up images of her. This guy really is scum. I also went back to his college years and pulled a bunch of sexual assault complaints filed against him. The women—all freshman—eventually dropped the accusations. They must've been paid off, threatened, or shamed into submission.

Noah likes to know the dirty details before he goes through with any eliminations. I hate knowing, but at least it gives me a solid justification for what we are doing.

After our family was murdered, and we realized the police weren't getting anywhere, I managed to get into the police system and pull their list of suspects. The main detective on the case had been keeping case notes in a Google docs file.

Google docs. A kid could hack into it.

We suspected that once they'd figured out that our father was a gambler and he owed a ton of money to a group of not-nice people, they tried a lot less hard to find the murderer.

Dad was an alcoholic and got sober when Sia and I were babies, Noah was a toddler, and Ivy not yet born. But when we were in high school, he fell into gambling. It started slowly, but eventually escalated until he owed more than he could possibly pay. Our parents had transferred the house into our mother's name years before, and the loan shark tried to get my father to sell it and hand over the proceeds. He refused, and soon after, someone came in and killed our parents and Ivy. Noah, Sia, and I were all out of the house by then, but Ivy was still there.

The case is still officially unsolved.

It's okay. We took care of it.

Noah had gotten a taste for justice. And vengeance. Just like my father, he was addicted. But when Sia found out what we were doing, she cut us out of her life.

In the end, it was like she was murdered that day, too.

I got better at hacking and digital detective work. So good that I dropped out of college to freelance.

"This guy in NYC actually kills women. Confirmed." I tap on the second target on the list, who we call Joe Killer. "I haven't found nearly as much information on him, but I got the police list of his suspected victims and where their bodies were discovered."

I've become an expert at perusing the dark web to look for information. Chat rooms are a good place to monitor conversations about criminal activity, especially true crime junkies who are trying to solve cases before the cops do. It's useful. Joe Killer targets homeless women and girls, and he finishes the job. Sometimes he's not sexually assaulting them, just fucking killing them and dropping their bodies all over the city, making it hard to predict where he'll hit next.

"Damn, that's good." Noah swallows the last bite of his pie and pushes his plate away from him. "Think you'll beat Ruth this year? If not, we can add her to our list." Noah tilts his head at me hopefully. "She's creepy as hell."

"I can't believe you're making a joke about killing an old

lady. She's legit evil, but still." I run my hand down my face. "Noah, about Chad—"

"I don't want to hear it." Noah shakes his head aggressively. "He's a scumbag."

"I get that. But I feel like we're going too fast these days. Florida was four days ago. We're so much more likely to make mistakes."

"Nah. Not with you on it."

I press my lips together. Arguing with Noah won't get me anywhere. I just have to do what I always do: research and plan and protect.

"Hey, who ate the rest of the pie?" Noah nods to the pie dish, which clearly has another slice missing.

I shrug and can feel my cheeks heat. I'm blushing? Fuck me.

"You fed her apple pie." Noah's eyes widen with glee and accusation.

"Shut the fuck up."

"She slept in your guest room, and you gave her pie."

"What's the big deal?"

"Did she pet Sir Fluffy?" Noah glances down at my cat, who is sitting on top of his feet, and immediately sneezes.

"Actually, he slept with her last night." I was the slightest bit offended my cat chose Callie over me overnight, but I guess I don't blame him. I would've made the same choice.

"I cannot believe she slept over. Have you ever had a woman sleep here?"

"It's not like she was my invited guest." I roll my eyes. And the answer is no, no I have not. "I told you. She followed me home from Portland, so I brought her in for some questions. And then there was a blizzard."

"*Brought her in*, you're hilarious." Noah snorts. "I'm sure she just walked right into your cabin."

"Not exactly. Tell me, brother, how's your internet girlfriend?"

A dark cloud passes over Noah's face.

"Oh, no. What happened?" I meant to tease him good-naturedly, but I didn't realize something had gone wrong with Noah's woman.

"She got weird after I left Cincinnati. I thought I'd managed her questions about our family, but then she kept pushing. She'd found an article."

"Ah, fuck."

"Yeah. She wanted to come here to visit. Said I needed to open up to her. She wanted to get to know me better."

"The fucking nerve of her."

Noah gives me an annoyed look.

"So it's over?" I ask.

"Yup."

Noah is less afraid to get involved romantically than I am, but he always keeps them strictly at arm's length. Five hundred miles of arm's length, to be exact, which I'll admit is a perfect way to keep his life separate. He'd been dating this one for six months and had been to Cincinnati to visit her a handful of times. I think it was his longest relationship ever.

"Sorry."

"I'm over it." Noah's been emotionally stunted ever since our family was murdered. I don't blame his girlfriend for bailing—he keeps walls up so thick I can barely find my way through them, and I've got the key to the main gate.

CHAPTER 10

BURNER PHONE

CALLIE

Nothing calms my brain like re-shelving a hundred library books. I squat down to a lower shelf and slide in three books from my cart about horses, and I know exactly who took them out. A sweet ten-year-old girl who just left and checked out a whole new stack of equine books. She comes in every week with her babysitter after school and is absolutely obsessed with horses. It's so wholesome and I absolutely love it. I love getting to know our regular patrons and thinking of them when we get new books in, or better yet, ordering books they want to read.

I stand and touch the spine of the next books on the cart, then can't help but pull out my phone from the pocket of my long cardigan and check for missed notifications.

It's been three days since I drove away from Wes's cabin, and my head's been absolutely spinning ever since. I'm pretending to be a normal human being. Thank god for work. Checking books in and out, shelving, helping patrons find what they need... the distraction of the library has saved me from spiraling into obsession. And it's not like I can talk about it with anyone. I don't want to give Jake the satisfaction of talking about Wes, the man he referred to me, or Lola, who would probably not approve.

As I slip my phone back into my pocket, I sense someone at the end of the aisle.

"Found you."

I gasp and jerk my head up at the deep voice.

Standing at the end of the aisle with his arms crossed in a black hoodie, black jeans, the ivy tattoo visible on one side of his neck, and the most genuine smile on his face, is Wes.

"Fuck. You scared me," I whisper—we're in a library, after all—and lay my hand on my chest. My heart pounds hard against my palm.

"Sorry, I didn't mean to." Wes shifts on his feet and slides his hands into his hoodie pocket. "You are exactly as I pictured you'd be in this environment."

"Which is as what?" I plant my hands on my hips, but it's mostly to calm the shaking. Uh, he's been picturing me?

"As a hot librarian." Wes says this with a completely straight face, like it's a simple fact.

I huff and look down at my outfit. Long, bright pink skirt, black tank top, and my favorite long pocketed black cardigan. I braided my hair and twisted it into a bun, which I now touch self-consciously.

"First of all, I'm not a librarian. I'm a library assistant."

"Okay, got it." Wes nods his head and scrunches his forehead like he's really trying to absorb my words. It's adorable. "Is there a second of all?"

"Uh... no?" Because the other part of his comment was that I'm hot, and while I know better than to argue with a compliment, it's not one I expected. Shane was such a dick about my job. He thought it was too low-level and boring and certainly did not think the clothes I wore were hot. Especially my work outfits, which I admit have a bit of a librarian flair to them.

Wes takes three steps toward me until he's only a few feet away, the cart between us. He runs his tongue over his teeth, and I can't look away from the movement under his top lip.

Jesus, why can't I breathe right now?

"C-can I help you with something?" I'm trying so hard to appear normal, but I sense my eyes are open too wide, and my fingers are splayed by my sides like some kind of frozen jazz hands.

Wes breaks out into a wide, genuine smile, his gaze drifting over my face.

"Yeah. I'm looking for a book."

"A book?" I manage to sound confused, even though we're standing in the book stacks of an actual library, and I get asked this very question multiple times a day.

"A book." He nods, his eyes squinting as he's clearly making this up on the spot. "On... pies."

I snort out a laugh and cross my arms.

"You need a book on pies?" I tilt my head. "Like how to make pies?"

"I already know how to make pies. And did you just snort?"

"No!" Yes. "So what kind of pie book?"

"Like... a coffee table book." His eyes light up. "With gorgeous pictures of fancy pies. For inspiration. I can keep it in my kitchen for when I need a little motivation."

"Motivation to beat Ruth?" I bite my lip. Why am I playing along with this? Is it just because he's tall—so freaking tall—and gorgeous? My eyes linger on his neck and the ivy curved along his throat. I have the intense urge to reach up and run my finger along the lines of ink.

"Yes, to beat Ruth." Wes gives me a sweet smile that's almost shy, and his cheeks pinken. This man can't be shy. That's ridiculous.

I reach up to touch my braided bun, ensuring I'm actually here experiencing this, and clear my throat.

"Hard to forget. Not that many—" I search for a word that isn't tall, hot, inked, or unhinged "—men like you would be competing in a pie competition against an eighty-year-old."

"Men like me?" Wes raises an eyebrow and crosses his arms.

"Anyway! Come with me to look up a coffee table book on pies." I step around the cart, and Wes is completely in the way. Does he move? Nope. I swallow, and his eyes dart to my neck to watch the motion. I press my back against the bookshelf and sidestep along the structure. He turns slowly so that—when my feet stop working—he's almost got me trapped against the stacks, kind of like he had me pressed against the doorframe last weekend.

Again, all breath leaves my body, which seems to be a common occurrence when I'm around this man.

"You know what?" His voice is low and gravelly.

"What?" I can feel the heat coming off his body and damn, it feels good to have my heart racing around a gorgeous man. I shouldn't feel this way. I shouldn't let myself be swept away with Wes's obvious flirting.

But then again, why not? Don't I deserve a little fun?

"I also wanted to ask you a question about the case."

Oh, right. The case. It's like a bucket of ice water dumps on my head as I scoot another few steps along the bookcase and step away from Wes. He turns to me, a half-smirk on his face, his light blue eyes dancing, probably at my flushed cheeks and the obvious way he's affecting me.

"Yes, of course. What's the question?" I stand straight and attempt to reclaim my dignity.

"I'm working on accessing Shane's phone carrier records. You mentioned that he called you a few weeks ago. Do you remember the date of that phone call?"

"Um, no, but I can figure it out." I pull out my phone and swipe to my calendar, then recall what it was like to receive the jarring call from my estranged husband on a Sunday morning. The library is closed on Sundays, and I remember lying in my bed with Honey Bunny snuggled next to me thinking that maybe Shane did me a favor by disappearing. "It was Sunday, February 1."

"Great. Thanks." Wes pulls his phone out and taps a few times on the screen.

"Have you figured anything out?"

Wes is the epitome of distracting, but he just reminded me why we even know each other. I should focus not on how hot Wes is, but the way he's trying to help. The slightest jolt of anticipation shoots through me. Maybe he'll actually find Shane for me.

Maybe I'll be able to move on with my life.

"Not yet, Callie. But I promise I will."

"Okay." I breathe out, hope dissipating.

"How about that book on pies?"

CHAPTER 11

LIBRARY CARD

WES

I am now the proud owner of a library card.

I haven't had one of those since I was a kid, but Callie hooked me up and sent me home with three different baking-related coffee table books.

Did I need to go find her at her place of work to ask my simple question? No.

Did I even need her to answer the question when I have the phone records at my fingertips? Also no.

But I got to see Callie Callahan in her insanely hot librarian getup. Fuck me. I wanted to reach over and pull her to me by her braided bun and push the sexy as hell cardigan off her shoulders and—

Deep breaths, dude. I slide into my car and deposit the library books on my passenger seat.

Wherever he is, Shane must be using a burner phone. I got into his records and saw the one phone call to Callie's number two and a half weeks ago, just like she said. That was the last phone call from his number.

The other option is he's dead. Which is possible, of course, especially in his line of business.

I've searched for other evidence that Shane is in Boston and haven't found any. However, I did get into an online chatroom where they were talking about a fight club. There aren't that many, so it's likely the same one.

I'll keep working on it. I don't want to make any moves until I have more information. I'll get into Shane's bank accounts and spend more time finding loose threads like social media, but something tells me he's disappeared. For now.

Found you. That's what I said when I located Callie within the library. I'm an ass. The look on her face was horrified. Terrified? But maybe also kind of into it? I'm a terrible reader of women, obviously, and I've learned to assume that everything I do is creepy to them. Especially showing up where I haven't been invited.

I speed up on the road out of Portland. I cannot believe Shane screwed things up with Callie. He didn't even seem to have good intentions to begin with. He tricked her, made her fall for him, then pulled her into his sticky, rotten web. If I could get a woman like that to marry me, I'd do everything humanly possible to get her to stay. And maybe some inhumane things as well.

"Fuck." I hit the steering wheel with my palm. I'm getting out of control, and it's been four days since I met her.

But I already need more.

CHAPTER 12
STALKER
CALLIE

"You have zero survival instinct, Cal." Lola's long, straight curtain of brown hair shifts as she shakes her head at me from across the booth at O'Connor's, the cozy Irish pub three blocks from Jake's apartment. Lola's bookstore is only a few blocks away, so we've been meeting here a few times a week after she closes up her shop.

I scrunch my face and don't try to argue. And I haven't even told her the whole story. I left out the part where I followed him home, he drugged me, zip-tied me, and that I spent the night in his guest bedroom in a t-shirt that he dressed me in while I was unconscious after he drugged me for the second time. She'd probably insist I call the cops, which is not something that people with my kind of family ever do. Lola knows that.

Lola was fascinated when I first let slip years ago that my family is involved in the underbelly of Boston and Portland, but it didn't scare her away. Her excuse was she's always had a thing for bad boys, which I hate for her.

"You know, in this day and age, you shouldn't meet up with strange men alone without backup, even in a public place."

"Really? You're like the queen of dating apps." I slowly spin my half-empty glass of red wine on the table.

"Nah. I scroll through them, but don't often meet anyone in person."

"Okay." I wave my hand in the air. I don't think that's the complete truth as I like to live vicariously through her robust dating life. "But it turned out fine. He was nice, and he said he'd help me."

It's not untrue. Wes *was* nice. When he noticed the zip ties were digging into my wrists, he (eventually) cut off the plastic restraints.

"What if he turned out to be a psychopath?"

"Define psychopath." I let out a squeaky snort at how close we are to the potential truth about Wes.

"He showed up at your work." Lola shakes her head.

"Yeah, but I work in a public library. Lots of people show up there."

"Callie." She raises her eyebrows.

"Don't Callie me. Surely psychopaths aren't that good-looking."

Lola laughs at this, as if I'm kidding. I laugh with her.

Wes *is* gorgeous. I keep thinking about those thick fore-arms and the way the tattoos snake up his arms into his hoodie and onto his neck. His height, broad shoulders... the way he undressed me while I was passed out was admittedly a little creepy, but it also seemed kind of sweet. He just wanted me to be comfortable, right?

Shit, I'm fucked up.

Wes is almost certainly some kind of psychopath. Casually drugging someone isn't normal, right? Even someone who's watching your cabin from behind a tree?

But he fed me pie. With a whipped cream heart on it. And scraped my car. And has a cute cat that he named Sir Fluffy, for fuck's sake.

"Honestly, I'm just glad he agreed to help. I don't know what else to do at this point."

Lola makes a sympathetic murmur. "So what happens next?"

"I wait for him to get back in touch."

"Hopefully he does soon, as now Shane's been gone for, how long?" Lola sips her vodka and coke.

"Almost five weeks." My stomach rolls. With each week that slips by, I lose confidence that I'll ever be free of that man. He's managing to control me without even being here.

"Don't be mad," Lola says, her cheeks turning pink. She waves at someone behind me.

"What?" I turn and swear under my breath. Speaking of fucking criminals. "You invited my brother?"

"Sorry, Callie." Her face crumples as she realizes that I'm pissed. *Obviously* I'm pissed.

"You know I'm furious with him!"

"I know, I'm sorry, but he was texting me asking how you are, and I mentioned we were coming here... shit. I shouldn't have told him. I'm sorry—hey, Jake."

Jake stops at our table, dressed in jeans and a casual but expensive-looking t-shirt. He smiles at Lola and gives me an apologetic look before sliding into the booth next to her.

Lola has had a stupid crush on my brother ever since I introduced them years ago. In hindsight, knowing Lola's preference for bad boys, this situation is not surprising. I've managed to keep them apart for all this time, but my current situation is giving them an excuse to have more contact with each other. I'm hoping he doesn't notice how sweet and beautiful she is. Because I don't approve. He might be my brother, but I know what it's like to be in a relationship with a criminal.

Zero out of ten stars, do not recommend.

"Hey, Callie. You okay?" Jake has the common courtesy to act remorseful around me these days, which is how I know he knows more about Shane's whereabouts than he's telling me.

"I'm fine, Jake." As the person who could potentially solve my problems but won't, Jake is the last person I want to see right now. Fine, I know, I live with him, but I don't need to see him *more*.

Jake's forehead crinkles, and Lola keeps staring at him longingly. Traitor! What happened to girl code? Honestly, she'd be better off finding some dude who rides a motorcycle or a rival book store owner or something instead.

The whole thing drives me nuts.

"We were just talking about how you won't tell me where Shane is."

Jake groans and leans his head back, his eyes shutting for a count of three.

"Did the Hawk person not work out?" Jake says once he opens his eyes.

"He's working out fine." I cross my arms and don't offer him more information.

"Be careful with him, I haven't worked with the guy personally—"

"Really? Be careful? I wouldn't have to work with him at all if you would help me."

My chickenshit brother sighs, genuine concern etched on

his face. Fuck his concern. He's scared of Shane because he's crazy, and Jones because he's now their boss and a scary asshole with no moral compass. The same way Jake was scared of our father right up until he passed away.

And now, he provided me Hawk's information, but that doesn't quite solve the problem.

As usual, I feel alone, ignored, and unsupported by those closest to me.

All my remaining hope is with Wes.

"Tell me, what do you think is going to happen here? That I'll just stay married to Shane forever? What's your endgame? Are you that afraid of him? Eventually, I'll get the divorce. It's just a matter of how long it takes. Now, as for Mom's ring, who knows if I'll ever get that back." I gulp my wine.

Jake's face falls, and he looks deeply unhappy. Good.

"Callie—"

"No." I scoot out of the booth awkwardly and stand. "I don't want to hear it. I gotta go."

"Oh, Callie, please don't." Lola's eyes widen. I finish the last sip of wine and deposit the glass back on the table, wanting to slam it but wanting more not to cause a scene by breaking it.

"Bye."

"Callie!" Lola calls, but I wave a hand behind me and stomp out of the bar, pulling on my pink puffy winter coat. The cold February wind whips my hair up and around my head.

Lola better not tell him any details about Wes. I'm glad I didn't share the whole story. My phone buzzes in my pocket when I'm only a handful of steps away from O'Connor's.

LOLA

hey, I'm so sorry, please come back

I grit my teeth. I can't believe she invited Jake to hang out with us. Lola just moved to the top of my list of traitors.

ME

it's fine. I need a minute to decompress. It's too loud in there. Just don't tell Jake anything about the guy who's helping me

LOLA

of course. Love ya

I sigh and put my phone back in my pocket as I stride further away from the bar.

I just need to think.

There was nothing online about Wes. I don't have his last name, of course, so my searches for things like *Wes-hacker-Lake Savage* haven't turned up anything. There's probably nothing online anyway, even if I had his last name. I'm willing to bet he's the kind of guy who isn't on social media.

I slow my stride. The sidewalk has icy patches, and I almost wipe out turning down another street. I need to pay attention to what I'm stepping on, as there are piles of snow everywhere and slick spots where snow melted and refroze.

My phone buzzes again and I pull it out, expecting another text from Lola, but it's a notification from Gone. I stop abruptly and click the message a little too eagerly.

It's from Wes. A picture of an apple pie with an intricate top crust woven in and out like a friendship bracelet. It's a beautiful pie, and my mouth waters instantly upon seeing it. I wait for another message, but nothing comes up. The picture of the pie disappears after a few seconds, like it always does in Gone. I get a rush of adrenaline.

ME

okay, I'll bite. What's up?

HAWK

did you like my pie last weekend?

My cheeks heat. Why does this feel sexual, like the whipped cream question? I get a rush of adrenaline. Finally, he messages. And it's about pie.

ME

your pie was the best I've ever had

Oh my god, and I'm playing along. The disappearing messages are giving me more confidence. I look up and continue walking.

HAWK

what are you doing right now?

ME

why?

HAWK

just wondering

I head down another dark city block, almost at Jake's apartment.

ME

heading home from a pub

did you find Shane yet?

HAWK

working on it

you know, a woman walking alone down
dark alleyways isn't smart, even in a safe
city like Portland

I freeze in my tracks, heartbeat speeding up, and I look around me. There's nothing except for shadows from the bare trees on piles of snow along the sidewalk.

ME

what the fuck? Are you following me?

HAWK

nah, just assumed

ME

how do you know where I'm walking

HAWK

I know everything

ME

except where Shane is

Now I put my phone away and start to jog, risking my life and trusting in the town's salt treatments. Five minutes later, I'm slightly out of breath and tapping in the code to get into Jake's apartment building. Up a flight of stairs and I'm inside, door locked behind me.

My chest is pounding. I try to convince myself that Wes wasn't following me, nor was anyone else. Portland is such a safe city, I almost never feel uncomfortable.

I strip off my jacket and gloves and head to the kitchen to grab water before hiding in my bedroom. I plan to get in comfy pajamas and snuggle under the covers with a book. I'll stick AirPods in so I don't hear Jake come in later.

Then I see the pie plate sitting on the kitchen counter.

I approach it slowly, like it's a sleeping bear I don't want to disturb.

It's an apple pie.

It must be a coincidence. Jake must've bought it at the

store, which is very uncharacteristic but not impossible. That is the explanation here. Or maybe someone sent us a pie.

It can't be from Wes. Obviously not. But Jake would've mentioned it, right? And—

Then I get close to the pie and realize it's got the same intricate friendship bracelet-like top crust as the picture Wes sent, the one that disappeared in Gone.

CHAPTER 13

BATHROOM SELFIE

WES

Should I have left one of my freshly baked apple pies in Callie's apartment? No.

Was it helpful in building trust with a new client? Also no.

But was it hot to sift through her underwear drawer, touch the pillow she lays her head on, wonder if she has any toys hidden somewhere, because her bedside drawer didn't have them?

Yep. Absolutely.

However, given the freaked-out messages she's sending me, maybe it wasn't the best choice. I run my hand down my face, then lean on the cold brick wall of the building that has the perfect view of her window.

But I'm doubting what I've done. What I'm *doing*. She liked my apple pie, but perhaps she didn't need me to break in while she was out and leave her one. That visit to her library on Tuesday was thoroughly enjoyable—I could've gone back there instead of creeping into her bedroom. Or, like, done none of that.

Sigh.

I've made a little progress this week with tracking Shane. He was definitely in Boston three weeks ago, but I don't think he's been at that fight club since. I managed to get the address from a chat room and hacked into security cameras in the area. While I've never seen Shane in person, the identification program I developed didn't find any potential matches for him on the security camera footage.

CC95

why is there a pie on my counter that looks exactly like the picture you sent me a little while ago?

were you in my apartment?? how do you even know my address?

wait—are you here right now??

Through the window, I watch Callie dart into her bedroom and throw open her closet doors. Damn. I fucked up. I wish I could see her face clearly. I guess I could check the camera I installed earlier this week (and adjusted during the pie delivery), but they are solely of her bed. I might go back and install more cameras, but that feels *too* intrusive.

ME

no, Callie, I'm not in the apartment with you

That would be preposterous. I'm across the street. I watch as she moves out of view. Hopefully she's calming down.

ME

and I thought you liked the pie

CC95

I did but—

ME

but what?

CC95

how did you get in here? I'm so confused

ME

think of it as my reference. It was easy as pie (get it?) for me to find out all about you and make a delivery

CC95

that's creepy as shit

ME

sorry. How can I make it up to you?

CC95

you can fuck right off

ME

come on. What can I do? Bring you another pie?

CC95

take a selfie in your cabin so I know you're not creeping around here

Uh-oh. That's not going to work at all.

ME

now now, weren't you the one who was creeping around my cabin just last weekend?

CC95

we're not talking about that

ME

fine, but I'm not at home

CC95

where are you? Take a picture now or I'll
think you're under my bed

ME

okay

I've still got the one problem. I'm in a freezing cold fucking alleyway across from her building, and I really don't want her figuring out that I'm right outside. Maybe she wasn't super observant when I first sent the pie picture on her own kitchen counter, but she'll pay more attention to the next image.

I dash around the corner and jog a block and a half before ducking into O'Connor's. She might recognize the bar she was just at, so I head straight for the men's restroom. This probably won't help me avoid appearing creepy, but it's the best idea I've got.

I lock myself in a stall and strip off my coat. I slip my arm out of the left sleeve of the henley I'm wearing and push it up, allowing me to take a picture of one full arm and half my chest. She's already seen my forearms, but my left bicep has an image of a bear standing on its hind legs with its teeth bared. It takes a few tries to get a picture where I'm flexing my ab muscles just so, which makes me hate myself more than a little.

I send it.

CC95

what the fuck was that. I didn't say to strip

and are you in a bathroom stall? Seriously,
what the fuck are you doing tonight

ME

no other comment on the picture?

CC95

what'd you want me to say? Okay, I'll try.

nice tat

I crack up and shake my head, slipping my arm back into the sleeve.

ME

now you send me one

CC95

you have got to be out of your mind

I figured I'd get that kind of response. I stare for a few seconds and am about to leave the bathroom stall when a picture pops up in our text chain.

Jesus fucking Christ.

It's the same view as what I sent her, but of her curvy body lying on her bed. She's wearing a plain bra, thicker than the one she wore the other night so I can't see her nipples, but it's pushing up her tits so they spill over the top. My hand clenches on my phone.

Fuuuck.

Her thumb is hooked in the waistband of her sweatpants, pushing them down enough to give me a full view of the phoenix tattoo I already saw the other night in my cabin. Her long hair lays flat down her side on the bright pink comforter. I bite my lip so hard I taste blood. This is fucking hot.

I immediately screenshot the picture just before it disappears. I shouldn't be able to do that, but I disabled the screenshot blocking feature of Gone with little trouble.

CC95

but you've already have seen my tattoo
when you FUCKING UNDRESSED ME last
weekend

ME

I don't know what you're talking about

Callie sends five eye-roll emojis. I snort. So she's thinking about that too. I decide to push my luck.

ME

have any more? Tattoos? Or pictures?

CC95

nope

So she's not mad? Noted.

I open the saved image and let my eyes feast on her while I adjust my half-hard cock in my jeans.

I want more of her, so I click through to the app that connects to the camera in her bedroom. It comes into focus, and I groan before remembering I'm in a public bathroom. She's on her bed with her shirt still pulled up over her breasts, and as I watch, she pushes her sweatpants down so they're bunched up around her knees.

"Fuuuuck," I whisper as she slides her hand down her belly and into her underwear. I moan and reach down for my cock, pulling it once hard, which doesn't help at all. I shouldn't be watching this, and definitely not in this bar bathroom. I really, really should close the app, but now she's got her whole hand moving on her pussy, and she's arching her back and grinding against her fingers. I put my fist in my mouth and bite down.

I want to hear her noises, smell her desire. I want it to be my finger inside her, my tongue, my cock.

Am I going to fully jack off in this bathroom? Gross. No.

Suddenly she stops and looks at her door, withdrawing her hand and pulling her sweatpants up and her shirt down. She stands and tiptoes over to her bedroom door, leaning an ear against it.

Dammit.

I switch to the living room camera, where her worthless brother is in the kitchen at the fridge. The asshole couldn't make sure Callie got home safely? He better not eat her apple pie.

It's gonna become a full-time job if I have to follow this woman around to keep her safe since no one else in her life seems to care.

I adjust myself one last time, then get out of there. The cold air hits me outside and helps calm my cock, and I head back to her place, tugging my hat further on my head and slipping my gloves on.

ME

I should have some more information for you in the next few days

CC95

and then we'll meet up again?

ME

yep. We can do Maine Coffee Co again, or you can try to break into my cabin, then I can catch you and tie you up

CC95

again

ME

again

CC95

just... let me know

I grin and make one last sweep of the outside of her

apartment. I stand in the alley across the street until her light flicks off in her bedroom and the cameras confirm she's burrowed under her thick comforter, this time sleeping. It'd be better if I could stand in the shadows of her room and watch over her.

Instead, I head home.

CHAPTER 14

NOT A GOOD STALKER

CALLIE

Instead of heading home after I get off work on Monday afternoon, I hop on the road out of Portland toward Lake Savage. Even though I talked to him via text—and picture, lord have mercy—on Friday evening. I'm getting antsy for more information about Shane.

The problem is I don't know exactly how to get to Wes's cabin. I have a general idea? So that might be enough.

Could I just message him for an update? Sure.

But this is me being assertive. Not a boring-ass good girl, but someone who goes after what she wants. Maybe I'm even behaving a little bit dangerous. I like it.

Not nearly as dangerous as that first time I followed him home, however, as I didn't know he was kind of not scary at all.

Even so, I should not be pursuing this man.

He broke into my apartment! And left a pie. I shouldn't let myself get distracted by delicious pies and killer abs. I've been so deprived of romantic love and affection for the last decade of my life that my brain must think that any attention is good attention.

I need to focus on my end goal, which is to find Shane and make him my ex-husband. But I am, right? If Wes likes me, he's more likely to work hard to solve my case, which will get me to Shane faster. I'm only interacting with Wes because he's the key to freeing myself from Shane and allowing me to start over.

Yeah. That's exactly it.

That's why I'm driving to his cabin uninvited. Again.

I was in Lake Savage once years ago, but there are so many cute little lake towns in Maine, it's hard to keep track. I zone out as I pass through thick woods, snow piled up on the side of the road.

When Shane first disappeared, after I found Honey Bunny and had a few days to process, I was almost relieved. *Almost* because we had shit to sort through. He had papers to sign. He had my mother's ring. It was not over. But not having to come home to an apartment with him in it was such a relief.

Now that it's been so long, I'm just anxious to be done with him for good.

I follow the county road that I remember following Wes on, but can't for the life of me recall where I turned off. His long, partially hidden drive was possibly off *that* road, but there might've been another turn in there. I wish I'd paid more attention that snowy morning, but I was so focused on driving safely that I don't remember anything else.

Instead of driving aimlessly, I follow the sign that points to the town center of Lake Savage. It's got an adorable Main Street. There's immediately a thrift store on the right and a coffee shop on the left, a tiny library, restaurants, boat rental, two gift shops, a bar, a bookstore, and a general store, where

I turn around to head back to find parking in front of the coffee shop.

The bell jingles when I walk into Killer Beans, and the high-school aged barista looks up from her iPad.

She stares at me curiously as I approach the counter, then sets her device down. The cafe is relatively quiet, with only a small group of giggling girls in the corner staring at one of their phones.

"Can I help you?" the barista asks after waiting for me to say something.

"Yes." I scan the quaint chalkboard menu that has a surprisingly extensive list of beverage options. "Can I have a mocha?" Might as well treat myself. The girl nods and turns to prepare my drink with the fancy coffee machine.

I check out the display case and spot an entire row of pies. Apple, blueberry, and cherry. I bite back a groan. I can't go five minutes without thinking of Wes.

What am I doing here? Am I really planning to ask the young barista if she knows someone named Wes who bakes pies? That would make me sound completely unhinged, and even if she knows him—which she probably does since this is a small town and how would someone not remember Wes —she might not want to tell a stranger anything. Then what?

She turns back around and slides my coffee to me. "Anything else?"

"A slice of apple pie, please." My stomach rumbles at the memory of the pie I finished just yesterday.

I touch my card to the reader, then gather my coffee and pie and head to one of the small round tables. Once settled at the table, I take a bite of pie and groan. Fuck, that's good. And after tasting from two of his pies, I'd be willing to bet it's one of Wes's.

I now have an unhealthy obsession with this man.

Here I am, sitting at a coffee shop in the middle of some deserted lake town with an overpriced coffee that's probably not even— ohhhhh my god, the mocha is amazing. I take another hot sip and appreciate the perfect balance of espresso and chocolate. Good pie and coffee. Certainly that's a sufficient excuse to have trekked to Lake Savage.

I open my message app and go to text Lola. I promised myself I'd tell someone next time I went off on a sketchy little adventure. But I hesitate. I'm still pissed at her for inviting Jake to our drinks the other night. I swipe out of the app. Nope. I'm not over it at all.

My finger hovers over the Gone app. I could just message Wes and ask him where he lives, or, like, his last name. And just as I'm about to tap the app, the door jingles with a new customer. I look up and my eyes land first on a man's heavy boots, perfectly fitted jeans, thick hoodie with a fleece vest on top, broad shoulders and—fuck me.

It's Wes.

His eyes land on me, and a slight smirk turns up the sides of his mouth. Instead of heading my way, he approaches the barista, who is looking way more interested in him than she was me.

"Hi, Wes," the barista says with a giant smile.

"Hey Maris. You hear from Colby yet?"

"I got in!" She smiles broadly.

"Nice work!" Wes high-fives Maris, who is practically hopping up and down.

Even the middle school girls in the corner are gawking at Wes. Then they all watch him accept a coffee from Maris and walk directly to my table, taking a seat across from me. The round table now feels ridiculously tiny with his large frame hunkered over it.

"Trying to find me, Calliope?" His voice is smooth and deep, and a shiver runs up my spine. He pulls his black beanie off and runs a hand through dark wavy hair, looking completely unsurprised to see me.

"No," I huff. "And no one calls me that."

"Kind of like no one calls me Wesley."

I shrug. "I guess." My stomach squeezes. No one's called me Calliope since my mother passed away.

"If you wanted my address—" He leans forward, close enough that I feel his warmth and smell that woodsy fresh scent. "You could've just asked me."

"That's not—I mean, I don't want your address. Why would you think I want your address?" I'm protesting too much, and a short giggle doesn't help. "Can't I have a coffee —a really good one, I might add—in this cozy lake town?"

Wes leans back and smirks. Under the table, his knees knock into mine and he adjusts so his legs are outside of mine, still touching. His eyes flit down to my plate, which has half of the slice of apple pie left.

"You like the pie here?" Now he's got a full-on smile on his face.

"I've had better, Wesley." I raise my eyebrows because I just know it's his pie. Wes bursts out laughing.

"Alright, I'll keep working on the recipe."

"I suspected it was one of yours." I fight to keep a smile off my face. His stupid grin is contagious, and the laugh is like a warm blanket on a snowy day.

"I bring a few once a week, plus anytime I have extra that I can't force-feed my brother."

"Well. That's... nice."

Wes shrugs. "It helps a small business. I know the owner pretty well."

"I bet you're like the mayor of this town, huh." I can just

about picture him stopping in each shop on Main Street and checking how business is going. Weird. I wouldn't have expected someone in his line of work to be so integrated in the community.

"Actually, a few people have asked me to run for mayor. Noah talked me out of it last time, so instead we elected a moose named Fred."

"There's a lot to unpack there." I sip my mocha. Still delicious. "You're close to your brother?"

"Yup. His cabin is less than a mile from mine, and we spend a lot of time together on some, well, joint projects, I guess."

"That must be nice." And he probably doesn't keep really important secrets from you like *my* brother, I think but don't say.

"It is."

I'm tempted to ask about the rest of his family, but I stop myself because Wes is not my friend. I need to keep that in mind.

"What are you doing here, Wesley?"

"What am *I* doing here?" He snorts. I ignore it.

"I might be in your little town, but there's no way you just happened to stop by this coffee shop—"

"Killer Beans."

"—Killer Beans ten minutes after I got here." I try to look haughty, but it's difficult when I'm obviously trying to track him down.

"Maris, what's your second choice for college next year? Is it still Boston University?" Wes calls to the barista.

"Yes, but I haven't heard from them yet." She gives him a bright smile.

"I'm sure you'll hear soon." Then he looks back at me and lowers his voice. "This is my town, Calliope. I know everyone. Those girls in the corner are eighth graders. Their moms all own a bakery down the road. The couple who just walked in?" He nods his head toward the two older women approaching the register. "They've lived here their whole lives. They used to own the general store but sold it a few years ago. They have a gorgeous lakeside cabin a mile up the road. In the summer they drive their golf cart in and out of town."

"I get it. What's your point?"

"That woman walking by with her dog?"

My eyes slide to a woman around sixty walking a tiny dog in front of the coffee shop.

"She runs the B&B with her husband and daughter. Her son is a professional hockey player in Colorado."

"Fine. You know some people. So what?"

"This is my town. I belong here. Why is it so hard to admit that you came looking for me?"

I groan. "Fine."

"Fine what?"

"Fine, I came looking for you."

"Why?" Wes leans back in his chair, taking a long sip of his coffee.

I try to come up with a reason why I'm here besides the truth, which is that I'm trying to hunt him down because of morbid curiosity and a little bit of an obsession.

"Oh! Shane. I wanted to see if you made any progress on finding Shane."

Wes raises a single eyebrow. "You didn't have to come here to do that. I bet you wanted more of my pie." He nods his chin to my plate. "I'd understand that. I can buy you another slice if you're still hungry."

I let out a laugh, noting that he'd buy back his own pie. "I do have a thing for your pie. And I finished the one you left in my apartment."

"What are you talking about?" Wes cocks his head and looks fake-confused. Oh, he's still pretending it wasn't his pie? Proof or not, I know it was him.

"Wesley."

"Calliope."

We stare at each other for a long few seconds, and I almost burst out laughing.

"I've been meaning to say." He leans forward on the table as he breaks our silence, and smirks. "You probably shouldn't eat random pies that show up in your kitchen. What if some lowlife tried to drug you?" His voice is a conspiratorial whisper.

"Who the fuck would do that?" I whisper back.

He shrugs and throws me a charming grin. Then a dark shadow crosses his face.

"But Calliope, you actually shouldn't be walking down dark alleys at night by yourself."

"And you shouldn't be following people around."

"Maybe. I'm honestly not sure how you've survived this long without someone like me to look out for you."

"I'm usually a lot more careful."

"I find that hard to believe, but okay." He has the decency to look worried, not annoyed.

No one has looked out for me since high school. Not my father, nor Jake, nor Shane. But Wes seems to want to. That is... fucking weird. And shouldn't make me as happy as it does. I can take care of myself. Kinda.

I swallow and shut my eyes, fighting back the memories of my father not protecting me from his associate when I was in high school. Pushing away the dread that cloaks me whenever I think of Shane's gaslighting and demands for my father's money. I punch back the anger I have toward Jake, who could help me find Shane but refuses to.

"Hey, where'd you go?" A warm hand touches my arm, and my eyes fly open. Wes stares at me with a furrowed brow, and the spot where his fingers touch my skin draws my eyes.

"Uh, nowhere." I shake my head and look up. "But I don't need your protection. I don't even know you."

A comical flash of hurt crosses Wes's face.

"You're right. I'm sorry if I overstepped."

At this, I laugh. A smile turns up the corners of Wes's mouth, and then he chuckles with me.

"What's so funny?"

"There are so many ways in which you've overstepped over the past ten days."

"Does that upset you?" he asks, paying careful attention to my reaction.

"Fuck, I don't know." I shake my head. "It should. It really, really should."

So why doesn't it?

CHAPTER 15

THE MAYOR

WES

Callie Callahan is doing some light stalking of her own, and it's adorable. It shows me she doesn't mind a little innocent obsessing.

Plus, she's gorgeous. I sip my coffee and let my eyes roam her face. Those dark, sharp eyes, a few freckles across the bridge of her nose, long dark hair in a braid lying over her shoulder. Her pink winter jacket is bunched up on her chair, and she's wearing another long cardigan, this one red, a snug white t-shirt, and long black skirt. She's perfect.

"What's your last name?"

"Winters." I only hesitate for a split second.

"Wes Winters?" Callie raises her eyebrows.

"Are you judging me? Because your name is Callie Callahan."

"Hey, I didn't choose it."

"It's adorable." I press my lips together.

"I'm a little surprised you shared your last name so easily."

To be honest, I usually wouldn't, but the woman has

already been to my cabin, so it's not like she can't figure out who I am via real estate records—if she can remember where I live. And I don't want to do anything to push Callie away. Not yet, anyway. Not when I'm so drawn to her.

Callie takes the last sip of her coffee, then tilts her head and narrows her eyes. "So nothing at all to share about Shane?"

I cock my head and consider if I should. I don't involve clients in the process aside from asking questions that help direct me here and there. There are often dead ends and leads that fizzle out. I push my hoodie sleeves up to my elbows before leaning lean back in my chair and linking my hands behind my head. Her eyes flit to my forearms.

"Shane was in Boston when he called you."

"Fucker." Her response is immediate and deeply annoyed. "Is he still there?"

"Nah." I shake my head. "I've been looking at security footage and haven't spotted him. But more so, he hasn't used his phone since that day."

"Think he's dead?" Callie almost looks hopeful, and I smirk. She rewards me with a small smile.

"It crossed my mind. But no. I'm guessing he's using a burner phone." If this was another case, I'd probably already be on the ground in Boston trying to sniff Shane out. But I want to take my time with this one. To get things right. I breathe deeply and admit it's also to spend more time with Callie.

"How much do you know about fight clubs?"

Callie's spine stiffens.

"I hate fight clubs." She picks up her coffee cup, remembers it's empty, then puts it back down and looks out the window at a man walking by the coffee shop. He's an Irish dude who is owner of the little bookstore in town.

I wait for her to continue.

"Dad ran the fight club in Boston. He asked me to work there multiple times over the past few years. As if I'd fit in."

I glance down at Callie's hot as hell librarian getup. She definitely doesn't belong in a fight club. Not dressed like that, anyway.

"Shane got involved. He gave me so much shit for not helping. Shane loves that stupid place."

"Is that what made you want a divorce? Him pressuring you to work for your family?"

"No. We had problems from the start."

I want to ask what kinds of problems. On one hand, I like hearing about how wrong her soon-to-be-ex-husband is for her. On the other hand, it makes me furious.

"And your father, did he like Shane?"

"God, no. Shane lived with Dad for a while after he lost his father. I think Shane thought of him as a new father figure, but Dad never felt that way. I think Shane married me to stay a part of our family, and I married him to piss off my dad, at least partly."

I grunt. He should've married Callie because he was hopelessly in love with her, not using her to advance his career. I ball my hands into fists under the table.

"I'm glad you're divorcing him instead of staying miserable. It's brave."

"It doesn't feel brave. It feels..." she trails off, staring into her empty coffee. I let my eyes roam her face. Callie's beautiful, but she's got dark circles underneath her eyes and deep lines between them, like she spends a lot of time with her brow furrowed.

"What does it feel like?" I bring my forearms onto the table and lean forward, watching her with rapt attention.

The coffee shop empties, the middle school girls heading out with giggles and the couple following.

"Almost shameful."

I have to bite my tongue to not jump in right here and contradict her. There's nothing shameful about making a mistake. Misjudging someone. Callie deserves so much more than to feel bad about that.

"I stayed married to him when I knew he was a terrible match for me. But I can't even divorce him correctly."

"I'm not sure there's a right way to divorce someone, Calliope," I say gently. I relax my fists and want to reach over and touch her hands, which are wrung together on the table.

She shrugs. "It should've happened a long time ago. I suspected he was cheating. The job required him to stay away overnight on a regular basis, but it became more frequent in the past year or so. Then I found woman's underwear in his pocket after a fight."

Oh, hell no. If I ever get in the same room as this man, I am going to fucking kill him. Cheating is never, ever okay. No matter what. And cheating on Callie? This beautiful woman, so pure and untouchable? She's managed to stay true to herself through a lifetime of being in the Callahan family. Somehow, she's clung to some kind of moral compass that has kept her from becoming a bad person. Somehow, she's remained good.

"I finally realized I needed to leave. But then—"

A shadow of sadness passes over her face, and she blinks a few times. I wait patiently for her to continue, my eyes not leaving hers.

"My father died. I asked for a divorce, and we fought about it. Then Shane disappeared."

"Fuck, Callie."

"He isn't going to let me go on my terms. It'll have to be on his, if at all."

I make a decision. This isn't going to be a simple job where I find someone and move on. It's not just a job anymore. Callie won't go through this alone. I was already invested, but now I'm committed.

"Shit, I don't know why I'm telling you this." Callie's cheeks turn a deep pink. "Please forget all of that. This is a job to you, not a sob story."

I shake my head, not willing to voice my thoughts: It's not just a job to me anymore.

"Think he's working at the fight club? God, that would be so obvious."

"No. He's not, I'm almost sure. But I have a feeling someone there might know something."

"Oh." Callie raises her eyebrows and hope creeps onto her face.

This woman might not want me to protect her, but I'm desperate to take that job. She deserves to have someone place her first. To watch her back. I can at least do that much for her while she's sorting out the end of her marriage.

"I was thinking I'd pay a visit."

"I'm coming," she says immediately.

"That's not a good idea." I shake my head, but it's a weak protest. Didn't I know she'd insist on coming? This woman who appears to be a good girl but also followed a serial killer to his isolated cabin and then came back looking for him a few days later? "Those places are dangerous. Violent. Filled with bad people."

"Yeah, I know." Storm clouds come over her face, and she narrows her eyes at me.

"It's not safe." The idea of taking a beautiful woman like

this to a nasty fight club filled with lowlifes is a nightmare. But she'll have me at her back. I can protect her.

"I said I'm coming," she says, and I huff, then smile. "What the fuck are you smiling about?"

"I like hanging out with you, that's all," I say, and she blinks with surprise. "So if you promise to stay close, I'll take you."

She breathes out, like she was holding air in her lungs waiting to see what I'd say.

"Thank you." Callie doesn't exactly smile at me, but the stormy look fades into cautious relief. "When?"

"They have fights on Friday nights."

"Okay." She nods. "So we go this Friday?"

"No. I need more prep time. A week from Friday."

"Uh—"

"This is my process," I say firmly. In all honestly, I could be ready for this Friday, but another week won't hurt. "I'll continue to monitor security footage from the area, confirm the fight club address, keep an eye on any activity on his cards or his mobile. I'm thorough, Callie."

"Ohhhhkay." Her mouth twitches, and I'm glad she finds me amusing instead of annoying.

"I'll pick you up next Friday afternoon."

"No." She shakes her head. "I'm driving myself."

"Of course you are."

"What's that supposed to mean?"

"Nothing bad, I promise. It just feels like something you would do."

"You don't even know me."

"I'd like to." I throw a charming grin at her.

"For fuck's sake," Callie murmurs but doesn't protest. "Now please tell me how you knew I was here."

"Huh?" I press my lips together and project innocence.

"Is it my phone? Are you tracking me through Find My phone?"

"Oh, Calliope, my sweet summer child."

"What? Is it something else?"

I have no intention of telling her about the spyware on her phone or in her phone case or the tracker on her car or the cameras in her apartment.

"So you're not going to tell me." She scowls.

I shake my head. "Isn't it enough I'm looking out for you?" I stand and pick up Callie's pie plate and our empty coffee cups. "Come, let's go for a walk." I walk the dish to the counter, toss the cups, then say goodbye to Maris. I swipe my beanie from the table and tug it on my head.

Callie shrugs her jacket on and watches me, stepping through the door that I hold open for her.

"But *why* are you looking out for me?" Callie asks once I'm standing with her on the sidewalk. I reach over and gently pull the hood of Callie's pink winter coat over her head.

"This way." I nod up the road.

"Why do you care if I get robbed on the streets of Portland?" She falls into step next to me.

I side-eye her, then grab her arm as she slips on an icy patch on the sidewalk. "Damn. This needs to be salted again."

"Is it the paycheck?"

"I'm not worried about the money." I reach for her arm again and stop us in front of my car. "Just give me a minute." I pop the trunk of my big SUV open and pull the bag of salt toward me, then open it and scoop with the plastic cup.

"You keep salt in your car?" Callie watches me curiously.

I walk back to the slippery part of the sidewalk and gently shake salt over the ice. The town did a pretty good job of shoveling, but this bit is always in the shade, so it's hard to keep clear.

It's useful to keep a big bag of salt in the car, for multiple reasons. I never know when my brother is going to call me with a dead-body-related emergency.

"Yup. Don't want someone falling. There's a lot of older people in town." I toss the cup back in my car and close the trunk, then hold out my arm. "Just in case there's more ice."

She slides her hand around my elbow and gives me a funny look.

We walk in silence for a minute, and I'm hoping she forgot her question about why I'm looking out for her. Because I'm not completely sure how I'd respond. It's true that I have an obsessive personality. I've scared off many women this way. But what's closer to the truth is that Callie is an anomaly as she hasn't already run screaming from me, and that's more than intriguing.

Which is why I need to be careful not to let myself actually care about Callie. Keeping Noah safe is a full-time job, I don't have room for anyone else.

"Wes?" Callie says in a sweet voice as she squeezes my arm, just on the verge of too hard. We're at the end of the shops and the sidewalk stops in about five feet. "Where the fuck are you taking me?"

"Here." I gesture down a path that leads behind the general store. Callie follows, and a gorgeous view of the icy lake spans out in front of us. It's a dramatic difference from what it looks like in the summer months, when tourists converge on the lake and there are jet skis, motorboats, canoes, families swimming at private docks, ducks, and the occasional loon. The general store bustles and families eat ice cream at the picnic tables down by the water. At this point in the winter, the lake is frozen. Solid with snow on top. No boats or people.

"It's beautiful," Callie says, her voice wistful. "But cold." She shivers.

"Here." I pull off my beanie and secure it onto her head. She looks up at me with big eyes while I do it. I adjust the hat gently.

"Thanks."

"No problem. Look. That's my cabin across the lake." I point to the distant short dock and pathway up to the screened-in porch of my cabin and the door which I snuck out of to catch her that first night she followed me home. "And my brother's cabin is there." Now I point a stretch further down the shore to Noah's dock.

"You're lucky he's so close," Callie says. "Do you have other family?"

I freeze with my finger pointed in the air.

"No," I say and drop my hand. "It's just us." And that's the truth. Our parents are dead, our little sister is gone with them, and my twin cut us out. I can feel Callie's gaze on the side of my face. I don't turn toward her. I'm not looking to share that dark part of my life, the series of events which turned Noah and I into what we are today, the sisters I lost.

Please don't ask anything else, I beg her silently.

"Welp, I'm an ice cube, even with your hat."

"Ready to go?" I finally have the nerve to turn toward her.

She nods and looks like she wants to say something else but doesn't. We walk back down Main Street in silence until we get to her car in front of Killer Beans.

"So I can't convince you to let me drive you to Boston next week?" Noah isn't going to be pleased if I do convince her. When I floated the idea of going to Boston, he insisted we go early to check out Chad Smith.

"Nope." She stops in front of her car and turns to me. "I can drive myself. We're not actually friends, Wesley, it might be weird." But she's got an exasperated smirk on her face.

I'm totally winning her over.

"Ouch, Calliope. We already have special names for each other. How can you say we're not friends?"

"They're not special. They're literally just our names." But she sighs when I give her a goofy grin. "Just send me the address to meet you at." She opens her car door and tosses me a withering look.

"Yes, ma'am."

Callie rolls her eyes and slides into the driver's seat. I knock on the passenger side window, and she rolls it down.

"We could be friends, Calliope. If you wanted to."

Callie makes a face. "You're exactly the type of person I should not be friends with."

"What? That hurts." I press my hand to my chest in mock pain, but in reality, her words do sting.

"Look." She grabs her phone and taps a few times, then hands me the device.

On it is a picture of an adorable small ranch house with a covered front porch, a tiny lawn, and an actual white picket fence.

"What's this?"

"It's a house in Seattle. The suburbs. I probably can't afford it right now, but that's the goal. Start over in a place like that. Leave all this drama far behind me."

"Got it." I nod and give the phone back to her with a smile, but it feels overly forced. Right. She's trying to get away from the criminal life. She's told me that already.

I'd never be the someone Callie would choose. Not after the life she's led so far with her asshole husband and her worthless father and brother.

She doesn't want to be here anymore, and certainly not anywhere near me.

Callie pulls away, and I feel something akin to regret. Regret for what? I am who I am, and there's nothing that would change that. And even if I did change for her, I can't erase all the things I've done in the past. All the white picket fences in the world won't bring back the people I've helped kill.

Someone like Callie doesn't belong with someone like me. I'll have to keep reminding myself of that. Maybe in a parallel universe she and I could be something. A universe in which my family is still alive, and Noah and I weren't pushed into becoming serial killers.

But not in this one.

CHAPTER 16

THE TATTOOS GAVE IT AWAY

CALLIE

You are exactly the type of person I should not be friends with.

Did I really say that as I drove away? After going to Lake Savage with the specific goal of finding Wes? I regretted those words as soon as they left my mouth. A hurt look flashed on his face just as I drove away.

I'm such an asshole.

My phone buzzes in my pocket as I'm stepping into the apartment, but I ignore it for now.

"Hello?" I call into the space, checking for my brother as I shrug off my winter jacket and hang it on a hook by the door. "Jake?"

There's no answer, so I head to the kitchen.

I realize something. I should avoid Wes because he's too distracting. Too tempting. Too much for my broken soul to handle.

I should tell him never to contact me again. Never to show up at Jake's apartment or Killer Beans or wherever I happen to be, because he'll definitely know where I am. He's tracking me, and that should scare me.

I could tell him to send me the address as to where I can find Shane when he gets it, then I can fucking Venmo him money. Something tells me he'd listen to me.

And I certainly shouldn't do things like driving around looking for him or openly flirting with him or drooling over the shirtless pictures he sends.

But it's been so long—forever?—since I had someone appear to be so interested in me. With Shane, once he secured his spot in my family thanks to our marriage, he lost all interest in me as a person. I was a tool for him. An in to the men in the group.

I wish I had more pie.

I fix myself a cheese sandwich—I really need to go grocery shopping—and settle at the kitchen island. My phone buzzes again when I have the first bite in my mouth.

UNKNOWN

glad you got home safe

I choke on the dry bread and am afraid I'm going to have to perform the Heimlich on myself, but I manage to swallow before I die.

I start typing an apology for how I acted as I drove away, then delete it. Then I try again, and delete it again. Shit.

What if it's not even Wes?

Of course it's him, but still.

ME

who is this?

Three little dots appear and disappear multiple times.

UNKNOWN

you know who this is

ME

seriously, Wesley? how'd you get this number?

UNKNOWN

have you met me?

I huff out a laugh, then the guilt for my last words to him makes my chest ache.

ME

hey, I didn't mean to be such a jerk as I drove away

There's a pause.

UNKNOWN

what do you mean?

ME

the shitty thing I said

UNKNOWN

can you remind me

ME

no! If you don't remember, good. But if you do, I'm sorry

UNKNOWN

apology accepted

His last text came without hesitation. The ache eases from my chest. I hope I didn't hurt his feelings. But I'm sure he's got thicker skin than that. A throwaway comment from me won't ruin his day like some sensitive little flower.

ME

so are we not using Gone anymore?

UNKNOWN

we can use whatever you want, Calliope

ME

I am a little sad I couldn't save the picture of
your tattoo the other day

UNKNOWN

if you want another picture of me without my
shirt on, all you have to do is ask

I crack up and take another bite of my sandwich. Yes please, Wes, another picture of you without your shirt on.

ME

unnecessary

Wes sends me a crying emoji, and I bite my bottom lip. Time to ask more questions as he's clearly in a chatty mood.

ME

hey, you never answered me when I asked
why you care so much about me being safe

He doesn't respond, and a minute later I'm regretting pushing him on the topic. He didn't answer before because he didn't want to. Why do I have to have an explanation for everything? I'm coming across needy and desperate for validation. I hate that.

But he does care. I know it.

And I also know that if I were a normal human being, I wouldn't be okay with how all of this is going down. Luckily, I'm not. I feel alone and isolated and lost, and Wes makes me feel safe.

Yeah, that's fucked up.

UNKNOWN

Is that so wrong?

ME

no. It's just that you don't even know me

UNKNOWN

something that can be changed

My stomach squeezes at his words. Does he want to know me? This is ridiculous. He's the guy I hired to track down Shane. But no matter how many times I remind myself not to get involved with Wes, I can't seem to stick with the rule. I set my phone down and push my hands in my thick hair, loosening chunks out of the braid and letting them fall around my face.

UNKNOWN

I think it happened the moment you were sitting in front of the fire in my cabin

ME

First of all, sitting in front of the fire is a cute way to describe what happened

Second of all, it's when you think what happened?

UNKNOWN

I started to care

I intake a sharp breath. Shit, why is that romantic? I was so angry when I woke up tied to that chair in front of his warm, crackling fire. But he confused me right away with how he checked my wrists when I complained and then set me free. And when I fell on my face as I tried to escape, he helped me up and made me hot chocolate.

Drugged hot chocolate, but still.

It was... sweet? And more than a little hot.

ME

you're fucked up

Kettle, meet pot. I save his information in my phone.

WESLEY

don't lash out at me

ME

I'm sorry. You're right. I was mostly thinking I'm fucked up

WESLEY

for what?

ME

for liking that you care

I drop my phone on the counter face down. Why am I telling him this? I shouldn't be encouraging my stalker. I stand and walk a circle around the family room, trying to convince myself not to pick my phone again.

The battle is lost in less than a minute, and I head to my room and collapse on the bed. There are messages patiently waiting for me from Wes.

WESLEY

of course I care

what else do you like?

I should close this chat and text Lola instead. I should tell her what's going on, and she will be appropriately appalled and tell me to cut it out.

Honey Bunny hops up onto my bed and pushes his soft nose into my leg. I gently scratch his little head.

Instead of texting Lola, I write back to Wes.

ME

I liked it when you went out to get firewood
wearing that black mask

Oh god, please stop, Callie, please stop. I splay my hand
over my face but peek through my fingers to watch the three
dots dance on my screen as he replies. Earlier today I literally
told him we shouldn't be friends. My resolve lasted only a
few hours.

I should be mad at myself. I should not be having so
much fun.

But... fuck it. I deserve fun with this hot masked man. Hot
masked *tattooed* man. I don't have a thing for tattoos, but
apparently, I have a thing for Wesley's tattoos.

ME

and your tattoos. I liked them too

WESLEY

good to know. we can arrange for all of that
to happen again

for what it's worth, I like your tattoo too

He sends through the image I sent him last week. Fuck!
How did he save it from Gone? I deleted it right away from
my camera roll, force of habit from when Shane used to
check my phone for anything he didn't like. I tilt my head. I
mean, I love my phoenix tattoo. I love everything it
represents.

I love that Shane hasn't ever seen it.

Still, I can't believe I sent it to him. I've never sent anyone
naughty pictures, but after seeing his, I couldn't help myself.
Again with something I never thought I'd do, but it was such

a rush. *I decided to send him that picture. I'm* taking control of my life, deciding what I do, where I go, who I talk to.

No one is going to control me ever again.

ME

> I would ask how you managed to keep that picture, but I'm guessing it has something to do with you being a hacker

WESLEY

yep

let's get back to how you like me half dressed and wearing a mask

ME

> did I say that?

WESLEY

I think you did. Scroll up

ME

> what kind of messed up person would like a man wearing a mask

WESLEY

you will not see me judging you for that

as a matter of fact, I am happy to be half dressed in a mask for you at any time

"Fuuuuuuck." I bite my lip and grin. I haven't smiled this much in months. Most of my interactions with people—people being Jake or Lola—include me complaining or yelling or sighing deeply or cursing out Shane.

By the time my text conversation with Wes ends, I'm giggling like one of those middle school girls in Killer Beans.

It's late, and the apartment is quiet. I scoop some food for Honey Bunny and get a text from Jake letting me know he'll be out of town for a few nights, so I sit at my desk and do a search for Wesley Winters.

There's nothing, of course. No social media, no professional profile, nothing.

Maybe I should be productive and browse houses for sale or apartments for rent in Seattle. My application for the program is complete, but I can't get myself to press submit. I just can't imagine myself there right now, so instead, I push the laptop away and pull out the latest book page art creation I'm working on. It's half of an adorable hedgehog, and I continue to fold the pages, first in half and then the corners, to work on its body. It's soothing and satisfying, and I manage to finish an entire hedgehog. I pull out my glue gun and attach big googly eyes, a black puffball nose, and a tiny pair of eyeglasses I bought online.

I crack up at the finished result, then climb into bed and turn off the light.

I AWAKE WITH A START. A thin ray of moonlight beams in from the window. My bedside clock says it's three o'clock in the morning. There's a weird stillness in the room, probably because the streets are pretty quiet in the middle of the night, so noise from the outside is minimal. I'm not usually up at this hour.

But—

Something is off. I sit up and glance around the room. My bedroom door is cracked open. Didn't I close it last night? Honey Bunny shifts in his cage, so I know he didn't use his rabbit magic to open the door. My heart pounds like a bass drum, my eyes scanning the room until I get to the long shadows from the curtains that frame my window. Did something just move? My hand shakes, and I reach for my phone on the nightstand.

My fingers grasp for something that's not there. Instead, I almost knock over my water bottle. I grab it to still it, then look back at the curtains.

I must've imagined it.

But then the shadow moves again and out of the darkness steps a tall, dark figure. I gasp, and my heart races as my eyes struggle to adjust.

"What the fuck," my lips part, and I mouth the words, but no sound comes out. The man is wearing dark pants, a dark face mask, and a bare chest. A bare chest? In February in Maine? But the moonlight shines on incredible chiseled abs and tattoos winding up both of his arms—oh god.

"Wesley?" My voice actually makes sounds this time, but it cracks. It's gotta be him, right? We were just talking about this. Mask and ab muscles and tattoos... it has to be him because the other option—that it's someone else—is way too dark. I squint but can't make out the details of his tattoos.

He doesn't answer, but instead walks slowly toward me, like a panther stalking its prey. I scoot back, my comforter kicked down my body to expose the thin tank top and underwear I wore to bed.

He stops next to my bed, and I crane my neck up to meet his eyes.

"What are you doing?" My voice wobbles.

He crosses his arms, and I take in the full view of his arms, covered in ivy and roses and thorny vines, the bear and the skull and dagger. His chest is clear of ink, which is surprising and hot. Who needs tattoos when he has all those muscles to show off?

I'd like to say my heartbeat slows now that I'm sure it's

Wes, but if anything, it speeds up. His light eyes drill into mine, then he slowly scans my body, his gaze lazily lingering on my breasts, then down. There's a deep ache between my legs, and I press them together for some kind of relief. I bet if I reached down and ran my finger over my underwear, it'd be soaking wet

Or if he did.

Damn. What's wrong with me? A man with absolutely no boundaries breaks into my house and—wait, is this my masked man kink coming to life?

He bends down, a hand on either side of me, and I lean back against the bed frame. I swallow as he gets close enough that I feel the heat emanating from his body onto my face, my neck. He moves down. He's breathing me in like some kind of hunting animal. He pauses at my abdomen before lowering his face to the intersection of my thighs and pussy. Can he smell me? I relax my legs and let my thighs open ever so slightly. He pushes his mask up to expose his mouth and nose and inhales deep, like he's trying to suck me up. I can feel his hot, feral breath on the inside of my thighs as he exhales. I desperately want him to touch me, but he doesn't make contact at all. I wonder if he could make me come without touching me. I want to pull him down and feel the weight of his body on mine. I want him to rip my underwear off with his teeth and bury his face between my legs. I want—

Then he's standing straight again, his balaclava shifting down but still exposing his mouth. I stare at his lips, red and plump, and his icy blue eyes that are clear even in the dark.

"Lock your doors." He practically growls at me. I'm frozen in place. Then he spins and walks out of my room.

"Hey!" I say, but my voice is weak, more like a whisper than the yell I intended.

It takes me a minute to convince my body to move. I jump up and run out of my bedroom to the door to the apartment. I open it but there's no one in the hallway, and I don't hear the door to the building open and close.

Did I imagine that whole thing? No way. I locked the doors before I went to bed... didn't I?

Wes did not come all the way here to make sure I was secure in this apartment. There's no way.

What if I imagined the whole thing? This is probably a dream. A wet dream.

I close the front door and double-check the locks before heading back into my bedroom, not sure I'll ever be able to fall asleep. My phone is on the corner of my nightstand, about to fall off.

Huh. It was there all along.

I check it and there's a message from Wes from hours ago, when I must've already fallen asleep.

WESLEY

good night, Calliope

did you double check your doors?

Wish I'd seen that reminder earlier.
Or maybe I don't.

CHAPTER 17

TOO MUCH?

WES

I shoulder open the door to Killer Beans with a pie balanced in each hand. The chime above the door jingles as I enter the coffee shop. I didn't sleep for a minute after my visit to Callie's bedroom in the middle of the night. I got home just before four o'clock in the morning and didn't even attempt it. I was too wired, too nervous, too turned on. The vision of Callie in only her underwear and that tiny scrap of a tank top is too much for my delicate soul to handle. I almost stayed. I almost kissed her. I almost buried my face in her pussy.

Fuck. Inappropriate!

I think it's safe to say she's terrified of me now, and once again, I crossed a pretty obvious line. A thick, bright white line on fresh black asphalt. Unmissable. Maybe it'll be better that I scared her off. The woman does not need me in her life.

Instead of sleeping, I headed right to the kitchen and started making dough for pie crusts with Sir Fluffy as my sous chef. When done, I threw them in the refrigerator to chill and moved on to the filling. With a fresh pot of coffee, I peeled and sliced all the apples in my house, and by the time the sun rose, I had four beautiful apple pies prepared.

At least I got to play around with some unique designs for the upper crust. That's where I'm going to shine this year at the Portland Springfest. It's hard to create art with crust, but I believe it's the way to stand out.

But four apple pies are too many, so I'm here to donate two of them to Killer Beans a few days earlier than usual. I'm a little embarrassed by the one with the top crust that looks like a fish but is supposed to be a loon. That design needs work.

"Wes!" Emma, the seventy-year-old owner of the coffee shop, gives me a bright smile as I approach. "What do you have for me today?"

"Two apple pies. I got in the zone this morning—I meant to make a blueberry as well, but I blacked out and created a row of apple pies." I chuckle and slide the disposable tins on the counter.

"They are beautiful. Is that a bear?" She peers down.

I groan. "It's meant to be a loon, but I can see where you got bear."

"You'll get there, dear." Emma reaches over and pats my arm.

"Can I have a coffee and a croissant while I'm here?" I always buy something when I walk into a shop in Lake Savage, especially in the winter when the tourists are away and traffic is slow.

"Absolutely. On the house, of course." She turns to pour me a coffee. "How much do I owe you for the pies?"

"You know the answer to that." I put a ten-dollar bill down as Emma chuckles. "And keep the change."

This is a game we always play. She always tries to pay me

for the pies, and I throw money at her instead. I'm just happy to support her business.

When Noah and I moved to Lake Savage a decade ago, we rented a place on the outskirts of town. We had little to our names until our family's house sold, and we were still deeply mourning the death of our parents and younger sister.

Mourning. Planning. Plotting.

We were a mess.

Emma was so kind. She somewhat forcefully invited us to community events like the quaint Christmas market and Fourth of July community street party. She dragged Noah to the local book club at the library, where he realized he hated book club fiction but had a thing for horror novels. Emma suggested a local baking class for me, which led me to my apple pie obsession and eventually entering the competition at the Portland Springfest.

Now that we're both in a much better place, we try to give back.

Emma thanks me and talks about her upcoming plans to hire more help so she can wind down her hours spent at the shop. She doesn't want to depend only on the high schoolers.

I nod and murmur in the appropriate places—I think— but I'm mostly wondering if Callie thinks I'm a total creep. I fucking smelled her. What is wrong with me?

A lot. A lot is wrong with me.

But the scent of that woman when I got close to her pussy? It made me feral. I was convinced if I pressed my face between her legs, I'd find her wet for me. She might have even wanted me to.

Probably not.

I sent her a good morning text a few hours ago. She read it, but she hasn't responded. I touch my phone in my pocket but resist the urge to check it while talking to Emma.

I'd never hurt Callie. Not in a million years. But she doesn't know that, so why do I feel the need to break into her fucking apartment and creep into her room like a stalker serial killer?

Which, I guess I am, but—fuck, I am.

It's too much, and she's never going to talk to me again. Between my behavior and the fact that she probably has some baggage from her marriage, she would never want to date me. Not that I'm thinking about dating her!

I leave Killer Beans with my coffee in one hand and croissant in the other and walk down Main Street, passing my parked car to head to the general store. There's a much bigger grocery store towards Portland, but I always get what I can here. I grab coffee creamer and a dozen apples, as I don't have a single one left in my house, and am checking out when my phone buzzes.

It's Callie.

I thank the cashier and step away from the register, eager to read the message. With my bag of groceries hooked on one wrist and my coffee and croissant in the other, I click through.

CALLIE

that was you last night?

No use lying about it. She'd figure it out and if I lie and say it's not me, then she'd probably freak out even more because that would mean someone else was in her apartment.

Plus, I didn't have a shirt on, and she'd seen my distinctive tattoos. The tattoos she said she liked.

Something's definitely wrong with me.

ME

yes

CALLIE

I can't believe you

I suck in a breath. Here it comes. A reminder I'm a psychopath. I'll stay calm, agree with her, get the job done she hired me for, and leave her alone. Even though I'm already attached to the fiery woman.

ME

about that—I'm sorry if that crossed a line

CALLIE

if that crossed a line? Are you fucking joking?

Maybe she's going to call the cops. Noah is going to kill me. I'm supposed to be the responsible one. But if she was going to call the cops, wouldn't she have done it by now? Also, I just confessed via text. Fuuuuck.

CALLIE

at least I now know to triple check my doors. or check them at all

ME

as if that would keep me out

Oops! Maybe that was (another) inside thought.

ME

sorry. I didn't mean to joke. I am sorry about what I did. I have boundary issues sometimes

CALLIE

it really freaked me out

ME

I know. I just thought since you liked my tattoos maybe you'd want to see them again? Obviously a bad call

CALLIE

as a surprise in my bedroom in the middle of the night was quite the choice. What the fuck, Wes

I search for the right way to respond to this. She's still talking to me, which is a good thing, but she's clearly pissed. I don't want her to cut me off, and she might be on the verge of that. She should be.

ME

how about you try to break into my cabin?

CALLIE

what??

There's not another message for a full thirty seconds. She's probably screaming into the void about how crazy I am. Then the three little dots start blinking.

CALLIE

I'm a shit stalker, as we both know

ME

cringing at being called a stalker

CALLIE

that makes you cringe? I mean, really?

I take a few steps and stop halfway out of the store, my back holding the door open. Is she... flirting with me? Fuck, I hope so. Someone appears behind me, and I step through the door onto the Main Street sidewalk to get out of the way, relief cascading through me.

ME

I can give you some pointers I guess, since you think I'm so good at it.

CALLIE

that's…really weird

But then she adds an eye roll emoji, and my mouth twitches up into a smile. She doesn't hate me. Not yet.

ME

I'll give you my address in case you need it, because obviously you couldn't find it last time

CALLIE

ouch

Then I text her my address. As if she could even get close to the cabin without me knowing. And she should not be doing something dangerous like that, especially as she doesn't really know me, and the skeletons in my closet are pretty dark.

This clearly is just some light flirting to go along with some light stalking. I bet beneath her spiky exterior, she's sweet as one of my apple pies.

But it's not like someone like her would actually go for someone like me. And it's not like I'd want her to. She deserves the pure life she's been fantasizing about, and there's no room for me.

CHAPTER 18
GUARD CAT
CALLIE

"I am not a boring-ass good girl," I whisper to myself as I quietly close the door to my car, which is parked on Wes's neighbor's driveway. He practically invited me to try to break in to his house, and while that would normally be a bonkers idea, I trust Wes.

I'm also feeling the inspiration to prove Shane wrong. I hate that some of his last words haunt me so much. That man made me feel like I'm not good enough, and I'm not sure I'll ever get over it.

It's almost pitch dark out, which makes sense as it's the middle of the night. Is it smart to go down a private driveway when I don't know for sure that the owners are down in Florida or wherever for the winter? Nope, it's sure not. But their driveway hasn't been shoveled recently, so I'm pretty sure they aren't here. Now, I'm not convinced I'll be able to drive my car back up the driveway due to all the snow, but that's a problem for later.

There are just so *very* many problems with this plan, but as I tiptoe through the woods toward the cabin with only a sliver of moonlight and my phone's flashlight at four o'clock in the morning in fresh ankle-deep snow, I ignore them all.

Because honestly, right now I'm most scared of running into a bear or a pack of coyotes. Or a moose. Or a very angry owl.

I'm such an idiot, but I feel more alive than I have in ages, and I have Wes to thank for that. He's made things lighter with that warm smile, those icy blue eyes, and the vulnerable way he looks at me, like I could hurt him somehow.

When I finally see the side of his cabin through the trees, a thin trail of smoke drifting out of his chimney, a wave of relief washes over me. I'm almost safe from wildlife.

An owl hoots in a nearby tree, and I almost scream.

"What is wrong with me?" I whisper, scanning my surroundings for a giant scary bird. I'm half tempted to just knock on Wes's front door and give up this game.

No way. I can do this. I used library resources to research how to stalk someone, after all! Literally. And how to break in! Could I get fired for that? Who's to know? All I have to do is pick his back door lock. I've also been watching YouTube videos for tips. Pick the lock, leave the present I have tucked away in my jacket, then retreat and wait for him to text me when he finds it in the morning.

Simple.

There's an outside light shining over the front door, but the back entrance is dark. My heart races as I approach the dark door with my newly purchased lock pick set. Why do they sell things like this?

I might know something more practical about being a criminal if I had let my father hire me. But the library is where I belong, not a fight club or gambling ring.

I take a deep breath and quietly choose a tool in the middle of the set to stick into the lock, wiggling it around a little. It's too loud, and I flinch at the sound. Nothing happens with the lock. I press my ear to the door and don't hear anything from inside the cabin. I pick a skinnier tool. Again, the metal scraping isn't great, but then there's a popping sound and the lock is open.

The lock is open.

So fucking easy! Maybe I have a secret talent for breaking and entering.

I turn the knob and quietly ease the door open wide enough for me to slip inside. There's not even a squeak, and I'm feeling pretty proud of myself. Then my wet boots squelch loudly on the wooden floor and I cringe, freezing for a second. When nothing stirs in the cabin, I push the door carefully shut behind me and lean against it, willing my heart to stop racing. It's dark in the house, the glowing embers of a dying fire in the living room providing the only light.

Something suddenly pushes against my calf, and I let out an involuntary squeak before processing that it's Sir Fluffy.

I bend down to pet Wes's cat on his head. Sir Fluffy meows, and I shush him, then he does it again.

"Shhh, kitty, hush," I whisper. This cat! What the hell?

But the cat keeps meowing, each one louder than the last. It's like he's a trained guard dog—guard cat?— screaming for Wes to come check out what he's found. Or maybe he's looking for breakfast.

Oh, fuck.

I stand and realize I need to get out of here. No time to find the perfect spot for my present. The counter right here will have to do. I pull out my gift and set it down. Now I just need to slip back out the door and run to my car. Through the woods and the leftover snow. In the middle of the night. And probably have to fight off bears or moose or owls.

But before I can even pull my hand back from the counter, everything goes dark.

~

MY EYES FLY OPEN, and I gasp as I try to figure out what's going on. Right away, I realize I can't move my hands or my legs and—

I'm zip-tied to Wes's kitchen chair in front of a warm fire, my jacket, gloves, and hat piled neatly on the couch next to Wes.

Again.

"Fuck," I say, noting the airplane pillow around my neck.

"Well well well, look who's finally awake." Wes is looking fucking adorable in sweatpants, a hoodie, glasses with slightly messed up hair, reading on his e-reader. "You were out so long I had time to get the fire going again."

My god, why is he so sexy?

"You didn't have to tie me up." I sigh loudly, trying to project frustration and nonchalance, not admiration at his beauty.

"I rather like seeing you tied up." Wes cocks his head and drops his device onto the couch cushion beside him, not making a move to stand.

My jaw drops, and it takes me a second to find words. He likes to see me tied up. Damn, that's hot. But the fact that he likes me tied up and the fact that I find it hot are both disturbing.

"Can you please untie me?"

"Of course, Calliope." Wes picks up a knife from the side table. I am zero percent afraid as he approaches and crouches in front of me.

"You drugged me. Again."

"You tried to break into my cabin. Again."

I growl, but he smiles and wraps a hand around my ankles, keeping them still while he cuts the zip tie. Then he drops onto his knees and reaches around the chair for my wrists, his torso pressing against my legs. I breathe out at the warm contact.

"I honestly didn't think you'd take my suggestion to heart." He frees my wrists with ease and gathers the plastic zip ties from the carpet. "But I really do think you could use some pointers."

"Forget it. I'm a terrible stalker, and I'm okay with that." I roll my wrists and narrow my eyes at him.

"Are you really going to be mad at me right now?" Wes remains kneeling in front of me. "It is four-thirty in the morning, and you tried to break in. I was sleeping comfortably in my bed. So was Sir Fluffy."

"Actually, I *did* break in." I'm feeling pretty smug about my breaking and entering, even if I did mess it up as soon as I got inside.

"Oh, sweetheart, I let you. I have about five more locks on that back door that I didn't use."

First of all, the way he called me sweetheart warms me from the inside out in a way I'm not proud of. Second, I guess I'm *not* good at breaking and entering.

"Also, I have cameras everywhere, and got an alert as soon as you crossed into my property from the Flemington's next door." Wes pats my knee and lets his hand linger there. I cross my arms and attempt to look annoyed. "By the way, they own a ton of guns, so you're lucky they're down south for the winter."

"Jesus." I pull my hair over my shoulder and cock my head at him.

"Listen," he says, hand still on my knee. "I hope you know you are safe with me."

I blink at him. I mean, yeah, I guess I do know that, otherwise this would be a really stupid position for me to be in. I nod.

"And I shouldn't have encouraged you. You're putting yourself in unnecessary danger, and as much as I love having you in my cabin, this could've turned out very differently if it were someone else." He looks at me so intently, eyes wide and locked on mine.

"Uh—" I swallow and my chest flutters. "Okay. Yeah."

"Right. Glad we've got that settled." Wes stands and holds out his hand. "How about a drink? Coffee? Tea? Whiskey?"

"That sounds nice, but I should get home." I glance at Wes's large, open hand.

"Why?"

I look up at him. Why, indeed.

"None of those drinks are right for this time of night." I say lamely, staring back down at his hand for a beat more before placing mine in it. I shouldn't be here, I shouldn't be flirting, and I shouldn't be imagining what things Wes can do with those large hands and thick fingers.

"Of course they are. Any of them. It just depends on what you're in the mood for. Plus, it's still dark out, and I don't think you should be walking through the woods or driving. What if you hit a moose? Or run into one?"

"Then I'd be fucked." I nod as I'd recently thought that.

"Exactly. Those motherfuckers are terrifying. Fred the mayor is real, you know, and he is enormous. Come on. Sit on the couch. I'll make tea."

I've officially run out of the strength to fight him—and whatever it is that's happening between us—so I let him gently pull me up. It feels so lovely that when he slides his hand out of mine I almost whimper.

I settle onto the couch as Wes puts his kettle on the stove to heat water. Sir Fluffy hops up on the couch next to me, sitting exactly on top of Wes's e-reader.

"Kitty, you totally sold me out." I scratch Sir Fluffy's head, and he presses up into my palm.

Wes chuckles from the kitchen. "Let's go over the plethora of mistakes from tonight, shall we?" Wes pulls out two mugs and drops a tea bag in each one.

"We're really doing the stalking lessons?"

"No, I just want to go over the ways you put yourself in danger." He shrugs. "You didn't even attempt to look for cameras as you approached the cabin. Not even a cursory glance up."

"I *was* looking up. For owls." I scrunch my face. He's right. I even remember reading that in my Google search, but I totally forgot.

"Owls are the least of your problems." Wes snorts.

"Wait, were you watching the whole time?"

"Yeah, obviously. I wanted to see what you'd do." The kettle whistles, and he pours steaming water over our tea bags.

"Next, you were so loud picking the lock with that amateur kit. Did you buy that on Amazon?" Wes judges me hard. I refuse to nod even though he's right. "Three, your shoes are so incredibly squeaky. Have there ever been squeakier shoes? Take them off before coming inside, wear different shoes, whatever."

"Listen—"

"I know. You're not a criminal." He grabs milk from the fridge and a container of sugar from his counter. "And you don't want to be one." Wes throws a look over his shoulder that I can't read. It's almost sad.

"I mean, basically, yeah."

"Milk? Sugar?"

"Milk and two sugars, please."

"You also didn't factor in animals. I happen to have a very vocal cat, but some people have dogs. You always have to bring a treat, sometimes with a light sedative."

I drop my jaw and gasp.

"Very, very light sedative. We are not about hurting animals."

"Fine. But I've already given up on my stalking career."

"Good. I did enjoy your gift." Wes nods to the book page art hedgehog I had placed on his counter before he knocked me out. "It's adorable."

My cheeks heat as he approaches and hands me a steaming tea. I accept it and wrap my hands around the warm mug. I shouldn't have brought the hedgehog. It's embarrassing.

"Did you make it?" Wes heads back into the kitchen to grab his own mug and the paper hedgehog, then sinks on the couch on the other side of his cat, placing my creation right next to Sir Fluffy. Wes reaches out and mindlessly scratches his head. The cat purrs so loudly I fear he has a whole airplane engine inside him.

"Yeah." I nod. Might as well just admit it now while we're in this surreal moment in time. I'm not sure why I felt the need to share something so personal with Wes, something that Shane hated and would make fun of me for. Maybe it was a test. Like, let's see how he reacts to this weird thing about me. "It's kind of my thing. I make book page art out of old paperback books."

"No way." Wes slides his mug onto the coffee table and

examines the hedgehog with two hands. "What book is this?"

"That one? It was an old thriller novel. I go to the thrift store or our library sales and buy a bunch of old books that I can use."

"You are really talented."

Wes is definitely passing the vibes test. I shouldn't care what he thinks about me, but obviously I do. Somehow, our little business relationship has turned very personal, very fast.

"Shane called it my stupid little hobby. He trashed all my stuff when he disappeared. The apartment was empty aside from my clothes, books, and a few other items." My cheeks heat as I remember the moment I got home and found the apartment empty. It was awful. "He even left my rabbit hopping around the hallway all by himself."

"He fucked with Honey Bunny??"

I nod solemnly.

"He is really an asshole."

"Yup."

Wes lays an arm across the back of the couch and sips his tea, watching me intently. I squirm underneath his gaze. It's like he's trying to figure me out.

This guy is contradictory. He's clearly not your average thirty-something bachelor. Even though he lives alone in an isolated cabin on a lake, he's got relationships with people. He's clearly close to his brother and integrated into the Lake Savage community. He smiles. A lot. He loves his cat and bakes pies.

But he's also dangerous. How easy has it been for him to drug me and tie me up? He's clearly an expert. A shiver runs down my spine. I haven't hated any of it. Which bothers me. I'm so eager to get away from my criminal family yet I'm drawn to Wes, who must have criminal leanings. No one knows how to drug someone and tie them up so well without having some previous experience executing it.

"How about you? Have a girlfriend?" I choke the word out, and he raises an eyebrow. "Ever been married?"

"No." Wes shakes his head, a tinge of sadness on his face. "I'm not good in relationships."

"Why not?"

"I can be, uh, kind of a lot, so I don't normally even get to the relationship phase."

"Is it the following? Tracking? Stalking? Breaking into women's bedrooms in the middle of the night?" It's an attempt to make him smile, but there's an unsettled look on his face.

And I absolutely hate the idea of him sniffing around some other woman's body in the middle of the night.

"Most women cannot look past that kind of thing. And I don't blame them."

"Yeah, well, most women must not understand you." I lean over to set down the mug and pull my legs underneath me. I'm not sure why I'm feeling defensive of this man, but I am. How dare other woman judge him for his uniqueness and passion? Dedication? Loyalty?

Wait, am I saying that *I* understand him? Lordy.

"So what else do you make out of book pages?"

I explain to him some of my creations, my face warm with embarrassment at first, but he seems legitimately interested. Then I ask him questions about his pie baking, and he tells me more about his five-year history of ribbons at different pie competitions around Maine.

It's only when the view of the frozen lake and pine trees becomes visible with the first light of the day that I realize we've been talking for hours. And that I'm exhausted.

"Do you want to crash here for a while, Calliope?" Wes asks when I yawn widely.

I consider it for a second, but I think I need a moment to process. It feels like every time I come in contact with this man, I need time to figure out what the hell just happened, and this time is no different.

"No, thank you." I shake my head. "I'm gonna go home to feed Honey Bunny and get some sleep in my own bed."

He nods. "I'll drive you to your car."

Fifteen minutes later, he hands me a hot coffee in another non-disposable travel mug—I really need to bring them back—and lets me leave as my car is warmed up and at the top of his neighbor's driveway.

"Calliope." Wes leans against his driver's side door as I slide into my car.

"Wesley."

"Thanks for stopping by." He grins at me.

I shake my head and pull out of the driveway, glancing in my rearview mirror until I round a curve and he's out of sight.

Last night was amazing. Wes listens to me, cares what I have to say, and seems to want to know me. I don't know why. He's all wrong for me, so I need to keep reminding myself that this is just a job for him and we are at most friends. But even as I think that, I know that it's not quite true. There's more happening here. What, I don't know.

Maybe he's helping me move on from my marriage so that by the time Shane signs the papers and returns my mom's ring, I'll truly be free. Maybe that's all this is. Maybe I'll look back on this weird in-between time of my life like it was some kind of fever dream.

Because it doesn't seem real.

CHAPTER 19

FIELD TRIP

WES

I really wish Callie would've let me drive her to Boston for our fight club visit, but then Noah and I wouldn't have been able to come in early and stake out Chad Smith, target number one on his list.

"We can grab him when he's with a sex worker," Noah says, taking a long swig of his beer. We're at a high-end bar that's busy with men and women in business casual mixed with groups on their way out for the night.

I nod. Being with a sex worker is not my thing, but it's fine on its own. Except not the way Chad Smith does it, which is drunk and full of rage. I lift a hand to get the bartender's attention and hold up two fingers.

Noah gives me a pointed look and pushes his glasses up his nose. I choose to wear contacts during the day, but Noah's never taken to them. "I don't know if he's still dating that high school girl, if you can call it dating. But the girl he was with last night looked really young."

"If it works out, fine." I nod. "But we're here for the fight club."

Last night, we followed Smith to a poorly lit area known to have sex workers. He found one, and instead of taking her to a hotel, he pulled her into an alley and fucked her against a wall. I was ready to step in to make sure he didn't hurt her, but Noah stopped me. He agreed that we'd help if things went too far, but we'd blow our cover. I couldn't watch. Smith was so rough, his face filled with focused fury, like it was all her fault, everything and anything he could think of. I wanted to beat the shit out of him.

I can't imagine treating a woman that way. I don't care what his kink is, he needs full consent to get rough before it happens, complete with safe words and clear agreed-upon boundaries. Something tells me he didn't have any of that. How can a man feel so comfortable spreading his hate? Taking it out physically on women and girls?

"Got it." Noah presses his lips together in a grim line. Since his recent breakup, Noah's had way too much time on his hands. And as it's winter, he doesn't have an active renovation project going on, so he's just getting himself into trouble researching targets all alone in his cabin. I've been stopping by more and badgering him to come over and taste pies.

He was too sloppy in Florida. We need to be way more careful.

The bartender slides two fresh bottles of beer our way. I glance down at my phone, the tracking app open on the screen. I know exactly where Callie is, but I'm giving her a chance to come to me before I go hunt her down. Not in a creepy way, but I'm not letting her walk into that fight club alone.

I've been riding a high all week from the other night. It was the best time I've had in years. I had fun. I was myself. And she seemed comfortable with me. Fuck, the image of her curled up on my couch with her legs tucked under her and her hands wrapped around a steaming mug of tea? I could get used to that.

She might not know it, but she's got a full-time bodyguard in me. For now.

"You have a problem, don't you?" Noah's voice pulls me out of my head.

"Huh?"

"That woman." He nods at my phone. "I truly cannot understand why you're bringing her tonight."

"She wanted to come. She has a right to know what's going on with her husband."

"Absolutely. But it's your job is to find out where he is and literally hand her, like, a Post-It with the address and other details. That's it. Her coming along is going to be a major distraction." Noah shakes his head, then narrows his eyes. "Don't lose your mind because you found the one woman who doesn't run screaming when you zip-tie her. It's not true love. You understand that, right?"

"It's not? Are you sure?" When his jaw drops, I laugh and wave my hand. Noah and I have zero filter with each other. "Just kidding. I swear."

"But you like her too much."

It's pointless to lie to Noah. He'll see right through me, especially as he'll witness Callie and I interact tonight. I'm pretty sure I can't keep my shit together around her. He'll recognize that right away. My brother is a true romantic at heart, and this is him taking it out on me that the last girlfriend didn't work out.

"Maybe." I stare at the back of the bar, my eyes scanning the bottles of liquor, hoping he changes the subject.

"Wes." Noah groans. "How bad is it?"

He knows I get obsessive. He knows I have a thing with

lightly stalking women I like. He's got no idea how bad it is this time, though. I'm not sure I even understand it.

"Bad?" I say, and Noah sighs deeply, shifting on the bar stool next to me. A new text pulls down above the map on my phone.

CALLIE

almost there

ME

I know

CALLIE

has anyone ever told you that you are too controlling

ME

yes

I snort and click back onto the tracking app. I probably shouldn't have made it so obvious that I can track her. But at this point, I don't really care. Unless she goes somewhere by foot and without any device, I'll know where she is.

And as much as she comments on it, she hasn't actually asked me to stop. It would be so hard to. My instinct to protect is part of who I am.

See, this is what gets me in trouble with women. This is why they back off as soon as they get to know me.

Movement by the entrance to the bar catches my eye. It's a crowded Friday night, but I'd notice Callie Callahan even if there were a thousand people around. She walks in, and I swear softly under my breath as the woman approaches us and shrugs out of her winter coat.

She's wearing a strapless black top with a dip in between her breasts. The shirt leaves a strip of skin showing between the bottom of it and her jeans. Black high heels add three inches to her height. Her long hair is curled and thick down her back. Her cheeks are pink from the cold, her lips plump and red, her eyes big and dark.

She looks hot as hell. Extremely inconvenient for this evening.

I growl and slide off my bar stool.

"Well, shit," Noah says from behind me. "So that's why you've been so distracted."

I ignore him and stalk over to her.

"Fuck. Calliope," I say with a warning tone when I get to her. She's got a smirk on that gorgeous mouth.

"Hey, Wesley. Why the grumpy face? You're usually smiling." She tilts her head and runs a finger through her hair, bringing it over her shoulder and exposing the side of her neck. There's just so much skin on display. Her neck, her shoulders, her collarbone, the curve of her tits, her belly.

"What the fuck are you wearing?" I say carefully. Yeah, I might smile more than your average guy, but not when I have a guess at the number of assholes I'm going to have to fight off her tonight, and that number is too high. The more time I spend with Callie, the more it drives me crazy how she seems to purposely put herself in danger. I talked to her about it last weekend when she tried to break into my cabin, but I guess it didn't really sink in.

"Well, this is an adorable shirt that I've owned for years but never had a chance to wear. I don't go anywhere that's appropriate for it. So I thought, why not?"

A trio of men slide by. One of them checks out Callie from the side. He looks soft and weak, like he spends all day at a desk job or in a classroom, and I step close and wrap my hand gently around Callie's arm. I narrow my eyes at the dude and shake my head slightly. He scans me up and down and quickly moves on.

"This is not appropriate attire for a fight club," I say through gritted teeth.

"Yeah, it is."

I swear under my breath. She's right, of course. But worrying about other men groping Callie will make my life much more difficult.

"You're killing me."

She snorts a laugh, and it'd be cute if it weren't so concerning. "Didn't you say your brother would be here? Is he as charming as you are?" She leans around me and waves at Noah, who is probably gawking at us.

I fully plan on being her bodyguard tonight, but I also want to pull her into a dark hallway and make her scream my name.

I shouldn't do that.

And I need to spend some time working through how I let myself get so attached after only a few weeks.

Instead, I take a deep breath and let my eyes linger on her face, then crawl over all that skin once more, spending extra time on her tits and the way her breathing speeds up when I do so. She's watching me eye fuck her, and it's getting to her.

When I finally look back into her eyes, her cheeks are even pinker than when she walked in.

"Are you okay, Calliope?" I've managed to regain my calm and am thrilled to see her physical reaction to me.

"Yup."

"Fine. Come meet Noah." I smirk and slide my hand off her arm.

NOAH AND CALLIE get along like old friends, which is

surprising because Noah is a weird dude and many women who meet him instinctively feel like something is off.

They're right, of course.

But Callie asks him if he watches the series on TV about Maine cabin renovations, and they immediately start discussing their favorite episodes. She's not just doing it to make conversation, she's citing episodes about specific cabins. Noah's delighted. She must've been paying attention when I talked about his line of work and either gone home and binge-watched the entire series or kept it to herself she's a fan. Either way—adorable.

I walk behind them on the busy Boston road in the direction of the bus that will take us to where we need to go. They're chatting, but I'm focusing. I want to get in and out of that place as subtly and quickly as possible. I don't think Shane Robertson is there, but I'm betting someone inside knows where he is, and my target is Shane's boss, Jones, the man who took Callie's father's job when he passed away.

After we make a few turns, the crowds thin and we hop on a bus. We get off in a quieter area of the city, with a darker vibe. The shadows are longer and there's a feeling that unseemly things linger in them. Callie and Noah have stopped their chattering, and she's got her hands wrapped around her arms. I continue to walk behind them, always scanning and paying attention to each dim corner and alleyway.

"Calliope," I say quietly. She slows and turns to fall into step next to me. "Stay close to me or Noah the entire time we're in there, okay?"

"Have you been to one?" Callie asks, her voice a whisper.

"A fight club?"

"Yeah." She nods.

"Yes," Noah says for both of us.

"But it's always felt unnecessary to go looking for trouble like that," I say. "Neither of us gamble. Neither of us needs more involvement in a criminal lifestyle. We stay away."

Noah gives me a sharp look over his shoulder.

"Or any involvement. It's not like we're criminals," I add. Callie snorts next to me.

"Right. You don't act like one at all." She looks up at me and bites her lip.

"Define criminal."

She chuckles, and Noah groans and gives me another dirty look. This is probably not the most appropriate place to be flirting with Callie, and especially about being a criminal, but I can't help it when she looks at me like that. That smile. That mouth.

Fuck me, it's going to be hard to do my job tonight and also look out for her.

"Do you think we'll find Shane there?"

"No."

"Me neither. I probably should've come here when he first disappeared, but I thought there's no way he'd hide in such plain sight." But the expression on her face hints that she's not totally sure of that.

"It's better that you waited to go with us. You have nothing to worry about tonight, Callie, I promise. Noah," I call to my brother.

He's leading the way, looking out for the side street that will lead to an alleyway with the hidden entrance to the fight club.

"If I step away, don't let Callie out of your sight."

"Obviously." He turns and rolls his eyes, and I'm so thankful he insisted on coming.

We follow Noah down a side street, two dark buildings looming on either side, and then duck down a much narrower alleyway, not even wide enough for a vehicle. There's a single flickering light shining over a short staircase descending to a solid door. Noah leads us down the steps and doesn't hesitate to pull the door open. Callie and I step through, immediately facing a giant, rough-looking bald dude with an earpiece and a gun tucked prominently into a holster.

There's cheering and shouting and sounds of a crowd of people down a long hallway behind him.

Callie's eyes widen, and I watch as her shoulders tense up. The bouncer glares at us suspiciously and ignores Callie altogether. Noah has a conversation with him that we can't hear because of the background noise. He hands the guy a few large bills before waving us along.

I really, really don't like Callie being here, especially as we walk down that hallway and she shrugs off her coat. Again with the bare shoulders and long gorgeous hair and plunging cleavage.

Fuck me.

So much for not drawing attention to ourselves.

It's chaos once we push through the doors to the underground fight club. We stop right inside the large open space. No one pays us any mind because the attention is all on the two men in the raised ring in the center of the room. One fighter is huge, with buzzed dark hair, bulging biceps and a wide, solid body, wearing tight shorts and nothing else. Sweat drips off his forehead and his hands are raised by his face in a fighter's stance. The other guy is much smaller and has his hair pulled back in a low, wet ponytail. Blood drips from his nose, and he looks much worse than the other guy, but he's energetically bouncing from foot to foot.

The crowd is majority men, fifteen people deep around the fighters. A pair of women in jeans and very small tank tops with their tits hanging out linger on the edge of a wall, but they don't spare us a look. There are a few more women sprinkled in among the crowd.

Callie presses up next to me and when I look down at her, she's staring at the fight. I don't think she realizes she's slipped her hand around my elbow, her fingers gripping my arm tightly.

"You okay?" I lean down to ask. She's taller with her heels so I don't have to go as far to speak into her ear. Noah's gone to prowl around the edges of the room.

Callie looks up, eyes wide, lips parted. Fuck, I want to kiss that mouth. I want to own it. I want to pull her in my arms and protect her from the world. I want to take her far away from this place, and I almost pull her back down that hallway right then and there, but someone says her name.

"Callie? What are you doing here?"

Her head whips around. "Jake?" She takes a few steps toward the man standing five feet from us.

Her brother. The one who referred Callie to me, even though I've never had direct contact with him. I've been wanting to meet the man who didn't do nearly enough to protect his sister.

"Looking for Shane. Obviously." Callie crosses her arms on her chest and glares at her brother.

"Shane's not here." Jake's a big dude, and he's the physical opposite of Callie with his light hair and blue eyes. The look on his face is exasperated, but there's also a layer of fear, and a hint of concern.

I step up next to Callie. Jake glances over at me.

"My brother knows where Shane is and won't tell me," she says to me without taking her eyes off him.

"That's shitty. I'm Wes." I don't hold my hand out, and I don't offer other pleasantries.

Jake narrows his eyes at me.

"Wes is helping me find Shane. You're the one who connected us." Callie throws her hands up at Jake, who is staring at me. "Hello?"

"You're Hawk?" Jake finally says.

I nod and watch a bunch of different emotions fly across his face. Regret, probably. Fear for his sister, maybe. Suspicion, definitely. And with good reason. He's got no idea I've been in his apartment many times to set up cameras, leave an apple pie, watch his sister fucking sleep.

He's got no clue how to protect Callie from the world.

"I'm Jake. And I don't know where Shane is."

He totally knows where Shane is. This man is not a good liar.

Callie steps forward and starts badgering him with questions. About Shane, about the club, about their father, and interestingly, about an inheritance. I'm assuming it has to do with her father. An inheritance might make all this more interesting. Divorce, siblings, and money will heighten emotions for sure.

Noah appears to my right, finished with his lap around the room.

"Any luck?" Noah and I pored over pictures of Shane so we'd recognize him, along with Jones, who Callie explained to me is her father's replacement and Shane's new boss. Jones is a tall, muscular man in his fifties. Both men are fairly good-looking, which says nothing about their character.

Noah shakes his head. "I didn't see him, but they might know." He nods to the far corner of the room, where a group of men linger, smoking and drinking around a tall table.

I nod once. "Stay with Callie?"

"Yup. Who the fuck is the guy?" Noah asks, looking at

Jake, who is listening to his sister whisper angrily at him. His cheeks are flushed, and he looks like he's getting a serious lecture. Callie is waving her finger, poking him in the chest every few seconds. She's furious, and it's fucking hot. Her brother, to his credit, looks shamed and like he actually cares. He could just walk away, but he's standing there taking it.

"Her brother. Don't fucking trust him."

I step away. At least I can trust *my* brother to look after my girl.

Wait—my girl? She's not my girl.

For fuck's sake, I've already mentally claimed her?

I head to the corner just as there's a huge uproar from the crowd. In the ring, one of the fighters goes down hard on his chest. It's the bigger guy, but he's immediately back up on his hands and knees, blood dripping from his nose onto the mat as the smaller dude dances around him.

I hate places like this. They're not safe for us. We're better flying under the radar and staying far from the underbelly of Boston.

The men look up from the table and stop talking as I approach, all watching me with deep suspicion.

"Too late to bet on this one, it's almost over." One man says, counting stacks of twenty-dollar bills on the table. He's got rough hands and strong arms, a crooked nose, and a popped blood vessel in his right eye. He looks like he's been in a good amount of fights in his life.

He's also got a gun tucked into his jeans. Why are all these men so obsessed with guns? I fucking hate guns.

I hand him a fifty-dollar bill and randomly pick a guy for the next fight from the iPad screen without reading or looking at the pictures.

"Where's Jones?" I ask once they tap my bet into the iPad

under the name Hawk. I'd also be willing to bet they know where Shane is.

"Who's fucking asking?" a little shit of a man with a cigarette in one hand and a glass of clear liquid in another pops into the conversation. He's got a black eye and is missing a tooth.

Again, I fucking hate this place. The black eye, okay, but go to a fucking dentist once in a while.

"Hawk," I spit out with clear annoyance. Black-eye guy turns and whispers something to the third man in the group, who looks like the twin of the bouncer at the front entrance.

There's a louder cheer from the ring, and I turn to see the smaller fighter kicking the shit out of the bigger guy as he's on the ground again, this time on his side. The crowd is chanting *kill him,* but eventually someone pulls the fighter off the man, who is no longer moving.

"Wait here," black-eye guy says as the bouncer-looking dude disappears. The crowd around the ring spreads out. I don't like it, because I no longer have a clear line of sight to Callie and Noah. I need another minute though.

"You got more of these places?"

"Why, you wanna fight?" Black-eye guy looks me up and down, like he's assessing whether or not I'd make a good enough fighter. He gives a slight nod.

"Nah. I just like to watch."

"There's a new one in New York," he says after a short pause.

"What a coincidence. I'll be in New York next week." At least now I will. "Got the address?"

He scribbles something on a scrap of paper. "Fights are on Thursdays."

"Thanks." I pocket the paper and turn to look around. I hate that I can't see Callie. There's a niggle in the back of my brain. Instead of waiting for someone to bring Jones to me, I head into the crowd. One of the guys calls to me, but I ignore him.

Before I get to the spot where I left Callie, I see Noah standing at the end of a dark hallway. "Where is she?" I ask when I get to him.

"In the bathroom," he says with a forced shrug. But he looks worried, not nonchalant.

The niggle gets bigger.

Something's off. Something feels wrong.

"Fuck," Noah says. "She insisted on going alone."

"Seriously? Stay here." I jog down the hallway and try all the door handles. Three are locked, but I finally find one that opens into a dirty, dimly lit bathroom. "Callie?"

I step into the dingy room and see a man facing the wall. At first I think he must be pissing or getting a blowjob or something, and then I realize he's got someone pressed up against the tiles.

He turns his head, and his eyes widen when he sees me. In fear or anger or what, I'm not exactly sure.

And it's Callie trapped against the wall, his hand on her mouth, his other hand pressing against her abdomen, his lower body smashed on hers. A million things run through my mind within seconds, but the loudest voice says MINE and PROTECT.

Callie's eyes meet mine, and they're wide and scared and—

Rage courses through my veins, and I black out.

CHAPTER 20

BLACK OUT

CALLIE

"Wes! Wesley! Hawk!" I wrap my hands around Wes's bicep in an attempt to hold him back from the beating he's giving my father's old colleague. As if *I* could stop him from continuing to pound Jones in the face.

Jones's angry question repeats in my head: *How much fucking money did your father leave you?* I was honestly confused at his reaction when I started telling him about my last fight with Shane and how we fought over Dad's estate. I told him too much, especially considering he was one of the people who stonewalled me when I asked about Shane's location. I guess for one stupid fucking second, I thought if I was right in front of him, Jones would care about me because of some leftover loyalty to my father or maybe because he's a human being. But the way his eyes widened at the mention of money? It was wild. Then he lost his mind when I didn't answer about the money.

Adrenaline courses through my veins as Wes pauses with his fist pulled back, appearing to register my voice. He turns, and the haze clears from his eyes. Jones deserves to be fucked up, but I don't want Wes to accidentally kill him. Wes is not a murderer.

Wes fully registers my presence and drops Jones to the ground with a thud. There's so much blood on Jones's face. I tell myself it's probably all from his nose and split lip. But from the way Wes was kneeing him in the chest, I bet he'll have broken ribs too. At least he's still breathing.

I thought Jones was going to beat the shit out of me to get an answer. He's never been a good guy and hardly said a word to me when Dad was alive and Jones managed another part of the business. I didn't love the way Jones looked at me then, but the violence with which he grabbed me from the hallway and shoved me into the restroom just now was terrifying. Maybe he only stayed civil previously because he was afraid of my father, but now he's dead, Jones is promoted, and both my brother and Shane work for him.

"Callie." Wes focuses on me.

"Thank god." I turn him away from the wall and lift my hands to his cheeks. "I'm so sorry. I shouldn't have gone off alone. It's not Noah's fault. It's mine."

"What do you mean?"

"I saw Jones duck down this hallway and made up a story to your brother so I could try to get Jones alone." God, that was stupid. I slide my hands off Wes's cheeks and let them hang by my side. "I thought I could get him to talk to me."

Wes gently grabs my hands and pulls them up to his chest, holding them in place securely. My eyelids flutter.

"You did this on purpose?" Eyes wide and deep, crystal blue, so focused on me. There's such an intensity there, but also anger.

"I thought that when I asked him where Shane is… but he got so ragey when I mentioned the inheritance…" I blink back the tears that sting my eyes. "He was screaming at me, and it was so fucking terrifying."

"You can't keep doing this, Callie."

"Doing what?"

"Putting yourself in danger." Wes clenches his jaw, and I can see him fighting for control. "This time, it wasn't by playing stalker outside of my cabin in a fake scenario that I was monitoring the entire time. This was real. He could've hurt you. He wanted to hurt you."

"Oh." I flinch, emotions swirling inside me. The way Wes is struggling to not freak out is scary but also fascinating. He truly cares about me being safe. He's tracking me, protecting me, invested in me. "Shane said some hurtful things to me before he left. I just want to prove him wrong."

"What did he say?" Wes's voice is low are dangerous.

"I think it was that I was a *boring-ass good girl.*" It sounds so ridiculous out loud. I need to get over myself. "So sometimes I try not to be one."

"I'm going to fucking kill him."

"Don't do that." I almost smile, but Wes looks dead serious.

"Calliope. Promise me you won't do anything like this again." His thumbs sweep over the insides of my wrists, and tingles run up my arms. "I swear you are not a boring-ass good girl. Not if you don't want to be."

He's so earnest, my chest tightens.

"I—I promise."

"When I saw that you weren't with Noah—" Wes squeezes his eyes shut. "So many bad things went through my head."

"But you came." It's a reverent whisper. My chest is tight, and I focus on the feeling of his hands.

"I'll always come for you." He practically growls the words before reaching down and lifting me up by the waist, then turning me around to press my back against the cold tile wall. I whimper and instinctively wrap my legs around him. The sudden ache in my center is more than I can handle.

"Wesley," I whisper. He'll always come for me? What does that mean? But at this point, I really don't care what it means, I care how it makes me feel. Safe. Protected. I wrap my arms around Wes's neck, and the move brings his face so close to mine. My throat tightens under his intense stare, and I can't help but glance down at his lips. I hear a noise and realize it's a desperate whimper coming from my throat.

"Fuck," he says. "Calliope." My name leaves his lips and it's magical, reverent, mystical. A soothing word for my hurting soul. I search his face, and his eyes are so full of life and passion, but there's also a battle going, and if it's fighting the urge to kiss me, I really hope he loses it. I *need* him to lose it.

I open my mouth to say something, then close it again. I'm in the middle of my own battle. Everything just became so much more complicated. Hiring someone to track down Shane was never going to be straightforward, but I didn't expect this.

I didn't expect *him*.

Wes swallows, and I track the motion, his throat rippling.

Fuck it. Right now, I don't give a shit if this makes things more complicated. I don't care if we're in the dirty bathroom of a fight club with a man unconscious and bleeding on the ground next to us.

"Fuck it," I say. "Kiss me."

Wes immediately presses his mouth to mine, like he was just waiting for permission. The kiss is wet and hot and his tongue is inside my mouth. I link my arms tighter around his neck, trying to get closer, more of him, anything he'll give me. In response, Wes presses me harder against the wall, his hands still cradling my ass, and pushes his groin up against my pussy. I can feel the hard length of him, and it messes with my head. But it's not enough pressure, not enough friction, not nearly enough.

Wes pulls back and presses his forehead against mine, panting.

"Callie," he growls, but I don't let him stop.

"More." Again, he doesn't hesitate before kissing me. I'm dizzy, and I hope it never ends.

Noah bursts into the bathroom.

"Jesus Christ," Noah says, relief and shock in his voice.

Wes moves his mouth off mine but doesn't shift his gaze from my face. I look over at Wes's brother, who is breathing heavy, his hands clenched into fists at his side.

"Thank god." Noah says. Then he sees Jones crumpled on the floor. "Fuck. I'm so sorry, Callie."

"It's okay. I'm fine," I say.

Noah looks despondent as he turns to Wes. He's not scared of his brother, but he's clearly remorseful. He wrings his hands together. "I was trying to give her privacy in the bathroom. Jones must've been in one of the rooms."

Wes doesn't say anything, but there's a low growl from deep in his throat as he turns to stare at his brother.

"Sorry, Noah, I ditched you on purpose," I say and touch Wes's face so he looks at me. "Okay? I ditched him on purpose."

"I'm sorry, Wes." Noah's voice is tight.

Wes glances briefly away from me, turning his head to look at his brother, and nods.

"Let's get out of here. We're not getting any more information out of Jones." Wes doesn't let me down from his arms or the wall.

"I'll go check our exit," Noah says and slips out the bathroom door.

"Are you okay?" Wes says in a calmer voice, his gaze flicking from my eyes to my lips. "I should kill Jones for touching you. Should I? I will do it without a second thought."

I shake my head. "No, don't." But I believe he would, and between that and the hard length pressed between my legs, my body aches for him.

"I would burn the world down for you, Calliope," he says to me in a raspy whisper, and everything inside me turns to hot liquid.

No one's ever wanted to burn the world down for me.

I can't respond. Not a single word forms in my mouth, but I stare at him, my gaze moving over his face, and I wonder what his thick lips could do to my body. I wonder what he would do for me. Would he really kill someone?

I move forward and press our lips together. This time, it's slow and sweet and intentional, somehow even more intense than earlier. But before we can turn the world into an inferno together, Noah flies back through the bathroom door.

"Let's go." He gestures to the door, not acknowledging our compromising position.

Unfazed, Wes slowly lowers me, letting my body drag over his, staring into my eyes the entire time.

Jones moans next to us.

"He's awake," I say, fear cascading over me like a wave. For all my attitude and rage, I know I'm playing with fire for even looking for Shane when he doesn't want to be found. Jones doesn't want me to find him either.

Wes sets me on my feet and gently nudges me toward Noah. Then he looks down at Jones, whose eyes are fluttering open, and kicks him hard in the ribs. My father's old colleague shrieks, and his sharp eyes land on Wes. There should be more fear there, but there's not. And that's as scary as anything I've seen tonight.

"You guys are fucked," Jones says calmly and attempts to sit up, but Wes kicks him again, this time in the groin. The man screams and curls into a ball.

I don't fully understand what's going on here. Shane wants my father's money, and I don't think he deserves it. But why disappear? And why is Jones protecting him? And so interested in my inheritance?

I should feel bad that Wes is hurting someone for me. I should be terrified. But I'm not, which is an unsettling feeling to sit with.

"Wes," Noah says, his voice laced with urgency.

Wes must understand the undertones in his brother's voice, because he glares down at Jones one more time, grabs my hand, and leads me through the bathroom door after Noah.

Another fight is about to start, and a man I vaguely recognize from my father's circle is walking around collecting money for bets. From what Jake and Shane have told me, these places make a shit ton of money and cost very little to run. You just risk getting caught by the authorities, especially since they count on enough people showing up who want to place high wagers to see men fight. They pay off a lot of cops to keep things running.

Wes doesn't stop, just pulls me through the crowd to the

door leading to the long hallway. His hand is tightly wrapped around mine, and he's keeping me close.

I glance around for my brother and spot him across the room. Jake takes a step toward me, but I lift a hand to him and let Wes lead me out the doors.

A minute later, we've passed the beefy bouncer and are out in the biting winter air. I have to jog to keep up with Wes and Noah as we put space between us and the fight club.

"Sorry, Calliope, we're almost there. Can I carry you?" Wes looks genuinely apologetic.

"No," I laugh. But my heels are killing my feet, except for my toes, which are going numb. Life choices with these stupid shoes, I guess.

We climb onto the bus a few blocks away, and everyone breathes a sigh of relief as the vehicle drives out of the neighborhood. I will my heart rate to slow now that we're safe now.

"Are you okay?" Wes wraps an arm around my shoulders and slides his other hand onto my thigh in a move that is more protective than seductive.

"Yeah." And I am, but my mind races, processing everything that happened. Seeing Jake, Jones, kissing Wes. I don't know what it all means, but as long as I'm with Wes, I know I'll be okay. At least tonight. We eventually get off the bus and head back toward the busier part of town. It's almost midnight.

"We have a small apartment close by. We're going to stay there tonight since it's so late." Wes holds my hand, and we walk at a much slower pace than before.

"What if I want to go home?" I ask, but I think we both know I'm in no condition to drive back to Portland.

"Then I'd take you home." But he looks exhausted, and so am I, so I nod.

Fifteen minutes later, we walk into a building and up to the third floor. Noah unlocks the apartment door and flicks on a light. It's clean, sparsely furnished, and overall pretty stark. There's no clutter or mess. No personal items. I hang my coat on a hook by the door and kick off my heels, which feels delightful.

"I'm crashing," Noah says, staring down at his phone in the middle of the kitchen. Then he opens the mostly empty fridge and pulls out three bottles of water, depositing two on the counter before disappearing down the hallway.

My heart flutters. I'm deeply tired, but now I'm alone with Wes, and I don't know what to expect. There's finally space and quiet to think about the way Wes lifted me in his arms, pressed me against that wall, and kissed me like we were the last two people on earth.

Wes leans against the kitchen counter and unscrews a water bottle, handing it to me before opening the other one and chugging down half. I wish I knew what he was thinking.

"Thank you," I finally say.

Wes's forehead creases. "For what?"

"For what you did for me at the fight club. For coming for me. For kicking the shit out of Jones."

"Hmm." He drains the rest of his water and sets the empty bottle on the counter. "I thought that would've freaked you out."

"You saving my ass?" I shake my head. Not only did it not freak me out, but I wish I could relive the bathroom scene. I want to experience him lifting me against the wall, wrapping my legs around his waist, and feeling him press against my center again. Heat rushes up my neck as we stare at each other across the kitchen.

Finally, Wes stalks toward me, and my heart pounds

louder with each step. He stops inches from me and touches his pointer finger under my chin, tilting my face to his. Time slows down, or speeds up, I'm not sure.

"I won't let anyone hurt you, Calliope." His voice is low and gravelly, and I wish—need—him to kiss me.

I grip his shirt and tug him forward, then slide my hands up his hard chest and around his neck. He reaches down and grabs my ass, lifting me easily so I'm sitting on the counter, and he can step between my legs.

My breath is fast as he leans his forehead against mine. I can feel the heat of him. His mouth, his hands still on my ass, his hips pressing against me.

I want this. I want him. This man has come into my life when it feels like I exist inside a hurricane, but he's taken me to safety. Sure, it might be the eye of the storm, but from the moment I met him, he's been there for me in a way no one else has.

And I fucking like it.

I know he's not right for me. He's the exact opposite kind of person I should be associating with as I attempt to start my life over. But maybe it's okay if he's what I need right now. Tonight, even. Maybe I don't need to think so hard about where I'll be in a few weeks or a month or a year.

I'm not going to change my short-term goal to find Shane, or my long-term goal to start a new life somewhere all by myself, but why deny myself someone like this while I sort it all out?

Wes buries his head in the crook of my neck and places a line of kisses down and over my bare shoulder, then moves to the hollow of my neck. I arch my head back and lean into him, the heat of his lips on my sensitive skin almost too much to handle.

"Fuck," I whisper when his mouth moves to the top of

my breast, his teeth biting down on the curve of my shirt and dragging it down, exposing a nipple. I gasp at his hot breath on my skin.

He stops and stares at my breast, then looks up at me, rabid hunger in his eyes.

"Calliope," he says.

CHAPTER 21

CAUGHT IN THE ACT

WES

Her exposed tit is perfect, and my cock's rock hard in my jeans, but before I go any further, I need to know what she wants from me. Can I touch her? Kiss her? Fuck her? Can I do more than that? Because I want all of it.

I am consumed by Callie.

And I'm on the edge of losing control. With every other woman I've had an interest in, it's usually ruined by now. When they see a hint of the real me.

But with Callie? She almost seems to want me more.

She flirted with me when I made it clear I'd followed her home.

She complimented me on the pie I left her when I broke into her brother's apartment.

She didn't get that horrified, disgusted look on her face when I beat the shit out of Jones.

The real tragedy is that she doesn't know the worst of it. She doesn't know I'm a serial killer, and I'm pretty sure that'll be a deal-breaker. I can't let her find out.

"What is it?" she whispers. Her breath is coming fast,

each intake moving her exposed nipple in a way that's mesmerizing. "Why'd you stop?"

"What do you want from me, Calliope?" I say quietly, meeting her intense gaze.

"Right now, I want you to fuck me."

I chuckle, partly relieved, partly disappointed. I guess I wanted her to tell me she wants me. All of me. That she likes me. Maybe even is a little bit obsessed with me, like I am of her.

"Tell me how you want me to fuck you." I lower my mouth to her tit again, kissing the perfect curve, circling her nipple with my mouth before sucking it in and flicking it with my tongue. She gasps, so I do it again. Her husband might have called her a boring-ass good girl, and I can imagine calling her a good girl… but it'd have a much different connotation.

"I—I don't know. It's been a long time since I had sex. A year, at least."

I pause for a second as I digest that. Her fuckwit husband disappeared six weeks ago. He wasn't sleeping with her for that long before that? He must be the stupidest man on the face of this planet.

"I'm probably going to come the second your dick touches me."

My cock twitches in recognition of being named.

I let her nipple slide out of my mouth and look up at her. "Good. We'll just have to make you come twice, at least."

She huffs, and I shove her strapless top down to her waist so I can give her other tit attention, sucking and licking while my other hand squeezes the other nipple. I do it until she's breathing hard and arching into me. It's a beautiful sight.

"I don't know how I want it. I just know I do," Callie says in a breathy whisper.

I look up at her and suck her nipple harder. At some point, I'll need her to tell me more. I want to know exactly what she likes and doesn't like. But for now, I'll do what she says. I stand upright and tug her off the counter.

"Take off your jeans, Calliope."

She glances down the hallway. "What about—"

"He won't come out. He's probably got his earbuds in." I cup her breast and lightly sweep her nipple with my thumb. She shivers and unbuttons her jeans, wiggling them down her thighs and off her body. She's wearing a scrap of fabric as underwear, barely covering her pussy. I let my eyes rake down her body, not touching her for a long minute. Then I reach down and touch her over her underwear, moaning when I find the material soaking wet.

"You're wet for me already, sweetheart?" I croon, moving my finger slowly back and forth.

She leans her hands back on the counter and arches her back, pushing herself down on my hand and sticking her breasts out. It's a beautiful sight.

I can't hide how I feel about Callie any longer. Not that I was doing a very good job before, but now that I've had a taste, there's no way I can give her up. And why should I? I might as well let myself fall into her while we're on this hunt for her that fucker of a man. And after we find him, I'll have to restrain myself from burying a knife in his gut. He deserves it after the way he treated Callie. Never again, though. He'll never get close to her again.

"Yes," she says, eyes fluttering closed. I shift my finger to the edge of her underwear and slide along the outside of her folds, then against the wet warmth of her pussy. I moan and swear underneath my breath. She's so hot and willing, it's almost too much to handle.

All I want is to give this woman pleasure, and if I can get

that done, I will. As long as she'll let me. She's slick and swollen underneath my touch, just fucking waiting for my cock.

But right as I'm pushing a finger inside, my brother walks in.

"Wes," he says, as if he's walking in on me reading a book. He's got no shame, no normal sense of boundaries.

Callie's eyes fly open and she gasps, an arm flying across her breasts, even though her back is to Noah. I sigh and regretfully pull my finger out of her, relishing how her eyes widen as I drag over her sensitive clit on the way out.

"Fuck, Noah, do you mind?"

"Nope, not at all." My brother has the nerve to sound annoyed.

"Oh my god," Callie whispers, her eyes locked on my face, frozen in terror. "Can he see my ass?"

"No," I chuckle, although I'm not actually sure that's true. "Just stay how you are, and he won't see anything," I say to her. But instead of listening, she slowly lowers herself down to a crouch so that only the top of her head is visible to Noah. Her gorgeous mouth is at cock-level, and I almost forget that my brother is still standing there.

"Wes." Noah sounds super serious.

"Seriously, what the fuck do you want?" I sigh. "We're busy."

"We're a go for number one. He's heading to Maple."

Well, shit. I curse and glare at Noah.

"What is it?" Callie says, staring up at me.

"I have to go." I clench my jaw. Why now? Noah and his fucking list.

"What? Go where?" Her brow furrows in surprise.

"We have an errand to run."

"An errand? It's two o'clock in the morning." Now she looks annoyed.

"I'll give you a minute." Noah backs up down the hallway. When he turns, I pull Callie up to a standing position.

"There are t-shirts in the back bedroom." I tug up Callie's top, covering her tits with a sigh. My entire body aches at the idea of walking away from her. I adjust my disappointed cock.

"What the fuck." She pushes me away and bends down to pull on her jeans.

"I'm so sorry. We've—we've gotta do this thing."

"You're seriously leaving?"

I nod, questioning all my life decisions.

"Wes." She buttons her jeans and shakes her head.

"I know. I know." I turn and stride down the hall, chickening out from discussing this further. In the bedroom, I pull out fresh black jeans and a plain black hoodie. When I walk back out, Callie's interrogating Noah, who is not giving her anything.

"And why are you both in head to toe black?" She points at me and then Noah. Callie's chest is flushed and red from my mouth. I'm going to fucking punch my brother later for interrupting us. Because I have a feeling Callie and I won't get to finish what we started. If I had to guess, she won't let me get away with not answering her questions, and I can't do that. Which means she'll guess the worst, and she'll basically be correct.

Noah fucked this up for me. My stomach clenches. Of course it's fucked up for me. I am fucked up. I don't deserve someone like Callie.

"We'll be back in an hour. Two, tops." I tuck my hands in my pockets. Callie's too smart. Too perceptive. Too inquisitive. I love all those things, but it's not helpful right now.

Although I guess it's pretty obvious we're up to no good if we're dressed in black running an errand in the middle of the night.

"Let's go, Wes." Noah's at the door, waiting impatiently, watching the app on his phone where he can see that Chad Smith is on the move. We've scouted him, we have a plan, and we are here. It still feels rushed, but at least I'll have Noah's back.

"Well I'm coming." Callie tries to walk toward the front door where her impractical heels are lined up next to my shoes.

"Absolutely not," Noah and I say at the same time.

"You are one hundred percent safe here," I murmur, stepping close and slipping a hand along her jaw, then letting my hand slide to gently envelop her throat. She swallows, and I can feel it under my palm. "We'll be back in a few hours."

Maybe I can fix this later. Maybe there's a chance.

Then her eyes narrow, and she swats my hand away. I consider pulling out the zip ties and making sure she stays put. She sighs and turns her back on us. I'll take that as agreement.

"Lock the deadbolt once we're out." I follow Noah through the door. I hate to leave her like this, but we've got a top-notch security system in the apartment, and she's truly safe here. When I hear the bolt slide shut, we leave.

HALF AN HOUR LATER, we're crouching in the shadows, watching Chad Smith fuck another sex worker from behind in an alleyway. She's moaning, but definitely not in a good way, and maybe crying. I clench and unclench my fists to stop from going over there and beating the shit out of him.

I adjust my black balaclava, and Noah does the same. There are no security cameras around here because all the businesses are shuttered and the city doesn't care about this poor-ass, broken-down neighborhood. But we still have to be careful.

Smith's sad cock slides out of the sex worker, and he roughly smacks her ass. He's only half hard and tries to shove himself back into her. I grunt in disgust. The poor woman, who looks very young but is possibly over eighteen, yelps and tries to get away, but he shoves her against the concrete wall, her head hitting hard as he pushes between her legs. He holds her there, growls in frustration, and reaches down to pull on his dick.

"Get on your knees and turn around," Smith says with fury in his voice. He pushes her to the ground. Like it's her fault he's soft? She braces herself on the ground but doesn't turn. He's going to hit her. Any second now.

"What the fuck are we waiting for?" I grind my teeth. Noah takes the lead when we're out on a job, but I can't just stand here.

"Hey!" Noah shouts, already in motion. Smith looks up and takes a step back from the young woman. She takes the opportunity to crawl away from him to the main road. Then she stands, pulls her dress down, and sprints away.

Chad is attempting to tuck his cock into his pants when we approach him. Struggling, it looks like, so he's either high or drunk.

Noah's eyes fall to Smith's tiny, limp dick, and I know he's thinking about cutting it off. But that would look too rough. Too targeted. Too... serial killery.

Then there's a soft cry from further down the alleyway.

"What the fuck?" I squint and make out another person with her back pressed up against the wall, a woman who looks like she's trying to melt into the cold brick wall. "Hey, are you okay?"

"No," she whimpers and backs further into the shadows. Her voice is young. Way too young.

Right. The teenaged girlfriend.

"That's my girl, stay the fuck away from her," Smith has the nerve to shove me in the shoulder, and I fight the urge to punch him. "Come here, baby." He waves his hands, and out of the shadow a very young woman—no, definitely still a girl —walks. She's shivering in a tube top, short skirt, and open jacket. The poor thing approaches Smith gingerly.

She's a fucking child. I want to strip off my hoodie and give it to her, but my tattoos are too distinctive to reveal.

"Sorry, just so we understand, you were fucking a sex worker while your underage girlfriend watches?" Noah's voice is soft and incredibly dangerous as he keeps a steady focus on our target. I know that voice. I'm guessing my brother is reconsidering cutting off this man's dick.

"I don't see what fucking business it is of yours." He pulls the girl against his body, his arm tossed around her shoulders. "Who the fuck are you guys?"

She looks terrified, big dark eyes flitting from Smith to us to the alleyway exit. She's scared of him. Of us. Of everything, probably.

"How old are you, young lady?" Noah asks, his voice suddenly soft and genuinely kind. He sounds like a kind grandpa calling her young lady, but her face relaxes a tad, so it's working.

"Legal," Smith says with confidence.

"I didn't ask you, I asked her." Noah doesn't look away from the girl. She looks up at Smith with fear in her wide eyes. He nods at her.

"Eight—" she breathes deeply. "Eighteen."

I scoff. No way in hell is this girl eighteen.

"Are you a sophomore?" Noah asks.

She nods, then her eyes widen, and she shakes her head.

Smith just rolls his eyes, not caring that she's outed him for dating a sixteen-year-old child. My blood heats to a slow rolling boil, feeding the fury coursing through my veins.

The girl being here complicates things, but it also seals Chad Smith's fate.

Our sister was fourteen.

I will never get over that.

Noah won't, either.

We could never walk away from someone like this.

CHAPTER 22
OH, HELL NO
CALLIE

I silently scream when the door shuts behind Wes and Noah.

What the actual fuck? What just happened? I was hooking up with Wes, and it was about to be fucking incredible, and he and Noah went out to run an *errand*? In head-to-toe black.

I pace the apartment, swiping my phone off the counter during one lap. I could text Jake. He's here in Boston, I could go stay with him, or ask him about Jones or Shane or whatever. Again. I could text Lola to commiserate, but I really need to extend an olive branch first because I've been ignoring her since that night at O'Connor's.

"Dammit!"

What is up with Wes? I know he's in shady shit, that's obvious. But this feels like more than shady. More than a little light criminal activity. Nothing good happens at two o'clock in the morning, especially dressed the way they are. They both walked out with black balaclavas in their hands, which, on the one hand is super-hot, but on the other hand is what someone uses when they don't want anyone to be able to identify them.

This man is a criminal.

I don't want to be with a criminal.

Maybe this little errand of theirs came just in time. Because once I cross that line with Wes, there's no going back. I can no longer pretend this is a business transaction. If I'm honest with myself, it's been more than that for weeks.

I'll leave. Book a ride to bring me to my car and then drive back to Portland. I'll tell Wes we need to keep things professional from now on. No more touching or kissing or long, lingering looks or spending time together talking or laughing. Pure business.

Yes. Exactly what I should do.

I pull on my jacket and pat my pocket to make sure my keys are there, then slip back into my heels. My feet scream at me. I slide the bolt open and slip out the door. Last chance to change my mind, but then the door clicks shut behind me. I spin and twist the knob, but it's locked.

Looks like I'm leaving.

I trot down the stairs and pull out my phone, fully intending to book that car. I open my map app real quick to figure out where exactly I am. But instead of clicking out of it, I think about what Noah said when he interrupted me and Wes. Heading to Maple? My eyes scan the map and there. I see it. It's farther than I'd prefer to walk, but I start in that direction anyway. It's almost on the way to my car.

Wait, no. It's not.

I tug my jacket tighter around me.

What am I doing? Even as I think that question, I continue walking. The mystery of Wes will be too much for me if I don't figure out what's going on. Sure, he made me promise just a few hours ago not to do stupid shit anymore, but that won't be his problem anymore soon enough.

The area around the apartment starts off okay, but within a few blocks it gets more broken down with busted street lights and boarded up buildings. This... might've been a mistake. My feet are killing me. I'm freezing. I'm definitely making poor choices. With a final glance down at my map, I turn onto Maple. Not a soul is around, and I slow my pace and walk pressed close to the buildings.

Then I hear something across the street just ahead. A slight woman crawls out of an alleyway, her dress up around her waist and no underwear, stands, adjusts herself, then runs down the road toward me in high heels. Her face is distressed and her hair is messed, but she's so fast. Whatever she's running away from must be really awful.

And she looks young enough to be called a girl, not a woman.

Adrenaline spikes in my veins. Someone needs to help her. Why isn't anyone helping? What if someone is chasing her? I stare at her departing form as she sprints past, panic coursing through me. Shit! Should I follow? But how can I help? I swallow thickly and step backwards onto a dark side street. I'm too chicken to follow. I can't bring myself to help, and my heart skips a beat when I turn back to where she just came from.

I'm having a hard time understanding what I'm seeing.

At the edge of the alleyway, two men in head-to-toe black are standing in front of another man, who has his arm around the shoulders of what could be his younger sister, but I'm afraid is probably not. The men have black balaclavas covering their heads.

It's Wes and Noah.

I'm sure of it. Wes is broader and Noah slightly taller. I

can hear snippets of the conversation between Noah and the man. Then the girl says the word eighteen, which surely can't be her age. Poor girl must be freezing in a tiny skirt and short open jacket which reveals a cropped top.

Who was the other young woman running from? It can't be Wes and Noah. They're protectors, not predators. I get that I can't know it for sure, but still, I do. They're not the bad guys.

Also, the girl tucked under that man's arm has the same terrified look on her face as the one who ran away.

Wes pulls out blue gloves from the pocket of his jacket and slips them on. Are those surgical gloves? Then he slips behind the man and grabs his arms, securing him and freeing the girl. She sprints out of the alley and pauses on the sidewalk. Noah approaches her from behind, says something in her ear, then hands her something—money, maybe?—before she books it past me in the same direction as the other girl went.

My jaw might as well be on the sidewalk.

"Bitch! Get back here!" the man screams, struggling in Wes's grasp to no avail.

But the girl is long gone. I take a deep breath and let it out in relief. I knew it. I knew they were the good guys. They just saved two girls from whoever the fuck this guy is. This was what they were doing? Sneaking out to save people, like some kind of hot balaclava-masked super heroes?

I almost chuckle.

Then, Noah stalks back toward the man. Some words are lost under the man's loud cursing, but I hear Noah clearly say, "You're a rapist and a predator and a horrific excuse for human being."

I gasp. Rapist? Predator? I mean, I don't doubt it, given what I just witnessed, but Jesus.

The man opens his mouth to shout or argue, but then he sees Noah sliding on a pair of blue gloves of his own. Noah says more to him, but his voice is low, and I can't make out the words. The other man is rambling and babbling, and with a dull ringing growing louder in my ears, I don't understand what's going on at all.

And then Noah starts stabbing.

I gasp and stumble backwards, squeezing my eyes shut and leaning against the building out of view. The bricks are cold and rough, and I try to manage the waves of panic, which have now returned.

Oh my god. What did I just witness?

I was just begging someone to save those girls, and then realized Wes and Noah were doing exactly that. But I didn't have "watching the masked man I'm obsessed with hold a guy so his brother could stab him in an alleyway after they saved two girls" on my bingo card for tonight. And that's something, because tonight's bingo card had some wild squares.

I'm honestly not sure if I should run back to the apartment or to the cops or to my car.

Tears fill my eyes and run down my cheeks. My chest shudders, and I'm so, so cold. I have to get out of here. I stumble through the alleyway, which thankfully connects to another road away from Wes and Noah and the man, and then I blindly walk down a block this way, and another block that way, and I'm so far from my car and the apartment, plus the blisters on my feet have popped. I can't take my shoes off because I'll get frostbite, but I can't walk any further, so I find a set of steps and sit.

I wait for Wes to find me.

Because I know he will.

And then he does.

CHAPTER 23
FOUND YOU

WES

"I like it better when we get to use pie," I say calmly. I feel like I always have to remind him that my way is the better way.

"You're obsessed with your pies."

"Yeah, and?"

Noah looks at me and shakes his head. "You're fucked up. Let's go." We cautiously make our way out of the alley, keeping our balaclavas on and ensuring no one is around.

"I'm sorry, *I'm* fucked up? You just stabbed a guy twenty times in the gut without blinking an eye."

"We can't use poisoned pie very often." Noah ignores my observation. "Otherwise we'll be known as the Mince Pie Killers or something stupid."

"I like the sound of that." My thoughts have already returned to Callie, waiting for me at the apartment. I need to decide what I'm going to say to her. Not the truth, obviously, but it can't be nothing or she'll never trust me.

"You would." Noah shakes his head, like *that* is the thing that makes me messed up.

189

"But it's been ages." We only use pie when we're positive the body will never be found. We shoved Chad Smith behind the dumpster, so he'll be discovered eventually. Otherwise, it's too unique of a way to die. I pull out my phone and stop short. There's a ton of missed notifications from the security system at the apartment.

"Oh, fuck." Adrenaline spikes in my veins. I urgently click and skim the video until I'm sure that no one got in.

Confirmed.

But she got out.

"What?" Noah says with a sharp edge. "Let me guess. Callie."

"Yes."

Callie left the apartment, and when I pull up the map, I swear. She's only a few blocks from here. I curse and start to jog, and Noah growls and follows. We're close to the blue dot. Is she running? Riding in a car? Trying to escape me?

But the dot isn't moving.

"She must've followed us." Fuck me. Did she see us take out Chad Smith? Callie's been okay with me stalking her, tracking her, obsessing over her, but I'm not sure she'll be okay with me killing people.

"Obviously." Noah's voice is exasperated and sharp. "But the question is, did she see what happened?"

"What if she did?" I challenge. Noah follows as I jog across the street and down another alley that'll cut through to where Callie is.

"I don't know, Wes, then what?"

"Then nothing. I'll talk to her." I focus on my breathing. "We don't murder innocent people. Especially women. Especially Callie."

I glance over at Noah, and he returns my look and nods.

"Obviously." Then he swears under his breath. "We'd never hurt her, Wes."

I dip my chin. But I'm terrified for what this all means. Callie's seen a lot of things in her lifetime, so I don't think she'd turn us in, but I don't know. And I'm dreading the way she'll look at me when we find her.

"She's down here." I point up to a better-lit road. Noah and I pull off our balaclavas in case we run into people.

I see Callie from half a block away. She's sitting on the stoop of a dark row house, shivering. Not even trying to run.

"Calliope." My stomach twists as I stop in front of the stoop and take her in. She's been crying. Her eyes are red, her hair mussed as if she's been running her hands through it.

Callie definitely saw us kill Chad Smith.

She looks up, a despondent look on her face. "What the fuck, Wes?"

Noah steps close to me and turns his head, speaking directly into my ear. "Do you need me?"

"No. Thank you," I say quietly. "We'll meet you back at the apartment."

Noah nods and strides away without a backward glance.

I step close to Callie, only five feet away now, testing to see how close she'll let me get. She looks up with wide, vulnerable eyes.

"Can I sit?" When she nods, I sink down next to her. "Did you see?"

"Yes." A violent shiver shakes her body. Sitting on this cold concrete step in early March in Boston is not the best choice. Or is her shiver from fear?

"Do you have questions?" I hope she asks the right ones. I hope she doesn't freak out. I hope she doesn't run.

"How did you know?" she asks after a minute.

"Know what?"

"That those girls would need saving?"

I blink and try to process what she's asking.

"And you guys—you killed him. Noah stabbed him. You held him still." She whimpers and covers her face with her hands. I slide my arm around her shoulders.

"Shhhh, it's okay, Calliope. I'm sorry you saw that." She leans into me, and I'm encouraged by the action. "He was a bad person. We knew that. And Noah figured out he'd be... out and about."

"How did he know that?" Callie looks up at me. I reach over with my free hand and wipe a tear from her cheek. Her eyelids flutter.

I don't know what to do here. I think I have to tell her. Because if not, she'll just guess anyway.

"Noah and I, we—" I breathe in deeply and her eyes open again. Waiting. Watching. Her breathing has calmed down. "We take care of bad people. Very bad people."

"What does *take care of* mean?" Callie whispers.

Uh oh. I sigh.

"We find individuals the world would be better without. Guys who like to fuck young girls. Guys who kill them, rape them, destroy them. And *we* destroy those guys."

Callie swallows, and I watch her throat move. Not long ago I was kissing that throat, and while she hasn't pushed me away, I'm not sure we'll get to that point ever again. I'm already mourning the us that never was. She was special. She *is* special, but she'll never be mine. Not now. Not ever.

"Why do you do that?" Callie sits up straighter. I keep my arm around her shoulders, as if it's a weight holding her down from flying away.

I've never spoken about what happened to my family to anyone. Not since we took out their murderer. Not since

Noah realized he liked killing, and I couldn't let him do it alone.

But I want to tell Callie. I want her to understand that I'm not a monster. Or maybe I am, but I have my reasons.

"Ten years ago, our parents and little sister were murdered."

Callie gasps. "What? Oh my god, I'm so sorry." She turns to me and slides her hands onto my thigh, scooting closer.

"And before he killed Ivy—" my voice hitches "—he raped her. She was fourteen years old." The words are so awful. So much worse out loud than in my head.

"Wes, that's horrible. That poor girl." She's crying again and gripping my thigh.

I nod, my eyes fixed on a lamppost across the quiet street. "The cops weren't getting anywhere. They had a list of suspects, but it was slow, and they kept messing up, and looking in the wrong fucking places."

I shake my head, remembering how furious we were. Me, Noah, Sia. Sia, my twin, who was just as devastated, just as upset.

"So Noah and I did something about it." I shrug. We had to. We couldn't go on while our family's killer walked free. "We asked around, followed people, did research. I hacked into phones and systems until we figured out who did it. Then we found the guy and ended him."

"Holy shit," she whispers.

"It was bad and messy. We were horrified at what we'd done, while also feeling like we got vengeance for our sister. Not that it would ever bring her back, nor change her devastating final moments."

Callie takes in a ragged breath, and I look at her. Tears stream down her face. She grabs my free hand with both of hers and squeezes.

"My twin—Sia—found out what we did. She was horri-fied. She wanted us to turn ourselves in. She said she couldn't." I shut my eyes, her horrified face always in the back of my mind. "We didn't, of course. And we kept going. Finding the worst of the worst and taking care of them ourselves."

"Your tattoo." Callie turns and wraps her arms around my waist. "Ivy." Surprised, it takes me a few seconds to turn toward her and return the embrace. She buries her head in my chest and cries. "I'm so sorry."

"Sorry for what? You didn't do anything." I rest my cheek against the top of her head, then kiss her gently.

"I'm sorry for your sister and your family and you and Noah and your twin. It's all so awful."

"It's why I watch out for Noah so much. I can't lose him, not after losing the rest of my family. Sometimes he can be reckless. I make sure he's safe."

"That's beautiful," Callie says, a hitch in her voice.

Callie's crying for us. Not running screaming because of what she just witnessed.

"Hey, it's okay. It was a long time ago."

"It is not okay, Wesley."

"Hmm." I shut my eyes. She's right. It's not. It never will be.

"You know what?" She looks up sharply. "I'm glad you guys got the man who killed your family. And I'm glad you did what you did tonight."

"You are?"

"Yeah." She nods. "Before I realized what was happening, I was hoping someone would help that girl. The first one was so scared, and so was the second one. You and Noah did that. You saved them." Callie nibbles on her lip. "Who knows how many other people you saved by getting rid of that guy tonight."

She fucking gets it? She gets it. My chest aches with emotion.

Then she leans in and kisses me, sweetly at first. I lift her up and settle her on my lap, straddling me. Our tongues mix together, and she arches against me, rocking back and forth as if it's enough to fuck me through our layers of clothing.

"Callie," I say, pulling her mouth off mine with regret. "We can't stay here. As much as I'm enjoying this. I shouldn't be out, not after—"

"Then take me back to the apartment." She slides her hand between us and rubs my cock through my jeans. "And hurry."

Fuck, yeah, let's hurry.

CHAPTER 24

IT WAS GONNA HAPPEN

CALLIE

Wes closes the door behind us and slides the deadbolt, then crashes his mouth onto mine. He bends down and picks me up again, holding my thighs around his sides so I can wrap my legs around him. Step, step, step. I vaguely recognize that he's walking us down the apartment hallway, but he's kissing me the entire time and it's hard to notice anything else.

I was both right and wrong about Wes. He's definitely a criminal involved in bad things. Worse than I'd imagined. By far. But he's also a really decent guy. He protects the right people and takes down the worst ones. He doesn't pretend bad things don't happen, instead, he chases the ones responsible for them.

We don't turn the lights on. I don't look around. He walks me through a doorway and in a smooth motion, pushes me onto the bed, pulls off my jeans and my shirt, and leaves me on my back in my bra and underwear. He pulls his hoodie over his head with one hand and kicks off his jeans, so he's left only in his boxer briefs. He pauses for a beat at the bottom of the bed, his chiseled chest on display in the moonlight, his expression heated and predatory as he stares down at me.

"Wes," I say as he lets his eyes soak in my body and then drops onto the bed and crawls over me. This is spiraling out of control. We should have a conversation before we have sex. Talk about… things. Make sure it's clear what we are doing. I feel his heat as he pauses above me, then lowers his body onto mine. The flesh-on-flesh contact is almost more than I can handle, but then he slides his hand down my abdomen, and into my soaking wet underwear. I moan as his fingers find the place they left off before we were interrupted in the kitchen, his thumb massaging my clit, his finger slowly slipping into my pussy.

"What, Calliope?" Wes looks down at where he's stroking me, and my eyes follow. I watch his fingers work my body, and I'm already half coming at the sight of his huge length pushing up against the fabric of his boxer briefs. He slides a second finger inside me, and I gasp, my eyes squeezing shut.

"This is just—" I moan loudly, unable to control myself. The friction feels so fucking good "—oh god. That feels so good."

Instead of answering, he presses his mouth to mine, then proceeding to slide his tongue in and out in the same rhythm as he pumps his fingers.

How can I already be on the edge? Fuck me. He breaks the kiss, and without removing his fingers from my pussy, he tugs his briefs down and reveals his incredible cock. It's engorged and thick, and I gasp at the thought of that thing inside of me. A second later, he's leaning over me again, lowering himself down to press his cock against my thigh, thrusting against me. God *damn* he is good at this. Just when

I'm on the edge, he pulls his fingers out with a sinfully wet squelch.

"I want to taste you, sweetheart," he says, and I almost black out. "Can I taste you?"

I nod, because god knows I can't come up with any words right now. Wes dips his head between my legs and fuck! I moan when his lips press against me, his tongue sliding between my folds, then a finger entering me, then a second. Now he's sucking on my clit, and I—I can't focus on anything, especially when he curls his fingers and sucks so hard I see stars, coming long and hard and on his face. He keeps licking long after I'm done, then crawls up over me.

"Good girl. Now, were you going to say something?"

I'm panting, looking up at him, his cock a hard rod between us.

"I... I can't remember." My breath is still coming fast, my heartbeat racing.

"Yes, you can." Wes leans down and kisses my lips. I taste myself on his mouth and shiver, and as he places gentle kisses on my cheek, jaw, neck, I remember what I was thinking before his fingers and mouth distracted me. I make a hmm sound.

"Well." This is going to come out so bad. I don't even want to talk about it anymore, especially with his dick sliding along my belly, the promise of more ahead of us.

"Tell me, sweetheart." Wes's lips find my right breast, and his mouth wraps around my nipple, his tongue flicking and sucking. I involuntarily arch my back and let out a low moan.

Focus! Fuck.

"Fine. I was going to say—but now wish I wasn't—that I don't know what this is between us." I'm jelly underneath him, and my breathing is accelerating. Wes drags a hand up my body and plays with my left breast. He's trying to distract me. Maybe he doesn't want to hear this as much as I don't want to say it. "But this is all I can give you right now."

He pauses and looks at me. "Fucking?"

"Yes." I lift my hands to his head and pull him up to my mouth, then reach down and tug his hips down until his cock is between my legs. I'm still so wet, it won't take much for him to slide right in. "Is this enough? Just fucking?"

Am I crazy? I watched Wes hold a man still while his brother stabbed him to death. It was planned and intentional. They're murderers. Serial killers. Wes is also a stalker and clearly a bit obsessive. I feel like I should care a lot more about that, but I want him so deeply that they all seem like good things, not red flags. Because when I think about it through the lens of him having my back, maybe they *are* all green flags.

Fuck the flags. I don't care what color they are. I want him.

"I'm not sure I accept that this is only fucking, but okay, for now, Calliope." Wes leans down and kisses me. "But I need you to say the words out loud."

"What words?"

"Tell me you want me to fuck you. Say you want my cock to fill your pussy. Tell me—"

"Yes. Yes. Fuck me. I want you inside me." Damn, am I begging? Yup! Sounds like it. "Do whatever you want with me. With my body."

"Good girl." Wes kisses me, and I can feel him smile against my mouth.

For the first time, I don't mind being called a good girl.

He pushes my legs together and nudges the tip of his cock at the intersection of my thighs and my pussy, pushing into the tight space, his cock sliding along my hot core. I'm still sensitive from coming, and it feels so good. As he thrusts, I lose the ability to think straight. His hands are everywhere, one of them pulling my wrists above my head, stretching me out so I'm even more bare than before.

Wes reaches down and shoves my legs apart, then drags his engorged cock along my swollen, desperate slit.

"Fuck me, Wes," I moan his name.

"You feel so good," Wes says, whispering in my ear. Moonlight shines in from the window, illuminating the side of his gorgeous face. I'm drunk, yet I haven't had a drink. I'm floating, yet I'm pinned to this bed.

I try to answer him, say that he also feels so good too, but I can't get a word out.

"I'm desperate to feel you from the inside." Wes slowly moves his hips so his cock rubs against my pussy. I whimper. "I haven't been with anyone in over a year, and I got tested after that."

"Yes, please. And I got tested as soon as I told Shane I wanted a divorce. I'm clear." Thank fuck I found my voice. "I've never gone off the pill. I want you bare inside me. Please, Wesley, do it."

He moans, and his cock twitches at the word bare. As soon as I consent, I feel the head of Wes's cock nudging my entrance. I gasp and try to hold it together.

"Say it again, Calliope. Tell me to fuck you bare."

"Please, Wesley. Please fuck me bare." I know what he wants me to do. Beg him some more. And I'm more than willing. "Please."

He pushes an inch into me, and my pussy stretches for him. I groan.

"Say it again. Louder."

"Fuck me, Wes. Fuck me, please."

He pushes in another inch, and the breath is stolen from my lungs. There's no way he's going to fit, no way—

Wes pulls out, and I feel horribly empty. He hangs his head for a second above me, taking a few deep breaths.

"Wes, please." Now I really am begging.

"I just need a minute so I don't come before I get fully inside you." Wes pushes back into me, farther this time, and he swears under his breath.

I buck up my hips and get him in deeper, but there's so much more to go.

"You feel so fucking good, Calliope. But I need you to take a little more, okay, sweetheart? I need your pussy to stretch and take all of my cock."

"Yes," I breathe.

He pushes further in, and I feel like I'm being torn in half in the best possible way. Wes reaches down and massages my clit. He's still got my hands secured above my head, but I'm not going anywhere.

Wes thrusts once more and takes a deep breath.

"You good, sweetheart?" Concern laces his voice, wavering for a second.

I nod, and he leans down to give me a messy kiss, licking my bottom lip, then pulls out before thrusting in again. He keeps going, and I feel like I'm in another world, on another planet, and it's just his cock and my pussy and the building of pleasure that starts deep in my center until it spreads and I'm coming, so hard, I might even scream, but he's grunting and coming inside me, our joint orgasm going on impossibly long until he rests on his elbows above me, his cock still inside.

"Fuck, Calliope. That was perfect." He's panting and struggling for control.

"Yeah, it was." I try to catch my breath. It was exactly

what I needed. A good fuck to ground me, get it out of my system, maybe break this weird obsessive relationship I have with Wes. I can't work through any of this now, not when we're still naked and sweaty and he's inside of me.

Later. I'll think about it later.

But then I meet his intense gaze, and with the way his blue eyes are locked on me, I think we just made it worse. We didn't break anything. And for now, I'm okay with that. More than okay with it. I'm drunk on it. I'm high. I'm fucked up on whatever drug Wes is made of.

He pulls out and reaches down to rub his finger in the mess of me and him on my pussy.

"You are a dream, Calliope. You're just dripping with us." Wes drags his finger up my body, leaving a trail of wetness. He leans down to kiss me, then scoots off the bed. "Stay exactly there. I'll get a washcloth to clean you up."

As if I could even move? I'm blown away by what just happened. By this entire evening, which feels like it lasted a hundred years.

Wes returns to run a warm washcloth up my thighs, over my stomach, and between my legs, gently cleaning me up. Then he cleans himself up before crawling back onto the bed and wrapping himself around me as the big spoon.

"I still have to brush my teeth," I say as I melt back into his chest, every inch of my naked back and ass pressed against him.

"Oh, sweetheart, we're not going to sleep yet. We're just on break." Then he slides his hand from my neck down to my stomach, gently swirling his fingers in soft circles on my skin. He's already growing hard behind me, his cock nestled against my ass, and when his fingers make their way back into my pussy, I'm ready for him.

This time, he takes me from behind, pulling a leg over his

hip, sliding in, and making me come with his cock in my pussy and his fingers massaging my clit.

When he's done, I'm a puddle of heat on the bed, and he cleans me up again, but not long after, his face is buried between my legs.

When we cuddle after that and I drift to sleep, he pulls me snug against his chest and murmurs sweet things into my ear.

This is fine. Everything is fine.

CHAPTER 25
ANOTHER FIELD TRIP
WES

I drive Callie's car back to Portland the next day, with Noah following so he can get me back to Lake Savage.

We talk for the two-hour drive from Boston. Callie asks me about my childhood with Noah and my sisters, and when I talk about Sia and Ivy, she reaches for my hand. She commiserates when I explain my father was an alcoholic and got into shady shit, and that was the reason our family was murdered. Callie tells me how her mother died when she was a senior in high school, and losing a parent relatively young was what originally bonded her and Shane.

Neither of us have had it easy in the past, and neither of us will likely have it easy in the future. I know it's too much to hope that I can find happiness with Callie. Easy happiness is not for someone like me. There's always going to be a catch, secrets to hide, a messy past to contend with.

When we get to the parking garage, I walk her to the apartment building's entrance. I'm hoping she invites me in, and I can send Noah away, but she doesn't.

Callie's got her arms crossed and gnaws on her lower lip.

She looks tired. A good tired, I hope, but maybe the high of our night together is fading and the worry over her current situation is weighing on her again.

"You want to hang out? Or are you going to try to get some rest?" I reach over and touch her arm.

"Rest." She leans into my hand. "For some reason, I didn't sleep much last night."

We were up for most of the night and only fell asleep for about an hour before Noah was banging on the bedroom door to get us moving.

"You okay with everything, Calliope?" I hold her car keys in my palm, not ready to hand them over yet. "What are you thinking?"

She presses her lips together and looks intently at my face, her gaze sweeping from my eyes to my lips and back up again. I give her time to respond. I'm a patient man.

Callie might not know it yet, but she's mine. And I'm hers. But even as I think that and know it's true, I also know it can't be. The contradiction feels heavy. Callie wants a different life from what I can offer her. There's no changing who I am or what I've done or what I will probably do in the future.

And anyway, I can't let myself fall for anyone. I can't be a guard dog for Noah *and* Callie. It'd be too much. I might lose one of them, or both of them, and I can't handle the thought of that.

"Last night was a lot," she says, but she bites her lip and has a soft look on her face.

"Last night was amazing." I move my hand up to cup her cheek. Her eyes flutter shut, and she reaches up and covers my hand with hers. A tingle runs down my spine, and I'm nervous about how much I like the feel of this. "You're not freaked out?"

I gotta know how she feels the morning after.

"You mean—" she stops talking as a group of people walk by with coffees in their hands, "—in the alleyway?"

"Yeah. That."

"No. Not freaked out." Color creeps into her cheeks, and she pulls away from my hand. "I—I think you're doing the right thing, in your own way. Not like Shane or my father. You're not like them."

"Nope. I'm not." I don't love getting lumped in with those assholes. Of course I'm not like Shane or her father. But the fact that it even crossed her mind isn't a good thing. Just another reminder I'm not what she wants, at least long-term. But for now? Maybe I can be something. I step forward and lift her arms so they're resting on my shoulders, and I pull her close against me by her waist.

"Wes," she says my name in a whisper, and tilts that full, sexy mouth up toward me. I lower my mouth to hers and place a long kiss on her lips. I'm not sure I want to hear what she has to say, but I release her mouth eventually.

"Yes, Calliope?"

"I don't want to live the kind of life I've been living."

"I know. You told me." Giving voice to it is a dagger to my heart.

"Hmm." She slides her hands up into my hair, and my eyes half shut at the feel of her fingers on my scalp. Fuck, she feels good. "I don't know what I can offer you. I'm kind of an empty husk these days."

That's not true, but I don't argue. She's got so much life in her eyes and passion in her heart. She just doesn't remember it's there. I can try to remind her. As long as she'll let me.

"Let's take it day by day, okay?" I kiss her gently again. "No pressure. No labels. No worries about the future."

I can do the worrying all on my own.

"Okay." Callie pulls my face back down to hers and we kiss long and sweet. But then she steps away, putting a sliver of space between us. I run my thumb over her bottom lip and note her intake of breath.

"Goodbye, Calliope." I hand her car keys over.

She blinks at me, as if surprised I'm actually letting her go.

"See you," Callie whispers. Then she turns and slips into the building.

"WE CAN TAKE care of Joe Killer while we're there."

Noah's sitting at my kitchen table drinking hot chocolate while I squat and feed fresh logs to the fire. Sir Fluffy is snoozing on the rug in front of the fireplace. There's nothing I like better on a cold winter day than a cozy, warm fire.

Except for having a certain gorgeous and spicy brunette zip-tied to a chair in front of it. I like that better.

"We hit a target literally last night. And less than a week before that." I stand and turn to my brother. He's jumpy, and his eyes are wide with excitement. He looks sort of crazed. "Way too fast."

I'm afraid he's been getting progressively more reckless since his breakup. It might've messed him up more than I thought. I think he let himself care too much about her, and now he's finally realizing women don't fit into our lives.

I realized that truth a long time ago.

Callie's a fluke. My brief intermission from the single life. At least that's what I *should* think. She wants a safe and legal life as a librarian and a white picket fence in the suburbs like the picture she showed me, plus probably a dog and a husband who's an accountant or a high school music teacher.

Not whatever it is I am.

I hate the suburbs. That's how Noah and I grew up. Give me the woods anytime, then maybe city as a second option. But the oppressive suburbs, with the carefully fenced yards and HOAs and neighbors watching everything you do and reporting back to the others, because they have nothing better to do? Hard pass.

Noah groans. "Come on, dude."

"I won't agree to anything right now. I want to make sure it's safe."

"The quicker we take care of targets, the more people we save. A little risk is worth it."

See? Reckless.

"Noah." I sigh. Arguing with him is hopeless, but I have to try. "Let's slow down. Be careful. Take all the precautions."

Noah rolls his eyes.

"I get that the quicker we get them off the streets, the better, but still. I don't want me or you getting off the streets as a result."

"Fine. Whatever." My brother shrugs. I'm not sure my speech actually worked, but maybe it delayed things. "Have you found anything online about the New York fight club?"

Noah dropped me at home this morning and then headed back to his place, returning a few hours later so we can talk about the NYC trip. I buried myself in research while he was gone.

"Some comments on message boards that refer to it." In the kitchen, I uncover the apple pie I baked from frozen and slide a knife in so I can serve each of us a slice. Sir Fluffy, now awake from his nap, weaves in and out of my ankles, meowing with growing intensity. "You are not getting pie, kitty."

Sir Fluffy strolls over to Noah and sits on his foot. Noah looks down and shakes his head grimly, then gently pushes the cat off. Sir Fluffy stalks off down the hallway toward my bedroom, probably to go pout. That animal is obsessed with Noah.

I settle at the kitchen table and slide my brother a plate.

"When do you want to go?" Noah's eyes are already red with allergies, if that's even possible.

"Soon."

Usually I'd locate the person, create a schedule of their lives and locations, then provide it to the client before walking away. They'd then proceed however they want without my involvement.

But that's not how things are gonna work this time.

My phone buzzes, and I flip it over on the table.

CALLIE

we didn't find anything out about Shane last night

Right. NYC. She doesn't know what I got out of the guy with the black eye before I stormed across the room to find her. And it didn't come up during our car ride this morning.

ME

actually, we did

CALLIE

really?

ME

yep. Want to take a trip to NYC soon?

CALLIE

is that where he is??

ME

I think so

CALLIE

when do we leave?

"Let's go next weekend." I look up from my phone. Noah is watching me carefully. "The conversation on the message boards seemed to confirm the Thursday fights. And we have the address."

Noah nods. "Callie coming?"

"Yes."

"Is that a good idea? After last night?"

"She's coming." He's not wrong. I expected him to push back. Things were fucked in Boston, but we got what we needed and were all safe in the end. Maybe this time Callie will listen to me and stay out of trouble. I think last night with Jones scared her enough.

And this time, they'll definitely be expecting us.

CHAPTER 26

OLIVE BRANCH

CALLIE

There are twenty brand-new books stacked in front of me. I love processing new titles for the library. Some are popular new releases from known authors, but there are always a few customer requests we approve for lesser-known or new writers. I have to enter them in the system, create a barcode, label, and get the books on a cart for shelving or display.

At the moment though, I'm staring glassy-eyed into the abyss, otherwise known as the giant dry erase board, that takes up an entire wall of the library back office.

I can no longer handle not talking to someone about what's going on in my life right now. And there's only so many people who I would even consider talking to about Wes.

It's been over two weeks since I've had more than a short text conversation with Lola, and it's driving me insane. I'd die to talk to her about all this.

I grab the next book from the pile and extract information from the copyright page for our database. My phone is on the table next to me, dark for the moment, but I'm tempted to go scroll through my conversation with Wes. He texted me a few hours ago, but I want more. More texts, more touching, more of him in all the ways.

Every time I close my eyes—like right now, with the new book clutched in my hands—I flash back to Friday night. Memories flood my mind. The way he saved me from Jones and pressed me against the wall in the fight club bathroom, then kissed me when I told him to. When he touched me in the kitchen of his apartment, his mouth on my breast and his fingers inside me. When he whispered my name like it was a prayer.

My eyes fly open as the librarian enters the small office, humming to herself. I swallow and take a deep breath.

"Hey, Callie. How's it going with the new books?" Rebecca, the middle-aged librarian working this afternoon, picks up her water bottle from the desk in the corner and takes a long swig.

She knows I've been thinking about going back to school to get my master's degree, but I haven't exactly told her I'm planning on moving across the country. It'll hurt to quit this job, but I will do it so I can truly start over.

"I'm almost done." I throw a smile at Rebecca and hope she doesn't notice my flushed cheeks or hear my racing heart from thinking about Wes.

"Good, because it's almost five o'clock. You can finish whatever is left tomorrow. I'm gonna go lock the door, but you're not closing tonight. Get out of here." She grins and disappears with the keys.

My phone lights up on the table, and I eagerly pick it up.

WESLEY

what are you wearing

I crack up and press my lips together.

ME

a long skirt, t-shirt, and long cardigan

WESLEY

fuck yeah

what's your hair look like?

ME

it's…in a braid

WESLEY

stop talking dirty to me

This time I laugh out loud. I was afraid it'd be awkward interacting with Wes once we went our separate ways after the night in Boston. But it hasn't. It's so much better. He's texted me multiple times a day to check in or say hi or make some comment about how hot I am.

So many things happened that night.

What does it say about me that I'm spending just as much—maybe more—time thinking about what it felt like to kiss and sleep with Wes as the fact that I discovered he's a serial killer? That I actually witnessed him and Noah in action?

And that it made me feel more for him, not less?

We had so much sex. I was sore all over for days. Shane wasn't interested in me or my body, was cheating on me, and I certainly didn't want him to touch me. Even before that, it was rare and unsatisfactory.

But that night with Wes was the best I've ever had.

I bring my hand to my neck and close my eyes.

This thing with Wes is the best distraction. Overall, this isn't a pleasant period in my life. Between my father dying and me divorcing Shane, it was always going to be a shit time. But having the attention of a six-foot-three, dark, tattooed, muscled man who adores his old rescue cat and bakes amazing apple pies? I love it.

So he's a serial killer. No one's perfect.

I stand and pick up my phone as it lights up. Nope. No one's perfect, but I should not officially date a criminal. Good thing I'm not dating Wes. We're just doing... whatever this is.

When I look at my messages, I see it's not from Wes, but Lola.

> **LOLA**
>
> hi! How are you?

It's like she heard me thinking about her. My best friend is eagerly and enthusiastically trying to win me over. She feels bad about the Jake thing, and it's time I got over it.

> **ME**
>
> hey
>
> I'm gonna stop by the bookstore in a bit, okay?

> **LOLA**
>
> yes! Great! I'll be here until seven!

I smile to myself. I miss my best friend.

"CALLIE!" Lola appears from behind a tall bookshelf and throws herself at me. "I feel like I haven't seen you in forever." She steps back and runs a hand through her straight brown hair. Lola is sweet and fiercely loyal. Well, except for that one night.

"Hey, I know, I've been busy." I search Lola's face, and her pinched look shows me she's worried.

"Busy with what?" She waves for me to follow her. "Sit for a minute?"

I nod and trail her to a back corner of the bookstore and sink into one of the two comfy chairs. I tuck my feet under my butt, smoothing my skirt over my legs.

"Well, I'm making progress finding Shane."

"Really?" Her eyes widen. "Have you talked to that hacker guy?"

I snort, and she stares.

"Oh, yeah, actually." I *so* want to tell her everything. She'd scream and jump up and down and be appropriately excited about it. And that's why I came here, isn't it?

My phone vibrates in my pocket, but I ignore it.

"Has he found him?"

"He thinks he knows where Shane is."

"Oh my god. Where is he?"

I almost answer right away, but then I press my lips closed. Jake can't know about this. There has to be a hard line in the sand, especially after Wes beat the shit out of Jones in Boston. It might get ugly.

"No telling Jake."

"Callie," Lola says, and her face crumples. "Of course not. We were only texting because we were concerned about you."

"Okay." I nod, deciding to trust her. "Wes thinks Shane is in New York."

"Woah." Her jaw drops. "So what are you going to do?"

My phone vibrates again.

"We're going to go to New York and find him."

"We?" Lola's eyes grow as wide as saucers.

"Wes, me, probably Noah."

"Oh my—wait, who the fuck is Noah?" Lola breathes out. "Callie, you need to give me more information about this. About everything. I'm dying!"

"Noah is Wes's brother." I chuckle at the expression on her face. Intense interest and awe. I'm probably giving way too much information, but I love her reactions. It's exactly how I'd imagined her responding.

"Are you sure you should be traveling with two strange men?" Her brow furrows.

"Um, I'm sleeping with one of them, so I think we're okay."

Lola leaps up from her chair and screams. Actually screams.

"Shhhhh," I crack up and wave her back down to her chair. She ignores me, probably because it's her bookstore.

"Callie! You're fucking the guy who's finding your husband?" She lowers her voice dramatically for the word *fucking*.

"I mean, yes?" I can feel my face heat, and I definitely can't wipe the giant smile off my face.

"You look... happy. Good. Oh my god, Callie. I'm happy for you." Lola throws her arms around me and practically sits on my lap.

"Easy, it's not like we're getting married. It's just sex. Just for now."

"Are you sure?" Lola returns to her chair.

"I'm sure."

"Maybe he's a reason to stay in Portland?" The hopeful look on Lola's face is painful.

"No. This changes nothing. It's just some entertainment while I'm still here."

Lola sighs, deflated. "Okay, I guess. Can you tell me, like, everything?"

"Not everything, no."

"Start somewhere, Callie!"

I smile and give her a cleaned-up version of my time with Wes. She doesn't need to know about the intense connection we seem to have. How he's stalking me, how I'm trying to be dangerous, how he's loyal and kind and is kind of obsessed with me.

How he's a serial killer.

I'll keep those things close to my heart.

CHAPTER 27

CUTE AND DELICIOUS

WES

I watch from a dark shadow across the street as Callie gives Lola a long hug at the entrance to the bookstore. She looks relaxed and happy, and I'm assuming she's made up with her best friend. Great. The woman needs more good people in her life, not fewer.

There hasn't been a minute of my time since I dropped her off last Saturday morning that hasn't been filled with thoughts of Callie. Her smiling at me, her laughing, the way her tits felt in my mouth, how her pussy clenched around my cock again and again. Her gorgeous dark eyes. The way she tastes. I'm so consumed, and forty-eight hours later, it's only gotten worse.

What I want Callie to do right now is call a car service. Her car's not an option as she walked the seven blocks from her apartment to the bookstore after driving home from the library an hour ago.

This might not fall in the same category as stalking a serial killer or tracking Noah and I as we eliminate a target, but it's still not safe. Why won't she keep herself safe?

Callie zips her pink puffy coat and looks around. The sun's just set. She pulls out her phone, and I think, yes, she'll call a car service, but instead she starts walking, still staring at her device. Not even paying attention to her surroundings.

"Fuck." I groan and watch her go down the block, only hesitating a moment before following her. Then my phone buzzes. I sent her a picture of Sir Fluffy while she was with Lola. Then I sent her a picture of an apple pie. It's like I can't stop.

> CALLIE
>
> cute. And delicious

> ME
>
> why thank you, I have heard that I'm cute and delicious before, actually

> CALLIE
>
> shut up. What are you doing?

I smile and stride after her, considering. I could stealthily make sure she gets safely home and then go back to Lake Savage. That's what I should do. But I have a chance to talk to her in person. Kiss her, maybe, if she'll let me. How can I pass that up?

I should. But I won't. I'm only ten feet behind now.

> ME
>
> making sure you're safe

She stops abruptly and looks up, spinning around until her eyes land on me.

"Wesley," she says, slipping her phone in her pocket and planting her hands on her hips. "You are insane."

I shrug and close the gap between us, stopping when I'm only two steps away.

"I would say I'm sorry, but it's quite literally who I am."

Her lips twitch. Fuck, she's so beautiful. I could stare at her face all day, every day. And the way she's looking at me? Like she's so happy to see me. Like she's relieved that I'm by her side again.

She huffs and takes a step toward me.

I'm suddenly afraid, because it's in this moment that I realize I'm falling for Callie Callahan.

Oh.

Shit.

"Walk me home?" she says, taking another step and sliding her hand around my elbow.

"Of course." I could use this time to talk to her about the security footage I've found of Shane around the New York City fight club. He's definitely working there. We'll find him later this week when we're there, not only because I've found him, but because I know he'll be expecting us. Jones will certainly alert everyone in the organization that I'm the one who kicked his ass in the bathroom, and they will all be able to put together that I'm the one who asked about the NYC fight club, including the address.

We'll be walking into a trap, probably. Who knows what we'll be walking into. And I have Callie to protect, which makes the stakes even higher.

But I don't want to talk about any of that right now, because I have a beautiful woman next to me, and her arm is wrapped around mine, and she's smiling at me. She's seen me hold a man while my brother stabs him, and she's still happy to see me. I entwine her fingers with mine. Neither of us are wearing gloves and the skin-on-skin contact sends shockwaves up my arm.

And I'm falling for her.

"Tell me something that happened at the library today," I say, squeezing her hand.

"Okay. I had a lady who was probably around sixty come up to the desk and ask if I had any gay romance recommendations."

I chuckle. "Hey, what's wrong with that?"

"Nothing at all." Callie looks up at me and smiles. "I didn't blink an eye, just went through a few recommendations of popular MM romance novels. I even threw in a MM monster romance, and she was all about it."

I'm not the biggest reader, but I'd happily build an entire library in my cabin if it meant I could tempt Callie to spend more time with me.

"How about you? What happened at your job today?"

I snort and raise my eyebrows. "I'm still working on my top crust for the competition on Sunday."

"The competition is this Sunday? Oh my gosh, I thought it was weeks away."

"Nope." I shake my head. "But I'm feeling good about it. Other than that, I helped Noah brainstorm some renovation ideas for his first project, which starts in a few weeks."

She makes a sweet murmur, then looks up at me. "Wesley? Are we ready for New York?" she asks in a soft voice.

Somehow, we're already at her building. We stop in front, and I glance at the door, desperate to be invited inside.

"We're ready. Don't worry." I turn to face her and let our eye contact intensify before sliding my hands along her jaw and into her hair. Her lips are so pink and full, and she licks them as I'm watching her. "Calliope."

She grabs my waist and pulls me toward her, and I take that as an invitation to press my mouth against hers. The kiss is soft and deep and sexy, and she lets me part her lips with my tongue and gently sweep inside her mouth. A soft moan escapes her throat, and my cock responds instantly.

Then Callie gently pulls her mouth away from mine. Her

eyes are heated and her lips pinker, but she steps away so my hands fall off her body.

"I'll see you Thursday," she says, and with not a small amount of regret on her face, she turns and disappears into her building.

My heart's racing so hard I can't bring myself to move from the spot I'm standing in. I touch my lips with my finger and close my eyes.

I am so fucked.

CHAPTER 28

IN THE RING

CALLIE

I've been avoiding fight clubs for years, but now I find myself heading to one for the second time in a week. Dad would be so proud.

Wes grips my hand and leads me down street after street, following his brother. New York City is overwhelming. So many people, neighborhoods, cars, buses, everything. I've only been a handful of times, and each time, it reminds me of how much I love the rugged beauty of Maine. And Portland. It's an actual city, but also quiet and cozy with a small-town feel. You can try to get lost in Portland, but it's more likely to feel like home.

Each turn leads us to a darker spot than the next. A fight club isn't going to be on a well-lit road with lots of people and a bright neon sign above the entrance. Still, I don't love descending into the bowels of this city.

"You okay, Calliope?" Wes murmurs, squeezing my hand.

I nod, trying not to think about the fact that I'll likely be face-to-face with Shane tonight. That he'll be expecting me. Us. I might get him to sign the divorce papers that are tucked inside my jacket. I might be able to get my mother's ring back. I look up at Wes and take in his sharp jawline, thick dark hair, and light blue eyes that meet mine.

"I'm nervous," I admit, squeezing his hand back. "They're going to know we're coming."

Wes stops in the middle of the empty sidewalk, leans down to cup my jaw with his free hand, and stares deeply into my eyes.

"Yes. For sure." He brings our mouths together with such tenderness that my insides squeeze. "I got you, Callie. You're with me and Noah. You have nothing to worry about."

I think I'm falling for this man.

I can feel it just like I can feel the late winter wind blow around us. Like I feel his hands on my face, his lips on mine. It should be just sex. A distraction while I finish up my life in Portland, just like I told myself last weekend.

But instead, it feels out of control.

I didn't stop thinking about him all week. When he showed up to walk me home from Lola's bookstore, the relief and joy I felt when I laid my eyes on his face were too much. I missed him, and it had only been two days. His smile, his touch, his voice. I wanted to invite him into the apartment so badly. Who cares that Jake was home? They met in Boston already. Fuck Jake.

But I couldn't. I can't let him into my heart any more than he's already there. I can't let myself fall completely for Wes. It just doesn't work with the vision I have for my life going forward.

I need to stop this before it goes too far.

But when he kisses me—like he does now—my body aches for him. When he makes me laugh and feel safe, all I want to do is be with him. I want more.

It's getting very confusing.

"Come on, Wes," Noah calls, and Wes breaks the kiss. "Down here." Noah's stopped at the entrance to an alley. He waves his hand, and we follow him into the darkness.

There's nothing until halfway down, then we stop at an unmarked steel double door with a dim light above. Noah knocks, and the door cracks open.

I give a quick glance to the bouncer who's holding the door for us and take in a sharp breath. He's big, like the guy in Boston, but looks like a fighter. Split lip, black eye, crooked nose. Rougher. Meaner. Like he'd punch someone for looking at him funny.

This place feels so much worse than the fight club in Boston.

Maybe because I know Shane's inside.

Noah talks to the bouncer in a low voice and hands him money. Then we head through another set of double doors. Once down the cold, dimly lit hallway, there are echoes of angry, excited shouts and cheers. I follow the men down a few concrete steps into what feels like a basement, the air damp and charged, the room filled with people.

A crowd of men and the occasional woman are packed deep around the ring. They're screaming and shouting and waving their fists in the air at the pair of men fighting in the center of the room on a raised platform. The room is easily three times as big as the Boston fight club and even louder. No windows, only flickering wall sconces in cages and some overhead lights on high ceilings with exposed pipes.

"Don't leave my side," Wes says into my ear, his hot breath tickling my neck.

"Obviously not." I shake my head. A pair of rough-looking men on the outskirts of the fight crowd give me a long stare until Wes turns his steely gaze at them. They look away reluctantly, but I wouldn't want to be caught alone in this place. I'm not looking for a repeat of what happened in Boston when Jones shoved me into that bathroom. There will be no sneaking away this time.

I turn into Wes and let him lay his arm over my shoulders. I wish we didn't have to be here. I'd much rather spend the night tangled up naked with this man, not looking for Shane, who is still technically my husband.

Because that's what Shane still is. I give my head a little shake and look around at the messy hordes of people. I'm not sure how we're going to find anybody.

Noah disappears into the crowd, and we follow the place where he got swallowed up by people.

"Keep an eye out," Wes says. "We've seen pictures of Shane, but you'll recognize him faster." Wes's eyes are darting all around us. He's on high alert.

I scan the room. There's a lot of drunk, angry-looking men. Tattoos. Sweat. Danger. No one I recognize. I start to lose faith—what did we think was going to happen here? We would walk in and Shane would be waiting to sign with a fresh pen and my ring in a pretty little box? There's no way this is that easy.

Wes tugs my hand and nods. Noah's talking to a man who looks sober and like he might work here. The man is shaking his head, and I hear him say *I don't know* as we walk up.

That's when I see the woman standing next to him. It takes my brain a few for the recognition to process. She's watching the fight with a hungry smile on her face. Tall and thin and blonde, pretty, with heavy eye makeup and bright red lipstick.

I haven't seen her in so long. And here? Why is she here?

A pang of regret stabs me in the belly, and as if she feels my stare, the woman finally looks at me.

"Holy shit!" Her face morphs into joyful surprise, and my half-sister leaps across the group and throws her arms around my neck.

"Meadow," I say with a laugh. "What the fuck? What are you doing here?"

"Working." Meadow takes a step back and smirks, letting her hands slide down my arms. I can sense Wes shifting on his feet next to me, watching our interaction carefully.

"Here?" I study her face and gnaw at my lower lip.

Dad never let Meadow work for him. It was almost insulting that he gave me shit for not wanting to work at a fight club, but Meadow was forbidden from doing so. As if he were trying to protect her, but he'd given up on me. Maybe he just wanted to keep his two lives separate. Meadow was the result of an affair my father had when I was a baby, and he kept her away from us. My mom knew all along. And in high school, Jake and I found out.

Meadow and I hardly know each other. She got a third of Dad's estate, and I saw her from a distance at the funeral, but she fled before we talked. Her being here now feels bizarre. Sure, our father is dead, so she can do what she wants, but still. She's here, working in the same place as Shane.

Shane, who was furious about me not wanting to share my inheritance.

"Yeah, only for a few weeks so far. And you're finally here!" Her eyes flit to Wes as I process her words. She examines him with open curiosity. "Who are you?"

Wait—did she say *finally here?*

"Meadow, this is Wes, and this is Noah." I gesture toward the brothers, my line of thinking interrupted. Meadow looks at me expectantly, maybe waiting for more of an explanation. I'm not gonna give it to her. The guy Noah was talking to slinks away, and both men watch his departure.

"Nice to meet you." She nods at Wes, her gaze shifting to our connected hands, her forehead crinkling. "Hmm." Then her gaze settles on Noah, and an interested smile lands on her face.

Noah looks grumpy and impatient, his arms crossed, his foot tapping the ground. But he's staring at Meadow intently.

"What's your problem?" Meadow says to him with an open smile, and I almost laugh out loud.

"I don't have a problem." Noah narrows his eyes at her, then pushes his glasses up his nose with obvious annoyance.

"You'd be cuter if you smiled." Meadow cocks her head at Noah. Wes snorts, and I chuckle. Meadow grins at us, seeming to be pleased at our reaction.

"What the fuck?" Noah says, glaring at us. "Who is she again?"

"My half-sister." I don't think he really needed me to remind him, but I play along.

"Do you need a drink?" She steps forward and slips her hand on Noah's forearm, like she's going to lead him away. Noah stares at her hand like it's a cockroach. His expression is annoyed with a side of deep confusion, but I don't miss the way his eyes scan her head to toe, and he doesn't pull away. She's looking super-hot with a cropped tank showing off her generous, perky breasts and toned belly, and a short skirt that bares much of her legs. Not sure how she survives in this place. I left my scandalous outfit at home and am wearing a high-necked tank top, jeans, and sneakers.

"No." Noah shakes his head and adjusts his glasses again. Is he nervous? Or annoyed? I've not seen Noah so flustered.

"Fuck, I love a hot nerd," she says, and his eyes widen.

"Have you seen Shane?" I blurt out. As fascinating as her

interaction with Noah is, we're here for a reason. And the sooner we get out of this awful place, the better.

"Yeah, of course." Meadow looks back at me curiously.

"You say that like I should know. I've been looking for him for six weeks." I hadn't even thought to check with Meadow. Why would I have? Or… why didn't I?

She blinks in surprise. "Really? He said he was getting everything set up for you here, and you'd move down soon." She looks at my and Wes's hands again.

Ah. Now the *you're finally here* comment makes more sense. Another one of Shane's lies.

Wes growls next to me, pulling me closer against him.

"But you appear to not be in on that plan?" Now Meadow scans Wes slowly up and down, thoroughly but not creepily. "Well. This should be awkward."

"Where is he?" Fucking Shane. A narcissistic liar who can't even admit to people that I'm leaving him. What does he expect will happen here?

"I generally try to avoid him because he creeps me out." Meadow covers her mouth. "Sorry, I know he's your, uh, husband?"

"Not for long." I shake my head so hard it hurts. "I'm divorcing him, and he's avoiding me. I need him to sign the papers."

"Oh, fuck, really?" She breathes out. "Good for you. He's the one who found me at the bar I used to work at across town and offered me a job here. I was excited because I love fight clubs," she says, a dreamy look on her face. "But I'm glad I don't work for *him*."

"You love it here?"

"Yeah. For sure." Meadow looks around and waves her hands, as if that explains why she likes this disgusting cesspool. "I feel fucking alive."

"Okay. That's... a lot to process."

"Oh. There he is." Meadow points at the ring.

And just as I look up, Shane walks into the ring to fight. A little whimper escapes my throat. He looks huge up there on the raised platform. Tall and wider than last time I saw him. He's got a mouth guard in and jumps from foot to foot, punching the air. Cheers sound from the audience.

"Fuck," I whisper. I've never wanted to run away from a place more. But I can't. Not now, not when he's right there.

Wes squeezes my hand, but I can't bring myself to turn away from Shane. His competitor ducks into the ring, and the referee shouts to start the fight.

CHAPTER 29

FOUND HIM

WES

I'm a big guy, and I'm pretty confident in my abilities to protect Callie tonight at the fight club, but I don't love that her husband is a fighter. I don't love the lies he told Callie's sister. I don't love the wild look in his eyes as he ducks the first swing from his opponent.

Callie's eyes are locked on Shane in the ring.

"Well. At least we found him." I squeeze Callie's hand, but she doesn't acknowledge my words.

"He's hard to miss," Meadow says over the noise of the excited crowd. "Callie? You okay?" She touches her sister's arm, but Callie's still frozen. Her eyes are wide and her breathing quickening.

"Callie." I face her and put my hands on her biceps, turning her toward me. "Hey, sweetheart, you okay?"

Finally she seems to see me.

"Yeah," she says in a breathy whisper. "Just feeling a little freaked out at the idea of actually talking to him."

"I understand that. But you won't have to right now. And there's no point in watching this fight." I turn to Meadow.

"Don't go anywhere. We might need to talk to you. Noah. Watch Callie's sister."

"What?" Noah says at the same time as Meadow protests.

"Hey! I don't need watching!" Meadow scoffs and plants her fists on her waist.

Before I turn to pull Callie away, I see Noah look down at Meadow as she stomps her foot. He reaches for her arm as she steps away.

"Fuck," Noah swears and follows her into the crowd. If it weren't for what happened to Callie in Boston, I think Noah would probably tell me to fuck right off. But he's freaked out about having let Callie get cornered by Jones.

"Come on." I grab Callie's hand.

"Where are we going?" She lets me lead her to a quiet corner of the room where there are a few old chairs along the wall. It's a disgusting spot in a disgusting room, but from here we can't see the fight, only hear it.

I sink into a chair and pull Callie down onto my lap. "We're going to get the papers signed," I say, sliding a hand up her back, then tugging her jacket off. It's too damn hot down here to be wearing a coat. Callie's shoulders sag, and she partially relaxes into me. "And we're going to get your mother's ring back." I push a chunk of hair off her shoulder and place a kiss on her neck.

She sighs deeply but then pulls away. "Don't, Wes. What if someone recognizes me?"

"They do."

"What??" Callie's eyes fly open, and her head swivels around us.

"There are multiple men in the crowd keeping watch." I speak softly into her ear, but I observe two beefy men who have their arms crossed and are standing watch on us. "This is what we expected. Jones will have warned them about us. Shane will certainly come find us after the fight."

"Fuck," she whispers.

"We're here to talk to your soon-to-be ex-husband." I touch the bottom of her chin and turn her gaze to me. "And that's what's going to happen. Just take a few deep breaths. I got you, okay?"

Callie nods.

"What are you thinking, sweetheart?"

"I'm thinking that if it weren't for you, I would never, ever have had the nerve to come find Shane here."

"I don't know if that's true. You are brave. And strong. But I'm so glad you asked me to help." Something tightens in my chest. I'll forever be thankful that fate delivered Callie to my doorstep. No matter how this turns out.

"He's crazy, Wes." She stares intensely into my eyes, pleading for me to understand. But I do. I understand men like him, and he won't respond to weakness. He'll respond to violence and bullying, like the kind he dishes out.

"Some might say *I* am crazy." I grin. "You, I think you have said that."

But Callie doesn't even crack a grin or acknowledge my teasing.

"Seeing him makes me realize he's not going to let this go. What if—" she stops speaking, her eyes wide and wild.

"Don't you believe I can protect you?" I rub my hand up and down her back, and her eyes flutter shut.

"Yes," she whispers.

"Good. Because I will. I swear to it."

There are cheers as someone hits the ground in the ring. Her eyes fly open, but I cup her jaw, preventing her from looking over. I suspect the match might be wrapping up.

"Come on." I put my hands on her waist and lift her up.

As I stand, the two—maybe three—men watching us perk up. "Let's go pick a fight with Shane Robertson."

Besides, I don't think we have much of a choice at this point.

WE FIND Noah and Meadow standing in silence, him with arms crossed, her with hands on her hips.

"Never leave me with her again," Noah says when we approach.

"What? Why?" Meadow asks, looking up at him and blinking her eyes dramatically. "Just because you're no fun and won't take shots with me doesn't mean I'm insufferable."

"That's exactly what it means." He stares down at her.

"No, it means you're not fun."

"I need to stay sober." Noah's got his jaw clenched and rips his eyes from Callie's half-sister. I kind of love that Meadow is harassing Noah. He's clearly not used to it.

But there's no time to think about that, because Shane pushes through the crowd, men slapping him on the back along the way. He stops at the man who was with Meadow when we first arrived. Shane accepts a wad of bills from him and slips it into his pocket. He looks around, nods at the thugs who trailed us back to Noah and Meadow, and then his eyes land on Callie. A nasty grin settles on his face as he heads our way.

"Callie." Shane is sweaty, has a black eye getting worse by the second, and is holding a towel to his nose. He's got old bruises on his face, and his other eye is clearly healing from a punch, the yellow and green seeping into his cheek.

It looks like he's recovering from a nasty fight. Or a beating.

A flash of an odd look crosses his face. Fear? Panic? Before disappearing and being replaced by a cocky crooked smile mixed with hostility.

He's not surprised to see her. Or me.

I look down at Callie, waiting for her to say something, but her eyes are wide and she looks terrified. Fuck. This asshole must've done a number on her if she's suddenly meek and scared, not the brave, feisty woman I've known. I touch her in the middle of her back subtly, and she comes to life.

She steps forward but doesn't close the gap between herself and Shane.

"Where have you been?" Callie's expression is wild, her breathing erratic. "What the fuck, Shane?"

"Hell, stop screaming." Shane has a nervous expression on his face and looks around, like he's worried about others overhearing. Spoiler alert: They definitely do.

She takes another step toward him and raises her hand to poke his chest, but he grabs her wrist, and she flinches.

I see red. He's touching her. He's got his fucking hand on her body.

"Get off her," I say, my voice sharp and dangerous.

"You're hurting me," Callie says, and my adrenaline spikes even higher than it already was.

"Aw, poor baby." Shane looks her up and down, ignoring me completely.

"Let. Her. Fucking. Go." I step forward and grab the wrist of the hand that's gripping Callie, and wrap my other hand around his neck. Callie's now tucked against my chest. "Now."

Shane drops Callie's hand, and she pushes back into me, but I don't stop squeezing his neck.

"I should kill you," I say.

"Wes," Callie says, a low-level of panic in her voice. "Please don't do that."

I growl and let Shane go, but only because his stupid thugs have pushed their way to the edge of the crowd, and if I kill him now, it'll be messy, and Callie won't ever see her mother's ring again.

Those are literally the only reasons I don't end his life.

"What the fuck?" Shane rubs his neck. He looks me up and down, clearly freaked out and definitely noticing me now.

"This is Wes," Callie says, then trails off. Maybe she's not quite sure how to explain me. I cock my head at Shane and glare at him.

"I heard about you." He narrows his eyes at me.

"Put your hands on her again, and I will rip your throat out." My voice is low and only for him and Callie to hear.

"Sorry, asshole, I'm talking to my wife."

Again, a red veil falls over my vision.

"Easy, Wes," Noah says from behind me. "Maybe let this… man, or whatever he is, talk."

"You're such an asshole, Shane," Meadow says from next to Noah.

"Shut the fuck up, Meadow." Shane shoots daggers from his eyes at Callie's sister.

"Hey," Noah says. I raise my eyebrows but don't take my eyes off Shane.

"I want a divorce." Callie's voice is shaky. I hate the effect Shane has on her. "And my mother's ring back. Why have you been hiding from me?"

"I'm down here for work, Callie. Jones sent me to set up the New York City fight club. So here I am."

"Fucking Jones," Callie says. I clench and unclench my fists.

"Hey, do you happen to know how he got his ass kicked in Boston? There are rumors, of course." Shane slides a sharp look my way.

"I don't care about Jones." Callie reaches for her jacket, which I dropped when Shane had her wrist, and fishes around the inside pockets. "Here. Divorce papers. Sign them."

Callie waves a packet of paper in the air.

CHAPTER 30

GUARD DOG

CALLIE

"Not until we have a chance to talk," Shane says. "We have unfinished business."

I flinch and hate myself for it. I also hate his arrogant fucking face.

But he's right. And there's no way he has my mother's emerald ring tucked away in the pocket of the joggers he pulled on after his fight. And the ring is half the point of even finding him. More than half the point.

Shane's eyes drag up and down my body, and Wes takes another step toward him.

"Eyes on her face, fucker," he practically growls at Shane.

Shane lets his gaze settle on me, then back to Wes. Then his eyes widen.

"Are you fucking him?" The rage that flares on Shane's face terrifies me.

How the hell did he figure that out so fast? He's going to hold that against me. He's going to refuse to sign the papers or threaten me in some other way. He's never, ever going to let me go.

Shane's face is smug.

"Shut your mouth," Wes says quietly. His words give me a rush of confidence.

"As if you didn't sleep with other women. As if—" I cut off my sentence as my voice gets squeaky. I don't want to acknowledge the way I felt when I found that pair of underwear shoved in his pocket. It shouldn't have hurt me, not after how long our marriage had been dead, but it did. And I shouldn't sound so hurt now.

"You hated when I stopped fucking you," Shane says in a low, cutting voice. He eyes flit to my breasts, as if he didn't hear Wes's warning before. I can't help but flinch.

Wes is instantly in Shane's face. Holy shit. I turn to watch Wes, the fury etched in the narrowing of his eyes and the disgusted turn of his mouth.

Movement to our sides catches my eye, and two giant men step behind Shane, glaring at Wes.

But Wes doesn't even give them a courtesy glance.

I flash back to when he beat the shit out of Jones in Boston. He might not have control over himself right now. I'm not sure I care, except for the fact that I don't want to see what Shane's bodyguards do if Wes touches him again. I look behind me just as Noah—who was apparently calmly observing the situation from the background—steps forward with his phone cradled in his palm. He says something quietly in Wes's ear, and Wes steps back from a frozen Shane and glances at his brother.

"Now?" Wes says, incredulous. Noah nods, and Wes waves his hand in the air. They exchange unintelligible words in hushed whispers.

"Jesus, Callie." Shane finally finds his voice again— unfortunately—and nods to Wes. "Who the fuck are you associating yourself with?"

I'm torn between responding to Shane and trying to figure out what Wes and Noah are arguing about.

"Hello? You came here to see me?" Shane waves his hand in front of my face.

I return my gaze to Shane. "Yeah, I did." I hate it here. I want to leave.

"Listen," Shane says, his tone much calmer now that Wes isn't fucking with him. "Can we talk somewhere else? Just us? About everything?"

"No fucking way are you getting her alone." Wes jumps back in the conversation just as Noah disappears into the crowd. Wes is speaking to Shane, but watching his brother walk away.

He's freaked out. I'm not sure I've seen him freaked out.

Meadow hesitates for a second, looking at me, then follows Noah without a word.

What is going on here?

"I'll sign the divorce papers after I get half of your share of your father's estate." Shane's glare bores into me. "Like we talked about. Because you owe me. Your *father* owes me for all I've done for him over the years."

"It was your job." I shake my head. He is the most self-centered human being I have ever encountered. "And you weren't in his will. I was."

"I went above and beyond the job," Shane spits out and once again, I flinch.

"Wrap this up, asshole," Wes says. "Callie, what do you want to do right now?" He touches my back, and I lean into the contact and take a deep breath. What do I want to do? We're not getting anywhere right now. Nothing is getting signed tonight; no ring is getting handed over.

"I need the money, and I'm not letting this go." Shane's

voice softens, and he now looks dead serious, the taunting expression gone.

He's delivering facts, I realize.

"Why?" My mind reels. What does he *need* the money for? *Want* the money, I get. But need?

"Transfer me the money, and I'll sign the papers." Shane snaps out of his serious tone, the casual asshole vibe back. "I'll get the money one way or another."

"Don't give him one dollar, Calliope."

I look up at Wes, and my insides soften.

"*Calliope*?" Shane looks Wes up and down. "She is *married*. To *me*. Back the fuck off."

This man has no sense of self-preservation. I wonder how he'd act if he knew what Wes and Noah do in their free time. He wouldn't laugh or chide or poke. He'd cower.

I'm so focused on this thought that I startle when Wes punches Shane in the jaw. Shane's face jerks, and his legs fly out from under him. I gasp and splay my hand on my chest. The thugs lurch forward and get between Wes and Shane. They don't, however, help Shane off the ground, where he's now on all fours.

Shane is low-level. Too low-level to have thugs there to protect him. So what are they protecting?

My blood runs cold.

My inheritance? That's what Jones freaked out about back in Boston. I wouldn't tell him how much, and that provoked him into attacking me. In all honesty, I was so surprised by the question that I didn't finish comprehending before he slammed me against the wall.

It's about money. All of this is about money.

I still don't understand, but I'm getting there.

Wes looks furious. Ragey. I'm a little terrified of him, but mostly because he's so fucking gorgeous and solid and there for me. That's the only thing he cares about. Me. Protecting me. My body aches for him in a way I've never experienced.

Shane gets up, holding his hand palm out to Wes in a gesture that begs him to stop. It doesn't look like Wes could get through Jones's thugs, but I bet he'd find a way.

"Watch your fucking mouth. You don't know anything about me, or Callie, or us." Wes looks at me. "You okay?"

I nod and my chest tightens at the intense way Wes looks at me.

The divorce papers are still gripped in my hand, and I know they're not getting signed tonight. I slip them back into my jacket.

Wes glances in the direction that his brother disappeared, a stoic look on his face.

Then the realization slams into me, making me sway on my feet. Wes let Noah go off in New York City by himself. He's tracking a target or staking out a building or something, and he's doing it without his protector. His brother.

Wes chose to stay here with me.

I've gotta end this conversation and get us out of here so Wes can go find Noah.

"Fine. We'll meet tomorrow." My hate for this man festers in my belly. "Bring my mother's ring."

"If I can find it." Shane smirks. "Come tomorrow ready to share, and I'm more likely to be able to."

If he can find it? I take a deep breath and appreciate that I now know for sure that Shane has the ring. I was almost positive, but there was always the worry that it was lost. I swallow and rub my arms. I don't want to meet Shane tomorrow. I don't want to see him ever again.

And then it occurs to me. Maybe he brought Meadow here as a backup plan. If he couldn't get the money from me, he'd figure out how to get it from my half-sister. A shiver runs down my spine.

I'm not sure how else to end this besides giving him some of my father's money. Maybe I need to do it to protect Meadow and Jake and get Wes out of this situation and just move on with our fucking lives.

"I'll text you the address of where to meet." Shane crosses his arms on his chest. Sure, he can be brave with two beefcakes standing between him and Wes.

"Let's go, Callie." Wes grabs my hand and guides me away from Shane before I can say another word. We walk side-by-side through the crowd and the first set of double doors. The two thugs follow us but stop when we head through the second set of doors. Past the bouncer, we step out of the building. The street is blessedly quiet after the noise of the fight club.

"You okay?" Wes stops and turns to me, cradling my face in his hands. The way his palms feel on my cheeks makes my stomach flutter.

"Yes." I nod and slip my hands around his waist. Relief washes over me that we're alone. "But I don't have a good feeling about tomorrow. What if he refuses to sign? Doesn't bring the ring?"

"We'll make him." Wes kisses me, his lips soft and gentle on mine.

How will we make him? I have so many doubts, but in this moment, I force myself to trust in Wes's words. He'll make this happen. I believe him.

"Shit, Wes, where's Noah?" My eyes fly wide open. How could I forget about Noah? Wes must be freaking out. I search his face.

"He got hotel rooms for us. Sent me the address. Said he's checking out—" Wes stops talking and looks at me.

"Another target?" I suggest, keeping my expression smooth. I maintain eye contact with him and tighten my grip on his waist. It's important that Wes knows I'm okay with this. I want to be a part of his life and that means accepting and understanding what he and his brother—

Wait, no, that's not right. I don't want to be a part of his life, not long-term. But for now. For now I'm okay with whatever it is he does with Noah.

At least for tonight. The last night.

Wes pauses, searching my face for something, then nods. "He said he'll see us later."

"But—are you sure? Should we go find him?"

This moment feels heavy. Wes should go find Noah. And the fact that he's even considering not doing that means that for whatever reason, he's choosing to be with me instead.

I'm not sure I like that.

"Don't you want to go find him?"

Emotions pass over Wes's face. "Yes. But I want to make sure you are safe. I don't feel comfortable with you being alone. Shane and Jones are out there somewhere, and they know you're here."

"Wes, I'll be okay. Or I can come?"

"No. I'm staying with you. I don't want you in any more danger. You've been through too much."

I throw myself into his chest, and he pulls me tight against him.

I've never felt safer than when I'm with Wes.

And that scares the shit out of me.

CHAPTER 31

UH OH

WES

We step off the elevator and into the long, dark hallway of the hotel. It's not in the best neighborhood, but it's nondescript, they take cash, and it's close to where Noah's staking out Joe Killer.

I should go find my brother. I should have Noah's back.

What if things go wrong tonight? What if someone catches him staking out the apartment building based on a stupid fucking tip from Scorpion?

Callie entwines her fingers with mine, and I tug her close to my body as we walk down the hallway looking for the room number Noah texted me. I glance down at her. I can't put her in danger. I can't leave her alone.

I'm being torn in two, just like I've always been afraid of, a reason I don't let myself date.

But here I am, with gorgeous and sexy Callie.

I will keep her safe. I have to.

So for tonight, Noah's going to have to take care of himself. I shudder at the thought.

I swipe the keycard and let us into the room, then turn to Callie standing next to me, watching, waiting. I reach down and pull her against me, and she hops up and wraps her legs around my waist.

"Fuck," I whisper and turn to press her against the wall, holding her against me by her thighs. "I want you so fucking bad, Calliope."

Her eyes shut as I press my cock against her center, a soft moan sounding from her gorgeous throat.

"Wes, god, fuck."

I bury my head in the warm spot where her neck meets her shoulder and press my open mouth against her skin. Fuck me. She tastes so good. I drag my mouth up her neck and tug on her earlobe with my teeth.

"Are you sure—" she gasps when I thrust between her legs. There are too many fucking layers between us. "—you don't want to go?"

"Absolutely fucking not," I growl. As if I'd leave her here alone? She's out of her mind if she thinks that's going to happen. I step away from the wall and walk her to the bed, my hands gripping her perfect round ass, then lower her supple body until her feet are on the ground. "Strip," I order, watching her every move as I slide my jacket off and pull the long-sleeved t-shirt from my body in one swift motion.

I can't take my eyes off her as she shrugs out of her jacket and pulls her tank top off her body, exposing her thin white bra. I rub my cock through my jeans with one hand as she unbuttons her jeans and wiggles out of them. I follow suit and step out of my pants, my cock straining against my boxer briefs.

"What now?" she says, her voice breathy.

"Pull your bra down."

She does what I say and exposes one heavy breast and

deep red nipple, then the other. Without me asking, she squeezes her breasts, her eyes locked on my cock, and rubs her legs together. Her phoenix tattoo is beautiful art on her body.

She's beautiful art.

"I've been fantasizing about something," I say and step forward, not touching her but moving my body close enough that I can feel her heat on the bare skin of my chest.

"What?" She touches her belly with one hand, then reaches for me. I lean forward, letting her grip my cock through my boxer briefs.

"Fuck, Callie." I step forward and reach behind her with one hand, sliding from the small of her back into her underwear, squeezing her ass, pressing her against me so her hand is trapped on my cock between us. Her tits are smashed up against my chest and the sight of it almost makes me come. "I want to tie you up."

She breathes out, bites her lip, and nods. "Yes."

"Are you sure?" I slip my other hand into her underwear and push the fabric down so the only thing separating us is my boxer briefs.

"Yes, Wes, fuck, yes. Tell me what to do."

I reach up and unclasp her bra, then step away.

"On the bed. Naked." My bag is on the ground along the wall, left there by my brother. I crouch to root around for what I'm looking for. When I find it and stand, I turn to find Callie lying on her back on the bed, naked, as I demanded, propped up on her elbows. Her knees are bent but together, not quite letting me see her pussy.

My cock grows impossibly harder at the sight of her laid out for me.

I stalk to the bed and crawl over her, pulling her wrists above her head and zip-tying them. What a fucking sight she is, tits spreading on her chest, hair mussed from the walk back, cheeks flushed, eyes dilated.

"Look at you, all tied up and waiting for me to fuck you, Calliope." I back up and kneel before her, nudging her legs fully open. Her pussy is wet and glistening. I can smell her, and I almost lose my mind.

"Wes," she moans. I bury my face between her legs and breathe in her sweet scent.

"Fuck," I say, my lips on her cunt, shoving my tongue into her soaking wet slit. I pull her thighs onto my shoulders and lick up and down her opening, tasting her sweetness, feeling her writhe against me. She smells like sex and heat and midnight and like she's mine, all mine.

I suck on her clit, caressing her with my tongue. She moans and reaches down to my head, but I stop.

"Hands above your head, pet, or I stop."

She whimpers but moves her tied arms back above her head. I get back to licking, pushing a finger inside her while I suck. Her legs shake, and I know she's already on the edge, so I add a second finger to her pussy and curl them inside, finding the spot that makes her cry out.

I stop licking for a second to watch my fingers move in and out of her, dripping with her desire. I can't wait to sink my cock inside her, but I want her to come at least once first.

"Ready, Calliope?"

"Yes," she breathes out. "Please, Wes, please let me come."

The view is gorgeous from here. My fingers in her pussy, her tits sliding on either side of her chest, her stomach soft and curvy.

I dive back in and pump my fingers in and out, licking and sucking around them until I can feel the walls of her cunt fluttering around me and she screams as she comes, wave after wave. I smile into her wet core as it finally fades away.

I could live forever here, pleasuring her, making her come on my tongue, my cock, my fingers. I crawl up over her.

Callie's gorgeous, panting and flushed from her orgasm. I lower my mouth to her right tit, taking my time sucking and licking, teasing her nipple with my tongue until she's moaning and arching her back.

"I love having you tied up for me." I reach down and free my cock from my boxer briefs, dragging the tip along her pussy, where it belongs. Her wet heat is waiting for me. It's made for me. "You feel so good."

"Wes, oh my god." She tries to wrap her legs around my waist, pulling me closer. "I need you inside me."

"I already was. Be more specific, sweetheart."

"Your cock. I need your cock."

"Well. All you had to do was ask." I thrust inside her tight, wet pussy and have to freeze for a minute to get myself under control.

Callie moans and thrusts her hips up.

"Fuck," I growl, pulling out and then pushing into her warm center, again and again. I won't let myself come until she does again, no matter what, but I don't have to wait long. Soon she's screaming and arching her back, and just as her pleasure is fading, mine explodes out of me, and I swear she comes again on my cock.

I prop myself up on my elbows, panting. I kiss her mouth.

"You're amazing, Calliope," I whisper.

"You too." Her mouth curves into a lazy smile. "I almost forgot about the shit day."

"Surely those two—three?" I look to her for confirmation, and she nods at three. "Okay, three orgasms at least partially made up for it."

"Yeah. But can you cut me free now?"

I smirk up at her tied wrists.

"If you insist."

"I do."

And so I grab my knife from my duffel and set Callie free, then lie on my side next to her and pull her against my body. There are so many more things I want to do to this woman, and I don't know how much time I have with her.

I don't want to let her go. Not ever.

But that's not what she wants, and it's not right for me, either. I'm already so attached that I let my brother go off alone in New York City to stake out an incredibly dangerous target. I should stop this from happening—all of this—but I'm incapable of doing so.

Anyway, it's too late.

I kiss the top of her head, and she wiggles further into me, her ass rubbing against my cock.

"You keep doing that, and I'm going to have to fuck you again." I slide my hand down her stomach and rub her clit slowly until she moans softly. "Oh, but you want that, sweetheart?"

"I do want that," she says.

Instead of tying her up, this time I spread her legs from behind and slide my cock right into her wet heat.

"You are perfect, Callie."

She lets out a soft huff and puts her hand over mine, pressing it down on her clit.

I fucking love this woman.

What?

Shit.

Yeah. I thought it, and now that I have, it's perfectly clear. She's never been just a client, not from the first night I laid eyes on her. She's always been different. Special. I wanted to pull her into my protective circle from the start. The rage I felt when Shane was talking to her tonight, when he fucking touched her. I would've killed him right then if she'd have let me. And the biggest evidence that I love her—I let Noah go alone tonight.

I am well and truly fucked.

I slowly move in and out of Callie, taking my time, massaging her as she moans and writhes against me. And as she comes and whispers my name, I know she's it for me.

I'm in love with Callie.

My orgasm hits me hard. I don't pull out right away, but keep her nestled against me, stroking her breasts, her belly, her thighs. She eventually pulls away and turns to face me. She traces the lines of my tattoos down my neck, over my biceps, forearms.

"My mom gave me her emerald ring as an early high school graduation present, that's why it's so important to me." Callie's face is relaxed, her eyelids heavy, like she's talking to me as she falls asleep. "She died a month later."

"I'm sorry, Callie."

"When she'd only been gone a few weeks, Dad was already basically pretending like nothing happened. Like she'd never existed to begin with. Like she hadn't been laughing in the kitchen one minute and dead the next."

I rest my hand on her hip and slowly trace circles on her skin with my thumb.

"Jake shut down so I couldn't even really talk to him. I kind of lost my shit. Didn't end up going away to college, even though I know that's what she wanted me to do."

"That's awful."

Callie's finger follows the lines of ivy from my wrist to my neck.

"So eventually, when Shane showed up grieving his

father, we bonded. He recognized my grief, and I recognized his."

I hate Shane deeply, but I almost feel bad for the man. Not quite. But almost.

"He'd only talk to me. His dad was murdered, you know."

"Damn. That sucks." And it does. Losing a parent is painful, but losing a parent to murder is worse. I think so, anyway. But it's not an excuse for what a bad human being Shane turned out to be. And especially not for how he treated Callie.

"He said he fell for me without knowing it would upset my dad. In hindsight, I think he went after me because it would secure his place in a new family. And then I got pregnant."

My hand freezes on her hip.

"We got married at the courthouse, then lost the baby shortly after." She shakes her head. "Everything was shit after that."

"I'm so sorry." Now I reach over and cradle her cheek in my hand, running my thumb on her lower lip. She shuts her eyes and a small smile twitches onto her mouth.

"Thanks."

"Come here." I pull Callie my way and wrap my arms around her, pulling her thigh up over my hip. I press my lips to her forehead. "I'm so, so sorry, Callie. Really."

She takes a ragged breath, and I look down to see a tear fall from her eye and run down the middle of her nose. I reach down and kiss it away, then rub her back. My cock is hard between us, but I just hold her.

Callie's been through so much. I want to make up for all the bad men she's had in her life. I want to be her rock, the man who puts her above all else, who protects her with his life.

"I've got you," I say, rubbing her back until her breathing steadies and her eyes sink shut.

I wish I could un-know what I just figured out. That I love her, that she needs me, that I need her.

Thank god I'm a good secret keeper.

CHAPTER 32

THE EMERALD RING

CALLIE

It's morning on the day after finding Shane at the fight club, and I'm nervously waiting for him to get in touch with me.

"That man doesn't deserve one penny of your money," Wes says to me earnestly. He's sitting on the second untouched bed in Noah's hotel room. I'm at the desk, and Noah's pacing. We're trying to come up with a game plan.

"I know." We've been going in circles with this. Wes is right, of course, but what else can I do? I want to end this. Be free of Shane forever. The only way to do that is to give him what he wants. "It's just money."

Wes growls.

"You should text him," Noah says to me, pausing mid-pace.

He's got a wicked black eye and a split lip, which Wes can't stop staring at. They had some angry, hushed words when we first saw Noah's injuries this morning, which he assured us are 'nothing' and 'fine'.

The last thing I want to do is text Shane. I scrunch my face and glance at my phone on the desk.

"Callie, you don't have to." Wes leans forward with his elbows on his knees.

"At least we got a tracker on his car, right?" Noah crosses his arms and glances at Wes, who winces as he once again looks at his brother's swollen eye. "If we don't hear from Shane, we—well, you—can go wait for him by his car."

"You shouldn't have left the fucking fight club without me." Wes glares at Noah, fixated on his face.

"Okay, maybe, but now we can track Shane's car." Noah shrugs and resumes pacing. "And I'm fine. I can handle two assholes trying to steal my wallet. They're lucky I didn't slice their stomachs open."

Meadow followed Noah out of the fight club last night. He told us he tried to shake her, but then she identified Shane's car parked along the road a block away. Meadow and Noah then separated, and Noah got into some kind of scuffle with a pair of dudes who tried to mug him on the way to the stakeout spot he was headed to.

The look on Wes's face when Noah told us about the mugging was lethal. And it's my fault. I'm the one who Wes stuck by last night when he should've been with Noah. I should've insisted he go check on his brother instead of spending the night with me, especially since he didn't even end up finding their target, but instead stuck a tracker on Shane's car. For me.

"Callie's fucking sister was trying to be sneaky and follow me, but she was as subtle as a herd of elephants." Noah scoffs and shakes his head, but I have the feeling that he's protesting a bit too hard.

"Stop trying to distract me." Wes is firm. "You cannot go

alone this morning. Wait until we hear from Shane to go anywhere."

"I can go alone, and I will if I need to." Noah shakes his head at Wes, like he's dealing with a petulant child. Or maybe Noah's the child, I dunno.

I'm a wreck. Again, Wes is having to choose between me and Noah? I'm desperate for him to come with me, but I feel awful that Noah is insisting he can go alone. I should tell them I can meet Shane alone today, but I can't get myself to do it.

I can't tell Wes I don't need him today, and he wouldn't leave me anyway. I know it.

This is it though.

I didn't think everything would get done during this trip, I really didn't. I thought it would all take longer. But the thing is, once I have the ring and Shane signs the papers, this all has to end. I can't let it stretch out longer. I might lose the nerve to actually leave.

Portland.

And Wes.

I am going. I need to go.

"Why can't you go later?" I ask Noah. I can hear the panic in my voice.

"Because the tip from Scorpion is about this morning. He said there should be a certain car at the apartment building that belongs to Joe Killer."

"Why didn't he know that last night?" Wes asks, a sharp edge to his voice.

"I don't know, you ask him." Noah shrugs.

"Okay, well, I can tell Shane I can't meet him until later."

"Sure, if that works out, fine," Noah says, looking not impressed. Wes, on the other hand, is literally growling across the room.

Just then, my phone buzzes, and we all stare at my screen. I click and read it out loud.

SHANE

Roots Cafe, 555 West Street, at ten o'clock

don't bring your fuck boys

ME

can we do it later?

SHANE

no

I look up from my phone, desperate. Wes glances between me and Noah.

"Welp, looks like I'm on my own this morning," Noah says, looking pleased.

Wes looks absolutely pained.

A HOT TEA sits in front of me, untouched. I'm waiting for Shane in the diner and ordered the hottest drink I could in case I need to use it as a weapon. I also have a knife that Wes slipped under my jeans and strapped onto my calf. As if I have any knife skills.

Wes is watching. I don't know where from, which he said is best so I don't accidentally look in that direction, but I've already gotten a text from him noting I haven't taken a sip of my tea.

I love how he watches me.

There might be some trauma there to talk to a therapist about at a later date.

Shane walks in, and I'm struck by his harsh good looks, strong with a hint of cruelty in his sharp jawline and prominent chin. Both eyes are bruised—the fresh one from last night and fading one on the other side. A new bruise is on his cheek and his lip is split. His eyes are a cruel gray, and his hair light and thick. He's noticeably more fit than when he disappeared six weeks ago. Back then, he wasn't a fighter. I would've noticed if he showed up at our apartment like this.

"Hey, Cals." Shane slides in across from me, glancing around the mostly empty diner. "Where are your guard dogs?"

I hate it when he calls me Cals. It was sweet at the beginning when we first got together, but he's used it contemptuously for the last years of our relationship.

"Not here," I say, trying to keep my face blank. But I can feel myself cringing, flinching, showing my discomfort.

Shane laughs bitterly. "Okay."

"Got the ring? Ready to sign?" I tap on the table where the divorce papers are waiting for his signature.

He leans back, arching his back and tucking his hands behind his head. He smirks.

Yeah, I know. The money. Worth a shot, I guess.

"Maine is a no-fault divorce state. If we split before figuring this out, everything will get divided fifty-fifty anyway. Your father died before any theoretical divorce, so..." He shrugs and takes his hands down, linking fingers on his abdomen. "I'd get half in the courts."

Fucking asshole. But he's probably right.

I can't wait to get as far away from this hateful man as I can.

But even as I think that, there's a stabbing in my belly because getting away from this life includes getting away from Wes. There's no restarting my life in a squeaky-clean way but also having anything to do with those serial killer brothers. Regardless of the fact that they are killing bad guys and saving young women and girls, Wes is still a murderer. And a stalker. And apparently has a kink for zip-tying me while he does unspeakable things—

"Hello?" Shane waves his hand in front of my face, and I return from the hot, sharp flashback of last night.

"And what do you need the money so bad for?" Money is money, so it's probably a stupid question. But all this drama of him disappearing to New York and calling me from Boston and waiting for me to find him... it's such a waste of time. Jones has leverage over him. That's gotta be the reason. "You already drained our bank account before you left."

A flash of something crosses Shane's face, then it's gone.

"Like there was any money in there anyway."

He's right. We didn't have much. But he left me with nothing except for my secret bank account, which he didn't know about. I open my mouth to argue, but he cuts me off.

"Fine. Take half of what was in our bank account off my share of the inheritance. Then it's fair, Cals. That's all. I'm only looking for fair." Shane's voice is hard. Cruel.

"What are you talking about? How is this fair?" It's frustrating because I feel like there's something else going on, but I can't put my finger on it. "Why did you even disappear if you wanted this money so bad? Wouldn't it have made more sense to stay in Portland?"

"I was sent here to New York, Cals." Shane's jaw is clenched, and he grinds his teeth together. "By my boss."

Never mind. I don't want to know what's really going on, actually. I just want to be free.

"Fine. Whatever."

"No courts, no lawyers. Easy."

"Fuck." I look out the window, wishing I could spot Wes's comforting presence.

Shane narrows his eyes at me. He's not bluffing about not signing the divorce papers. My phone buzzes in my pocket.

"I'll do it now." I swallow the hard lump in my throat and pull out my phone. There's a text from Wes.

WESLEY

what's going on?

I don't respond. I need to finish this right now. So I click through to my bank app and accept the piece of paper Shane shoves toward me with all the numbers I'll need. It takes a few minutes to enter the information correctly. I show him, he nods, I press submit.

He signs the divorce papers. A copy for him, a copy for me.

Then Shane yanks a chain out from his hoodie and pulls it over his head. A ring dangles from the cheap chain. My mother's ring. I take a sharp breath and reach out my hand.

He looks like he really, really doesn't want to hand it over. He's got the money, so it's out of pure spite. A desire to make me miserable. Punish me for things I never did wrong.

But he extends his arm, and I grab the ring and clutch it to my chest.

No more words are spoken.

CHAPTER 33

MISSION ACCOMPLISHED

WES

Noah was absolutely giddy going off on his own this morning again. Black eye and all, he practically skipped out the door to follow Scorpion's tip about Joe Killer.

Up until this point, we've had very little productive information on Joe Killer. No solid clues or leads, just the list of his suspected kills from the police database, with the latest being about two weeks ago. He's been killing more frequently, so the man's gotta slip up soon.

Last night was a bust except for Noah sticking the tracker on Shane's car. Now he's back at the apartment building looking for a certain make and model of car that Scorpion claims belongs to Joe Killer.

Once again, I'm not with him because I'm watching Callie as she meets with her fuckwit soon-to-be ex-husband.

I hate that I'm not with Noah.

I hate that I'm not sitting right next to Callie.

Instead, I'm leaning against the building across the street from Roots Cafe, where Callie's waiting for Shane. Not the most subtle hiding spot, but I don't really care. Shane's gotta know I wouldn't let her meet with him all on her own, just like I'm relatively sure Jones's thugs are lingering around somewhere, although I can't spot them.

I won't take my eyes from Callie. Not for a second.

I DON'T EVEN WAIT until Shane is clear of the restaurant before striding across the street and ducking inside. I intentionally bump into his shoulder as we pass each other.

"The fuck, man?" Shane says with a glare, then his eyes briefly flash when he recognizes me. Fear and fury, but he just shakes his head and flees. Coward.

"You okay?" I slide into the booth across from Callie.

Callie nods but looks miserable. She's spinning a ring on her finger, her eyes fixed on the jewelry. The ring.

"Can I see?" I hold out my hand, and she hesitates for a beat before putting her hand in mine. I touch the ring gently. It's a green emerald set in gold with tiny flowers etched along the band. "It's beautiful. And he signed?"

"Yes," she squeaks out.

"Good." I squeeze her hand, but then she pulls away from me. "Then all you gotta do is file the papers."

"And wait two weeks for the hearing. He doesn't have to be there for that. I don't either—I can just send a representative. Jake said he'd do it."

"You're done with him, Calliope." But as I speak, I realize the reason she asked Jake to attend the hearing for her is because she'll be gone from Maine.

She'll be *gone*.

We've done what she hired me to do.

I found Shane. She got her ring back. He signed the

divorce papers. I stayed with her far longer than I ever had with a client before. That's because she's not just a client.

She's the woman I'm in love with.

Her expression morphs into a frown as she continues to spin her mother's ring on her middle finger. It really is beautiful. I'm not surprised she fought so hard to get it back, especially as it's the last gift her mother gave her before passing away.

Is Callie thinking that this is the end for us? Is she even thinking about us at all? Maybe I'm reading too much into her expression, her forehead crinkled and a downturn to her gorgeous mouth. Suddenly, I'm desperate.

Is this over?

Do I need to let her go, even though she's fucking mine?

I can't force her to be with me. But maybe she'll have changed her mind. She could stay in Maine. Stay with me.

"Callie—" I start. I'll have to convince her. I must.

"Can you send me your bank information or Venmo?" She cuts me off. "Plus how much I owe you. I can get the payment over right away."

"I'm not taking your money, Calliope." My voice is a low whisper.

"Please, Wes. Send the information." Callie lays her hands flat on the table, as if she's about to stand. "I'm—I'm going to go see Meadow. Thank you. Thank you for everything."

These are not the words I expected to come out of her mouth.

Thank you? Like this was some kind of transaction or favor.

"Where does she live? I'll get you there." My voice cracks.

"Wes—" she closes her mouth and shakes her head.

"I can't let you wander around the city by yourself, Callie. There's some fucked up people here."

Fuck. Fuck fuck fuck.

I can't accept this is happening right now. The edges of my vision darken, and I fight to stay calm.

"Fucked up people?" Callie chuckles without humor. "Like you and your brother?" Her face grows pink, like she's shocked or surprised or embarrassed at her hurtful words.

They settle on my chest, burning like acid. I let them tear through my flesh and reach bone.

I thought she understood what we were doing. That we're the good guys. We're helping people. Helping women and children, so fewer people like my mother and sister end up murdered in their beds.

My stomach twists. I told her who I am. I showed her. And I thought she'd accepted me. I guess I was wrong. I was so desperate for love and acceptance that I made myself believe in an us that never existed.

"I thought you were different." My words come out sharp, and she flinches.

"I'm not." Callie shakes her head. Her eyes brim with tears, and even though her jaw is set and her words are firm, the tears escape and roll down her face. "I could never be with someone like you, Wes. I just can't."

Her words are a nightmare. My world shifts as I struggle to accept what she thinks of me. It was inevitable, I guess. And I can't convince her—or anyone else—that murdering bad guys is ethically okay. It's at best morally gray. And if I have to try, then this thing between us doesn't have a chance.

My phone buzzes in my pocket, but I ignore it.

"Let me come with you. I don't have to go in, but I can keep watch, then get you home safely to Portland."

"Is that my home anymore?" Callie asks, and I don't think the question is directed at me.

"Okay, then we grab your stuff and Honey Bunny, and you can come with me to Lake Savage." I present the option, knowing she won't take me up on it. Knowing I'm begging and it's not dignified.

"I—" But then she stops. Looks at her hands. Shuts her eyes.

"Calliope." What more words are there? Haven't we said them all? But no. We haven't. Not all of them. I reach over and cover her hand with mine, feeling the ring under my palm, but she withdraws after a few seconds, the edge of the stone setting scratching my skin.

Callie raises her big dark eyes to mine, and my heart breaks in two along the fissure that was already there. Her eyes are begging me to understand, but I shake my head. I don't. I won't.

While Callie's goal is to get her divorce and start over, mine has always been to protect my loved ones, which was a lot simpler when it was just my brother.

For some stupid reason, I thought she'd choose me.

She stands, and I panic, the black along the edges of my vision creeping in. This is happening too quickly. I thought I'd have more time.

My phone buzzes in my pocket again, and I want to throw it across the room. I struggle to find the words for how I'm feeling at this moment. How can I convince her to give us a chance?

And maybe more importantly—should I?

Callie steps closer and grabs my hands. I link our fingers together, the feeling both familiar and foreign. She might have been mine, but it was only ever going to be for a short period of time. I see that now.

I shake my head, and she presses her lips together at the motion.

"Please, Wesley."

I bring our linked fingers to my mouth and press my lips to the back of her hand.

"Callie," I say, finally able to voice words. "I will get you to Meadow's."

"I don't need you to protect me, Wes." Her voice is soft and regretful. "You need to leave me alone. Understand? This is over." She squeezes my hand, then withdraws and turns away.

But if I'm not there to protect her, who will be?

No one.

She's so reckless, and she's got no one in her life to protect her.

"Fuck!" I say. The older couple at the table next to me stops talking and stares. Callie hesitates with her hand on the door, but then she pulls it open and slips through without turning around.

"Sorry," I growl at the older couple, whose eyes widen. I slide my phone out of my pocket, intending to track Callie. There's a text from my brother.

NOAH

found the car

He sends me a dropped pin for a mile away. I check Callie's location before leaving the diner, and with a last glance at where Callie disappeared around a corner, I turn in the opposite direction and jog down the city street, my heart breaking with every step that takes me away from her.

CHAPTER 34

THE TRUTH

CALLIE

"He said he was handling a situation, and if I told you where he was, he'd hurt you." Jake stares at me intently. His jaw is clenched, and he's opening and closing his fists while sitting on the edge of the couch in his living room.

My brother's blue eyes are so different from Wes's light icy ones. Jake's are a deep, marine blue that annoys the shit out of me because I've always wanted remarkable eyes like that.

"I guess I'm not surprised." I let my head drop back onto the soft cushion and shut my eyes. I spin my mother's ring on my right ring finger. It feels so good back where it belongs. It's the only thing that feels right in my life right now.

"I should've told you what I knew. I should've gone after him when he threatened you. I'm so sorry, Callie." Jake runs a hand through his thick hair. "I still can. I can try to get the money back."

"No!" I shake my head. "Please, don't. It's okay. Who

knows what he would've done." My brother is maybe a bit of a chickenshit, but not an asshole. I suppose his heart was in the right place when he decided not to tell me the whole story.

"I'm sorry he made you give him Dad's money."

I open my eyes and turn my head.

"He said he needed it. Any idea what he meant? Was it just something he said, or is there more there?"

I don't know why I'm asking. I shouldn't care. I don't care. The money is gone and, hopefully, so is Shane.

Jake swallows, and his lips grow thin. "There are rumors he fucked up on an assignment. I don't know details, I promise. But you know the family isn't kind to members who fuck up."

I wonder if there's something else Jake's not telling me. I can see a shadow of fear in the lines on his face. Jones knows about my inheritance, therefore he knows about Jake's. But if it was really Shane's fuck up that made him desperate for money and my half of the inheritance covers it, maybe that'll keep Jake safe.

"I really don't know anything else."

"Okay, I believe you." But do I? It doesn't matter, I suppose.

I thought I'd feel a deep relief once Shane signed the divorce papers, but I don't.

I'm devastated to have walked away from Wes.

I'm furious because Shane doesn't deserve any of my father's money.

I'm confused about my life choices going forward.

Yesterday, after I met with Shane and ended things with Wes, I texted Meadow and went to visit her at her apartment. She was kind and open, and we promised to make more of an effort to see each other. Then I got on a train at

Penn Station to head back to Maine. It was a long-ass journey that had me change trains in Boston and deposited me at the station in Portland at one o'clock in the morning.

I took a car back to the apartment and collapsed in bed, exhausted from the past few days. Weeks, really.

My insides twist when I think about the look on Wes's face when I ended things in the diner yesterday. I can't believe I had the strength to do that. The look on his face was heartbreaking. The lies I told him! I could tell he was fighting himself to let me go. I wish he hadn't. I wish he'd fought me harder.

"You okay, Callie?"

"Fine. I'm fine." I sit up and focus back on the laptop resting on my thighs. I want this conversation to be over. "Thanks for telling me the truth."

Jake lingers, and I just want him to leave me alone. Finally, he stands and walks back down the hallway to his bedroom.

I stare at the laptop screen. My finger hovers over the submit button to the master's program I've been planning to apply to. I talked to someone from the program weeks ago, and they said there's no reason I won't be accepted. The application itself has been complete for weeks, and I've been procrastinating, my version of Jake's chickenshit by not pressing the stupid submit button.

I can do it. It's time. Everything is wrapped up here except for filing the signed divorce papers.

The lawyer's office is closed until Monday morning, and there's no way I'm putting the document in the mail and risking it getting lost. I emailed the lawyer to see if we can meet up, but he hasn't responded. I'd go to his house and knock on his door if I knew where he lived.

And once that's done, I leave.

My stomach twists. I'll miss Lola and Jake, but I know I'll stay in touch with them. But Wes? What about him?

I met Wes only four weeks and one day ago. It feels like a lifetime.

I feel awful right now, but I have to trust in the decisions I made when I was calm and rational and not in lo—woah, nope. When I wasn't sort of obsessed with a gorgeous serial killer.

What a fucking joke. I truly am a disaster. First I marry a lowlife mob guy who my father did not approve of, then I fall in with a stalker serial killer.

Which just reinforces that I need a fresh start.

So why doesn't it feel right? Not like it did a month ago before I'd met Wes. I knew what I wanted then.

Now, it feels like I want him instead of a brand-new life across the country. It's probably because being with him is exciting, and even with the murders and drugging and zip ties and breaking in, he feels safe. I feel safe.

But you know where I'll also feel safe? In my own apartment, far, far, away from known criminals.

In the moment, it felt like Wes and Noah were doing good when they took out that guy in Boston. But now, away from them, it feels far more in the gray than black and white. It's vigilante justice. Murder. Definitely against the law and associated with very long jail sentences. I want him, but I don't want someone who's a criminal like my family.

See? I can logic my way out of this. I nod my head, my eyes laser focused on the submit button.

Before I can continue to overthink it, I click. A little cry escapes my throat, but I push it down and pick up my phone.

Does Wes know where I am? Is he still tracking me? I can't believe he hasn't texted or gotten in touch. Except I can. The man might have zero boundaries, but I told him I don't want him, and he respects the things I say. But I never told him not to track me, and the knowledge that he might still be doing so is a fucked-up kind of comfort.

I send a text to Rebecca, my boss at the library, asking her to chat. She responds right away. Instead of hiding in my room, I pull on a hoodie and leave the apartment.

It's beautiful outside. The sun is high in the sky and it's warm enough to not wear a jacket. The official start of spring is only a few days away. Spring represents new beginnings, and it's fitting that my life will restart just as the season turns.

Then a cool breeze rushes over me, and I shiver. How dare winter try to hang on, pulling me back just as spring is right there to pull me forward.

"Hey, Rebecca," I say when the librarian answers my call. "I'm giving my notice."

Rebecca freaks out, telling me how much she loves me, will miss me, wants what's best for me, etc.

This feels all wrong.

CHAPTER 35
DOOM SCROLLING
WES

I'm doom scrolling Ruth Roy's social media.

"Fuuuuuck me." Sir Fluffy weaves between my legs, dragging his tail under my knee. "That has to be fake." Her feed is image after image of perfect pies against cozy backgrounds. There's one of her baking in her pristine kitchen. She has an apron on that says *TGIF: this grandma is fabulous* and a spot of flour on the tip of her nose. Totally posed and annoying as shit.

I know better than to look at her socials. But she tagged me in a post. Tagged. Me. Noah thinks I'm nuts for even having a social media presence given our dark activities, but it's purely baking related.

And what did Ruth fucking Roy tag me in? Well. She stopped in at Killer Beans—*my* fucking local coffee shop— and tasted a slice of pie. She mutilated it, then took a picture and called it ugly, dry, and tasteless. Said it was like swallowing a forkful of sawdust and that she has *tomorrow's apple pie competition in the bag for the fifth year in a row.*

I'm furious, but it's a welcome emotion from the despair

that's blanketed me since I left Callie in New York City yesterday. After she walked away from me, I met up with Noah, checked out the Joe Killer apartment location and car, then we headed back north.

My timer goes off, giving me a good excuse to walk away from my phone. I adjust my apron and slip on an oven mitt so I can pull the apple pie out. The only difference between this pie and the other two that are already cooling on the counter is the top crust. A big part of the Portland Springfest pie competition is appearance, including what the crust and topping look like before and after slicing. I step back to assess the pies.

The first one is a classic loose, laced topping, baked just until it started to brown. There's a hint of the tender spiced apples underneath. I nod. Can't go wrong with that one. Classic, if not a little boring.

The second one has a delicious crumbly streusel topping, chaotic perfection made of flour, sugar, butter, and spices. This is Ruth Roy's specialty, and while it's tempting to try to beat her at her own game, I think I want to do something different.

The third, which I just pulled out, is my attempt at art on the top crust. I tilt my head and try to see it from the judges' point of view.

It is... not good.

I tried again to carve a loon into the dough, which, while better than the first few times, looks only slightly better than what a five-year-old child might create. Nothing against five-year-olds, of course.

I love this idea, but it needs some work. I bet I could get it on the next try.

The competition is tomorrow afternoon, so tonight I'll prep the dough and the filling, and early in the morning I'll assemble the pie and bake it so it's as fresh as possible. I have just a few hours to make final decisions and adjustments.

I tap out a quick text to Noah.

ME

> I need you here assessing pies immediately. It's a pie emergency

I don't even put my phone down because I know Noah's probably sitting at his kitchen table plotting to take over the world.

NOAH

> you are a weird fucking dude

> also, be right over

I snort and head to my coffee machine to prepare a fresh pot to go with the pie assessment.

I tracked Callie long enough yesterday to make sure she got back to Portland safely. She visited with her half-sister—which I know because Noah had Meadow's address as he's apparently as much of a stalker as I am—and then she took the train home. I haven't been able to bring myself to disable the tracking devices and software on her phone, which I know is fucked up, but I'll get there eventually.

I press the blue blinking light to start the coffee machine and sink into one of the kitchen chairs. This is the chair that I zip-tied Callie to on that first day, after I slid a needle in her neck out in the woods. She was so angry.

In hindsight, I wanted her from the first second I saw her watching me outside of Maine Coffee Co, and even more so when she was screaming at me to untie her instead of crying or begging. Even when I *did* untie her, she was still mad. Especially because I then gave her spiked hot chocolate.

She has trust issues for sure, but Callie never looked at me like I was a monster. Even when she followed me and Noah to that alleyway in Boston and watched us take out Chad Smith. She was far more pissed that I'd left her alone in the apartment than the fact that I'd helped Noah murder a guy. It was only in our last conversation that she looked at me like I was something bad.

Part of me wonders if she was purposely pushing me away, but the thing is, I *am* bad. For her, at least. I'm not what she wants or needs, and I have to respect that, because I can't change it. I drop my head into my hands just as the door swings open.

"Christ." Noah shakes his head and closes the door behind him. "Are you crying about Callie?"

"I'm not crying." I lean forward and press my palms to my cheeks. Yup. I'm crying.

"Wes—" Noah's face softens, and he approaches the kitchen table.

"No." I hold up my hand. "I don't want to hear what you have to say about this. I know letting her go is the right thing to do. I'm doing that. But I don't have to fucking like it."

"If you—"

"Please. Noah. I don't want to talk about it." Part of me is desperate to know what he was about to say, but there's no point in torturing myself further. "Not yet, anyway. I'm not ready."

Noah takes a breath as if to talk but seems to think better of it.

"Can we just taste the pies?" I plead. "Ruth Roy's been posting again and it's driving me nuts."

Noah stares at me for a long minute, then nods.

"I swear to god, that old lady is a serial killer." He slides his jacket off and tosses it onto my couch.

I chuckle. "She's a horrible human being, but I highly doubt she's a serial killer."

"I found out more that I haven't told you."

"Yeah?" The coffee pot steams and beeps as it finishes brewing. I head to the kitchen as Noah sits across from my chair. "Go on. What do you think you know about Ruth Roy?"

"Well. There was a serial killer who stopped killing around twenty years ago. It would've put Ruth in her sixties. The killer targeted men who were total scumbags. Domestic violence, rape, etc. Murder too, but it was the everyday abuses that triggered her."

"Is this what you do in your spare time?" I pour coffee from the carafe into our favorite mugs—*hacker* and *I just want to take naps and watch serial killer documentaries*—and glance over at my brother. "Although I guess it's better than adding people to your list."

Noah ignores my comment.

"They were active for at least a decade. It was a couple. A man and a woman." His eyes are wide and eager. Jesus fuck. I would say Noah needs another hobby, but he already has one that I struggle to keep a handle on. "Sometimes it would be a year or two between killings, and the authorities would think they died or retired or whatever. But then they'd hit again, up and down the Northeast."

"First, how did they know it was a couple? And second, how'd they know it was the same people? Did they leave a calling card?"

"I've got answers to all of that." Noah raises his eyebrows and rubs his hands together, looking self-satisfied. "Two pairs of footprints. It was winter, and they found frozen prints of impractical high-heeled boots and a man's Timberlands."

"Cool. A serial killer couple." I splash some creamer into Noah's and my coffees and add a sugar to mine.

"And get this." He accepts the mug and sips noisily. "They left *recipes* as their calling card."

"What?" Standing next to the table, I pause with my coffee halfway to my lips. That is weird. Still, it's not Ruth Roy. Obviously.

"Yeah. I couldn't find anywhere that says what the recipes were for. But I'd bet a lot of money it was apple pie. Killings stopped the same year her husband died. Twenty years ago."

"Shut the fuck up." I burst out laughing, and to his credit, so does Noah.

"I'm serious!"

"Stop. Please. You have sufficiently distracted me. Thank you. Now go look at my pies and tell me which one you like best."

Noah stands and strolls over to the counter. Sir Fluffy is sitting on the wooden floor with his tail swishing back and forth like a Swiffer, staring up and probably wishing his hind legs worked better so he could jump up to lick some pie.

The knot of dread in my chest is looser now that Noah is here.

"Is this supposed to be a duck?" He scrunches his face at the third pie in the row.

I groan.

CHAPTER 36
PACK IT UP

CALLIE

"Are you sure about this, Cals?" Lola sits on my bed, her face scrunched. "Portland has always been your home."

My throat feels tight as I stack books in a heavy-duty box. I've lived in this room in Jake's apartment for less than two months, but considering how little I came here with, it feels like home. Besides my book page art creations and my bookshelf, I also bought a few cheap canvas prints to hang on the walls, one of a pink sunset over a lake, another a trio of lop-eared rabbits against an artistic pink background. It feels more like home than the apartment I shared with Shane.

The answer to Lola's question is no, I'm not sure about this.

I'm the farthest thing from sure, actually. But I have to trust in the decision I made when I was calmer. The decision that said I need to start my life over somewhere else. Of course it feels all wrong right now. This is the hardest part. Following through with the plan I made that is best for my future.

The thing is, change is hard. It's hard to think about, and harder to actually make happen, even if you know it's the right thing to do. The average person doesn't change, as a general rule, and there's a reason for that. It's way easier just to keep on doing what you've already been doing. An object in motion remains in motion unless something gets in its way and forces it to adapt.

But I'm not an average person.

I understand that right now, things are clouded by a tall, tattooed, muscled serial killer who is a walking contradiction. I know him as sweet and kind and funny and so protective of the people he cares for.

Then there's the other version of Wes. The Wes who holds people down while his brother stabs them, or destroys anyone who hurts someone he cares about. That side is dark. Violent.

I surprised myself when I didn't find the morally gray part of him a deal-breaker. Because Wes looks at me like I'm his and dammit, I am. But I can't be, even though I care about him so much.

There's a knock at my bedroom door.

"Callie?" Jake says, slowly pushing my cracked door.

"Come in," I call, even as Lola's eyes widen.

Jake pushes the door open the rest of the way, his gaze flitting between me and Lola.

"Hey, Lola."

"Hi," Lola says with those damn hearts in her eyes again. Lordy.

"What's up, Jake?" I try to keep my voice steady, but the sad puppy dog look he's giving me hurts my heart.

"Um." He sticks his hands in his pockets and shifts from foot to foot. "Do you need any help?"

"Nope."

"I just wanted to say—" He casts another quick glance at Lola. "That you're welcome to stay here for as long as you want. Forever, even."

I squeeze my eyes shut. I can't handle the looks from these two. The guilt trips. The subtle pressure to not follow through with my plan, which they have both known about for months. They should understand.

I'm still upset about everything with Jake. I know why he did what he did. It was to protect me. But I hate that he lied to me for so long, and I fucking *hate* Shane.

Now Jake and Lola look at each other. For fuck's sake. I'm encouraging an alliance between them. It'll be a disaster when I leave town and they have no supervision.

"This is happening." I glance back and forth between them. "I'm leaving."

"When?" Lola manages, her voice cracking. "When do you think you'll go?"

I look around the room. My eyes land on the blue folder sitting on top of my dresser. The divorce papers will be processed on Monday after I drop them off. I'll leave Portland then, destination Seattle. The long cross-country drive will clear my head. I'll sign up for summer classes, which start in June. It'll be enough time for me to get settled and then dive into the program.

My stomach flips. Will I really be able to drive away from here? Away from the city I've lived in my whole life? Maine? My brother? Lola?

Wes?

Now it's not my stomach that flips, but my heart. This was always going to feel awful while it was happening, right? But it's the right thing to do.

And it *is* happening, so my heart better get on board. But no matter how many times I try, I can't get excited about moving on. I don't feel the same joy and freedom that I thought I would.

I kick Lola and Jake out of my room but can't focus on packing anymore. A short drive will clear my head. I'll go to the water and listen to the waves crash on the rocks at my favorite spot along the coast right outside of town.

Jake isn't in the family room when I head to my car with a few things in my arms. The cold air is a welcome relief outside of the apartment building, but I speed up my walk when I get to the dark parking garage. I pull out keys, my car within sight.

That's when everything goes dark.

CHAPTER 37

AMERICAN PIE

WES

"Hello, dear." Ruth appears next to me, her white curls tight to her head, reading glasses halfway down her nose.

She's really playing up this whole fucking sweet grandma persona. I squeeze my hands into fists.

"Ruth." I nod my head and cross my arms. Noah's conspiracy theory crosses my mind. Maybe he's fucking right about this woman being a fellow serial killer.

We're standing with the other bakers a respectful distance from the pie contest table. There's also a rope barrier, as if the queen's jewels are in the center, not a bunch of apple pies. Half a dozen judges with clipboards look at each pie, whispering to each other and scribbling notes.

"It's wonderful to see you again, Weston," Ruth says loudly enough that a few people look over.

"It's Wesley," I say through gritted teeth.

Ruth ignores my correction and lowers her voice, not looking at me, but turning in my direction so her voice carries to only me. "But your top crust looks soggy. Did you carve a child's rubber ducky into it? Wait—no. You weren't attempting a *loon*, were you?"

She looks straight ahead again, and I let out a low growl.

I will not fight with a mean grandma. I will not fight with a mean grandma.

"At least I'm trying to elevate my pie game. You bring the same pie every year." I attempt to keep a smile on my face while I deal with this monster. It won't look good if a thirty-year-old man is being nasty to a seemingly sweet old lady. Does no one else realize she's a cutthroat monster?

Of course they don't. Look at her.

"And, if I'm not mistaken, I tend to win. Four years in a row now. Am I counting correctly, dear?"

I first entered the Portland Springfest pie competition five years ago, not too long after Noah and I bought our cabins in Lake Savage. Ruth immediately approached me at the festival and introduced herself, saying all the right things. I thought I'd made a friend.

Then I got first place in the competition.

The next year, she stuck a finger in my pie when no one else was looking, screwing up the top crust completely. She dared me to report her, but I didn't because it wouldn't be a good look for the new, younger baker to accuse sweet Grandma Ruth of cheating.

I got sixth place that year. The following three years I've gotten second place.

Ruth and I have been enemies ever since.

"Do you like mince pie?" I say to her, keeping my eyes glued on the pie-judging table.

"Why?" she asks sharply.

"Just wondering."

I'm not going to poison the grandma. Definitely not.

A man steps away from the table and toward the small audience watching the judging from behind the rope divider.

"Now we will begin the taste portion of the competition. Judges will look at crust, filling, and consistency. This section of the contest is worth twenty-five points out of seventy-five points total. Another twenty-five is the overall appearance of the pie, and the last twenty-five points is our overall assessment including creativity, originality, and anything else that stands out." He nods and turns back to the table, where a woman in an apron is about to cut into the first pie.

"I bet your pie tastes like you fucked it, like in that *American Pie* movie where the kid sticks his dick in," Ruth hisses at me, then cackles quietly.

"What?" I whip my head to Ruth. She didn't really say that, did she?

Ruth ignores me and watches with a fake-ass smile on her face as the woman in the apron slices into her pie and doles out portions onto small plates. The judges all make delighted faces as they chew, nodding and whispering and taking notes.

I shake my head at Ruth, but she pretends I don't exist. What a crazy lady. She looks so calm and sweet in her grandma outfit and her... heeled boots? My eyes fix on her black boots with the pointy heel, sticking out from her long floral dress. Isn't she in her eighties? Shouldn't she be wearing some very stable, flat, supportive, and incredibly ugly shoe?

And... didn't Noah talk about the Recipe Killer lady wearing high-heeled boots?

My eyes widen, but Ruth still ignores me, that angelic smile on her face as she watches the judges.

Nah. Can't be.

I bite back a chuckle—which earns me a quick glare from

Ruth—and pull out my phone. I tap out a message to Noah about the boots and the dick-in-pie comment for a laugh.

NOAH

I KNEW IT

ME

can you imagine?

NOAH

yes, yes I can. I told you. She definitely looks like a killer today

ME

wait, are you here?

NOAH

I'm back by the donut food stand, come find me when you're done whispering about dicks in pies with Ruth

My head whips around, and I spot my brother. He raises his hand.

I grin and turn back to the pie contest table, where the judges have moved on from Ruth's pie. They get through a few more, and another older lady in the crowd comes to talk to Ruth.

When the judges get to my pie, I can't read their expressions. But it's absolutely my best work. After so many attempts, I think I finally got the iconic Maine loon design right. It definitely looks like a loon, not a duck. Fuck Ruth.

One judge—mayor of another lake town near Lake Savage—steps forward and clears his throat. He announces the third-place winner, who is a pretty middle-aged mom with a group of teens and tweens cheering for her.

There were two dozen entries, but I'd be shocked if Ruth and I aren't in the top two. What I would do to beat Ruth this year! She's paused her conversation with the other lady and is waiting with a big smile on her face.

"Second place goes to... Wesley Winters. Judges' comments included the impressive loon top crust design and the perfect consistency of the apples. Congrats, Mr. Winters."

The group claps quietly, and Noah whoops from behind me. I toss a look over my shoulder and grin. It's not first place, but at least I'm holding my position from last year.

"First place, Mrs. Ruth Roy! The perfect streusel topping and flawless filling earn her the record-setting five-year repeat title of best apple pie in Portland. Congratulations!"

Yep. Sounds about right.

Ruth Roy tosses me a sweet smile and touches me on the arm in a grandmotherly way—all for fucking show—on the way up to receive her blue ribbon, but I know her secret.

She's a wolf in sheep's clothing.

As I accept the red ribbon, I scan the crowd again and find Noah. I'm glad my brother is here, but I was really hoping I'd see Callie.

I know I'm supposed to have let her go.

As of a few hours ago, she was still at her apartment. So she hasn't left Maine yet, but I'm sure it's coming soon. The pie competition was a good distraction, but now my fingers are itching to click on the tracking app.

I miss her.

I love her.

"I didn't beat Ruth," I say when I get to Noah.

"Maybe next year, and if you reconsider feeding her your mince pie, you'll definitely win" He hands me a ridiculously ornate donut. Thick chocolate icing and bits of bacon.

"Murder an old lady? Nah." But I crack up anyway. Noah's my original ride or die, the only family I have left. "That would be a step too far."

"Just one, though."

We wander through the festival, held inside a high school gymnasium, as end-of-March weather is never predictable in Maine.

"Have you heard from Callie?" Noah asks.

I jolt to a stop and turn to him. "Why?"

"I dunno, just asking." He shrugs and points to a drinks table. "Let's get hot chocolate."

I nod and take another huge bite of donut to experience the taste explosion in my mouth.

"I was perfectly happy before I met her," I say, my mouth still half full. "And I'll be perfectly happy now."

"No, you weren't, and no, you won't." Noah hands money to the girl at the table. She pours steaming hot chocolate into two paper cups. "You think you were happy, but really all you did was follow me around and bake sad pies in your sad cabin all alone."

I'm speechless for a minute. "My pies aren't sad," is all I can think of to respond.

"Listen." Noah takes a hot chocolate from the girl and hands it to me, then accepts the other one. He puts a five-dollar bill into the tip jar before nodding toward the doors that lead to the parking lot, where there are a few food trucks, tables, and a bonfire with hay bales as seating.

It's freaking freezing outside. I shove the rest of my donut into my mouth and hand Noah my hot chocolate so I can slip my jacket on. My brother's been trying to talk to me about this. He's probably not going to let it go, so I might as well hear what he has to say.

"Go on." I take my drink back and follow him toward the fire. The first sip overwhelms me. I've been drinking hot chocolate all my life, but right now, just the smell of it reminds me of Callie on my couch the first night we met.

"You might be thinking about the Callie thing all wrong." Noah gestures toward the hay bales in front of the fire. I follow him and sit on the makeshift seating.

"It's over between us. There's nothing to think about."

"I think you're underestimating her." Noah sips his drink. "She knows the truth and isn't afraid of you. Isn't afraid of *us*. Do you realize how crazy that is?"

I stare into the fire, the heat warming the front of my body. Thoughts of Sia, my twin, flow in. A few years after she realized what we'd done and fled, she came back to Maine. I think she had it in her head that she would reconcile with her brothers. But when she found out that we were still killing, she got this horrified look on her face. She cut us out of her life again. Permanently, she said. The way she looked at us was heartbreaking, like she could forgive us killing our family's killer, but after that there was no leeway. Even when we explained what we were doing, who we were protecting, all of that.

It didn't change anything. She was terrified, and she fled. I track her occasionally, but even though I can figure out where she is, she's gone from our lives.

"That *is* crazy. But the last time I talked to her—" I shut my eyes at the final conversation where she implied Noah and I were the scary people in New York City. "I don't think she gets it. I think she's scared of us."

"Tell me, have either of us had any luck dating? Ever?" Noah stares at the side of my face.

"No." I shake my head. To say Noah keeps women at arm's length would be a massive understatement. "Last time I tried, I got accused of stalking."

"How dare she," Noah deadpans.

"Exactly. I was just—" I narrow my eyes at Noah. It was a trap.

"But Callie is different. So different. Wes, she saw us take care of business in Boston."

"I know." I duck my head and bury my hand in my hair. "It took her a minute to understand."

Because she did seem to understand at the time. And it didn't take her long.

"She barely batted an eye, which is pretty fucked up, don't you think?"

"But at the end..." I say, then see what he's getting at. "On Friday she acted differently. About what we do."

"And why do you think she acted different?"

I let silence sit between us for a moment, really thinking about his question.

"So she could break it off with me?"

"Yes. She probably wanted you to think she isn't the right person for you. Otherwise, you'd never let her go."

"She wants to go." It comes out as almost a question.

"I'd be willing to bet she's just as obsessed with you as you are with her."

I snort, then stare into the fire. Could Noah be right? Did Callie say those things to force me to let her leave? *I can't be with someone like you.*

"I love her," I say. I look at Noah. His shoulders lift and fall as he absorbs the words. Then he nods.

"I thought so."

"But it's because I love her that I need to let her go." The flames of the fire hypnotize me. "Callie wants to start over and live a different life. She was miserable being her father's daughter, and she was miserable being married to a criminal. And like it or not, I am a criminal," I whisper the last word.

"Can I tell you what I think, Wes?"

A sliver of hope cuts through the darkness of my heart.

Fuck, I want Noah to convince me there's a chance. I want that more than anything.

"You're going to anyway." I attempt to sound gruff.

"I think Callie had a rough childhood and a terrible marriage," Noah says carefully. "None of the men in her life look out for her. Not like they should."

"Yeah." I clench my fists thinking of all of them. How dare her father let her suffer with Shane? Her brother not do anything he could to help his sister? Her husband pass up a life with someone as incredible as she is?

"But then you came along, the psycho stalker serial killer that you are." Noah elbows me in the side, and I stare down at my hands. "And she's accepted every part of you from the start."

I swallow and try to breathe past my tightened chest. Yeah, it was wild she didn't react differently to my stalking and drugging and zip-tying, but—

"She liked that I was looking out for her. Protecting. That I obsessively cared about her."

"Exactly. She should've run screaming, like every other woman you've tried to date." Noah chuckles.

"But she tried to stalk me back." I can't help but smile as I think of Callie trying to break into my cabin, as if she could pull that off without me noticing. How she brought me one of her book page art hedgehogs, which sits on my mantle. Then how we stayed up the rest of the night talking and drinking tea and getting to know each other.

"Who fucking does that?" Noah shakes his head and tips the rest of his hot chocolate in his mouth.

"Calliope." Her name is precious on my lips.

Could Noah be right? Am I letting her go too easily? Maybe she does want to be with me, but she's so stuck with her previous plan she can't see that we are meant to be.

Maybe I just need to convince her to change her plan.

Because Callie Callahan is mine.

I thought that from the start. I never wanted to let her go, but I knew that I loved her too much to force her to be with me. I wanted to respect her wishes.

But maybe I really need to fight for her. Not just a battle. A full-on war.

"Wes?"

"Fuck." I jolt up and stand. "I gotta go."

"Thank fuck."

"Thank fuck what?" I turn to Noah, but my mind is already racing.

Relief is written all over Noah's face. "I kept warning you to be careful around her, and I was afraid I was the one responsible for you letting her go. And I don't think you should."

"Good thing I ignore what you say half the time."

"Good thing. What are you going to do about it now?"

"I gotta find Callie before she leaves town."

I just hope I'm not too late. I pull out my phone to figure out where she is.

CHAPTER 38

MISTAKES WERE MADE

CALLIE

I did exactly as he asked me to do, yet I think there's a good chance Shane is going to kill me.

"Fucking bitch." Shane has me duct-taped to a folding chair in the cold, dark barn, and he's pacing back and forth in front of me.

I have no idea where we are. Last thing I remember is approaching my car in the dimly lit parking garage, and then nothing.

I woke up about ten minutes ago with my hands, wrists, and mouth duct taped. There's an ache in my head that indicates Shane hit me with something to knock me out. As an aside, I much prefer Wes's less violent drugged hot chocolate.

I'm freezing, but adrenaline races through my veins as I observe this completely unhinged man. And not unhinged in a good way. Unhinged in a he-might-murder-*me* way. My whole body shakes with fear and cold, and I clench my jaw to stop my teeth from chattering.

When I saw Shane at the fight club in New York, I felt

confident, protected, furious. But that was with Wes and Noah by my side. Now it's just me and Shane, who's muttering under his breath as he continues to pace.

Where the fuck is my phone?

I concentrate on taking deep breaths through my nose. I can't think straight with my heart beating so loudly. After getting some air in my lungs, I scan my surroundings. We're inside a dark barn, the low light coming from flickering bare bulbs hanging from the barn ceiling. There are stacks of hay bales to my left along one side of the barn, and to my right is a tractor and snow plow equipment. I look over my shoulder into the dark back of the barn. I can't tell what I'm looking at. A sliver of moonlight streams in from a door behind Shane, but all I see is dark outside of the barn.

I have a feeling we're in the middle of nowhere.

My eyes settle on a pile of items by the door. My purse. A shadow of a duffel bag on the ground. A gun on top of the duffel.

Fuck.

For a second, hope surges through me as I spot my phone resting on the dirty floor next to the bag, far away, but at least here in the barn.

"Don't worry. Your phone is off. No one is finding you here." Shane strides over and reaches down to pick my phone up and hold it out to me. "Want it?" He laughs. "Nah. Not yet."

My throat tightens. Fear grips my chest. Even I know that you can't track a phone if it's powered off.

"Oh, and I took the liberty of stopping by your apartment and grabbing these." Shane walks over to the duffel bag and pulls out a blue folder. My stomach flips.

The divorce papers.

A whimper escapes my throat, and he drops them back on top of the bag.

"What's that, Cals?" Shane strides over and rips the duct tape off my mouth, the sting eliciting a gasp from me.

"What the fuck," I say in a voice so small it barely exists. Tears spill down my cheeks, and my mouth burns. "How—"

"I know how to break into an apartment, Cals. Fuck, you're stupid as shit."

"What about Jake?" And Honey Bunny. I suppress a pathetic whimper.

"In and out of the window, Cals. As easy as walking through the front door. Don't worry, no one noticed me."

My fear for my brother and rabbit morphs to despair. So Shane broke into the apartment and Jake didn't notice? Par for the course. And I bet Jake won't check on me tonight. Sure, maybe it's because of the way I blew him off earlier, but maybe it's just always how it goes with people who are supposed to love me. I'm not anyone's priority.

You know who didn't do that? Wes. In the most important moment at the fight club, Wes even chose me over his brother, the one person he's sworn to protect no matter what. I'm not proud that he did that. But it showed me he would choose me over everything else. No one's ever done that for me.

And what did I do? I said the worst thing to him that I could think of. Because if I didn't scare him away, I wouldn't have been able to leave.

I could never be with someone like you.

What did I even fucking mean? I could never be with someone who chooses me first? Who is kind and deep and gorgeous? What is wrong with me? And now here I am. In a situation that I'll probably never get out of.

My regrets come crashing over me. I wish it were Wes's zip ties on my wrists right now instead of Shane's duct tape.

Wes found Shane for me.

He protected me.

He chose me over his brother.

He made me feel like the center of his universe, not a side quest.

And I broke it off with that man.

What a fucking mistake, on so many levels.

"Fuck you, Shane." Tears well in my eyes, then spill down my face.

Shane stops pacing and strides over to me. Without a word, he raises his arm and brings the back of his hand down hard across my face, his knuckles digging into my cheek, my head whipping to one side. I can't breathe and panic as I struggle to take in air. Shane's never hit me before. Something's changed. He's changed.

He bends down in front of me, a hand on each of my thighs, leaning with his full body weight and squeezing hard. I can't help the tremor in my body, from fear and anger and cold.

"I'm not even mad that you fucked another man. Not really."

"You cheated on me all the time. You don't even *like* me." I turn my head and try not to sob. "Just let me go."

He squeezes harder and harder until fresh tears stream down my cheeks. Rage flames on his face, but also excitement. He's been waiting for me to fight back for years. Starting now is not my best decision.

"You don't get to be happy." He spits out *happy* like it's a dirty word. "Not on my watch."

"What do you want from me?" My brain is starting to clear from his hit. I gave him the money to get rid of him. To meet his divorce blackmail. So what more does he want from me?

"Oh, I want all the money, Cals."

I scrunch my face up as I try to comprehend. He thinks I'm going to give him all the money?

But then he leans in close to my ear, and for a second I'm afraid he's going to bite me. Instead, he whispers, "You see, I owed that money to Jones. Now he has it. But he wants interest. More money, more time, more of my fucking soul."

Shane stands and resumes pacing.

"What? Owed him for what?" My voice sounds like it belongs to someone else. Small and meek and inconsequential. Actually, that's an accurate description of me.

Shane spins around and steps back to me, grabbing my chin with one hand. I whimper and shut my eyes.

"You don't know anything, *Calliope*." He squeezes my chin when I try to turn away. Hatred flares inside me. How dare he use my name the way Wes does? "Jones blames me for that cocaine shipment getting seized. I owed him a whole fucking lot of money."

Oh, damn. I open my eyes. It's hard to meet Shane's intense, rage-filled gaze, but I do.

"But you gave it to him?"

"Yes! I gave him some money when I first left Portland."

"The money from our account," I say, but I don't think Shane hears me. Probably for the better.

Shane releases my chin and turns, taking long, aggressive strides, shaking his hands, scrunching his face.

"And he sent me to New York City to work off the rest of my fucking debt." Shane spits out those words, like he doesn't believe it was really his debt at all. "When he heard that your father's estate had cleared, he fucked me up. Told me I needed to be ready to get it from you when you showed up with those fuck boys of yours.”

I let out a ragged breath. I am so, utterly, completely screwed.

“And then I gave him the money from your father. But was that enough? No. It fucking wasn’t.”

“Shane—”

He rounds on me and gets right in my face.

“Shut the fuck up, Cals.” Spittle flies out of his mouth and onto my cheek.

I keep my eyes focused on a spot behind him, the dark entrance to the barn. I don’t respond. I try to sink into the chair, disappear into the dark shadows behind me. But there’s no way for me to move.

“This is your fault. This is all your fault.” His voice is dangerous, and then Shane raises his hand and slaps me across the face on the other cheek. The contact stings, and for a moment I can’t breathe, can’t comprehend what just happened. Shane must’ve been holding back all these years.

“You don’t understand anything. All you’ve done your whole life is hide from who your family is. Who *you* really are. And now look at you. Pathetic. Weak. Fragile like your fucking rabbit.”

CHAPTER 39

NOT WHERE SHE SHOULD BE

WES

"Why the fuck is she there?" Alarm bells are ringing as I stare at the blue blinking dot showing Callie on the map in my spyware app.

"Maybe you don't know everything about this woman. Maybe she's hanging out with a friend." Noah's tone is light, but I recognize an edge of concern. Like he's trying too hard to dismiss my question.

"No way." I've been tracking this woman enough over the past month to know where her usual haunts are. Besides her brother's apartment, she goes to the library, her friend's bookstore, the grocery store, that one Irish pub, and a few coffee shops within a mile or two radius of there.

So why is she at a remote location outside of Portland?

And why isn't her phone tracking? The spyware is picking up the signal of the slim tracker inside her phone case, not her phone.

"Her phone is offline," I say without looking up.

"What are you still sitting there for? Let's go."

I look up from the hay bale. My brother's standing there,

waiting. He shifts from one foot to the other, and I recognize the worry on his face.

"Where?" I ask and shoot to my feet. Suddenly the flames are too hot on my cheeks, the laughing of families too grating, the night too dark.

"To find Callie. Obviously."

"Together?"

"Lordy fuck. Yes. Just in case." Noah gestures for me to follow. "I'll drive. We can grab your car later."

"Fine." I follow Noah around the building and slip into the cab of his pickup truck. I send him a dropped pin and he connects his phone to the truck.

"Got it," he says, and Red Daisy announces the first set of directions. Once he's out of the parking lot, he floors it.

I send Callie a text, which goes unread. Unsurprising if her phone is off or dead. I click onto Gone and send her a message on that platform as well, just in case.

Maybe she's blocked me, and that's somehow interfered with the spyware? I wouldn't blame her for doing so. She knows I don't do well with boundaries.

Still, that's not what this feels like. She's in trouble. I can feel it in my bones.

I zoom into her location. The map's satellite view shows a broken-down barn next to an abandoned-looking farmhouse, surrounded by thick woods and a long, skinny lane leading to a county road.

Something is definitely wrong. She should not be there.

"Thirty minutes away. Fuck!" I smash my hand onto the dashboard. "Can't you drive faster?"

"First of all, respect Red Daisy. She didn't do anything wrong."

"Sorry, Red Daisy." I sit back in the seat, but I feel like I'm crawling out of my skin.

"Second of all, I'm doing seventy-five in a fifty-five, and getting pulled over will not help us." Noah glances at the side of my face, then at my bouncing knee. "I'll get us there in twenty. This might be nothing, Wes."

"It's not nothing." I turn to look at my brother, and he nods once.

We trust our guts. It's something we've had to learn to do over the years, and that gut instinct often saves us from trouble. Noah sometimes pushes through and ignores the warnings, but I never do.

Noah's phone dings with an alert. His forehead immediately creases, and he glances at the cupholder.

"What's the look for?" I grab Noah's device and look at the notification. It's from the same tracking software I use. Without asking permission, I enter his password and click through.

It takes me a minute to understand what I'm seeing. There's only one blinking dot on Noah's screen.

It's labeled JK.

Joe Killer.

I glance back at my phone, in my right hand, then back at his, in my left hand.

Joe Killer's red dot is blinking in the same spot as Callie's blue dot.

"Why the actual fuck is Joe Killer showing in the same location as Callie?" There's a ringing sound in my ears that makes it difficult to focus on what Noah says in response. I feel like I'm floating above myself, being taken away on a wave of adrenaline.

The truck jolts forward, and Noah swears under his breath.

He knows the assignment.

Get to Callie as soon as possible, because she's with a serial killer.

I focus on my breathing. My brother reaches over and squeezes my arm. The contact brings me back to the truck, and I fight to push the panic down. It won't help Callie.

Why did I let her walk away? I should've refused to leave her side, even when she pushed me. I should've at least stayed close and protected her. No one's *ever* protected her, and I just proved myself to be another useless man in her life who let her get hurt, when all I ever wanted to do was to keep her safe.

"Fuck!" I grind my teeth together. "Is it just some terrible coincidence that Joe Killer is targeting Callie? Did he know we were tracking him?" Even as the words come out, I know they aren't true. I can't quite make the connection. I'm almost there.

"No. It's not."

"Why is Joe Killer in Portland?" I drop my phone in my lap and clench and unclench my fists. My entire body is tingling, and I recognize it as spiked adrenaline ebbing in my veins as I fight back a full-blown panic attack.

"I have a theory." Noah's voice is low and dangerous.

"What, Noah?" I don't know how he can sound so calm when everything is falling apart. "Fucking spit it out."

"Okay. Check Shane's car location."

I click the box for Shane's car tracker on my app, and his vehicle appears all the way down in New York City, where it's supposed to be.

My brain is slowly connecting the dots. I don't want to understand what Noah apparently already does. I block it out and squeeze my eyes shut.

"And?" Noah asks.

"He's in New York." But it's not true, is it?

"His *car* is in New York."

"Noah." I push aside the cloud of denial and let the truth crash into me.

"Shane Robertson is Joe Killer," Noah says simply. The car jolts forward again as Noah pushes the pickup truck even faster.

I let out a roar, and Noah swears under his breath.

"Did you have any idea?" I'm gripping the car door, willing the vehicle to fly and get to Callie faster.

"No." Noah shakes his head.

Both of us contemplate what it means that we didn't catch on to this.

"And he's got Callie," I finish my understanding of the truth with words that drive a stake of horror and fear through my heart. Shane is Joe Killer, and he has Callie in a remote location with her phone off. "Drive faster."

Noah does.

CHAPTER 40
THE WORST KIND OF BAD

CALLIE

Shane squats in front of me. His eyes wander from my face down to my chest, where my long-sleeved shirt is taut against my breasts with my hands pulled behind my body.

I shiver in the cold barn air, struggling to swallow. He's right. I'm weak and stupid and all alone. I have no leverage. No way I can refuse this man whatever he wants.

"Now, what're we going to do? Where are your watch dogs? Not here, huh. That's a pity for you." He grins but there's no joy in it. It's a wicked smile.

My face still stings on both sides where he hit me. What is Shane capable of? Even I don't know. Fighting in the ring seems to have unleashed something even more monstrous in him. It was probably there all along, just barely contained.

And it scares the shit out of me.

Will he kill me? It certainly feels like that's where this is heading. Fuck.

"I'll give you the money." My voice comes out as a whimper, and I hate it, hate myself for the choices I've made. I couldn't control who I was born to, but I could've not married Shane. I could've divorced him years ago.

But I didn't, and here I am.

Shane reaches over and grabs my breast, squeezing hard and then twisting my nipple. I cry out and close my eyes.

"It's been a while since we fucked. Should we give it one last go before we get you logged into your bank account?"

"No, Shane." I let out a pathetic whimper. He laughs and squeezes again.

"Then again, I'm no longer interested in your dry, loose cunt. Not like your fuck boy is." He slides the finger off my chin and releases my breast with a disgusted look on his face.

A single tear escapes my right eye, followed by another and another until streams of tears run down both sides of my face. I don't want to be the kind of woman who needs saving, but I need Wes to save me. Now. My train of thought splinters as Shane walks over and picks up the divorce papers he took from my apartment.

"Let's take care of these, shall we?" Then he pulls the papers out of the folder and unceremoniously rips them in half, then in half again. He watches with a smirk as my shoulders heave with sobs.

I'll never be free of him. Never. Shane will always own me. And my always might not be very long.

Wesley, please come. I'm sorry. I want you. I need you. I love—

Then, I see a shadow moving behind him at the open door.

What the fuck?

Shane must've seen my eyes dart over his shoulder, because he spins to the doorway and pulls out a long knife that was tucked somewhere underneath his jacket. He curses and watches the entrance, his eyes flitting down to the gun on top of his bag.

"Who's here?" he spits out, shoulders raised and tense, his body in his fighting stance.

Maybe I imagined the movement. Maybe it was nothing. I take a few deep breaths. Despair threatens to drown me. I definitely imagined it.

Please save me, Wes. Please.

And as if I conjured him out of thin air, Wes steps out of the shadows.

"Hello Shane, you piece of shit." Wes's eyes flash to me, and I feel the fury radiating off him.

"He's got a knife, and a gun, Wes. There." I nod to the bag that's a few steps away.

But Wes doesn't move, just continues to stare at me, his fury at Shane dimming, replaced with concern and relief. There's more there. Anger and heat and much—

Shane takes advantage of the distraction and throws himself at Wes, knife first. Wes reacts quickly and manages to grab the wrist that has the knife, but Shane gets a powerful punch into Wes's gut. His whole body doubles over and for a second, I think he's going to fall to the ground. Shane reaches for Wes's neck in slow motion.

I gasp and struggle against my restraints, but moving only pulls the duct tape against my skin. Watching this happen is torture. What if I'm about to watch Shane kill Wes? Wes doesn't have a weapon. How could he come here without a weapon? And where's his brother?

"Fuck," I whisper, but no one pays me any mind. This is a nightmare. It was already a nightmare, but now it's even worse.

As soon as Shane gets his hand on Wes's neck, Wes comes at Shane with a fierce uppercut to the jaw, causing

Shane's head to fly back and his hand to slip. Then Wes bends Shane's wrist until he screams. The knife falls to the dirty barn floor with a dull clatter.

Wes lets Shane go, and the man stumbles back. I expect Wes to finish the job, but instead, he stands at the ready, watching the scene unfold.

Then Noah strides up from behind me and swings a baseball bat at Shane's head, making contact with his skull with a sickening thud.

Shane crumples to the ground, unconscious.

"Sorry about that. I had to get the bat from the bed of the truck."

"Fuck, took your sweet time, huh?" Wes growls.

Noah shrugs and looks down at Shane. "I wonder if he's dead?"

I let out a crazed laugh, trying to process it all. They came for me. He came.

"Calliope." Wes appears in front of me, dropping to his knees. "Are you okay?" He reaches up to cup my face with his hands, rubbing his thumbs along my sore cheeks, wiping away the tears.

I nod because there are no words.

"I'm sorry it took us so long to get to you." Wes leans around me and pulls a knife out of nowhere to cut me free of the duct tape.

It's in this moment that I realize that I'm completely in love with Wesley Winters.

CHAPTER 41

SOME ANSWERS

WES

My rage fades as I touch Callie's face. I stare into her eyes, searching for answers.

"Did he hurt you?" I force out. Her eyes are wide, her cheeks wet with tears.

Fuck, I love this woman so much.

Behind us, Noah is loudly securing an unconscious Shane with strips of duct tape. Without looking, I'd guess he's targeting the ankles, wrists, and mouth.

"Not really." But she flinches when my thumbs skim her cheekbones.

"Callie. Your cheeks are red." There's a faint bruise forming in the middle of one cheek, and—oh fuck no—a *handprint* on the other side. Black spots start on the edge of my vision. "Callie."

"Fine. He hit me." Her eyelids flutter.

I completely black out for a second, the rage taking over, and when I come back to my body, I'm kicking Shane viciously in the ribs. Noah pulls me away from him half-heartedly.

"No, Wes. No killing him." But he doesn't sound super concerned, and he probably wouldn't fight me too hard if I shrugged him off and kept kicking.

"Yet." I grind my teeth together and settle. Shane's awake now, and he's whimpering like the pathetic scumbag bully he is. "You did not hit him hard enough with the bat."

"I know, sorry. Maybe later." Noah's voice is soothing.

"Wesley," Callie says from behind me.

With one last lethal glare at Shane, I turn back to Callie.

"I'm going to rip his throat out for hurting you." This man is as good as dead. I'm going to kill him with my own two fucking hands.

Shane makes gasping sounds through his taped mouth. I hope he's having trouble breathing.

"Guess he's not dead," Noah notes with disappointment in his voice. Then Shane quiets after a thud and the sound of duct tape ripping resumes.

"How did you know to look for me?" Callie asks, sounding stronger than before as she rubs her red skin.

"I needed to talk to you." I shrug out of my jacket and drape it over her shoulders, holding it open so she can slip her arms in, then tugging it around her. "After the pie competition—I got second place, by the way—Noah made me realize I shouldn't have let you go. And when I checked your location..." I stop speaking to see how she reacts to me continuing to track her. She nods for me to continue. "I realized you weren't where you should be."

"Second place, huh." Callie attempts a small smile. "Sorry about that."

"It's not important." I shake my head and pull off my beanie, tucking it onto her head.

"Thank you," she says. Her eyes flutter as I lean forward and place a soft kiss on each side of her face. She sighs softly.

"Done," Noah says from behind me. "He's coming with us."

"So you shouldn't have let me go, huh?" Callie's gaze flits from my eyes to my lips. I can't fully read her expression, but it's definitely sad.

"Yes. We need to talk, but not here." All I want to do is tell her I love her and kiss her, but we have some pretty fucking urgent things to take care of first.

"Wes." Callie's voice catches. "I wanted you to come get me. But I thought—after all the horrible things I said to you —I thought you'd respect my wishes and leave me alone..." she trails off.

I offer her a hand and gently pull her to standing. Her knees buckle, but I wrap my arms around her waist, pulling her against me. Her mouth trembles, and I run a finger along her lower lip while still supporting her with my other arm. The words she said to me have run through my mind like a ticker tape ever since. *I could never be with someone like you. You need to leave me alone. This is over.*

Maybe she didn't really mean them. Fuck, it's hard to control the surge of hope that almost knocks me over.

"I am not a noble person, Calliope. I realized I couldn't let you go, even though you told me to. I know that's fucked up. I know that's not what most women want. But I need to do everything I can to convince you to stay with me before I let you go."

Callie takes a sharp breath, and her gaze dances between my eyes.

"I hate to interrupt," Noah says in the same calm tone as before.

"Do you, though?" I don't look away from Callie.

"Yeah, well, we have a dude—unconscious, again, but still—duct-taped on the barn floor, so maybe you can help me get him into the truck and then move this conversation to my cabin?"

"I thought he was awake?"

"Well. My baseball bat took care of that."

"Ouch." Callie peers around me at Shane, who is indeed once again knocked out.

After we get Shane loaded into the bed of the truck and pull the cover down, I sit in the front with Callie nestled against me for the drive to Lake Savage.

My panic comes in waves as Noah weaves his way out of the long, overgrown lane and turns on the radio. No one would've found Callie, and I shudder to think of what Shane was planning.

What Joe Killer was planning.

He was going to fucking kill her.

"Hey. Are you okay?" Callie slides her hand on my thigh and looks up at me. "Are you shaking?"

"I'm okay," I say, but it's clearly a lie. All the adrenaline of the past hour is leaving my system, and I feel weak. She's right, the hand not gripping her to me is shaking. I open and close my fist to try to get the blood flowing.

"Wesley, you got there in time." She lifts her hand and slides it onto my cheek, pulling my face down so she can press a soft kiss on my mouth.

I take a ragged breath in, our lips still touching. So much could've happened if we'd been a few minutes later. If I hadn't checked her location at all. If Noah hadn't kicked me in the ass to go tell her how I feel. Even if Ruth Roy hadn't won the pie competition and I was busy with the winner's photo shoot or schmoozing with the judges.

"Thank you," Callie whispers.

"There's nothing to thank me for." I press my forehead against hers.

"There's more that you don't know." I have my hands around Callie's waist, and we're standing in Noah's oversized garage as the door descends. He's run inside to prepare the room for Shane, who is currently kicking around in the bed of the truck, his muffled shouts music to my ears. I'm tempted to use the baseball bat on him myself since I didn't get to earlier, but Noah gave me strict orders to wait for him to come back out.

"Like what?" Callie's forehead furrows

I reach down and tuck a stray chunk of dark hair behind her ear. How the hell am I going to tell her what Noah and I figured out? She knows her ex is a fucked-up human being, but I don't think she has any clue just how much.

"Callie—" I start, but Noah appears at the door to the house.

"Let's get this piece of shit out of Red Daisy. She hates him." Noah walks around to the back of his truck. "Callie, can you hold the door open for us while we get him inside? We're pretty isolated out here, but I don't really want to give him a chance to cause too much of a ruckus. We respect our neighbors in Lake Savage."

"Sure." Callie's mouth twitches, and I'm impressed my brother almost made her smile.

Noah and I walk around and pull back the truck bed cover. Shane's face is red with fury. Not only is he still duct-taped all over, but Noah secured him in the truck bed with tight ratchet straps so he wouldn't roll around or bounce up and out of the truck. Shane's got a huge knot forming on the top of his head where Noah got him with the baseball bat—twice—and he winces as he struggles against the duct tape. His ribs probably don't feel great from when I kicked him repeatedly and the straps are holding him down.

He's having a bad day.

Noah unhooks the straps, and we pull Shane to the edge of the truck bed by his feet. I grab his feet, double checking the duct tape is holding strong, and Noah takes his arms. We pull him out of the trunk and accidentally drop him face down on the cold, hard garage floor. Oops. Shane screams—muffled by the duct tape, of course—and kicks his connected feet. I snort a laugh and look up at Noah, who is also smirking.

We are so fucked up.

I shoot a look at Callie, who has her arms crossed and is staring at Shane on the ground, throwing daggers with her eyes. She's absolutely stunning when she's angry. Then I take in the bruise on her cheek that's darker than it was in the barn, and I give Shane another sharp kick in the abdomen. Her eyes flash to mine. I shrug.

"Ouch. I really wouldn't want to get kicked by you," Noah notes.

"I promise not to kick you."

I flip Shane over—don't want to be mean and drag him face down—and groan at the mess that is his bloody nose.

"For fuck's sake," Noah grumbles. "Let's not get blood on my carpet inside, okay?"

"Noted," I say. We grab his legs and drag him through the garage and up the single step into the cabin. He shrieks when his head bounces on the step. Oops again!

"Hey—" Callie follows us in with her bag from the truck and shuts the door behind her.

"Can you lock that?" Noah asks.

"So, what are we doing with him here?" She locks the

door as we drop Shane's feet and toss our jackets on the coat rack.

"We'll explain it all soon." I hold up a finger to have her wait, then jog to Noah's kitchen and turn the oven on to preheat at 350 degrees. I practically squeal with excitement when I open Noah's freezer and locate two pies: a mince pie and an apple pie. We need a snack, obviously.

The mince pie is wrapped in layers of red plastic, and even though I spelled out *no* on the top crust in flakey, delicious dough, I also added black X marks on the plastic wrap and tin since these live at Noah's cabin.

I unwrap the pies and pull out a tray from Noah's bottom cabinet, then place the pies onto the tray and slide it into the oven. It won't hurt them to be inside as the oven preheats. I set my timer for an hour and return to Callie, who's standing in the family room watching me with a shocked expression. Noah's got Shane halfway down the hallway to his special room.

"Did you just put a pie in the oven?"

"Two pies, actually. One's a snack for us—the apple pie —and one's a snack for Shane. A mince pie."

"I love mince pie."

"Jesus fuck. Of course you do." I swear under my breath and glance to the ceiling. "Listen to me: You can never have these mince pies."

"Why?" She scoffs and plants her hands on her hips.

"Damn, Wes." Noah chuckles and calls from down the hall. "You found the one woman who loves mince pie?"

"This mince pie is not for eating," I try to explain, keeping my voice down so Shane doesn't hear.

"You drug your mince pies?" Her eyes widen. "Yeah, of course you do."

"Mmmmm let's go with that." I cringe. Callie doesn't ask follow up questions, thankfully.

"Come on. We've got things to discuss." Noah calls.

I grab Callie's hand, and we watch Noah pull Shane feet-first into the room with only the smallest of bumps on his head on the doorframe. My brother's restraint is impressive. Once inside, I help Noah lift Shane up and secure him to a heavy chair in the middle of the room. Duct tape is child's play, and I won't tarnish my love for zip ties by using them, so Noah pulls out handcuffs and takes care of Shane's ankles and wrists. Our prisoner's eyes are wide and crazed as he looks between the three of us, grunting and whimpering and trying to say something.

The room is bright from recessed lighting in the ceiling, but no daylight gets in. Noah did a ton of work sound-proofing this room by sealing the window and covering it with black-out curtains, adding an extra layer of drywall all around, and installing heavy-duty and easy-to-clean floors. The door to the room is thick and seals completely, plus there are multiple locks on both the inside and the outside of the door. No one from the outside would be able to hear a thing that's happening in here, which has proven unfortunate for more than one person.

This room should terrify anyone not on Noah's good side.

"Shane told me he fucked up a cocaine shipment and owed shitloads of money to Jones." Callie crosses her arms and glares at him. I love seeing her confidence come back now that her torturer is handcuffed to my brother's murder chair. "And Jones demanded more money. Not that it excuses what he did, but it at least explains it a bit."

Shane screams under the duct tape. Not sure why he cares that she's telling his secrets, but he seems to.

"No excuse." I shake my head. "But there's more to the

story. This is going to be hard to hear." I turn to Callie and put my hands on her biceps. "We're pretty sure that Shane is not only the asshole who stole your mother's ring and withheld a divorce from you to scam you out of your father's inheritance and probably planned to kill you just now, but we think that Shane is also Joe Killer."

Callie looks at me, confused, as she processes what I just shared. That information would be traumatic for anyone to hear about their spouse, even a soon-to-be ex. Her face scrunches as she tries to understand.

"The—the guy you were looking for in New York?" She looks at Noah, who nods. "The one who's killed a bunch of homeless girls?"

"Yeah."

Callie's face drains of all color as she turns to Shane, pulling out of my grasp. Shane's shouting intensifies, and he looks even angrier than before. He makes eye contact with Callie and shakes his head violently.

"While you were with Shane at the diner on Friday, Noah was busy getting a tracker on Joe Killer's car."

"Okay. And you also got a tracker on Shane's car the night before, right?" Callie looks back and forth between us. I can almost hear her brain working and making connections, but something's stopping her from connecting the dots, just like what happened to me. Logic and sanity, probably.

"Yeah. That car is currently parked a few blocks away from the fight club in New York City." Noah taps on his phone, then holds it up showing the tracking app and a blue dot blinking to indicate the location of Shane's car.

His *other* car.

"Okay. But—how does that make him Joe Killer??"

"Because he's driving Joe Killer's car," I say. "When we were driving here, we knew Joe Killer had you. Shane must have two cars. He uses one as Joe Killer, and one as himself." I reach over and take Callie's hand. We all ignore Shane freaking out a few feet away in the chair.

"He was going to kill me," she says with horrified wonder. "Which I knew back in the barn, I guess... he was going to either get me to transfer him the money and then kill me, or just kill me and claim the money as my spouse."

"Probably," Noah says with a casual nod.

We're all silent for a moment. I stare at Callie and wait for her to process. Shane struggles in the background, and I'm really tempted by the baseball bat and pie back in the kitchen.

"Are you okay, Calliope?" I ask quietly.

She shakes her head and crosses her arms over her chest.

"I think it should be up to you what happens next," Noah says. "And that should be that he dies."

"No way." I shake my head and glare at my brother. "We can't put that on Callie. We already know what we do with men like him."

"He's still technically my husband," Callie says, and both Noah and I turn to her. "I should get to decide."

I squint my eyes shut for a beat. I can't let her take this burden on. She doesn't want this. She said it a million times. We can't turn her into a murderer. She didn't want this life.

I need to protect her from this.

"Shut the fuck up!" I growl at Shane, who hasn't stopped making noise. Jesus, he's annoying as shit.

"Why don't we discuss it back in the kitchen?" Noah gestures out of the room. "I don't need to hear this nonsense."

CHAPTER 42

MINCE PIE

CALLIE

S hane's a serial killer.

All these years I've been married to a murderer. And then, just as I'm trying to escape the criminal world, I go ahead and fall in love with a serial killer.

Shane kills women and girls. The worst kind of criminal. But Wes is a different type of serial killer. He kills bad guys like Shane. And yeah, I hear myself trying to justify Wes's actions. Maybe I shouldn't. Maybe I should stick to my plan to start over. Finish whatever the fuck is happening here at Noah's cabin and then leave.

But there's no way I'm doing that.

I love Wes.

I'm in love with him.

Wes leads me to the sofa in the family room and sinks down next to me on the comfortable cushions.

"How do you like your tea?" Noah asks from the kitchen, clicking his kettle on. His cabin setup is different from Wes's. There are nooks and crannies and hallways leading off the main kitchen and family room area. This cabin is bigger and quirkier than Wes's more straightforward two-bedroom square floor plan.

"Milk and two sugars," Wes answers for me. I can't even manage a thank you when Noah hands me a steaming mug of tea a few minutes later. I look into the milky liquid and sip gratefully, the burn on my tongue a reminder that this is all real. Noah settles on the single chair next to the coach, presumably waiting for me to say something.

"You're sure he's Joe Killer?" I glance between Wes and Noah.

"Yes." Noah presses his lips together and furrows his brow.

"Noah doesn't make mistakes about things like this." Wes stares at me intently. "Callie, we got here as fast as we could. I'm sorry it wasn't faster."

"You got there in time," I say. He came for me. I begged the universe to send Wes to save me, and he appeared. I'd be dead if he hadn't come to that barn when he did.

The way he looks at me. The times he's saved me. Chosen me.

I should never have sent him away.

Because I think this man might love me like I love him.

I'm getting ahead of myself, and also, I don't want to think about the implications for my future if I decide I want to be with Wes. The way my entire life plan is sinking to the bottom of the frozen lake.

Before any of those conversations can take place, we need to deal with the man duct-taped and secured to a chair in Noah's creepy murder room.

"Joe Killer's murders have gotten more frequent. A year ago, it was once every three months. Six months ago, it was up to every other month. And the past six weeks, it's almost one a week. Which is why I've been so anxious to get things moving." Noah gives a pointed look at his brother.

"That's around when Shane moved to NYC." My stomach drops out as Noah moves to sit on the other side of me with his laptop and points at a map of New York City, indicating where Shane was living and where the fight club is, then where bodies have been found over the past year.

It basically forms a circle around Shane's apartment.

"How'd you know where to look for Joe Killer's car?"

"Scorpion," Noah says, and when I give him a confused look, he continues. "I have a contact online who drops me tips." Noah shrugs.

Quiet descends on our weird little trio for a few beats. I get caught up in memories of the last year. How often did Shane disappear, and I assumed it was a work trip, but he was off murdering some poor homeless girl?

"He'd go away on business," I hear myself say. "It was supposed to be for my dad or stupid fucking Jones." I shake my head. "It became more frequent."

"It's a newish fight club." Wes shrugs. "He probably was going to New York to help set things up even before he left town."

Noah slams his laptop shut and stands, heading back to the kitchen with it. Wes puts his arm around my shoulders and squeezes.

"You okay?"

"I guess."

I lean my head onto his shoulder. He's warm and comforting, and I feel so damn safe with him. Like I'm home. The delicious smell of pies helps the feeling settle deep inside me. Will I ever smell pie and not think of Wes?

We all exist in silence for a few minutes, Noah doing something on his laptop in the kitchen, Wes and I cuddled on the couch together. I should feel bad that Shane is tied up in the other room, not having a very good day, but I simply don't. He was probably going to kill me and steal the rest of my share of my father's estate. Maybe he was getting extorted by Jones. But I was his wife, and he was more than happy to extort me.

Wes gets up, collects all of our mugs, and pours us whiskey in new glasses. Then he works on getting the fire going. When he finally settles back down next to me, I turn and lay my legs on his lap. At the kitchen counter, Noah scrolls through Shane's phone. Once in a while he swears under his breath, but I just don't want to know what he's finding.

A timer goes off.

"Can you get those?" Wes calls to Noah. I snuggle closer to him as the whiskey warms my belly, Wes's solid form and the cozy fire comforting me in a way nothing else ever has. There are so many conversations to be had, but for now I'm taking this moment by moment.

"Yup." Next come the sounds of Noah opening a drawer, then the oven, then letting the oven door click shut and turning it off with a beep.

"Calliope?" Wes says softly, kissing the top of my head so sweetly. "What are you thinking?"

"I'm thinking I need to be the one to decide what to do about Shane. I just... get him more. There's more to Shane than what you've seen." Fuck, I hate how defensive I sound, but I'm working through this all in real time. I loved him once, long ago, and I'm trying to understand how that man became a vicious serial killer.

Wes stiffens next to me. "How so?"

"I should've divorced him years ago. That much is true. But when I think about how he was when we first got together... he was so vulnerable. So hurt." I glance at Noah in the kitchen. He's closed his laptop and is leaning on the counter watching me, the whiskey glass clutched in one hand.

"We've all been hurt, sweetheart," Wes says softly, rubbing my shins on his lap.

"I know." I run a finger from his neck to his belly, feeling his muscles shift under my touch. "He had a total shit childhood. His father had him in the business from the time he could read, practically. And when he was murdered, Shane totally fell apart."

How he was raised wasn't his fault. The fact that his father was murdered wasn't his fault. The adult he became? That part was.

Wes nods. He's heard this before.

"Murdered, huh? Who killed him?" Noah walks toward us, leans against a pillar, and crosses his arms.

"He didn't talk much about it. Something about how his father messed up an assignment, and someone killed him for it." I breathe out. "He even changed his name once he came to live with my father. Shane used to be James Shane Sorentino, if you believe it." I huff. That name never seemed to fit Shane. He'd always gone by Shane to his family and close friends, so he only had to get used to his new last name, Robertson.

The men are quiet. I rest my head on the back of the couch and scoot as close to Wes as I can get without climbing in his lap. I shut my eyes.

"Which is probably why when he messed up the drug shipment, it pushed him over the edge." I'm almost sleepy, which is wild considering the current situation. But I'm freaking exhausted, and warm next to Wes. "Shane was probably afraid he'd end up like his father."

"How'd his father die?" Wes asks in a weird voice.

"Beaten with a shovel, which is brutal." I shiver and open my eyes to stare at the floor of the cabin. Shane told me the whole story once, and that was enough. Those were dark days, But for better or for worse—definitely worse—Shane and I found each other.

"When, exactly, was his father murdered?" Noah's voice is tight, like it's being forced out of clenched teeth.

"Like ten years ago?" I open my eyes and look at Wes, who is staring at Noah with an odd expression. I sit up straight but leave my legs on Wes. "Why are you guys being so weird? Weirder, I guess, since you're already serial killers." I whisper the last two words to be funny, but neither of them even looks at me.

"Calliope, do you remember anything else about that time? Details about his father's murder besides the shovel?"

"Tell us everything. Anything," Noah says.

Why is my heartbeat speeding up? There's something about their calm voices that is sharp and dangerous.

"Uh, they found his father in the woods about an hour away from Portland." I scrunch my face and let myself remember. "His car was ditched nearby, and they never figured out who did it. I don't know anything else."

"What was Shane's father's name?" Noah steps close to the couch and sits on the coffee table, elbows on his thighs, staring intently at me.

"Sammy Sorentino."

Wes takes a sharp breath.

"Do you think?" Noah says earnestly to Wes.

"I do." Wes nods.

I swing my legs off Wes and sit on the edge of the couch cushion. What the fuck is this about? Can this night get any more fucked up?

"What's going on?" A deep sense of dread spreads from my center, like poison rot seeping into the earth around a beautiful field of purple flowers.

I almost don't want them to answer.

"I think Shane's father killed our parents, then he raped and killed our little sister," Noah says while looking at his brother. "Ivy. Shane's dad raped and killed Ivy."

"No," I say. A whimper comes out of me involuntarily. It doesn't even sound like me.

"And that would mean—" Wes starts.

"You killed Shane's dad," I finish in a whisper.

CHAPTER 43
MORE ANSWERS
WES

This just got so much more fucking messy.

Callie's shaking her head. Her face has lost any trace of color, and she keeps glancing back and forth between me and Noah.

I know what Noah's thinking. My brother is clenching and unclenching his fists and trying to contain his emotions, the primary of which is likely rage. He doesn't give a shit that we killed the father of the man tied up in his back room. He cares that the man tied up in his back room is the son of the man who murdered our family.

He also likely doesn't care that he's the one who suggested letting Callie decide Shane's fate, because I know my brother, and Noah doesn't want to let that man leave here alive.

"Shane didn't kill them," I say to Noah, working hard to control the rage flowing in my own veins. A consistent thing in all the police reports is that it was a single person who broke into our family's home.

"Nope. But he sure killed a bunch of women since." Noah's furious. "He might as well have."

"You are correct. But let's think this through." I'm not sure what there is to really think through, and I say nothing to kick off *thinking through.*

Shane might not have killed our family, but he's an awful person, just like his father. He targets homeless girls and young women. Young, vulnerable, and with no one to look out for them.

He has no right to take their lives away, just like his father had no right to rape and murder Ivy.

"What are we going to do?" Callie asks, her eyes wide with a mixture of fear and horror. I wish I could whisk her away from this situation so she doesn't have to witness or be involved in what happens next.

Should she have a say? Part of me screams no. I need to protect her from any responsibility in the crimes that are currently occurring and the ones that might occur in the future.

But the other part of me says she has every right to be here.

With this new information, the rules have changed. I know it. Noah knows it. And by the look on her face, Callie knows, too. The entire game has changed now that we know who Shane's father was.

"Shane doesn't deserve to die for what his father did." I look at Noah as I finally come up with something to say. "But he might for what he's done since."

"Might? Of course he deserves to die. How can we let someone like him go? He's exactly the kind of scumbag we try to eliminate. He killed our father. Our mother. *Ivy.*" Noah's eyes are wide and feral.

That was all true even before we found out about Shane's

connection with our family's murder. But we brought him here because he's Joe Killer, not Sammy Sorentino's son.

"Shane didn't kill Ivy," I correct. I'm not very convincing. "We should punish him for his own crimes."

"Hello? Do I no longer have a say in this?"

Noah flicks his gaze to Callie, eyes immediately softer. He nods to me, and it's a relief.

"Callie." I turn to her, the woman I love. I have to tell her how I feel before we make a decision about this. Because maybe it'll be too late once Shane's fate is decided. She might not want to hear a thing I have to say.

I memorize her face. Those few freckles across her nose. Wild, long dark hair tucked behind her ears. Those dark eyes.

This woman deserves all the protection in the world.

Please, let me be the one to protect her.

"Wes." She looks cautious.

"I think you should let Noah and I take care of this situation without your involvement. You can drive away right now in Noah's truck—"

"Hey! No one drives Red Daisy," Noah cuts in.

"Shut up, Noah." And he does. "You don't want this life. You don't want to make a decision about a man living or dying. Let me send you away. Then we can talk later. Tomorrow. And pretend this never happened."

"No, Wes." Callie shakes her head and watches me with a pained expression.

"You guys need a minute. I'll come back out in a few." Noah backs away from us into the kitchen, but I keep my attention strictly on Callie.

I reach for her hands, which she gives me. Maybe how I feel will matter to her, maybe it won't. But it might be too late if I wait. I squeeze her hands to get her attention.

"I just don't know, Wes." She turns her face up to me, her eyes wide and innocent and full of emotion.

I shake my head. "Forget about Shane for a second."

"Okay." She nods, although I'm not sure she'll be able to do it.

"This might not seem like the best time, but I also feel like it's important I say it now." Noah's in the kitchen making some noise, but I ignore him. He's probably slicing pie.

"Say what, Wesley?" Her expression is clear of pain for the moment.

"You are like no woman I've ever met before." I search her face and sigh when a ghost of a smile appears. "I've never had to hide who I am with you. You never gave me that look —the one of fear or disgust or confusion. You were never freaked out by the way I kept track of you."

"You made me feel safe," she says, her voice so soft. Now it's my turn to smile, and I lift my hands to her face, cupping her jaw.

"All I want to do is protect you. From everything. I'd tuck you in my pocket and carry you around if I could."

She huffs a sweet laugh, but her eyes are filling with tears. That can't be a good sign. Or is it? Who fucking knows. I've never been good at any of this.

"I'd burn the world down for you, Calliope. Do you know that?"

"I think I do." She nods.

"Some might say I stalked you—and I don't condone stalking—"

Now she fully laughs. Glad she finds me entertaining? Fuck. But I can't help but smile with her.

"At least you're good at it. I was the worst stalker ever."

"Being good at stalking isn't something to be proud of." I

run a thumb over her bottom lip, and she takes a ragged breath.

"You made it fun." Her mouth turns up in a sad smile. I love her smile, but hate that I'm making her sad.

"You played along. You're perfect." I run a hand down her long locks.

"I'm not. I'm a mess."

"You're perfect for me, Calliope. I love you. I'm in love with you. I think I was from the first time I found you trying to spy on me from the woods in the middle of a snowstorm in a bright pink parka."

Now the tears spill out of her eyes and down her cheeks as she stares at me with an intensity I've never seen before. I swipe the wetness from her face before pulling her arms up so she can wrap them around my neck. She moves her body so she's straddling me on the couch.

This feeling of her in my arms. I thought I'd never feel it again. And maybe this is the last time. I don't know. But telling her the truth about how I feel? I might not get right from wrong like the average person, but this is the right thing to do.

"You don't have to say anything back. But I wanted to tell you all of this before the rest of today unfolds. After tonight, things might be different. You might feel differently about me."

She nods and presses her lips together.

"But to make it absolutely clear: I love you. I'm in love with you. I want you in my life in whatever way I can have you. In an ideal world, you move into my cabin immediately, and we take care of Honey Bunny and Sir Fluffy—I think they could be friends, maybe, but I'm a little nervous your giant rabbit will eat my cat—and bake pies and drink hot choco-late. You can get a job in Lake Savage. Or Portland. Or whatever you want to do. We can turn the guest room into your book page art space. I'll keep doing what I've been doing and we'll live happily ever fucking after."

"Oh my god, Wes." Another tear escapes from the corner of her eye. "I can't believe—"

Both of us turn toward a loud shout coming from down the hallway inside the room where Shane is. My eyes dart to the kitchen counter where the pies are. I expect to see Noah, two pies, a stack of plates, and maybe even a few slices of apple pie served.

What I see is close to that, but not quite right.

No Noah. No mince pie.

"Shit." I drop my hands from Callie's face and lift her off my lap. I stand and stride to the kitchen counter.

"What? Wes?" Callie's behind me in an instant, not understanding what I just realized.

"He gave him mince pie."

CHAPTER 44

A BIG DECISION

CALLIE

We dart into the murder room, and my brain scans the space to understand what's happening. I flinch as the smell of the room hits me, which I soon realize is Shane's vomit. He's still handcuffed to the chair in front of me, looking like he's having way less fun than the last time *I* was tied up.

I gag and cover my mouth and nose.

"Callie, thank god," Shane says, hair around his face sweaty. He looks like shit. Wes swears softly beside me.

"Did you give him the mince pie?" Wes asks Noah, like he's speaking to a child who did something a bit naughty.

"He deserves to die." Noah answers Wes's question, but looks at me, almost apologetically. "I know originally I was for letting you decide, but that was before I had all the information. I couldn't let you choose to release him without consequence."

"Callie," Shane begs, but his voice is weak.

"Oh," I say, glancing between Shane and Noah.

"For fuck's sake, Noah," Wes growls.

"I'm not sorry. This is the right thing to do for so many reasons."

I scan Shane from head to toe. He's… definitely not doing great. I search my soul for how I really feel about that. Do I want him to die because of everything he's done? Or do I want to forgive him and move on with my life with a clear conscious? And if it's the first one, what does that say about me as a human being?

"Cals. Please. After all we've been through."

I let his words sink in. This is a man I once loved, or at least thought I did. I married him. I felt deep empathy for Shane over the death of his father, as it reminded me of my grief for my mother. I touch my mom's emerald ring and spin it on my finger. Shane and I were a team at the beginning, however briefly.

I search and search. But I feel nothing positive for Shane anymore. There's not a shred of empathy or sympathy inside me. Does that mean something's wrong with me? Shouldn't I care? Even if I don't love him anymore, I should feel something, right?

And I do. There's something there. But it's not anything good.

"You are a terrible person." I step forward and cock my head to the side. I sound calm. Too calm. Maybe a truly good person wouldn't be this emotionless while watching her husband suffer. But if I've learned anything over the past month, there's a pretty big gray area when it comes to what makes a person good or bad.

"Wh-what?" Shane says with confusion on his face. Noah snorts.

"Shut up," Wes hisses at Noah.

"What?" Noah's the picture of innocence as Wes gives him a firm head shake.

"No, Cals." Shane scrunches his face. "I mean, yeah, I know, I've done some bad things, but I don't deserve this." Some kind of seizure seems to take over, and Shane's face is frozen for thirty seconds.

"Is the amount he ate fatal?" I turn to Wes for an answer. His eyes dart to the plate, where there's what looks like a quarter of the small pie gone.

"Probably."

Shane whimpers. "I knew that pie was fucked up! There was something disgusting about it. What's wrong with you people?"

"Hey," Wes says, looking wounded. "My mince pie is not disgusting."

"Did you think I was giving you a little treat?" Noah, arms crossed and shaking his head, glares at Shane. "And if it was so *disgusting*, why'd you keep eating it?"

"I was hungry," Shane says in a whiny voice.

"Is there a way to counteract the poison?" I ask.

Wes glances at Shane, who's looking more fucked up by the second. His face has gotten redder, and there's a bit of foam at the corners of his mouth. Fucking gross. I look back at Wes.

"There's an antidote of sorts." Wes maintains eye contact with me while the information sinks in. "It could probably save him. Maybe. If you wanted to."

"Please. Please! Can I have it?" Shane appears to be having trouble breathing, but finds some energy to beg, his eyes going from me to Wes. He definitely seems to know better than to look to Noah for help.

"Your father killed our parents and our little sister." Noah sends Shane a death glare. "You don't deserve an antidote."

To his credit, Shane stops begging and his eyes bug out,

making him look even freakier than he already does with the poison coursing through his veins.

"Come on," he says—although it's hard to tell with the slurring—as if he doesn't believe Noah's words.

He's dying. And now, there's a battle going on inside me. If I were really looking to leave a criminal life behind for good, I should beg Noah to let Wes save Shane. Or at least try to.

I want to feel bad. I want to *want* to stop it.

Maybe Noah wouldn't let me. But the fact that I don't even want to? Wes is staring at me with a deeply concerned expression.

"Ivy was fourteen years old." Noah's voice cracks. He uncrosses his arms and runs one hand down his face, rubbing his eyes under his glasses. "Your father came into our house and shot our father. Then our mother, who was next to him in bed. Then he went into our sister's bedroom. He... assaulted her, then shot her in her bed while she begged and cried. Why would he do that? Why didn't he leave her alone? She was a little girl." Noah takes a step forward. "Did you know what he did?"

"Of course he didn't know," I say, but when I look back at Shane, he's got an actual remorseful look on his face. There's clarity there. For how much longer, I'm not sure.

"I told him not to do it." Shane's eyes shut for a few seconds. "He killed your parents. That was supposed to be it. Then he heard crying and realized there was a girl there, hiding."

"How do you know exactly what happened?" I whisper.

"I was there."

I let out a half-cry and cover my mouth. He knew. All along, Shane knew. He knew what his dad did because *he was there*. And all those deep conversations we had, all that bonding… he wasn't telling me the full truth about what happened.

"I tried to get him to leave, but he wouldn't." Shane seems to fade out, then back in. "And then my father got killed for it." His voice cracks. "I hated her for that. Your sister. If she'd just stayed quiet, she'd still be alive, and so would my father."

Noah steps forward and punches Shane in the face. His head whips backward. A gasp escapes my mouth, and I step toward Wes. He drapes his arm around my shoulders and pulls me against him.

"I'm so sorry," Wes says to me, kissing the top of my head.

I look up at him, incredulous. "Why are you sorry? I'm sorry. For you and for Noah and for Ivy." The two of them carry this pain around every day of their lives. I don't know how they manage it.

"We killed your father." Noah's standing in front of Shane. He bends down, his palms resting on his thighs, so he can look right into Shane's face. Then Noah slaps him again to make sure he's awake. "Your father was our first, you know. The first horrible man we rid the world of."

"What?" Shane shakes his head, his eyes darting around the room, appearing to have trouble focusing. They finally land on me. "Cals?"

"I'm not going to save you, Shane." I press my lips together and gather my thoughts. He was devastated about his father's death. But he must've known his father deserved it. And all the horrible things he's done since? "You don't deserve it."

I think about how he hit me in the barn just a few hours ago. How he grabbed my breast and threatened to assault me. How he did much worse to a dozen or more girls before today, none of whom had someone like Wes to save them.

I'm not going to save him.

It's over for Shane.

"You tried to blackmail me out of my father's inheritance. Yeah, I get it was partly because of Jones. But you could've talked to me. Instead, you chose violence. You chose this."

I saw it in his eyes in the barn. They were black. Soulless. I would be dead right now if it weren't for Wes.

"No," Shane whimpers, but it sounds more like nah than no, probably because of the poison that's working hard to kill him.

"I don't forgive you for what you did to me. You didn't protect me. You actively tried to harm me in every way. And you would've done worse if it weren't for Wes and Noah."

His eyes plead with me. I'm not sure he can even talk anymore. His face is turning an unnatural red. Again, I look for any part of me that cares.

I can't find it.

Once again, I realize I don't think Wes and Noah are bad. I think they're ridding the world of horrible people. And while that isn't the kind of justice that's widely accepted, there is a sweet satisfaction to it. Noah and Wes are the judge, jury, and executioners, and I trust them.

"We found his copy of the divorce papers in the car," Noah says, his voice calm.

I startle at the statement and stare at Noah, then Wes.

"It's true." Wes nods. "You can still file it."

"Where is his car?"

"We'll take care of that." Noah says. "No one will find it. We'll make it look like he took off."

I'm done with Shane. I want to move on with my life.

And I want to do it with Wes. I don't care if that makes me good or bad or somewhere in the middle.

I turn toward Wes and place my palms on his chest, marveling at the feel of his hard chest beneath my hands. "Wesley, when I first met you, I was hurt and timid and angry. I didn't want anything to do with a man ever again. But almost immediately, you started chipping away at the wall I'd built around me."

Wes takes my wrists in his hands, running his thumbs on the sensitive insides. Electricity tingles down my arms and to my core. I marvel at the fact that every time he touches me, my body reacts with joy and desire and love.

"I can't believe you could make me laugh. I was a hot mess, searching for Shane, mourning my father, lost in every way. I hadn't smiled in months. But you—you made me play." I chuckle. "And I could do it and feel safe. I could rest. Even when I was in my bed at Jake's apartment, I knew you were protecting me. You were probably watching me."

"I was definitely watching you. But I will do a better job of it from now on."

"That's fucking hot." I feel my cheeks heat as Wes pulls my arms around his neck and slides his hands along my waist.

"Fucking hell," Noah mutters behind us. "You two really are made for each other because that's creepy as fuck."

"Spoken like a true serial killer," Wes says, his eyes locked with mine. "Keep talking, Calliope."

"Knowing you were always there in some way made me feel the safest I've ever felt in my entire life. And I only wanted to be in your arms. When I sent you away in New York, I've never felt worse. I thought it was for the best, but every moment after that was worse than the last, up until the moment you found me at the barn. Walking away from you was the biggest mistake of my life."

"Fuck, Callie," Wes reaches down and pulls me up against him by my ass. I wrap my legs around his waist and link my hands around his neck.

"I love you, Wesley. I'm so fucking in love with you."

"You love me?" His eyes are wide with wonder. I nod vigorously. "But you told me you wanted to start over and live a different kind of life." Desperation is etched in his face alongside hope and fear.

"Fuck that." I run my hands up his neck, hanging onto him, burying my fingers in his thick hair. His eyelids flutter. "I want to live a good life. And that good life is with you. I want you. Whatever life I can have with you."

Shane makes a pathetic sound behind us, but neither of us look his way.

"Lovely, wonderful." Noah slow claps. "You're in love with each other. That's just great. I'm so happy for you. Callie, welcome to the family."

Wes leans down and gently brings our lips together, kissing me once softly, then more insistently, swiping his tongue in my mouth. I let out a soft moan and arch my back so I'm fully pressed against him.

"This is like a fucked-up Hallmark movie ending, but can we put a pin on your celebration for now?" Noah sighs dramatically. "Because we gotta deal with this asshole before you two can fuck."

I chuckle into Wes's mouth, and we pull away.

"I love you," I whisper.

"I love you more," he says, placing one last kiss on my lips before lowering me down.

I turn to Shane. He's—well, he looks like he's dead. I stare at the face of the man I was married to.

"Is he—" I stop and look at Noah.

"I think so." Noah steps forward and puts his hand on Shane's neck, looking for a pulse. When he can't find one, he nods.

"You okay?" Wes entwines his fingers with mine.

Am I okay? I think so. I do a check. My heart is full. My mental state—it's the calmest I've felt in months. The constant feeling of restlessness and unfinished business has disappeared. Even after I got Shane to sign the papers and had Mom's ring on my finger, I didn't feel settled. I thought it was because I hadn't left Portland yet. But I think it was the fact that his existence would hang over my head forever. And maybe I suspected what he was truly capable of all along.

We rid the world of a monster. And now I can live my life.

Physically, I'm exhausted. My legs are wobbly, I've got the start of a headache, I'm thirsty, and all I can smell is that apple pie. I'm starving.

"Can we have pie when we're done getting rid of him?"

"Not the mince pie," Wes says with a grave face.

"You're gonna have to make me a non-poisoned mince pie one day." I giggle and bump him with my shoulder.

"For you, I'll do anything." He brings our linked hands to his mouth and kisses the back of my hand.

CHAPTER 45

BEST FRIENDS

WES

Each of Callie's wrists is zip-tied to a bedpost, and she's spread out naked before me. Her legs are wide open, and her pussy is wet and glistening, even though I haven't even touched it yet.

"Wes, come on," she says, bucking her hips up toward me. "Touch me or I'm going to die."

I stroke my bare cock, which is hard as fuck. She watches me and moans, rubbing her thighs together, her eyes glued to the motion of my hand.

"Soon, Calliope." I release my dick and crawl up the bed toward her, reaching for the bowl from my nightstand and dipping my fingers into the sticky apple pie filling. I drip some of the sweet filling down the center of her chest and over each nipple. "I'm hungry for an appetizer before I have my main meal. First, you taste."

I lift my fingers to her mouth and she opens immediately, sucking on each finger as if she's starving.

I curse under my breath at the sight of her sucking, wishing it was my cock instead of my fingers.

When she's licked them clean, I lower my face to the side of her right breast to catch the pie filling that's threatening to drip onto the sheets. I lap up the sweet goo, dragging my tongue up the side of her breast and onto her nipple, which hardens into a tight peak.

"Fuck, Wes, that feels so good." She bucks her hips against me, and I let myself press my cock against the inside of her thigh. I have to stop for a second and take a few deep breaths.

Making her feel good is my main purpose in life, today and every day. It's been a week since we got rid of her scumbag husband, and every moment with Callie has been bliss. We've spent a lot of it here, in my bed, so there's that.

I move to her other breast, taking her nipple in my mouth and teasing it with my tongue.

Callie is perfect for me, and I'd like to think I'm perfect for her. She accepts me exactly as I am. I know that's not easy to do, and most women wouldn't even try.

As I suck her nipple, I slowly slide a hand down her abdomen until I get to the center of her and drag a finger up her slick slit. She's so fucking wet and ready for me, it's all I can do to not bury my cock in her right now.

"Wesley, fuck, I love you so much."

And as I smile with my mouth still locked on her tit, I continue stroking her pussy with one finger, ever so gently, while rubbing her clit with my thumb. I could do this all day long. I would, but she insists we eat regularly, and Noah badgers me to keep researching his target list.

It's going to be harder to make sure both my brother and Callie are protected. But I'm up for it. I was made for it. Made for *her*.

I add a second finger and push both inside her, pulsing

them slowly until I find the spot that makes Callie gasp and moan even louder.

Her chest is perfectly clean, so I lift my lips to her mouth, kissing her pleas away when I remove my fingers from inside her. I lick her juices off my fingers and groan at the taste of her.

"Fuck, Calliope, you taste so good."

"You're such a tease," she whines, pulling her hands against the restraints and lifting her legs up to pull my hips down against her. "One day I'm going to tie you up and see how you feel."

"That sounds hot as fuck." My cock twitches and grows impossibly harder at the idea. "But for now, I'm in control."

I drag my cock over her entrance, and we moan simultaneously. She's too damn delicious, too tempting, too willing to let me do whatever I want to her. I can't get enough.

I lower myself down, and Callie locks her ankles together behind my back, pulling me close so that the tip of my cock notches into her.

"Oh my god, Wes." She moans so loudly I wonder if the animals are getting worried.

I push in further, barely able to form coherent thoughts, let alone voice them. All I can think about is how she feels. How I feel inside of her. We are the perfect fit. She can take all of me, every fucking inch, and the anticipation of it is delicious.

"You're so tight, Calliope."

"Stop messing around and fuck me before I die right here on your bed. And I don't want to die in zip ties, so you better do it."

I chuckle and push all the way in, so deep I might just get lost in her.

And I do what she tells me to, pulling out, then sliding

back in slowly, the friction feeding the fire between us, then pausing when I bottom out. I do it again and lean down to give her a wet, sloppy kiss, and with the third thrust, she starts bucking against me, whimpering my name.

"Faster, harder, more, Wes," she says, arching her back.

I do as I'm told and slam into her again and again until she cries out. I feed into her orgasm, pumping against her, milking every last wave of pleasure. And only when she's almost done do I let myself come, filling her up until we're both finished.

"That was amazing," she whispers in my ear.

I lift my body so I don't crush her, but can't bring myself to slide out just yet. Inside her body is where I belong. Protecting her, loving her.

And if I stay here long enough, I'll get hard again.

"You are amazing, Calliope."

"Mmmm." Her body is relaxed and limp beneath me, her smile soft as she stares up. I fucking love this woman. I lean down and trail kisses from the edge of her jaw into the crook of her neck and then nip at her breast, which is slightly sticky from the apple pie filling.

"The pie was a bit messy," I note after running my tongue in a circle around her nipple.

"Worth it," she says, shifting her hips beneath me. I reach down and slowly rub her clit, watching her eyes flutter shut. "Are you hard again, Wes?" she moans as I move my hips.

"Yes." I reach up and grab the knife from my nightstand so I can cut each of the zip ties. Her eyes open as she lowers her arms and grips my waist. I flip us over until she's on top of me, where she immediately starts rocking.

This fucking view. There's nothing better than it.

I reach up and grab her hips, helping her move. She massages her breasts and throws her head back. When I can tell she's close, I take one hand and reach down to rub, her clit wet from both of our cum, and don't stop until she screams as she comes.

"Fuck, sweetheart. You are magnificent."

She leans down and holds herself up with her hands on my chest.

"I love fucking you, Wes." She turns her head to me. "I love you."

"I love you too, Calliope."

Callie rolls off me and lies on her back by my side as we both catch our breath.

There's a scratching sound at the bedroom door, and I turn my head to look at her. We both crack up.

"Sir Fluffy and Honey Bunny are ready for dinner," Callie says. "We can't keep them waiting."

The introduction of my old man cat and her giant lop-eared bunny went better than expected. Sir Fluffy just sort of stared at the rabbit at first, but then started following him around as Honey Bunny explored the house.

Now they're best friends. Their food bowls are next to each other, and they even sleep in a bed cuddled up together. It's freaking adorable.

"At least they waited until we got two rounds in." I sit up and swing my legs off the bed. "Stay there," I order her and head to the bathroom.

"I don't think I could walk if my life depended on it," she says as I wet a washcloth with warm water.

I return to the bed to clean her up, starting with her breasts where the apple pie filling was, then gently wiping her thighs and her pussy, loving the sight of my cum dripping out of her.

"I'll feed them. You stay in bed as long as you want."

With a gentle kiss to her forehead, I pull a blanket over her naked body and leave the bedroom.

Sir Fluffy weaves in and out of my legs, and Honey Bunny sits patiently next to the food bowls, his little nose sniffing the air.

I still feel like I'm dreaming this life, but when I return to the bedroom and watch Callie snoozing just where I left her, I know it's the real thing.

CHAPTER 46

GOLD DIGGER

CALLIE

The high school girl who I met the first time I came into Killer Beans stares at me with narrowed eyes and her hands on her hips.

"Why are you working here, anyway?" Maris tilts her head. "Why don't you have a real job?"

"Why is this not a real job?" I suppress a grin and continue staring at the iPad, scanning the menu so I continue to get familiar with it.

She blinks at me, ignoring the question I threw back at her.

Fucking hell, teenagers these days.

"My mom said you're living with Wes, and you've only known him for, like, a month. She thinks you're a gold digger."

Wes warned me about living in Lake Savage, the smallest town ever, but I guess I didn't really fully understand how much everyone knows about everyone else's life. Right now it's still charming, but I can see how it could be challenging sometimes. There is none of the anonymity of living in a city, even a small one like Portland.

"Wes has gold?" I glance up at Maris, but she just rolls her eyes. "Emma—Mrs. Stonewall—is trying to cut back on her hours. So she wanted someone who could be here during the day when you and Juno are at school."

"Hmm. I guess that makes sense." Maris looks me up and down in the completely unsubtle way of the teenage girl. "How'd you meet Wes, anyway?"

I can't say the truth: that I hired him to track down my husband and our relationship culminated when we discovered that my now-dead husband is a serial killer—but the bad kind?—and he was there when his father killed Wes's family. Oh, and Wes and his brother killed my dead husband's father a decade ago.

"We worked together." I go with a three-word, less-illegal summary instead.

She narrows her eyes further.

The bell above the coffee shop door jingles, and I'm relieved when a woman with two young daughters walks in to interrupt the awkward conversation. It's Saturday and almost closing time after my first week of work at Killer Beans. It was kind of fate when I stopped in a week or so after the Shane fiasco was over. Emma was here all alone, and she looked so tired. After I explained to her that I'd just moved to Lake Savage and was living with Wes, she immediately warmed to me and raved about his pies.

Then she asked if I needed a job. Which, I did.

"Maris, why don't you help this family?" I look up and smile at the mom with her girls. "And then you can head home."

Maris rolls her eyes and humphs, but then takes the family's order with almost a smile. I turn and wipe down the coffee machines as part of the closing checklist Emma prepared for me.

So much has changed in my life, and the changes keep coming. I'm still processing the acceptance that came in yesterday to a Master of Library Science program in Portland. Classes are in-person two days a week, plus online.

The tiny library in Lake Savage is run by a librarian who is about seventy-five years old, and when I stopped in to introduce myself and tell her about the program, her eyes widened, and she said she'd be retiring soon. It seems like fate.

Maris is adding generous amounts of whipped cream to two hot chocolates when the bell jingles again.

I turn with a smile, expecting to see another local customer.

Instead, it's my half-sister.

"Meadow," I say, shock in my voice.

"Hey, Callie." She gives me a tentative smile. Her cheeks are pink, and she pulls a long blonde braid over her shoulder, so similar to mine except in color.

My heart squeezes at the sight of her. Being in New York during the whole fight club drama with Shane made me realize I've neglected my relationship with Meadow. We didn't grow up together, but that's no reason for us not to get to know each other as adults.

"It's so good to see you. What brings you to Lake Savage?" When I realize that sounds sort of aggressive, I add a big smile. "You're always welcome here, of course."

"I wanted to come see where you live." Meadow sniffles. Her eyes are slightly puffy, the skin around them pink.

Maris is watching the interaction with keen attention, having handed off the hot drinks to the family. I'm sure she's going to report back to her mother or her friends or whomever and there will be a whole new rumor about Wes's gold-digger girlfriend.

"Maris, thanks for your help today. See you next week, right?"

I swear to god she rolls her eyes at me again and mutters something under her breath as she takes off her apron and reaches under the counter for her bag.

Maris walks out with a final curious glance at Meadow.

Meadow and I are left standing in front of the register. She's smiling brightly and looking around like she's never seen a coffee shop, and I'm trying to figure out what to say since she's not offering an explanation for why she's here.

"You okay, Meadow? It's so good to see you, but—"

"I'm sorry for just showing up." Meadow interrupts. "I —" She turns to me with wide eyes that are filled with tears. "Well, things kind of fell apart for me in New York."

"Oh. Shit. Hey, why don't you sit?" I gesture to a table. There are no more customers in sight, and we're almost at closing time, so while Meadow pulls up a chair at the round table, I flick the sign on the door to closed and click the lock. "Tea? Coffee?"

"You don't have alcohol, do you?"

"Nope, it's a coffee shop only."

"Damn." She rubs her hands together. "Tea would be nice then."

I make two mugs of tea in silence, preparing hers like I like mine, and then join Meadow at the table.

"So what happened in New York?" I wrap my hands around the ceramic mug that says Killer Beans.

"That asshole Jones got really handsy. Like literally, he'd walk by and touch me every single time. He's kind of hot, but it was gross."

"Asshole. And he's like twice your age." Fucking Jones. He was the source of so many problems.

"Plus gross and sketchy."

"For sure." I kind of wish I had asked Wes and Noah to take care of Jones. I'm sure they would've, but I didn't want things to look even more suspicious given Shane was gone.

Plus, I don't want to distribute any more death sentences.

"I thought I'd found my place at the fight club. I'd wanted to be a part of it for so long. It felt like home for a minute."

I make a sympathetic sound even though I don't understand that at all.

"Did you know Shane quit?" Meadow asks. "He didn't even say goodbye. Not that I needed him to, I'm just surprised he sort of disappeared."

Nope, Shane didn't quit. That dick is literally dead and buried.

"I don't talk to him anymore. The divorce is final." I go with that instead of acknowledging his murder.

"That makes sense," Meadow says. "And congratulations?"

"Thank you." I examine her face. "Did... did something else happen in New York?"

She shakes her head, her eyes wide.

I'm betting something else happened in New York, but I'm not close enough to Meadow to push her on it yet. If she wants to keep it a secret, that's her business.

"Can I stay with you for a while?"

I let out a surprised squeak. "What?"

"I'm sorry, forget it, never mind, that's too much to ask, I get it—" She shakes her head aggressively.

"Hey!" I wave my hand at Meadow to try to get her to stop. "I didn't say no. Of course, you can stay with us."

I probably should ask Wes, as I've been living with him for only a month and it's technically his cabin, but he won't deny me anything.

"Really?" Meadow looks at me with her big blue eyes. This poor thing. She's barely thirty and both of her parents are gone—which I can relate to—and it doesn't sound like she has anyone else to depend on. I get it.

"Yes." I nod firmly. "Absolutely."

"Okay. My stuff is at the bed-and-breakfast down the road."

"Yeah? When did you get here?"

She bites her lip. "Two days ago. I was too nervous to call you."

"Meadow, you can always call me." I reach over and pat her hand. Two days ago? And she's only just come to me? Girl is definitely hiding something. "Why don't you grab your stuff, and I can take you home with me after I'm done closing."

"Can you give me the address, and I'll come later? I have a few things to do first."

I give her the details and watch her leave, my curiosity piqued.

A half hour later, I walk out into the spring afternoon. It's April in Maine, so I'm still wearing my puffy coat, but I left behind my beanie and gloves, and my jacket is unzipped. It's almost no jacket weather. My phone buzzes as soon as I step out, so I pause to read the response from Wes about Meadow staying with us.

WESLEY

yeah, sure. Whatever she needs

that's gotta be a good story

ME

I bet

WESLEY

is she coming now?

ME

no, in a few hours

Wes is amazing. Every day I'm with him is better than the last. Being with him is a fantasy. Being loved by him is everything.

WESLEY

Calliope

ME

yes?

WESLEY

when are you going to be home? I miss you
and now we've got a guest coming soon

ME

just dropping off some book page art at
Brutal Reads, then I'll head home

WESLEY

I'm dying for you

Then he sends me a picture, which is a selfie of him lying back on our bed, one hand tucked behind his head, his impeccable triceps and gorgeous abs on full display, a blank slate between the beautiful tattoo artistry on his arms. I click on the picture, then zoom in, scanning every inch of his body on display, heat washing over me. His eyes are hooded, and the look he's giving the camera steals my breath.

ME

I'm hurrying

I slide my phone back into my pocket and continue walking until I get to Brutal Reads. The inside of the bookstore is cozy and warm, and the bookseller looks up from his spot at the register. He's got a paperback open and closes it when he sees me approach with the shoebox. The book he's reading has a cartoon cover with a couple kissing, but I'm betting there's some spice between those covers. A man who reads romance novels? Maybe I should try to set him up with Lola and get a rival bookstore owner love story going.

Lola was so happy when I told her I'm staying in Maine. She screamed and threw her arms around my neck. I didn't share the whole story of what happened, of course. Jake didn't jump up and down or cheer, but I could see the relief in his eyes. My brother and I have work to do on our relationship, but I'm happy I'll be around to do it.

"Callie, hello." Finn slides off his chair, and his cute dog lifts his head from the ground to watch our interaction, tail wagging.

"Hey, Finn. I brought the items we talked about the other day."

"That's grand, let's have a look." Finn's Irish accent is charming, and he seems like a good guy.

I reach in to grab the book page art I created since impulsively stopping in last week and word vomiting to him about my hobby.

"Here's a hedgehog." I pull out the animal creation made out of the pages of an old romance novel. "I thought it'd be cute. I can make other animals, larger or smaller."

"That's adorable," Finn says, picking up the paperback hedgehog with googly eyes and glasses.

"This one is more intense, but there could be tourists that want to take it home as a souvenir, or summer families looking to decorate their lake houses." It's an open book, the pages carved out and folded to look like a birdhouse with origami birds on the house and flying around. I even wrote Lake Savage in calligraphy as if the birdhouse has a name, like so many of the houses here do.

"Gorgeous. You really have a gift." Finn takes the creation from me and glances around the shop, as if picturing where he would hang it.

I love the stillness that doing book crafts gives me. I'll never forgive Shane for making me feel bad for it and then taking it away when he fled to New York City. Fuck him for trashing all my supplies and hating on my hobby.

I guess it's enough punishment that he's dead.

"How about we do it on consignment? If I sell an item, you get sixty percent of the sales."

"That sounds amazing." My cheeks heat. I never imagined selling my creations, and it'll certainly not pay my bills, but I love the idea of it.

"Can you bring in a few more little animals?"

"Absolutely."

He holds up the birdhouse. "I think I'd like to buy this one to decorate the shop. I can pay you for it today."

I nod, my heart full.

"I bet we'll sell a load of these in the summer."

I walk out a few minutes later and head to my car, texting Wes that I'm on my way.

ME

I'll be home in ten

WESLEY

fucking finally, Calliope

drive safely, but hurry because I want to
ravage you multiple times before your sister
arrives

I bite my lip and throw my car in gear, my heart beating faster as I make my way to the cabin.

Wes hasn't stopped tracking my every movement, and I'm here for it. He's obsessed with me, and I'm obsessed with him. More than a little bit, too.

I feel completely safe for the first time in my life.

"Hey!" I call when I throw the door open. The cabin smells delicious, a sweet potato turkey chili cooking in the crock pot mixed with the scent of apple pie, as usual.

"Hey, Calliope." Wes is facing away from me mixing something in a bowl. If I had to guess, it'd be fresh home-made whipped cream for the pie.

He's wearing an apron... and nothing else. This man's ass is so muscular and perfect, it should have its own social media accounts.

I chuckle and leave my coat and shoes at the door, then pull off my sweater so I'm in my bra, then wiggle out of my jeans on the way to the kitchen.

"You have a great ass." I walk up to him and wrap my arms around his waist, pressing my body against his bare backside. Our skin pressed together feels divine.

Wes turns from the counter and takes my face in his hands before leaning down to kiss me.

"I see you understood the assignment." He lets his hands drift down to my waist.

"I always understand the assignment when it comes to you, Wes." I slide my hands down to cup his ass and press him against me.

"Mmm. You do, sweetheart." Wes leans down to place a soft kiss on my mouth. "I still can't believe I found you."

"Yeah, your life was pretty boring before you met me." I wrap my arms around his torso, and he layers his arms on top of mine. This man is the least boring person I've ever met.

"It was... incomplete before you. Now I have you and Noah. That's all I'll ever need."

I tug on his neck until he leans down to kiss me again.

Wes is my family now.

Jake is, too. Lola. Meadow. Honey Bunny and Sir Fluffy.

I feel like I have a true family to support me.

We stay with our lips locked together for a long moment, the calm before the storm as I can feel the hard promise of what's to come pressing against my belly.

I am so lucky to have Wes. I'm lucky we found each other, and that he managed to break down those impenetrable walls I'd built around my heart.

He convinced me I am worth loving.

Worth protecting.

Both by him.

EPILOGUE

WES

I'm slamming into Callie from behind on our bed, one hand holding her in place by the hip, the other hand reaching around to rub her clit.

"Fuck, Wes. Fuck!"

"Does that feel good, Calliope?"

"So good. Please, Wes..." She moans, and the view of my girlfriend bracing on all fours is almost too much. I concentrate so fucking hard on not coming before she does.

I pull out and flip her around, tossing her on the bed and immediately sliding back into her soaking wet pussy. She's so tight, and I can feel her starting to contract around me.

"I'm going to come, Wes." She reaches over her head to ground herself on the headboard and arches her back.

"I know, sweetheart. Good girl. Come now, Calliope. Come all over my cock."

She's so sweaty and gorgeous, and when she screams out and starts coming, I immediately follow.

"Holy shit," she whispers, turning completely limp underneath me when we're both done.

I lean down and kiss her on the lips before pulling out and lying next to her.

"Holy shit," I agree and turn to face her. "I will never get over your incredible pussy, Calliope."

She laughs and reaches over to grab my cock, still half hard. "And I'll never get over your dick, Wesley."

I chuckle and pull her closer, careful not to disturb her hand on my cock, which loves anytime Callie touches it.

These days, my heart is full, but I don't always have enough time to track the movements of both my brother and Callie. Noah laughed at me when I brought up the concern, reminding me he is, indeed, a serial killer and doesn't need my protection.

I'll never stop protecting the people I love.

Three hours, five orgasms (three of them Callie's) and one joint shower later, Noah shows up while Callie's out picking up last-minute things for our family dinner. We're checking out his list before everyone else arrives.

"You added five more targets within the past week?" I examine the updated list in Noah's notebook.

"There's a lot of garbage humans out there, Wes." My brother sneezes and glares at Sir Fluffy, who is at his feet staring lovingly up.

I snort.

"We need to prioritize. Some of these are just a few descriptive words. Like when you wrote '*Rhode Island murders —campus killer?*'" I look up.

He shrugs and pours us each whiskey from the bottle in the middle of the table. "I'm not sure about that one yet. It was a tip from Scorpion, and I haven't been able to vet it yet."

"Just promise me you'll control yourself. No sneaking away and trying to do any of these on your own."

"I could totally do this on my own," Noah says. "Well.

After you help with the locating and hacking into systems and all that shit. Then I could do it on my own."

"But it's safer to do it with me." Sometimes I can't believe I'm the younger brother. "You need to have someone there to back you up."

"For fuck's sake, fine."

A key jangles in the lock and a second later, Callie walks in. She's got a reusable grocery bag in her arms, and it should have fresh garlic bread from the bakery in town to go with the lasagna.

"Calliope," I say, my heartbeat skipping when she pauses on the welcome mat and meets my eyes. Honey Bunny hops over to greet her, and Callie bends down to pet her rabbit. Sir Fluffy notices the movement and follows Honey Bunny, as usual. Those two have some kind of bromance going on. Or maybe it's one way, I'm not sure.

"Hey." Callie smiles at me as she slips her shoes off, shrugs out of her jacket, and comes right over. I shift back in the chair to give her plenty of space to settle on my lap. Which she does, placing a sweet kiss on my lips.

"Hi, Callie," Noah says, attempting to interrupt us.

"Hey Noah." Callie pulls back from our kiss and smiles at my brother.

"We were busy before you came in and distracted Wes." Noah pretends to be annoyed, but I know he adores Callie.

"So sorry I interrupted your murder talk."

"You better watch out or I'll put you on the list."

Callie laughs. "Noah? You are the least scary person ever."

"My god woman, that's not what quite a few people would say, if they weren't already dead." Noah sighs. "But I actually love that Wes is so wrapped up in you that he can't stalk me as thoroughly as he's done for the past decade."

"Wow, now we're saying the quiet part out loud, huh." I make an unimpressed grunt.

"You're the best, Wes." Callie nuzzles into my neck before hopping off my lap to unpack the groceries. Noah rolls his eyes.

These are the only two people in my life who understand my deep need to be their guard dog.

The front door opens again, and Meadow enters the cabin with a bottle of wine in each hand.

"Hey!" she calls in her cheery voice.

When Callie asked if her sister could stay with us for a while, the answer was obviously yes. I'd never say no to that woman. I am a little bummed that we can't get naked in the kitchen or living room whenever we want, but Meadow gives us our space.

Noah lets out a frustrated sigh and closes the notebook.

"Be nice," I whisper as a slight flush appears on his cheeks.

"She's such a pain in the ass." Noah's not even trying to be quiet. But even though his words are negative, he doesn't take his eyes off Meadow. "I can't believe she just showed up at my cabin earlier. She can't just do that. What if I was... busy?"

I cock my head at Noah. We might have sent Meadow over to his cabin earlier today so we could have alone time, and we might not have given him a choice in the matter, or even more than a five-minute warning that she was on her way. Both of us are highly entertained by the idea of forcing the two of them together. Callie seems to think they'd be perfect, but I'm not convinced. My brother seems to detest Meadow.

"Hasn't she been helping you with plans for the upcoming renovation?" I say, also not softly enough.

"Help is a strong word." Noah shakes his head and glares at Meadow as she approaches us.

"Hey, my design ideas were spot on." Meadow slips into a chair next to Noah. "Maybe you are good at cabin renovations—"

"Of course I'm good at it." Noah scoffs.

"—but haven't you had to hire a designer in the past?" Meadow plays with her braid, taking the elastic out and unbraiding the sections.

"Traitor." Noah says to me, but doesn't look away from Meadow's hands.

I might have let it slip to Meadow that Noah is shit at that final step of his cabin renovations, and we often have to pay someone to come finish things off.

"It just so happens I'm looking for a job," Meadow says.

"No." Noah shakes his head aggressively.

"What do you mean no? We had fun together, didn't we?"

"We did not."

"Why are you such a pain in the ass?"

Callie's sister doesn't know that she's hanging out with a pair of serial killers. Besides personality conflicts, that fact might get in the way of anything happening between Noah and Meadow.

There's another knock. Callie jumps up and opens the door to Lola.

"Hey!" Callie throws her arms around Lola, then hugs her brother, who appears behind the women. Then Callie grabs Lola's hand and drags her to the kitchen to open wine. "Come on, Meadow!"

Jake stands awkwardly in the front door for a moment, but I gesture to the table, and he follows and sits in the chair Meadow just vacated. Noah pours him a whiskey without a word, and Callie's brother accepts it gratefully and throws it back. I head to the kitchen to check the pies, flicking the oven light on. The apple pie looks beautiful. Perfect.

Callie slips next to me and wraps her arms around my waist. Meadow and Lola are chattering away across the kitchen. Next to the apple pie is a mince pie. This one has a gorgeous top crust and decidedly no poison in the filling.

"Fuck, that smells good," Callie says. It's true. The smell of the pies mingles with the lasagna baking in the second oven, and it's an incredible aroma. "Both safe to eat?" she whispers.

"Of course." I kiss the top of her head. She turns her face up to me, waiting for a kiss on her plump, pink lips. I give the woman what she wants, and she sighs against me.

"I love when you kiss me," she says.

"And I love kissing you. I do have one problem."

"What?" Her brow furrows, and she looks into my eyes intensely.

"I'm going to have to come up with another disgusting pie flavor to add my special ingredient to."

"Mince pie is not disgusting." Callie laughs and shakes her head.

"Agree to disagree." I push a chunk of her hair behind her ear. "I was researching recipes, but some of them sound so good I don't want to ruin them."

"Like what?"

"Chocolate Haupia pie, which is a chocolate coconut pie from Hawaii."

"Oh my god, that sounds amazing." Callie licks her lips, and I'm obsessed with the movement.

"I know. I'm gonna make it sometime. But I think I decided on something called funeral pie."

"That's almost too perfect. What's in it?" She smiles,

and I love the open and pure joy on her face. I hope I can continue to make her happy. I hope I can help her create a life here that's so much better than the one she was considering across the country. I don't want even one single second of doubt to enter her mind about choosing this.

Choosing me.

Choosing us.

"Raisins and custard."

"I mean, raisins are also in mince pie, but I'm not sure about raisins just, like, floating around in custard." Callie scrunches her nose.

"Exactly."

"So I guess I'm on board with funeral pie being your new mince pie."

"Glad we agree." I grin and lean closer to her, pausing just before our lips meet. "I love you, Calliope."

"I love you too, Wesley."

And then I kiss her.

🖤 Preorder *A Little Bit Dark*, Noah & Meadow's book, out March 2027!

📖 Check out one more chapter with Wes & Callie by signing up for Chrissy's newsletter at www.ChrissyHopewell.com.

✏️ If you enjoyed *A Little Bit Obsessed*, leave a review, it helps so much.

Fort Collins Blizzard Hockey romance series (ongoing):
Just One Season is Lucy & Kellen's love story. It's a fake dating,

brother's best friend, single dad, found family hockey romance.

Any Second Now is Raleigh & Atticus's story. It's a second chance, twice-divorced FMC, hockey romance with chickens.

The Hart Sisters Trilogy (completed):
If We Pretend is Reese & Oliver's love story. It's a fake dating, divorced mom, ex pro soccer player light sports romance set in Scotland.

Unless It's You is Stella & Ethan's love story. Set in London, this romance is a second chance, enemies-to-lovers, bucket list novel.

Since We're Here is Maddie & Patrick's love story. It's a grumpy sunshine Irish romance.

One Hundred Lights is a prequel novella to the Hart Sisters Trilogy and is a holiday romance featuring Britt & Adrian, both slightly morally grey characters who can't stay away from each other.

Stay in touch:
Instagram: @ChrissyHopewell
Facebook: ChrissyHopewellAuthor
TikTok: @ChrissyHopewellBooks
Email: Chrissy@ChrissyHopewell.com
BookBub: ChrissyHopewell

ABOUT THE AUTHOR

Chrissy Hopewell started her love for romance novels by sneaking her mom's steamy books in middle school. She has spent varying amounts of time overseas, including working at a pub in Dublin, waitressing at a hotel in the Scottish Borders, and studying and living in London. Because of these experiences, international flair and accents often show up in her writing. Chrissy now lives in the suburbs of Cincinnati, Ohio with her family, and she no longer has to sneak what she reads.

instagram.com/chrissyhopewell

tiktok.com/@chrissyhopewellbooks

facebook.com/chrissyhopewellauthor

www.ingramcontent.com/pod-product-compliance
Lightning Source LLC
Chambersburg PA
CBHW020903060726
47591CB00004B/1068